## SOMEONE'S WATCHING

He watched the light go out in the master bedroom on the second floor.

They'd left a lamp on in the living room just to throw off someone like him. It was the Mission-style lamp with the Tiffany shade. He'd noticed it while inside the house two nights ago. They weren't throwing him off at all. He'd been here long enough to know nobody was in that living room—or on the entire first floor. The two of them had gone upstairs to their respective rooms about forty minutes ago. Though their bedroom lights were off, he was pretty sure neither of them was asleep yet.

He was parked across the street from the town house. He'd been there for almost an hour, and only twenty or so cars had passed him—none of them police cars. It was a far cry from three weeks ago, when this place had swarmed with cops and reporters. How quickly people forgot.

But he didn't forget. He held onto things.

Andrea and Spencer had foiled his break-in the night before last. But he would get inside that house again. It just wasn't happening tonight.

He'd get the two of them while they were home—with their guard down.

And then he'd go a little crazy . . .

**Books by Kevin O'Brien**

ONLY SON

THE NEXT TO DIE

MAKE THEM CRY

WATCH THEM DIE

LEFT FOR DEAD

THE LAST VICTIM

KILLING SPREE

ONE LAST SCREAM

FINAL BREATH

VICIOUS

DISTURBED

TERRIFIED

UNSPEAKABLE

TELL ME YOU'RE SORRY

NO ONE NEEDS TO KNOW

YOU'LL MISS ME WHEN I'M GONE

Published by Kensington Publishing Corporation

# KEVIN O'BRIEN

# YOU'LL MISS ME WHEN I'M GONE

PINNACLE BOOKS
Kensington Publishing Corp.
www.kensingtonbooks.com

PINNACLE BOOKS are published by

Kensington Publishing Corp.
119 West 40th Street
New York, NY 10018

All Kensington titles, imprints, and distributed lines are available at special quantity discounts for bulk purchases for sales promotions, premiums, fund-raising, educational, or institutional use.
Special book excerpts or customized printings can also be created to fit specific needs. For details, write or phone the office of the Kensington sales manager: Kensington Publishing Corp., 119 West 40th Street, New York, NY 10018, attn: Sales Department; phone 1-800-221-2647.

This book is a work of fiction. Names, characters, businesses, organizations, places, events, and incidents either are the product of the author's imagination or are used fictitiously. Any resemblance to actual persons, living or dead, events, or locales is entirely coincidental.

ISBN-13: 978-0-7860-3881-7
ISBN-10: 0-7860-3881-0

First printing: August 2016

10 9 8 7 6 5 4 3 2 1

Printed in the United States of America

First electronic edition: August 2016

ISBN-13: 978-0-7860-3882-4
ISBN-10: 0-7860-3882-9

*This book is for my friend Tom Goodwin.*

# ACKNOWLEDGMENTS

What I love about the acknowledgments section of my novels is that it's like giving an Oscar acceptance speech in which I get to thank a lot of wonderful people—and there's no orchestra to cut me off.

This is my twentieth year with Kensington Books. I'm so lucky to be with a publisher who believed in me back when I was a railroad inspector moonlighting as an author. They stuck with me, built a career for me, and always had my back. My thanks to everyone there at Kensington Books. You guys rule! Of course, I have to give a special shout-out to my brilliant editor and dear friend, John Scognamiglio.

My thanks to Meg Ruley, Christina Hogrebe, and the terrific team at Jane Rotrosen Agency. You guys are amazing.

Thanks also to my Writers Group friends, who saw early drafts of this book and came back with marvelous suggestions on how to make it better: John Flick, Cate Goethals, Soyon Im, David Massengill, and Garth Stein.

I'm also grateful for the support, encouragement, and friendship of my fellow Seattle 7 Writers, especially the Core members: Garth (again), Jennie Shortridge, Erica

Bauermeister, Dave Boling, Carol Cassella, Randy Sue Coburn, Laurie Frankel, and Stephanie Kallos.

A special thank-you goes to Doc Doolittle for helping out with some of the nautical nomenclature in this book.

Another very special thank-you goes to Doug Mendini.

I'd also like to thank these fabulous friends and groups who have been incredibly supportive. Without you, I'm nothing! Thank you: Dan Annear and Chuck Rank, Ben Bauermeister, Pam Binder and the Pacific Northwest Writers Association, Marlys Bourm, Amanda Brooks, Terry and Judine Brooks, Lynn Brunelle, Deb Caletti, George Camper and Shane White, Barbara and John Cegielski, Barbara and Jim Church, Pennie Clark Ianniciello, Anna Cottle and Mary Alice Kier, Tommy Dreiling, Paul Dwoskin, the gang at Elliott Bay Book Company, Bridget Foley and Stephen Susco, Matt Gani, Bob and Dana Gold, my friends at Hudson News, Cathy Johnson, Elizabeth Kinsella, David Korabik, Stafford Lombard, Paul Mariz, Roberta Miner, Dan Monda, Jim Munchel, my friends at The News Group, Meghan O'Neill, Midge Ortiz, the folks at ReaderLink Distribution Services, Eva Marie Saint, John Saul and Mike Sack, the gang at Seattle Mystery Bookshop, Suzanne Selfors, John Simmons, Roseann Stella, Dan, Doug and Ann Stutesman, George and Sheila Stydahar, Marc Von Borstel, Michael Wells, Susan Wiggs, and Ruth Young.

A great, big thank-you and lots of love to my wonderful sibs.

And finally, thanks to all my loyal readers. You know who you are!

# CHAPTER ONE

*Thursday, October 8—12:21 p.m.*
*Seattle*

There was no backing out of it now.

She'd already mentioned to Luke that she had something important to discuss with him over lunch. Of course, that had been this morning before he'd had his coffee, before he'd gone off to the theater to work on rehearsals and rewrites for his new play. Luke might have forgotten by now. Hell, he probably didn't even remember they had a lunch date. So she'd texted him a quick reminder before leaving his place. She hadn't heard back from him yet.

Andrea Boyle had her phone in the cup holder of her car—in case he called. Sitting at the wheel, she focused on the road ahead. It was a short drive from his town house apartment to the theater in the Seattle Center. As her eight-year-old, red VW Beetle took the steep descent on Queen Anne Avenue, a few drops of rain hit the windshield. It wasn't quite enough to switch on the wipers yet. Andrea had been in Seattle only a few months, but she'd already figured out that true Seattleites didn't use their wipers or umbrellas until the rain started coming down heavy and hard.

She'd moved here from Washington, DC, with her seventeen-year-old nephew, Spencer. Andrea was a copyeditor. She polished manuscripts for authors before they sent their work off to publishers. She copyedited everything from textbooks to thrillers to bodice-ripper romances. It was a job she could do anywhere, which made moving to Seattle a bit easier. In fact, she'd first met Luke at a party in the home of her one and only Seattle client, a true-crime writer.

Andrea had relocated with the hope that she and Spencer could start fresh, where no one knew them. She'd made a dozen calls and filled out a pile of documents to have Spencer's last name legally changed. Too many people had heard of Spencer Rowe. He was Spencer *Murray* now. Murray was his choice, because he worshiped Bill Murray. Spencer claimed that while in the hospital, the only thing that could cheer him up was a Bill Murray comedy. He must have seen *Stripes*, *Caddyshack*, and *Rushmore* at least a dozen times each.

She and Spencer had a distinct family resemblance, both of them lean, tall, dark-haired, and blue-eyed. Traveling together and renting an apartment together, they must have looked like a slightly odd pair. Andrea was thirty-six, but thanks to good genes, her Fitbit, and Clairol's "Chestnut Shimmer" hiding the gray in her shoulder-length hair, she passed for someone in her late twenties. Most people in Seattle assumed Spencer was her younger brother—until she told them he was her nephew. The story people got was that his parents had died in an automobile accident back when he was eleven, and she'd been taking care of him ever since.

At least the part about Spencer being her nephew was true.

No one asked any probing questions after hearing about her family tragedy. As far as Andrea could discern, no one in Seattle knew the real story—including her dear, handsome Luke.

But she needed to tell him the truth today—before someone else did. Thinking about that discussion made a knot form in her stomach.

The rain came down faster now, and Andrea switched on the wipers. She tried to think of where they could go for lunch: Tup Tim Thai, or maybe the 5 Spot. Whichever restaurant they ended up in, she'd be too nervous to eat. And from today on, it would always be the place where they had "the talk." If, by some miracle they survived this and didn't break up, they probably wouldn't want to set foot in that restaurant again.

Would he ever forgive her?

She'd been dating Luke for over four months—and deceiving him the whole time. He'd gotten close to her nephew, and she didn't want anything to foul up that friendship. Sometimes Spencer seemed more like Luke's son than Luke's real offspring, Damon. Spencer and Damon were both juniors at Queen Anne High. They hadn't exactly hit it off, which wasn't Spencer's fault. Early on, he'd tried to reach out to Damon.

"I figured the guy could use a friend," Spencer had told her near the beginning of the school year. "I could see he was getting picked on and all. So in the hallway, between classes, I introduced myself, and said, 'I know this is awkward, because my aunt is dating your dad, but we might as well at least acknowledge each other or whatever.' And all I got from him was this snooty, blank stare. Then he rolled his eyes at me and wandered away. I mean, God, no wonder people hate him. I'm sorry, Aunt Dee. Please don't tell Luke I said that . . ."

*Aunt Dee* was what he'd been calling her ever since he'd learned to talk. He'd had a hard time saying *Andrea*.

Spencer had a point about Damon Shuler.

She and Spencer had moved in with Luke about three weeks ago. Under ordinary circumstances, cohabitating with a guy after knowing him only three months would have been way too soon for her.

But the circumstances were far from ordinary.

She hadn't had much time to get used to their living arrangement. And she hadn't had much time to get used to Damon, who—so far—had spent two of his "alternate weekends" with them.

He'd declared he wasn't comfortable sharing his room with anyone. So even though Damon's room had twin beds, Spencer had to sleep on the couch in Luke's study for those weekends. Technically, it wasn't even Damon's room. It was a guest room—with only a few of Damon's possessions in there. During those designated weekends, Damon acted as if staying with them was a huge ordeal. He was icily polite and in total said about a hundred words to her. She was the recipient of much eye-rolling as well. He wasn't a bad-looking kid— with his skinny build, pale complexion, and wavy brown hair. But his demeanor was so off-putting, he seemed unattractive.

Damon had a bit of OCD, which wasn't noticeable at first. But then Andrea realized he had to touch everything he came in contact with—as if testing how hot it was. Damon touched a pencil before picking it up, touched a chair before sitting down in it, touched a door before pushing it open, and sometimes he just test-touched something and then after that, didn't handle it at all. He also washed his hands about forty times a day.

Apparently, the kids at school had picked up on it, and they teased him mercilessly. In fact, Luke and his estranged wife, Evelyn, had had a few meetings with the school principal about it. Those were the only times Luke ever saw Evelyn—at these conferences to discuss the bullying inflicted on their son.

As the newbie in their class, Spencer had been harassed by a few bullies, too, but he said it was nothing compared to the treatment Damon endured.

It broke Andrea's heart to know that her sweet, vulnerable nephew was being harassed at school. He'd already suffered enough. But Damon was so arrogant, she couldn't help feeling he'd sort of set himself up for the abuse he got.

Still, Andrea did her damnedest to be nice to him. After all, he was Luke's son—even though he could get bratty toward Luke at times. Andrea was pretty certain it was Damon's mother's influence that made him so strange and standoffish.

To his credit, Luke Shuler never complained about his soon-to-be-ex. He admitted he'd only stayed with his wife for Damon's sake, and things had been pretty awful for a long time. "Let's just say I'm in a much better place now," he'd told Andrea. Of course, Andrea was curious about her predecessor. Obviously, the woman was still very connected to Luke—after nearly nineteen years of marriage and having a son together. They'd been separated for only seven months. Andrea couldn't help wondering if Luke might end up going back to her.

She'd found herself admitting as much to a new friend, Barbara James-Church, manager of the Seattle Group Theater, over lunch at Café Lola. The petite, attractive, fortyish brunette had already set up Andrea with two new Seattle author-clients.

"I love Luke and hated seeing how miserable he was with Evelyn—for years," Barbara had said. "Evelyn was very clingy and possessive. She's always been a cold fish to me. But then I compared notes with people, and realized she was that way with *everybody*—at least, everybody who had anything to do with Luke. Evelyn wanted him all to herself. I've known her for six years, and the first time Evelyn was ever nice to me was two weeks ago. She donated five thousand dollars to the Seattle Group Theater. She comes from money, you know. Five thou is a drop in the bucket for her. We've never gotten a dime out of her before. But suddenly, once they split, she was so bighearted. Anyway, the very day the check arrived in the mail, she phoned me—all chummy-chummy, wanting to know if I'd gotten the donation. Then she asked about Luke and started grilling me about you. I mean, could she be any more transparent? Anyway, I said you seemed 'nice.'

Of course, Evelyn wasn't too happy with that reply. But to her credit, at least she didn't stop payment on the check. Anyway, in answer to your question, I don't think Evelyn is ready to give him up—not without a fight. But it's a losing battle, because Luke is so much better off now—with you. He knows it, too. And I'm not just saying that because I like you and you're buying me lunch . . ."

Andrea wondered what Luke had ever seen in Evelyn. He didn't seem to need her money. But then Andrea had seen photos of Evelyn among the family snapshots that Luke had saved. Evelyn Shuler was a knockout—blond, elegant, and chic. The only possible physical flaw Andrea could find was a slight overbite—which some men found attractive.

As curious as she was about Luke's almost-ex, Andrea had no desire to meet her.

Then just a few days after the informative chat with Barbara at Café Lola, Andrea had received an email from Evelyn with the subject line: *Free for Lunch?* How Luke's wife had gotten her email address was a mystery:

Hi, Andrea,

I'm sure by now you've heard a lot about me! Before you form an opinion, I think it would be a good idea if we met. I was married to Luke for 19 years & know him better than anyone else. You're just starting to know him. For example, can we talk about how every morning he needs to have his coffee in that cup with Bruce Lee's picture on it? And how about the way he's always humming to himself? Anyway, I think you could learn a thing or two from my knowledge & experience. Plus if you continue seeing Luke, I'd like to meet the woman who might end up spending some time with my son, Damon. Do you think we could meet for lunch or coffee next week?

I look forward to hearing back from you!

Cheers!
Evelyn Shuler


At the time, Andrea had been living with Spencer in an apartment in Ballard. She'd been dating Luke for only six weeks and hadn't yet spent the night at his place. She hadn't witnessed Luke's morning routine with the Bruce Lee coffee cup. However, they'd shared many extended lunch hours at his apartment or at the Westin. It was no secret they'd been seeing each other. She'd merely been reluctant about leaving Spencer alone in the apartment for a night—or having Luke in her bed while Spencer slept across the hall from them.

Maybe she had read too much into a friendly email, but it seemed a bit manipulative and meddling. Andrea might have had a little more respect for Evelyn if she'd focused more on Damon in that note. Instead, she didn't mention him until the very end. Her son seemed like an afterthought.

Andrea didn't tell Luke about his wife's email, not until after she'd sent Evelyn a reply. She spent forty-five minutes carefully wording the short response:

Dear Evelyn,

Thank you for your nice note and for the invitation to lunch. I appreciate the offer, but I'm afraid I'll have to decline. I just don't think it's a good idea at this point. However, I'm looking forward to meeting Damon. If you have any special instructions or concerns about that, please let me know through Luke. Thanks again.

Sincerely,
Andrea Boyle

She'd shown both emails to Luke that evening. "Well done," he'd said, kissing her on the forehead. "Let me know if she tries to get in touch with you again."

She never heard back from Evelyn.

That wasn't to say Evelyn had backed off. The email had been harmless. What came later was far more disturbing. In fact, things got so bad that she and Spencer had to leave their apartment in Ballard and move in with Luke.

Though it was "Modern Cookie-Cutter" in its construction, Andrea had liked their first Seattle home. It was part of the Briarwood Court, a complex of six tall, thin, identical buildings, each with two apartment units. She and Spencer had an upper unit. Once through the outside front door, they had to climb up a stairway to the living room, kitchen, and powder room. Another flight of stairs led to the two bedrooms and another bathroom.

The manager had pointed out that the beige Berber carpeting throughout the apartment was brand new. He asked that they and their guests remove their shoes be-fore going upstairs to the unit. After two weeks, there was a different pair of shoes—belonging to either her or Spencer—along the edge of each step nearly halfway up the stairs. In fact, Spencer had more shoes on the stairs than in his bedroom closet. Though it was a bit messy, Andrea found the display of footwear on the steps a comforting, homey image when she came through the front door—a sign that they were settled in.

She got the manager's okay to plant some iris, chrysanthemums, and pansies near the bushes beside their front door. She loved to garden—to the point that Spencer jokingly called her "Fanny View" be-cause she was always bent over, tilling the soil. But to her knowledge, she'd never actually mooned anyone.

Briarwood Court was walking distance from shop-ping, restaurants, and the bus to downtown Seattle. An-other plus about the location: it was a mere ten-minute drive to Luke's town house on Queen Anne Hill. She'd had her first date with him just a week after she and Spencer had moved into the apartment. She remem-bered thinking at the time that everything was finally going their way. She'd met a great guy, and she and Spencer had found a terrific place to live.

But with its own separate, outside entrance, the big windows and a designated uncovered parking spot, the apartment in Briarwood Court also made her and Spencer vulnerable to anyone who had it out for them.

They were still relatively new to the complex when somebody broke a headlight on her VW during the night. The car had been in its parking spot. As if a broken headlight weren't enough, the culprit had also scratched

the driver's side with a key or a box cutter or something. Andrea reported it to the police and her insur-
ance company. The police asked her if she had any
idea who might have inflicted this damage on her car.
She thought of Luke's wife, but quickly dismissed the
notion as silly. She told the police she didn't have a
clue who the perpetrator was.

Around this same time, Andrea experienced a surge
in hang-ups on her cell phone—always from a CALLER
UNKNOWN, according to the caller ID. Even when she
answered, they hung up after a moment. It was as if
they just wanted to hear her voice—or make certain
she was home. She got one of those anonymous hang-
ups at two in the morning; after that, Andrea switched
off her phone before going to bed at night.

But she couldn't flick a switch and turn off the eerie
feeling that someone was watching her whenever she
set foot outside the apartment. Or maybe they were out
there in the dark, studying her through the living room's
big picture window. There weren't many streetlights on
their block, so at night all she could see outside were
some trees and the lights from the apartment building
across the way. But she knew her every move was vis-
ible to anyone out there. In the darkened glass of the
living room windows, she'd notice her own reflection
in the room.

She imagined it was exactly how a stranger lurking
outside saw her.

Andrea started closing the drapes once dusk settled.
It made her feel closed in, and not all that much safer.
But at least she knew no one could see her.

One morning, Spencer started off for school and almost stepped on a dead squirrel on their front stoop. And someone had trampled all over her newly planted flowers. Andrea talked to the manager, who seemed to think she was paranoid. She asked if the previous tenant had ever had a stalker—or any enemies. The manager said a quiet seventy-something widower had lived there for eight years before her. "And *he* never gave me any problems," he added, scowling at her.

At least Spencer didn't think she was paranoid. In fact, he couldn't help wondering if someone in Seattle knew about him after all—and maybe this was a campaign to make him feel unwelcome.

Andrea tried to assure her nephew that it wasn't about him. He wasn't the one getting ten hang-ups on his cell phone every day.

Then about five weeks ago, Andrea heard from a friend and client, Sylvia Goethals in Washington, DC. Andrea had copyedited seven of Sylvia's travel books. At the time of Sylvia's call, Andrea had thought her friend was in India, researching her next book. But no, Sylvia was home: "Andie, I think you should know, some private detective came to my book signing at Barnes and Noble this afternoon, asking questions about you."

"You're kidding," Andrea murmured, bewildered. She stood at the living room window with the phone to her ear. It was early in the evening, and she hadn't closed the drapes yet. "What—what did he want? Did he mention who he was working for?"

"No, he wouldn't say who hired him," Sylvia replied. "But that didn't stop this joker from asking a ton of questions about you. He was very clever about it. Unfortunately, I didn't have that good a turnout at the bookstore, so he started talking to me and I was a captive audience. He didn't say who he was at first. I thought he was looking for an editor when he asked about you. He must have Googled you and found your name in the acknowledgments section of one of my books. He knew we were friends. Anyway, when he started asking personal questions about you, that's when I put the brakes on . . ."

"Did he know about Spencer?" Andrea started pacing around the living room. "Did he give any indication?"

"Yes, he clearly knew. He even mentioned that he'd talked to some of the witnesses at the trial. Anyway, he gave me his business card, and I realized he was a private detective. He asked me about the men you've dated and if you had any long-term boyfriends. I told him if he was so curious, maybe he should ask you . . ."

Andrea wondered why in the world he'd asked about her love life. Until she'd met Luke, there had been just a few *short*-term boyfriends. Considering her family history, she'd always felt so grateful when a guy—any guy—wanted to go out with her. Usually, it took her a few dates for the blind gratitude to wear off. Then she'd realize the guy was totally wrong for her.

"Andie, are you still there?" her friend asked on the other end of the line.

"Yeah, sorry," she murmured, moving to the window again. "What else did he ask about?"

"That was it," Sylvia said. "Obviously, he realized I wasn't going to cooperate. I told him if he wasn't going to buy one of my books, he could move on . . ."

Andrea stared at her reflection in the darkened glass. She looked frightened and haggard. Her chestnut-colored hair was in a ponytail, and she wore a long-sleeve white T-shirt and jeans. Spencer was up in his room, tinkering with his portable keyboard. She'd been putting together one of her favorite "quick dinners" when Sylvia had called—Trader Joe's Mandarin Orange Chicken, to which she added fresh, steamed vegetables and rice.

Now she didn't have any appetite at all.

"Do you think he knew that we live in Seattle?" she asked.

"He seemed to, yeah," Sylvia replied.

Andrea was about to turn away from the big window, but then she saw something on the other side of the glass—a small, white object hurtling right toward her. She wasn't sure what it was, but automatically stepped back. The thing—it must have been a rock— hit the glass with a loud snap.

Andrea let out a startled little scream, and almost dropped the phone.

The stone ricocheted off the window. Lightning-bolt splintered cracks shot out from the point of contact.

Spencer called down from upstairs, asking what had just happened. On the other end of the phone line, Sylvia wanted to know if she was all right.

Her heart racing, Andrea retreated all the way to the kitchen counter. She kept expecting another object—

maybe a brick this time—to come crashing through the window. She heard a rumbling upstairs.

"Spencer, don't come down here!" she yelled. "And stay away from the windows!"

Her friend was still on the line. "For God's sake, what's going on? Are you okay?"

"Listen, I have to hang up and call the police," she said, catching her breath. "Someone's been harassing us lately, and they—at least, I think it was them—they just threw a rock at our window. I'll call you back in a little while, Syl."

"A little while" was an hour later, almost 10:30 for Sylvia on the East Coast. By then, Spencer had ventured down to the living room to join Andrea. The police had arrived—and left already. Andrea had told them about the other incidents: the vandalism to her car, the dead squirrel left on their front stoop, the trampled garden, and the countless hang-ups on her cell phone. The two cops responding to the 911 call had taken notes and given her a card with her "incident number" on it.

On the phone, she assured Sylvia that she and Spencer were okay. By that time she was so frayed she couldn't think straight. She kept wondering why this was happening. Who had she made so angry? No one in Seattle really knew her well enough to hate her. Was there a connection between the private detective asking questions about her and the harassment they'd endured— including tonight's episode?

She remembered her lunch conversation with Barbara James-Church at Café Lola: *"I don't think Evelyn is ready to give him up—not without a fight."*

Andrea couldn't quite picture Luke's chic wife vandalizing cars and tossing rocks at windows. If she was behind any of this, she would have had to hire some lowlife to do her dirty work for her. Suspecting Evelyn seemed like a knee-jerk reaction. She wondered if Luke's son was behind everything that had occurred. But it didn't make sense. His parents had split up long before she'd come into the picture. Besides, what about the private detective? She couldn't see a high school kid having the means to hire a private investigator.

When Luke phoned a little later that night, she told him what had happened. She didn't share with him any of her shaky theories as to who might be responsible. Luke wanted them to spend the night at his place, but Andrea refused to be bullied out of her apartment. So Luke came over. She put the Mandarin Orange Chicken back in the freezer, and they ordered a pizza from Zeek's. The three of them ate in front of *High Fidelity* on cable, and at one point, Andrea realized they were all laughing. And it was nice to sleep with him in her bed.

Things calmed down after that—for nearly two weeks. Andrea welcomed the peaceful lull. Even the anonymous calls had stopped. The living room window and the Volkswagen were repaired. She even planted some new perennials in the little garden. But that didn't mean she wasn't constantly looking over her shoulder, ready for the next "incident."

She phoned Sylvia to find out more about this pushy private detective. But her friend didn't reply until two days later—by email—saying she was back in India. She didn't remember the investigator's name, but she was pretty sure she'd stuck his card in a drawer at home. She would be coming back to the states in three weeks, and could search for it then. "If it's an emergency, I can ask the building manager to let himself in and look around the apartment for the card," Sylvia wrote. "But it might be a lost cause. Anyway, let me know what you'd like me to do. Meanwhile, here's hoping you haven't had any more broken windows or things of that sort . . ."

Andrea emailed her friend that it could wait until she was home again and settled in. "Everything's fine here for now" she wrote. "We're okay." At the time, she felt as if she were jinxing things by putting that in writing.

Perhaps she had.

A few days later, while Spencer was at school, Andrea went out to run some errands. She was gone for just over an hour. Returning home with a bag of groceries from Safeway, she stepped through the front door and started to kick off her shoes. Then she noticed the footwear on the steps. The pairs were all mismatched, lined up alongside the wrong corresponding shoe. It was as if someone were playing a joke on her.

Or maybe they just wanted her to know they could get inside her place now.

Andrea set down the grocery bag and backed out the front door. She kept thinking the culprit might still be inside the apartment. She hurried toward the sidewalk in front of Briarwood Court. With a shaky hand, she grabbed her phone from her purse and called Spencer at school. They usually texted each other, but she couldn't really explain in a text what she needed to know. Fortunately, Spencer was between classes, and he picked up. He told her no, he hadn't messed around with their shoes before catching the bus that morning. He didn't know what she was talking about.

Andrea felt silly, calling the police because someone had rearranged their footwear on the stairs; nevertheless, she phoned them. She said she thought that someone had broken into the apartment and that they might still be in there. She gave them her incident number and waited outside until a patrol car showed up. The two cops went inside the apartment with her. No one was there. Nothing else had been disturbed. Nothing was damaged or missing. She sensed her credibility with them slipping after each room inspection. She pulled the quilt and the sheets off her bed, just to make sure the intruder hadn't slipped anything in there—like another dead squirrel. She was afraid they might have done something to her soap or shampoo, her eyedrops or her perfume. Anything that was open in the medicine chest, the kitchen cupboards or the refrigerator might be tainted.

The two cops recommended that she change her locks and have her home security system upgraded. When they asked if she had any idea who might be harassing her, she thought about Evelyn Shuler again. But she told them she didn't have a clue.

Once the police left, Andrea phoned Luke and admitted her suspicions that Evelyn may have been responsible for these strange, unsettling incidents. "I'm sorry," she said. "It's an awful thing to say about someone who is still a very important person in your life. And I'm not accusing her. I'm just wondering. I can't think of anyone else who would do this—"

"Honey?" he interrupted.

"Luke, I'm sorry. I have absolutely no proof—"

"Andrea," he interrupted again. "To tell you the truth, I wouldn't put it past her. I'm so sorry if she's the one who put you through this. I should have seen it earlier. But I have a history of blinding myself to some of the things Evelyn is capable of. I'll have a talk with her. She'll deny it until she's blue in the face and be furious with me. But I'll have a talk with her."

This time, he insisted she and Spencer come stay with him—at least until all of this was resolved. Spencer could sleep in the guest room, where Damon stayed on alternate weekends. Luke pointed out that, at last, he'd actually have her sleeping in his bed. His room was far enough away from the guest room so she needn't feel self-conscious. Spencer was practically an adult. He knew the score. He knew they were involved. Luke told her, "After what he's been through, I don't think he'll be traumatized because we're sleeping together."

But Luke had no idea how fragile Spencer was— and neither did she, for that matter.

"Just so you know," she told her nephew as they were driving to Luke's town house that first night, "I'll be sleeping with Luke in his room tonight. Do you have any problems with that?"

"God, it's about time," Spencer sighed. He had one arm dangling out the window on the passenger side. The wind whipped at his unruly, dark brown hair. Their suitcases were piled in the tiny backseat. "You guys have been going out for—like, three months now. I can't believe you've waited this long . . ."

And so, though it seemed to be rushing things, Andrea and Spencer "temporarily" moved in with Luke.

In her effort to scare off Andrea, Evelyn had only thrown her and Luke closer together. But Evelyn still had an advantage—if she'd been the one who had hired that private detective. Luke's soon-to-be-ex knew Spencer's and her history. And it was just a matter of time before she told Luke.

Last week, when Luke had asked her and Spencer to consider living with him on a more permanent basis, Andrea had come very close to telling him the truth. It had seemed like the best time, and she'd wanted him to hear it from her. But she'd lost her nerve.

Except for this awful thing hanging over her head, she was the happiest she'd been in years. She was in love. After a sporadic series of "wrong guys," she'd finally hit the jackpot with Luke. She cherished what they had together and didn't want to see it ruined.

Evelyn Shuler could do that with one phone call.

Andrea knew she had to tell him the truth today.

She found a parking spot a block from the theater, grabbed her umbrella from the floor of the passenger side, and stepped out of the VW. She made a mad dash in the rain. For this lunch she dreaded, Andrea wore—under her trench coat—a floral print sweater and khaki slacks. The pants were damp from the knees down by the time she reached the theater. The Seattle Group Theater was in a complex of buildings under the shadow of the Space Needle. Andrea knew which door they kept unlocked during the day. As she collapsed her umbrella and ducked inside, her phone rang. It played the refrain from the Beatles' "Hello, Goodbye."

Checking her cell, she paused in the lobby by a life-size, black-and-white cardboard cut-out of Jack Kerouac, advertising the theater's current play. Andrea pressed a few digits on her phone and saw she had a text—from Luke:

C U Soon! XX—Me

Andrea felt another little pang in her stomach. She took a deep breath and headed to the main level door to the theater. She wondered if it wouldn't be better to get him alone for a few minutes and just tell him here. Why wait until they sat down at some restaurant for lunch? Why prolong this agony?

Opening the door, she saw several actors seated in a semicircle of folding chairs on the illuminated stage. They all had bound scripts in their hands or in their laps. Some held Starbucks cups or bottled water. In the center of this group was a pretty, thirty-something redhead wearing a blue T-shirt and jeans. She was reading aloud part of a monologue Luke had written for his new play: ". . . I guess I've always been jinxed in the love department. My first boyfriend turned out to be gay. We were freshmen in high school. He was the first guy I ever made out with. I remember we were tangled up on the couch in his basement, listening to Air Supply sing 'Making Love Out of Nothing at All.' I mean, how prophetic was that? Still, he was one of the most considerate, sweetest—"

"Lisa, I really like what you're doing with the start of this," Luke interrupted. "But you're kind of turning the last sentence into a punch line. It's got to be both heartbreaking and funny at the same time. You know what I mean?"

He was in a pocket of people seated in the middle of the otherwise-deserted theater—about ten rows from the stage. The others, with scripts in hand, were in the seats on either side of him and behind him.

Luke was tall, sturdy, and offbeat handsome—with receding brown hair and sexy, sleepy eyes. He reminded her of Yves Montand or Liam Neeson. He had that same smoldering, continental look, which was kind of funny, since Luke grew up in Omaha and didn't even visit Europe until he was in his forties. He always dressed impeccably—even in casual clothes, like today's blue-striped shirt and jeans.

Andrea had told him that story about making out with her first boyfriend. Luke had asked if he could use it in his play, and she'd told him to go ahead. It was interesting to hear an actress revealing this intimate detail of her life.

A young man in the seat behind Luke whispered something to him, and he glanced over his shoulder. Then he spotted her, broke into a grin, and waved. He looked so happy to see her.

Andrea waved and smiled back at him. She wondered if this would be the last time she'd see that look from him—like she was the most important person in his world.

Would he hate her after today?

Luke motioned for her to join them.

Andrea shook her head and pointed toward the lobby. Then she ducked back out the door.

She retreated toward the lobby bar, which at the moment was just an empty counter—devoid of any alcohol or glassware. Leaning against the bar, she nervously rubbed her forehead. She kept wondering how she'd break it to him: *"Luke, I have something very difficult to tell you. I've been lying to you all this time . . ."*

She still wasn't ready, damn it.

Her cell phone rang with the "Hello, Goodbye" refrain again.

She figured it was Luke, wondering what in God's name was wrong with her and why she wouldn't sit with him. Without checking the caller ID, she clicked on the phone. "Hello?"

"Aunt Dee?"

"Spence?" she replied, baffled. Why was he calling her in the middle of a school day?

"Is Luke watching this?" he asked, a little out of breath.

"I don't understand. Watching what? Honey, are you all right?"

"It's Damon," Spencer said, an edge in his voice. "He—he sent out a link to a live-streaming webcast. Practically everyone in school got it. I'm watching him on there, and he says he's going to kill himself. I figured he must have sent a link to Luke, because he acts like he's talking to him on the webcast . . ."

"Are you serious?" she asked.

"Yeah, and so is Damon, I think," Spencer replied. "I'm pretty sure he's going to do it. This isn't a joke. He's gotten hold of some explosives. He keeps saying he's going to blow himself up . . ."

"Has anyone called the police?"

"I'm not sure," Spencer answered.

"Well, where is he?"

"That's just it. Damon isn't here at school. I don't know where he's doing this."

Andrea was shaking her head. "Oh, God, I—I don't think Luke has any idea. Can—can you send this webcast link to him? Send it to me, too . . ."

"Okay, hold on," Spencer said.

Andrea rushed back to the lobby door and flung it open.

All the performers had left the stage—except for the redheaded actress, who was now up there with Luke and the director. He must have switched off his cell phone after that last text to her.

Andrea heard her phone chime, and on the small screen she saw an email message:

SPENCER SENT YOU A LINK.

"Luke!" she cried out. She clicked on it to connect to the webcast.

*"Are you listening to me, Dad?"* Damon Shuler ranted. The pale, gangly teenager was just a tiny, slightly blurred image on the small screen of Andrea's smart phone. He paced in front of a black BMW, parked along some wooded road. *"I'm going to kill myself, and everyone will see it. Just think of all the people who have seen the plays you've written, Dad. And that still won't be as many people who will watch me die."* Damon laughed manically. *"I'm going to have a bigger audience than you've ever had for all your plays combined!"*

Andrea looked up toward the stage again. "Luke!" she screamed.

He stood and squinted toward the lobby door.

"Come here!" she cried. "Your phone, bring your cell phone . . ."

"What is it?" he called, frozen up there on the stage.

"For God's sake, hurry!" she answered.

She watched him grab his phone. Then he bolted toward the steps at the side of the stage. He hurried up the aisle—toward her.

*"I'm going to be more famous than you, Dad!"* Damon was saying on the webcast.

"What's going on?" Luke called to her as he came closer.

Staring at him, Andrea took a deep breath. Her hand shook as she held out her cell phone for him to see.

"It's Damon," she whispered.

# CHAPTER TWO

*Thursday—12:42 p.m.*

With so many kids in the school cafeteria always focused on their mobile devices, Spencer couldn't tell just how many of them were watching Damon's live webcast.

Spencer Murray was always surprised whenever someone—like the cashier at the Safeway two days ago—pointed out to him that he was handsome. He never thought of himself that way. He did his best to blend in and avoid attention. That carried over into his wardrobe. Today he had on jeans and a white shirt with the sleeves rolled up. He sat in an orange plastic chair at one of the cafeteria's long, faux-wood-topped tables. He shared the table with five others—all losers like him. At one end were three pint-sized freshmen boys, who seemed oblivious to their own nerdiness as they excitedly talked over each other about some Xbox game. Across from him was a husky girl with short, curly brown hair. Her food tray held only some white bread slices and a bowl of lime Jell-O. She kept her head down as she ate, seemingly fascinated by some textbook. Spencer wondered if she was really reading it—or just using it as a prop so she didn't feel too conspicuous sitting alone.

Tanya McCallum sat directly on his left. She was wearing another one of her weird thrift shop outfits: a pair of beige "mom-type" stretch slacks and a red blouse with puffy, short sleeves. She had a plain, slightly chubby face. Pale green streaks highlighted her shoulder-length mousy brown hair. She kept it back from her face with a couple of cheap, blue plastic clips—the kind little girls might wear.

Spencer figured she dressed that way to be eccentric and gain attention. But it only seemed to invite trouble, which she got—in doses that almost matched the woes heaped on her best pal, Damon Shuler. The two of them hung out together. One of the cheerleaders, KC Cunningham, maintained that Tanya was Damon's "fag hag." Spencer was pretty sure Damon wasn't gay. Of course, that didn't matter. The kids in school still called him "fag" and "freak." Damon and Tanya always bore the brunt of abuse. Damon got hassled for his OCD tics. But Tanya almost seemed to set herself up for teasing.

Just a week ago, nearly everyone had already taken their seats in Mr. Dwoskin's world history class when Tanya shuffled in alone, wearing sort of a big girl's Marcia Brady–style jumper and clutching her books to her chest. It was the only class Spencer had with Damon and Tanya. Dwoskin wasn't there yet.

"Yo, Tanya!" Ron Jarvis bellowed from his seat, four rows back. "Tanya!"

She paused in front of the blackboard. Gawking at the handsome, dumbass jock, she gave a mock curtsy.

Seated near the back of the classroom, Spencer had to admire Tanya for that defiant response. But at the same time, he figured she was pushing her luck. Ron was one of Damon Shuler's constant tormentors. Spencer had also been targeted in the corridors by Ron his first week at school. He'd been shoved once and had had his books knocked out of his hands on another occasion. Spencer had done his best to avoid the guy. But there was Tanya in Mr. Dwoskin's class, smirking at Ron, for God's sake—just inviting him to pick on her.

Spencer figured she was either very brave or very stupid.

"Yo, Tanya, you're ugly!" Ron announced. He made a howling sound like a dog. "You're ugly as shit, Tanya!"

People started to snicker.

Tanya glared at Ron and said something—probably a very biting, sarcastic zinger. From some of the remarks she'd made in class, Spencer knew she had a quick, lethal wit. But he couldn't hear her because of the laughter. Plus Ron was shouting over her: "Tanya, you're ugly . . . *ugly!*"

A few others joined in. Some of them howled and barked.

Spencer watched her friend, Damon, on the other side of the room, sinking lower in his seat. Though Spencer always did his damnedest to blend in and not make trouble, he couldn't hold back. He had to say something. "Jesus, give it a rest!" he yelled. "What's the point?"

But no one seemed to hear him over all the taunting, jeering, and barking.

With her head down, Tanya started toward her desk. But she burst into tears before she could make it to her seat. Spencer thought everyone would let up now that she was crying, but they didn't. Tanya swiveled around and bolted for the door.

She must have heard the wave of laughter crescendo before the door shut behind her.

Spencer glanced at Damon, who kept his eyes on his desk and nervously tapped his foot. Damon had it a lot worse than her.

Spencer had a unique insight into Luke's son. When he and his aunt had spent that first night at Luke's place, he'd slept in the guest room Damon used for his alternate-weekend visits. Spencer stripped the bed the next morning, figuring he'd change the sheets for Damon. Under the mattress he found Damon's journal. He would have left it alone and unread. But it turned out they didn't go back to the Ballard apartment that day. They stayed, and curiosity got the best of him. So Spencer read snippets—enough to know that Damon didn't want to leave the journal in the house with his mother, because he was afraid she periodically searched his room. God only knew what he thought she was looking for. Apparently, he didn't have a high opinion of the women in his life, because he wrote that Tanya was "overbearing" and "frumpy." And yet Damon and she were together practically all the time. Spencer didn't quite understand that.

But he certainly understood Damon's reluctance to tangle with Ron Jarvis—and his pal, Reed Logan, who was just as bad. They were relentlessly cruel to him. Spencer cringed as he read a blow-by-blow account of how the two of them once locked Damon in a cramped storage space in the school's auditorium and left him there for three hours. "I could hardly move," Damon had written. "I couldn't breathe. It was so dark in there. I thought I was going to die in there . . ."

There was another incident—earlier this year—when the two of them attacked and stripped Damon naked in the restroom. Apparently, KC Cunningham mercilessly made fun of him on Twitter and Facebook.

For good reason, Spencer didn't have any social media accounts, so he never actually saw KC's venomous posts. But Damon described in his journal how humiliating they were.

Spencer was no fan of Damon's, but he didn't think anyone deserved such treatment. Maybe it was because he'd been protective of his journal—among other things—that Damon had made him sleep in Luke's study the first weekend they'd spent together in the town house. That Sunday night after Damon had gone back to his mother's, Spencer had noticed—big surprise—the journal was gone.

He wondered if Tanya had a clue how much and how often her best friend criticized her in his diary. Yet every lunch period, they usually snuck away to eat someplace in private.

Spencer couldn't figure her out. Damon didn't want a damn thing to do with him, and yet for the last two weeks or so, Tanya wouldn't leave him alone.

Spencer found her part flirty and part friendly—and a bit obnoxious. He couldn't trust her. He was cordial toward Tanya, but kept his distance—which wasn't always easy.

She'd sat—uninvited—at this same table with him two weeks ago when Damon had stayed home sick. She'd planted herself in the chair next to Spencer and started asking questions about his aunt and his former school in Virginia. Spencer managed to be vague and elusive in his responses. He switched the subject to the play she'd been rehearsing. On that topic, Tanya wouldn't shut up. She went on and on, criticizing her costars, their names tripping off her tongue as if Spencer was supposed to know who they were. She talked endlessly about someone named Randy. It was brain-numbing, because Spencer couldn't figure out if Randy was a boy or a girl. Was Randy in their class—or was it the name of a character in the stupid play?

He wondered how the hell Damon put up with her.

This morning, he hadn't seen Damon in world history. Spencer figured what with her best friend home sick today Tanya would be inflicting herself on him during lunch hour again.

Taking a cue from Ms. Jell-O & White Bread, Spencer had brought along a copy of *Jude the Obscure* to read during lunch—in case Tanya sat next to him once more. "I really need to have this finished by sixth period," he imagined telling Tanya, as an excuse for why he couldn't talk to her.

That had been fifteen minutes ago.

Spencer had read only a few pages of *Jude* and gotten halfway through his plate of mac and cheese when he'd spotted Tanya barreling toward him, weaving around the crowded tables with her cell phone raised in her hand.

"Oh, my God!" she'd cried—for half the cafeteria to hear.

Plopping down in the chair beside him, she'd grabbed hold of his arm. "Have you seen this? Does Damon's dad know about this?"

Baffled, Spencer had stared at her.

Even after Tanya had explained everything to him, Spencer still couldn't believe it.

Apparently, Damon had gotten hold of a student list and emailed the entire junior and senior classes a link to a live webcast. Spencer realized he must have missed the email—he didn't have an alert for them on his phone. He rarely received emails—except spam.

On the tiny screen of Tanya's phone, he watched the bizarre broadcast. Damon claimed he was going to kill himself. He said he'd gotten his hands on some dynamite.

All of it seemed so surreal. Spencer couldn't be sure whether or not he was on the level. Checking his phone, he found Damon's email in his inbox. He called his aunt. He probably didn't make any sense trying to tell her what was happening. But as soon as he hung up, Spencer emailed the webcast link to her and Luke. Then he started watching the webcast on his own phone.

His aunt had said Luke didn't have any idea what was going on. Ironically, so far, most of Damon's ranting was aimed at his dad.

"You and my mother are responsible—*culpable*—

for all this," Damon decreed, staring at the camera. Spencer could almost get used to Damon's OCD tics, but he had a strange way of talking, too. He'd come up with weird words most kids didn't use—words like "culpable." It was another thing that made him different.

On the webcast, Damon was outside, standing near a black BMW parked on what looked like a remote, wooded, dead-end road. Usually, Damon was a pretty fastidious dresser, but now he was wearing jeans and a gray sweatshirt that drooped on his skinny frame. He had a manic, frayed look—like someone who had pulled an all-nighter and then downed too many Red Bulls to stay awake. He had dark circles under his eyes and kept twitching as he spoke into the camera. Spencer imagined the camera or smart phone in Record mode, propped on a tree stump or a fence post.

"You knew what was going on, Dad," Damon hissed, his eyes narrowing. "And you didn't do a damn thing to stop it—except for a few conferences with Principal Dunmore." He let out a bitter, ironic laugh. "Yeah, Dunmore, talk about useless. Done-Nothing! That fucker, he knew they were making my life shit. Yet he sat back and allowed them to keep on—*brutalizing* me . . ."

Tanya stared at the phone in her trembling hand. "I can't understand why he didn't talk to me first," she murmured. "If he's serious about this, he should have told me."

On the webcast, Damon stepped closer to the camera. "I hope you get fired after this, Dunmore. Let the record show I came to you for help again and again, but you didn't lift a finger to stop any of the bullying. You shouldn't be running a school, Dunmore. You couldn't run a lemonade stand, you worthless piece of shit . . ."

Spencer heard an eruption of laughter at a nearby lunch table. He glanced up and noticed Reed Logan, Ron Jarvis, and several others from the cool clique at *their* table. Reed was particularly obnoxious. He was kind of wimpy, but made up for it with his big, loud mouth. He always wore—even during classes—a Dodgers baseball cap, because he was originally from Los Angeles or something. And talk about innovative, he wore it *backward*. The guy really was a tool. He didn't excel in any sports, but for some insane reason the "cool" crowd seemed to like him.

Practically all of them were on their mobile devices. From the timing of their laughter, Spencer was pretty certain they were reacting to Damon's tirade against the principal.

It was quiet at the other tables—except for some hushed murmuring. The word must have gotten around about the webcast, because nearly everyone was glued to their phones. The only people who seemed to think it was funny were the ones sitting at the "cool" table. Spencer couldn't fathom how Damon's persecutors— the very people who had driven him to this pitiful, public spectacle—could find his diatribe so amusing. Maybe they just didn't believe he'd go through with the suicide.

Yet Spencer knew from his own experience that people could be capable of anything when pushed too far.

Everyone at that table must have bullied or teased

Damon at one time or another. The only student who didn't seem to find the situation funny was Ron Jarvis's cheerleader girlfriend, Bonnie Middleton. Pretty, with long, straight chestnut hair, she stood on her tiptoes and glanced over Ron's shoulder at the cell phone in his hand.

"Five bucks says the freak will chicken out," Reed Logan loudly proclaimed. Everyone at the table laughed—except for Bonnie. She scowled at the others, shook her head, and muttered something.

"Oh, get over yourself!" Reed bellowed at her while adjusting his baseball cap.

Spencer glanced back down at his phone screen.

"I hold my parents and *Principal Done-Nothing* responsible for a lot of this," Damon was saying. "But let's be honest here. A number of assholes at school are really to blame, and you know who you are—Reed Logan, Ron Jarvis . . ."

The group at the elite table hooted and howled at the mention of these names. Smirking, Reed bumped fists with one of his buddies.

"It's not funny!" Tanya screamed at them. "What in God's name is wrong with you people?"

"Cow!" shot back KC Cunningham from the cool table.

Blond, sexy, and impish, KC reminded Spencer of Miley Cyrus. KC seemed unfazed when Damon named her among his tormenters.

Then he mentioned Bonnie Middleton. Everyone at the table laughed and teased her. With a hand on her forehead, Ron's girlfriend turned away from the others and ran out of the cafeteria.

"There are others, but those four are the worst offenders," Damon continued. "You made my life utterly miserable. And why? Because I have OCD? It's an *affliction*. And who are you anyway? Small, cruel, petty, insecure creeps! You're pathetic. And you'll be sorry. You'll miss me when I'm gone."

"Shut up and kill yourself already!" Ron retorted. His friends laughed.

They were the only ones being rowdy. Silverware had stopped clanking, and a hush had fallen over the big room.

Spencer gazed at the phone. Damon went out of focus for a moment as he moved closer to the camera. "I want you to understand the full impact of what's about to happen here," he announced. He picked up his camera or phone, and everything turned blurry for a few seconds. Finally, the black BMW came into focus. But the image was shaky in Damon's unsteady hand. He opened the driver's door to show five sticks of dynamite, rubber-banded together, resting on the front passenger seat.

"It's fake!" yelled some guy in the cafeteria. "I'll bet it's fake!"

Someone else shushed him.

"Oh, God, no," Tanya whimpered, squeezing Spencer's arm. "He's serious about this. He's really going to do it. Can you tell where he is?"

Spencer shook his head. Queen Anne and nearby Ballard both had a lot of woodsy cul-de-sacs. But most of those were residential streets. Damon couldn't have pulled off this webcast anywhere residential—not without drawing someone's attention and having them call the cops. He was just too loud in his denouncements. He seemed confident nobody was around to hear him. Not once had he even looked over his shoulder.

If anyone watching the webcast had called the police, it wasn't like they knew where to send them. Damon could be anywhere.

"I'm not alone here, you know," he said, a tiny smile tugging at one corner of his mouth. "No one cares about suicides anymore unless the person killing himself takes at least one other person down with them . . ."

The camera panned from the front interior of the car to the back, where a thin, forty-something blonde was sprawled across the seat. A piece of duct tape covered her mouth. Squirming, she rolled over on her side. The camera zoomed in on her hands, tied in back of her. Then the unsteady camera panned up and moved in close to her face—until Spencer could see the terror in her eyes.

"I think some of you already know my mother," Damon said.

# CHAPTER THREE

*Thursday—12:45 p.m.*

"It looks like someone's trying to get in touch with you, *Mom*," Damon said over Evelyn's "Ode to Joy" ringtone. The ringing came out slightly muffled on the webcast. But Damon's voice was loud and clear—and dripping with irony. He turned away from the camera to glance at his mother, bound and gagged in the backseat of the BMW. She was a bit out of focus on the webcast.

Damon reached into his back pocket and pulled out the ringing phone. He still had the scowl on his face as he turned toward the camera again. "Too bad you can't talk right now," he continued. "In fact, you've already uttered your last words ever. You're going to die with that tape over your mouth, Mother. But not to worry, you won't be alone. I'm going with you."

"C'mon, Damon, look at the caller ID," Luke whispered into his phone. "Please, pick up, c'mon."

Luke and Andrea were alone in the gloomy theater. The director and leading actress had wandered off a couple of minutes ago, dimming the stage lights before they left. Luke stood at the back, near the lobby doors. Andrea hovered beside him, holding up her smart phone so that he could see the webcast. But the screen was so tiny he couldn't make out any details in the background that might give away the webcast's locale. He had no idea where his son and wife were. They didn't seem to be anywhere near the house on Garfield Street in Queen Anne, where Damon and Evelyn still lived.

Luke had tried twice—unsuccessfully—to get ahold of Damon before realizing the camera on his son's cell must have been recording this webcast. So he'd tried Evelyn's number, figuring Damon would have confiscated his mother's phone before tying her up.

The phone was in Damon's hand, still chiming "Ode to Joy."

Tears in his eyes, Luke listened to the ringtones on his end.

Damon seemed determined to go through with this murder-suicide. And the poor kid was right to point the finger of blame at him. He was *culpable*. He should have guessed that allowing Evelyn custody would lead to something like this. But Damon had insisted on staying with her.

Luke had known for years that his son was troubled. Yet at times, he could be a very lovable kid. He still had a chance at a good life. Damon needed to know that. Whatever awful thing had led him to want to kill himself and his mother, it was reparable. This grand exit—this horrible, broadcasted murder-suicide—was no solution.

Luke couldn't let it happen.

With the phone to his ear, he counted a fifth ring-tone on Evelyn's line. All the while, he anxiously watched Damon on the tiny screen of Andrea's phone.

His son still hadn't looked at the caller ID. He didn't know his father was trying to get ahold of him. "C'mon, Damon, pick up," Luke said under his breath.

On the webcast, "Ode to Joy" stopped playing.

At the same time, over the phone line, Evelyn's voice mail recording came on: *"Hi! Sorry I missed you. But if you leave a message after the beep . . ."*

It was strange to hear her, so perky and confident—and then see her in the backseat of that BMW, trembling, terrified and utterly doomed.

The beep sounded on the other end of the line.

"Damon, it's me," Luke said into the phone. "I—I'm looking at you right now. Please, son, we can fix this. We can make it okay. C'mon, you—you don't have to do this. Please, call me. I love you . . ."

But Luke wasn't even sure if Damon knew how to retrieve messages on his mother's phone. He clicked off the line and then speed-dialed Evelyn's number again.

He squinted at his son on the tiny screen of Andrea's phone. "Damn it, I still can't make out anything familiar in the background . . ."

Andrea glanced at something on the stage. Then she set her phone on the ledge of a half wall behind the last row of seats. She left the screen side up so that Luke could still see the webcast. Before he could ask what she was doing, she raced down the aisle to the stage. One of the folding chairs made a loud ding as she accidentally bumped it. The sound echoed through the deserted theater. She made her way to the chair where Luke had been sitting, where he'd left his laptop. It was still open. He'd been taking notes on the rehearsal before she'd interrupted them.

Dropping to her knees, Andrea furiously worked her fingers over the computer's keyboard.

Luke still couldn't figure out what she was doing. He looked back at the webcast.

Damon seemed annoyed to hear "Ode to Joy" chiming from Evelyn's cell once more. This time, he glanced at the caller ID.

Luke's heart leapt. At last, his son would see that he was calling him.

"Well, well, well, it's the Seattle Police," Damon muttered. "So somebody decided to call them."

Luke was crushed when he heard the busy signal. He wondered if the police had any notion where Damon was. Or were they as frustrated and clueless as he was right now?

On the webcast, Damon stared at the phone in his hand. "All I can say is that I'm very touched someone cared enough to contact the local authorities on my behalf. Where the hell were they when I really needed some help—when I was everyone's punching bag at that fucking school? How many of you stood by and watched me get shit on, huh? How many of you did nothing?"

Andrea raced up the aisle, carefully holding his laptop in front of her. The illuminated screen glowed in the darkened theater. Luke heard Damon's voice echoing—almost overlapping—as it came from two different sources. "Well, the police can leave a message," his son announced. "They're too late anyway . . ."

"You can see better on this," Andrea said, out of breath. She tilted the laptop screen toward him. Her hands were shaking.

She had pulled up the webcast on his computer. Luke desperately searched the road and the trees in the background for a clue—any clue that might reveal where his son was.

Evelyn's phone stopped ringing. Damon paid no attention to it. Instead, he scowled at his webcast audience. "I blame some of you teachers, too," he said. "All of you at one time or another allowed them to call me *freak* in front of the rest of the class. Did you think it was funny? Did you for one minute consider my feelings?"

Andrea nodded at the laptop screen. "It isn't raining," she said.

"What?"

"Wherever Damon is, it's not raining there. You've been in the theater all morning. It was pouring on my way here ten minutes ago." She pointed to the BMW behind Damon—without a single raindrop on it. The windows reflected the sun's glare. "He's not in town, Luke. He isn't in Seattle . . ."

Luke kept examining the scenery behind Damon. He spotted three dilapidated, rural-style mailboxes at the edge of the screen—behind the car. He'd always wondered about those mailboxes.

There was a dead end a couple of blocks from their

summer home on Lopez Island. When he was just a kid, Damon had been fascinated with one of the three houses on that dead-end road. Whenever they'd gone to the island, the first thing Damon would want to do was "see the big dog." So Luke would take little Damon by the hand and walk him to the road so he could look at the huge statue in the side yard of someone's house. It was a twelve-foot-tall replica of the RCA Victor dog, sitting in front of a Victrola gramophone. Luke had no idea why it was there, but the kitschy monument fascinated young Damon. That was the last house on the block, but the road curved around for another two hundred yards to a dead end surrounded by a wooded lot. A short path through the trees led to the edge of a cliff—and a spectacular view of the water and the other San Juan Islands.

But at the end of the turnaround—at the beginning of that path—Luke remembered the three slightly battered mailboxes. He never knew why they were there—maybe for an old triplex that had been torn down or a trio of cabins lost in a landslide. Whatever, those three mailboxes were all that remained of what had once been there.

And he saw them now—in the background, at the edge of the laptop screen. Damon had taken his mother to the family's island getaway.

"They're on Lopez," he said. "Oh, God, Andrea, call the Lopez Island Police, and tell them. He's on—on Timber Trail Place or Timber Trail Court or something like that. It's a dead end. They should know where it is . . ."

Andrea snatched her phone off the ledge behind the

last row of seats, and then she set the open laptop in its place. She started working her thumbs over the phone's keypad.

On screen, Damon was still accusing his teachers of negligence: "Did you think *freak* was a—a term of endearment? What's your excuse? Mr. McAfee, you were the worst. I think you actually encouraged guys like Jarvis and Logan. You want to know something, McAfee? In addition to being a bad human being, you're a bad teacher. You didn't come back to high school to educate anybody. You came back for another shot at being popular, and if that meant letting the cool crowd get away with murder, then it was fine by you, wasn't it?"

Luke was about to speed-dial Evelyn's number again when the phone rang in his hand. He checked the caller ID: SEATTLE POLICE DEPT.

"Who is it?" Andrea asked, stopping to stare at him.

"The police," he said. Luke hesitated for a moment, and then clicked on the line.

"Is this Luke Shuler?" the caller asked—before Luke even said anything.

"Yes. Is this about my son?"

"This is Detective John Reich with the Seattle Police—"

"I don't think my son's in Seattle," Luke interrupted. "I'm almost positive he's on a dead-end road called Timber Trail Place or Timber Trail Court. It's on Lopez. You need to get ahold of the Lopez Island Police. Do you understand?"

He noticed Andrea putting her phone down.

There was a silence on the other end of Luke's line. "Hello?" he asked anxiously.

"Timber Trail—on Lopez," the cop said finally. "We'll let the Lopez Police know. Mr. Shuler, do you have any idea where your son could have gotten his hands on that dynamite?"

"No, none," he replied.

"Was your son in Tacoma this past Monday night?"

"I—I have no idea," Luke said, baffled at the question.

"Seven sticks of dynamite were reported stolen from the Bourm Construction Company storage facility in Tacoma on Monday evening. Security cameras didn't get a good shot of the culprit, but one picked up a car parked near the site for an hour. It appeared to be a black BMW . . ."

"I'm sorry, I can't—I can't account for my son's whereabouts on Monday night," Luke said, flustered. "He lives with his mother. Listen, you need to contact the Lopez Island Police, and tell them where my son is—"

"It's being taken care of right now, Mr. Shuler," the cop said, cutting him off. "We appreciate your help. Can you tell us where you are?"

"I'm in the Seattle Group Theater building on Mercer—in the Center. Listen, please, I'm trying to get ahold of my son. I think maybe I can talk Damon out of this, but I can't get through to him, because you guys are on the line. If you could only—"

"Mr. Shuler," the detective talked over him. "Mr. Shuler, we've been monitoring this broadcast since a student at Queen Anne High sent us the link several minutes ago. We don't have much time. We counted five sticks of dynamite in the front seat of that car. If your son stole the dynamite from Bourm Construction, that still leaves two sticks of dynamite unaccounted for. He obviously has a grudge against a lot of people at the school. Do you know if he was there earlier today—or perhaps late last night?"

"No, like I said, he's living with his mother. You—you might try his best friend at school. Her name is—Tanya, Tanya—um, *Tanya McCallum*. She might know something."

"Do you have a phone number for her?" the detective asked.

Luke sighed. "No, I don't, I'm sorry . . ."

All the while, Luke was watching Damon on the laptop. His son had gotten quieter. He didn't seem as annoyed by the "Ode to Joy" ringtone chiming over his mother's phone once again. He just seemed sadly resigned to it. "It's the police again," he murmured, checking Evelyn's caller ID. "Too little, too late . . ."

Damon looked directly into the camera. "They can't save me," he said with a tiny smile. "Remember what I said earlier? No one cares about suicides unless the person killing himself takes at least one other person down with them. My mother's not the only one going with me."

He glanced back at Evelyn, helplessly struggling in the backseat of the car.

Then he turned to his webcast audience again. "I mean, c'mon," he said. "Did you really think I'd leave this world without getting back at some of you?"

\* \* \*

"What the hell is that supposed to mean?" yelled Reed Logan at the cool table. His voice rose above the murmuring and the occasional clang of flatware in the school cafeteria.

Hunched over his phone, Spencer watched Damon's tirade. All the while, Tanya sort of pressed herself against him. He was barely aware of it. He was too focused on Damon's thinly veiled threat against his classmates—and the school. Unlike Reed Logan, he had a pretty good idea what Damon meant when he'd said, *Did you really think I'd leave this world without getting back at some of you?*

If Damon had gotten his hands on a few sticks of dynamite, he could have procured several more sticks—enough to take out a substantial number of people in the high school. And what part of the school was most crowded at this time of day? A bomb set to detonate in the cafeteria right now would kill or maim dozens of students.

Spencer suddenly felt sick to his stomach. "Listen, we've got to get out of here," he said to Tanya.

She squinted at him. "Why? What are you talking about?"

He stood up. "Haven't you been listening to him? He's out to get even with the whole school. We're sitting ducks here—"

"Someone's trying to call me," Tanya said, distracted. She pressed some digits on the keypad of her phone.

"Jesus Christ, never mind that," he pleaded. "We need to leave—*now*."

"It's the police," Tanya murmured, checking her caller ID.

Spencer pulled her to her feet.

She almost dropped the phone. "Hey, watch it!"

With a tight grip on her arm, Spencer glanced around the cafeteria at all the students—so oblivious to the danger. "Listen, everybody!" he yelled. He'd spent the last five weeks here trying to maintain a low profile. Most of the people in the cafeteria didn't know him. "Haven't you heard what he's been saying? We're not safe here . . ."

"Shut your hole!" someone yelled back. A few people laughed.

"Who the hell is that?" someone else asked.

"Attention, students, faculty, and staff." Principal Dunmore's voice boomed over the PA system.

Spencer froze.

"This is Principal Dunmore. Please listen to these important instructions. In a few moments, the fire alarm will sound. It is imperative that you evacuate the school in a quiet, orderly fashion. You are to head to the play-field north of the parking lot and wait there for further instructions . . ."

At least three hundred students were eating lunch in the cafeteria, and Luke guessed only fifty of them got to their feet. Were the rest of them really that stupid? Nearly all of the upperclassmen had to be watching the webcast. Didn't they realize they were being evacuated for a reason?

"Oh, yeah, sure!" someone yelled out. "Make us do this bullshit during our lunch hour!"

He got a big laugh. But only a few more people got to their feet.

Spencer started to pull Tanya toward the fire exit—a set of double doors that led outside. She was still preoccupied with the phone call from the police. "Should I answer it?" she asked.

Spencer suddenly stopped in his tracks. He stared at the fire exit. No one had opened those double doors yet. Had Damon rigged the doors to activate an explosion? It was one way to ensure a high body count. Spencer wanted to scream out a warning to the others, but who would listen?

He steered Tanya toward another exit, one that led to a hallway that eventually accessed a side door. At the moment, it seemed safer. Or had Damon booby-trapped that, too?

He couldn't shake the terrible feeling in his gut. Damon was going to unleash something catastrophic on this school. The people in charge must have felt the same way; otherwise they wouldn't be emptying out the building. More and more of the students seemed to be catching on to the seriousness of the situation—and the potential danger. The chatter got louder in the cafeteria. People were gathering up their books and backpacks. Chairs scraped against the floor as students got to their feet.

More than anything, Spencer just wanted to get out of that cafeteria before the first blast went off. But Tanya was slowing him down. "Hello?" she said into her phone, talking loudly over the increasing din around them. "Yes, this is she . . ."

"I'll bet the freak planted a bomb!" Reed screamed. But he was cackling, too—as if amused as well as panic-stricken. "Holy shit, he set us up—"

The sudden, shrill blare from the fire alarm drowned him out.

Someone screamed. But people were laughing, too. Over the incessant alarm, Spencer heard the clatter of chairs falling over and the rumble of feet as kids hurried toward the emergency exit.

Spencer winced as he watched the double doors fly open.

But nothing happened. A bomb didn't go off.

It didn't matter. Spencer still wanted to get out of there. Damon might not have booby-trapped the cafeteria doors, but that didn't mean he hadn't planted a bomb somewhere in the vicinity. All it took was a backpack under one of the cafeteria tables—or an explosive device in a locker.

"I can't hear you!" Tanya was shouting into the phone. "They're evacuating the school."

Spencer held on to her arm. They were overrun—almost crushed—by a mob of students moving in the opposite direction. Everyone was struggling to make their way to the double doors. It was next to impossible for Spencer and her to make it to the exit on the other side of the cafeteria. He gave up and pulled Tanya along with the wave of bodies heading toward the double-door fire exit.

Despite the panic, chaos, and deafening noise, he noticed several people talking on their phones or texting as they made their slow, clumsy escape. The horde seemed to reach a bottleneck at the doors.

"Yes, Damon and I are friends," Tanya was yelling into the phone. "But I haven't seen him outside of school this whole week . . . What? I can't hear you . . ."

Spencer kept tugging her by the arm as he worked his way through the crowd. They finally made it through the double doors, where a few teachers were directing the flow of traffic.

"C'mon, keep moving," one of them shouted over the fire alarm. "Don't block the doorway!" It was Roger McAfee, the English teacher Damon had taken to task in his diatribe. McAfee was in his late thirties and slightly paunchy. He wore a navy blue Windbreaker with QUEEN ANNE HIGH SCHOOL on the back in gray letters. As he waved the students on, directing them like a traffic cop, he stopped to grin at Ron Jarvis, lingering by the doorway with a teammate from the varsity football squad. "C'mon, keep moving, Jarvis. You know where the playfield is . . ." He slapped him on the shoulder.

McAfee, like several others, didn't seem to take Damon Shuler's webcast very seriously. Spencer wondered how McAfee could be smiling right now.

He felt the rain dampening his shirt and matting down his hair as he moved along with the rest of the herd down the sidewalk toward the playfield. Tanya was still on her cell phone with the police, talking loudly to compete with the fire alarm: "Okay, I can hear you better now . . . No, I didn't have any idea he was planning anything like this . . . As I said, I haven't seen him outside of school in over a week, maybe two weeks even. That's unusual, because I'm his closest friend . . ."

Something about the way Tanya spoke—she seemed to relish the attention.

Spencer noticed all the others around him were talking and texting on their phones. From what he could tell, no one was tuned into Damon's webcast anymore. They were too busy checking in with each other.

It was as if they'd already forgotten about him.

Spencer pulled out his phone and tried to retrieve Damon's webcast. He figured he was probably the only one in the school who still cared.

Poor Damon, he'd lost his audience.

He was taking too long to kill himself.

"The Lopez Island Police estimate they'll be there in about three or four minutes," Detective Reich told Luke over the phone. "We have a professional standing by on this end. She has a good success rate intervening with potential suicides. We'll clear the line, and if you're able to get through to him, stall him. If you need help, we'll break in and let the pro take over. Understand?"

Luke nodded, even though he was on the phone. "Yes—yes, thank you," he said. Then he hung up. He stomach was in knots. He tried to take a few calming breaths and told himself to count to fifteen before dialing Evelyn's number again—to give the police time to get off the line.

Andrea stood close by with her phone in hand. She turned to him. "I can't get ahold of Spencer at school."

"The cops would have said if anything had happened there," Luke replied hurriedly. "Listen, the Lopez police should reach Damon in about four minutes. Could you count down the minutes for me?"

"Sure, of course," she said, checking her wristwatch.

Luke glanced at his laptop—on the partition ledge behind the last row of theater seats.

His son looked tired and defeated. Damon's voice had gotten hoarse from his long, emotional tirade. He seemed to be winding down. With a sigh, he shut the back door to the BMW. Luke wondered if the Lopez police would make it in time. He speed-dialed Evelyn's number again. There was a click as it connected on the other end.

Over the webcast, he heard the slightly muffled "Ode to Joy" ringtone.

"C'mon, Damon, look at the caller ID," he whispered. "Pick up, pick up . . ."

"Thirty seconds," Andrea said under her breath.

Damon finally frowned at the phone in his hand. He let out a sad little laugh.

Luke counted two more ringtones. "Please," he whispered. "You can see it's me. Please, Damon . . ." One more ring, and it would go to voice mail.

Luke heard a click on the other end. "Well, hey, Dad," Damon said in a quiet voice.

"Damon," he gasped. He couldn't hold back. He suddenly started crying. "Son, I'm so sorry about everything you're going through. But—but we can make it okay. It isn't too late . . ."

"But it is, Dad," he said, sounding listless—almost like a robot. "Things have already been set up."

"It's nothing we can't fix," Luke insisted. He quickly wiped his tears away.

"No, I have to go through with it now," Damon said.

"You don't have to do anything . . ."

"A minute," Andrea whispered.

Luke glanced at her, and he tightened his grip on the phone. "What's 'been set up,' Damon?" he asked anxiously. "A minute ago, you said things had already been set up. What did you mean by that?"

On the webcast, his son glanced into the camera. "You'll see," he murmured.

"Damon, I know a lot of people have hurt you. But you're better than them. If you—if you set up something at the school to—to hurt people, to get back at them—you need to tell me. Please, buddy, tell me, before it's too late."

Damon turned away from the camera. "It's no good, Dad. It's already been done."

"Ninety seconds," Andrea said in a hushed voice. She had tears in her eyes.

"Damon, please," Luke said, wincing. "You're a good kid. You have a chance at a good life. I love you. I don't want to lose you. I don't want my son to be responsible for hurting a lot of innocent people . . ."

"These people aren't innocent," Damon replied.

"They're still just *kids*," Luke argued. "And so are you. You have so much to live for, Damon. Please, call this off . . ."

"You're talking in clichés, Dad," Damon muttered. "You'd never write that kind of dialogue in one of your plays."

"Two minutes," Andrea whispered.

On the webcast, he saw Damon, still standing in front of the BMW. He held his mother's phone close to his face. He wasn't looking into the camera. Twisting his mouth to one side, he seemed pensive. Luke hoped he was getting through to him. If he could just keep him on the line for another two minutes, the police would get there in time to put a stop to this. Maybe their suicide-intervention expert could even persuade Damon to divulge whatever he'd set up at the school to get revenge on his tormentors.

"Damon, I owe you an apology," he said, his voice still shaky. "You're right. I could have been a better father to you. I could have done more—much, much more. I knew you were having a tough time at school—"

"It's not really your fault," Damon sighed. "I was probably exaggerating earlier. You and I both know who's mostly to blame. I mean, let's face it. I'm doing you a favor, Dad, taking her out of the picture." He glanced back toward the car. "You can marry that other woman—and be like a father to what's-his-name— Spencer. He's more like the son you always wanted than I ever could be. At the end of the day, you'll come out better than anyone else. And just think of the publicity, Dad. All those people who have never heard of you and never seen your plays, they'll know you after today . . ."

"You know I don't care about that," Luke said.

"Two and a half minutes," Andrea whispered, checking her wristwatch. "Just keep him talking, Luke . . ."

"*At the end of the day*, more than anything, I want you to be all right—recuperating from all of this," Luke said. "And everything will be okay, you'll see. Please, son. You mean the world to me, Damon. I love you . . ."

Damon said nothing.

On the laptop's screen, he was nodding over and over again. Luke hoped against hope that he was coming around.

But then, Damon grimaced. All at once, he hurled Evelyn's phone into the woods on the other side of the BMW.

"No, God, please, no, no, no!" Luke yelled into the phone—though he knew it was in vain.

Damon couldn't hear him.

His son opened the front door of the car again. Then he stepped to one side, out of the camera's range.

"Three minutes!" Andrea cried.

The other end of the line went dead. But Luke still clutched the phone in his hand as he anxiously watched the laptop screen, waiting for his son to reappear. He thought he heard a distant wail on the webcast. Could it possibly be a police siren?

On screen, the image went out of focus for a moment. Damon was repositioning the camera. Now, Luke could see only the top half of the car—from the passenger side. Damon came back into the shot and calmly walked around the front of the BMW. He approached the open door on the driver's side and bent down to climb into the front seat.

At that moment, Luke realized it was the last glimpse he'd ever have of his son.

"Three and a half minutes," Andrea whispered. "Oh, Luke . . ."

The car door slammed shut.

With the sun reflecting off the windows, it was impossible for Luke to see what his son was doing inside the vehicle. He stepped closer to the laptop screen. He could still hear that siren in the distance. But it sounded too far away.

"God, no," he prayed under his breath. "Please, Damon, don't—"

Before he got another word out, Luke saw the bright flash inside the car.

All at once, flames shot out the windows, and the BMW jumped off the ground. The sound of the blast erupted over the webcast. Then the laptop's screen went blank.

Past the gray static on the laptop, a shrill screeching came over the speakers.

It was the sound of Damon's camera phone melting.

# CHAPTER FOUR

*Thursday—3:07 p.m.*

"Where's Luke?" Spencer asked as he jumped into the passenger side of his aunt's VW Beetle. He was soaked and shivering.

From the driver's seat, Andrea reached over and rubbed his shoulder. "Thank God you're safe," she murmured.

"You, too," Spencer said, patting her hand. He pulled away to shut his door and then buckled his seat belt. He glanced at the rain-beaded side mirror. "We're holding up traffic, Aunt Dee."

Andrea's Volkswagen was at the beginning of a long line of cars in a police-designated pickup area one block from the high school's playfield. The entire school had been in lockdown. Actually, it was more like a lock-out. All six hundred and eighty-something students had been corralled inside the fenced playfield. They'd been standing in the rainy drizzle for the last two hours while the police bomb squad searched the school.

Spencer had seen the BMW blown to bits on the webcast. Looking over his shoulder, Tanya had still been talking to the police when it happened. At the moment of the blast, she'd dropped her phone. She started screaming and sobbing. Spencer tried to calm her down, but she pushed him away.

"Where are they?" she cried, barreling through the mob—toward Ron, KC, Reed, and their group. They all looked a bit shaken and subdued. "Are you fuckers happy now?" she shrieked at them. "Look what you did to him!"

Tanya lunged at Ron and started hitting him on the chest. It took two of his friends and a teacher to pry her away. They led her off the playfield. The last Spencer saw of her, Tanya was sitting in the back of an open ambulance with a rain slicker over her shoulders, talking with a policewoman.

After the initial shock, most students became impatient standing out in the rain. But they weren't allowed to leave. Spencer overheard several of them on their phones, complaining to their parents or friends. Some of those outraged parents must have gotten in touch with Dunmore, because eventually he announced over a bullhorn that everyone would be going home soon. But each one of them had to give their name to a cop or teacher stationed at the exits. Kids had their backpacks searched. Spencer noticed they stopped Bonnie Middleton, the pretty cheerleader Damon had named in his tirade as one of his tormentors. She'd been smart enough to grab a sweater with a hood before evacuating the school. She wasn't with the others from her group. Though visibly distressed, she seemed to be cooperating as a policeman led her off the playfield toward an open tent they'd hurriedly set up by one of the fire trucks. It must have been their impromptu command center.

Spencer figured everyone Damon had mentioned in his webcast was being stopped and questioned. Damon had referred to him, too: *You can marry that other woman—and be like a father to what's-his-name— Spencer. He's more like the son you always wanted than I ever could be.*

That much was more or less true. Spencer had enjoyed being sort of a surrogate son to Luke. He knew he got along better with him than Damon ever did. And Luke was a real nice guy. Until today, Spencer had felt content—and yes, even kind of smug—about the bond he'd formed with Damon's dad.

He could have told the young, curly-haired brunette policewoman at the playfield's northwest exit that he and his aunt were living with Damon's father. But he knew they would just detain him. Andrea was coming to pick him up, and he didn't want to keep her waiting while the police questioned him. Besides, he had absolutely nothing useful to tell them. So when the policewoman asked for his name, he told her, "Spencer Murray." He didn't say anything else. He didn't say anything about his strained relationship with Luke's son. And he didn't say anything about how Murray wasn't his real last name.

"How are you getting home?" she asked, briefly glancing up at him from her iPad, which must have had a list of student names on it.

"My aunt's picking me up," he said.

"We're routing that traffic to Eleventh Avenue," she said, nodding toward her left. "Go on ahead, Spencer."

"Thank you," he said, heading down the sidewalk. He numbly glanced back through the chain-link fence at the hundreds of students still milling around the playfield in the drizzle. They looked miserable, like prisoners.

He was still in a daze over what had happened. He couldn't believe Damon had actually gone through with it. He kept thinking he should have tried a little harder to be Damon's friend, but the guy hadn't exactly made it easy for him. Still, he felt bad, especially for poor Luke.

Spencer took his place with dozens of other students gathered on the corner of Eleventh and Franklin, waiting for their rides. He scanned the gridlocked cars for his aunt's VW. Then something occurred to him. If the police thought Damon might have planted a bomb somewhere else—and it wasn't in the school—where was it?

He imagined Andrea climbing into her VW and turning the key in the ignition—only to set off some kind of detonation device. He'd seen what had happened to Mrs. Shuler's BMW. Or had Damon rigged Luke's car to explode? He'd killed his mother, what would have stopped him from making sure his dad was blown to pieces as well?

After waiting on that corner for another fifteen ago-

nizing minutes, he'd become convinced that something horrible had happened to Andrea or Luke—or
both of them. Spencer had watched one kid after another—and sometimes groups of kids—jump into their
respective cars and drive away. Only about twenty students had been left when he'd pulled out his cell phone
to call his aunt. But then, to his utter relief, he'd spotted the VW.

"Where's Luke?" he asked again as Andrea pulled
away from the curb.

"He's with the police—in a seaplane on their way to
Lopez Island," Andrea answered. She was watching a
cop ahead of them directing traffic. She looked so
tense.

"How's he holding up?" Spencer asked.

She sighed. "How do you think he's holding up?
He's devastated."

Spencer didn't know what to say to her. He turned
and stared out the window.

Apparently, the police had determined it was safe
enough to route traffic down a road that ran along the
side of the school. Three police vehicles were lined up
in the teachers' parking lot. Spencer caught a glimpse
of two guys from the bomb squad coming out of a side
door to the school. They were covered head to toe in
olive green protection gear that resembled space suits.
In front of them was a bomb-detecting machine—a
wheeled device that was a cross between a go-cart and
R2-D2. Spencer had seen one in the movie *The Hurt
Locker*. A pair of cops—each with a bomb-sniffing
German shepherd on a leash—were going from one
parked car to another in the lot.

Spencer squirmed in the passenger seat. "Listen, I know you've got enough to worry about," he said. "But do you think Damon might have done something to Luke's car—or maybe the town house? I mean, if the cops believe he could have set up another bomb . . ."

Andrea nodded. "The police who met us at the theater were thinking along the same lines." She nodded in the general direction of the dashboard. "They already checked out this heap—along with Luke's car and the house. We're okay, Spence. I think we've seen the worst of it. I just hope Luke gets through this okay . . ."

Spencer sat back, but he still couldn't breathe easy. He pressed his forehead against the car window. Three blocks from the school, they passed a car he recognized—parked on the side of the road. It was Mr. McAfee's black Mustang. Though it was about fifty years old, the vehicle was in pristine condition—except for a scratch that ran three feet along the driver's side.

McAfee had made a big deal about it during his English class one week into the school year. Spencer had just started attending Queen Anne High. At first, he'd thought McAfee was kind of laid-back and cool. But then, someone had keyed his precious Mustang in the teachers' parking lot, and McAfee showed his true colors. He spent the first ten minutes of class time vowing to track down the "worthless punk" who had keyed his car. He was certain that someone in that class was responsible—or at least, that someone in the class knew who was responsible. Then to prove just how much of a dick he was, he gave everyone a writing assignment. "I want a minimum of five double-spaced pages analyzing *Beowulf*, due Friday," he decreed. "And I'm sorry if it puts a crimp in your weekend, but you'll have a four-page paper analyzing the character of Grendel due on Monday. There will be another four-page paper due on Wednesday, analyzing Grendel's mother. And I'm going to keep this up until someone comes forward with information on who scratched my car . . ."

True to his word, for nearly two weeks, McAfee kept demanding a new four-page essay—every other day. It was a total pain in the ass. What was worse, they never got the papers back. McAfee didn't bother to grade them. In fact, Spencer was pretty sure McAfee didn't even read them. He overheard someone talking about it in the cafeteria: "Dan Flick said he wrote 'Screw Beowulf and screw you' in the middle of page three in his paper on Hrothgar or whatever the hell his name is—and he never heard a thing from McAfee about it."

Spencer also overheard—from several different sources—that after the first of these punishment papers were turned in, McAfee secretly excused the guys on the football team from writing the essays. At least that was the rumor, and Spencer believed it. The jocks seemed to get away with murder in McAfee's English class.

Damon wasn't in that sixth-period class with Spencer. Damon had McAfee for second period—along with Reed, Ron, and that tribe. Spencer could only imagine what those creeps must have put Damon through during second-period English while McAfee turned a blind eye. He wondered how McAfee felt now—after Damon's speech and his suicide. Was he sorry—or embarrassed? Or did he just turn a blind eye again?

They never did find out who keyed McAfee's car, but after that incident, he stopped parking in the teachers' lot.

Back when it had happened, Spencer had wondered if it was merely a coincidence that someone had keyed his aunt's VW outside the apartment just a month before.

As he looked at the sporty black Mustang behind them, growing more and more distant in the side mirror, Spencer wondered if the cops and their bomb-sniffing dogs were inspecting all the cars in the vicinity—or just the ones in the teachers' lot.

# CHAPTER FIVE

*One year earlier*

Damon Shuler kept a journal. He could pinpoint the time and date when his life at school took a drastic turn and went to hell. It was sophomore year, during Mr. McAfee's fourth period English class, Wednesday, October 23.

He'd squeaked through freshman year without anyone really noticing or bothering him. A few people knew that his dad was a famous playwright, but that hadn't really won him any friends or admirers—except maybe for Tanya, who was crazy for theater arts. He and Tanya hung out a lot, but he didn't feel all that close to her. In fact, sometimes she was kind of a pest. The truth was he really didn't have any friends.

He figured people like Ron Jarvis and Reed Logan didn't even know he was alive.

In September of that year, he had his first bad brush

with Reed Logan. It was sort of a precursor for when things would become terrible a month later.

Reed was the first one to notice Damon's OCD tic— or at least, he was the first one to say anything, and he said it loudly. It happened right before McAfee's class, when Damon was taking his seat.

"Shuler, what's with you and the weird way you have to touch your desk every time you sit down?" Reed asked—for all the students in their English lit class to hear. "Could you possibly be any more of a *freak*?"

Damon didn't realize anyone had been watching him. He'd barely been aware of his own actions. It was automatic. He had to touch the chair and the desk before sitting down. He couldn't help it. Every time he was about to come into contact with something, he needed to touch it. He couldn't explain why. He didn't feel safe grabbing a doorknob until he'd touched it first—and *tested* it. Even if it was a doorknob he used ten times a day, he had to touch it first before he'd take hold of it.

When these tics had started to manifest themselves during his early adolescence, Damon's parents sent him to see a shrink, who prescribed some medication. But the pills made him groggy and kind of stupid. Instead of the meds, another therapist recommended meditation. But that seemed like a waste of time. Damon figured he was fine—so long as no one noticed his tics.

But Reed Logan had noticed.

The next day, as Damon went to take his seat in McAfee's class, Reed offered a play-by-play commentary for all the classmates within earshot: "Watch him touch the chair first—and then the desk, then the chair again . . ."

Damon pretended he didn't hear. But Reed's buddies were cackling. One of the people laughing was Mr. McAfee, standing there at the front of the classroom with his arms folded. Damon thought McAfee looked like an ex-jock gone to seed. He was wearing a loosened tie and had his shirtsleeves rolled up. Damon kept thinking: *He's the teacher. Why doesn't he say something to shut them up?*

By the time he was seated, Damon knew his face was red. Still, he refused to look at anyone.

From then on, he did his damnedest to be one of the first students in their seats for that class. If he got there before Reed and his friends, then no one would be reminded of his little idiosyncrasies. No one would make fun of him.

Reed was hardly one to point fingers. He had a fixation with this stupid Dodgers baseball cap he always wore— backward. The blue cap was his trademark. Some of the teachers made Reed take it off while class was in session. But McAfee let him wear it.

It was on that day in late October in McAfee's English lit class when Damon inadvertently made things worse with Reed—and officially horrible for himself.

With his dumb baseball cap on backward and a little askew, Reed was slouched in his desk chair, trying to bullshit his way through an answer to McAfee's question about *The Great Gatsby*. It was obvious Reed had watched the movie in lieu of reading the book. Damon couldn't help rolling his eyes while Reed babbled on and on.

"Damon, I see you making faces like you disagree with Reed," McAfee pointed out. "Would you care to comment?"

Damon let out a nervous little laugh. "Well, in the first place, while he was talking, Reed said *irregardless* twice—and there's no such word. It's *regardless*, not *irregardless*. I'm kind of surprised you didn't correct him, Mr. McAfee, since this is after all, an English class, English lit . . ."

McAfee narrowed his eyes at him.

But the remark got some snickers from his classmates, and Damon smiled. It felt good to be the one getting the laughs for a change—instead of the one getting laughed at. "And I'm pretty sure he didn't read the book," Damon continued, "because he slipped and called Gatsby 'Leo Gatsby,' after Leonardo DiCaprio in the movie." He rolled his eyes again. "*FYI*, Reed, Gatsby's first name is Jay . . ."

Several students giggled.

Squirming in his chair, Reed glared at him. "And *FYI*, your first name should be *Freak,* you weird, pasty-faced fag!"

The classroom erupted with laughter.

Suddenly Damon was the one squirming in his seat. He nervously glanced at McAfee, sitting at his desk and staring back at him with a tiny smirk on his face. He didn't do anything to silence the guffaws. It was as if he enjoyed watching the humiliation of this kid who had dared to criticize his capability as a teacher. *This is, after all, an English class . . .*

Damon realized right then that Reed would always have the upper hand—especially in McAfee's class.

After that, it seemed Reed's number-one mission was to make Damon's life miserable. He was chummy with a lot of jocks, cheerleaders, and people in the cool crowd. Suddenly these people Damon barely knew were pushing and tripping him in the school hallways and the cafeteria. He couldn't pass Ron Jarvis in the corridor without the hulky, good-looking football star knocking the books out of his hands.

It got so every morning, he dreaded going to school. He found hallway routes between classes where he could avoid most of his tormentors. He rarely ate in the cafeteria, and when he did, he didn't sit anywhere near the "cool table." But one place he couldn't avoid his tormentors was McAfee's English class. None of his other teachers tolerated outbursts and name-calling. But in McAfee's class he was called *freak*, *freakazoid*, or *fag* by Ron, Reed, and their buddies. They always got away with it. After a while, McAfee sometimes discouraged them by smiling tolerantly and saying, "Okay, you guys, enough . . ." Then, after class, he'd be laughing with them and slapping them on the back.

Damon put up with it for the rest of the school year.

And then, at the beginning of Damon's junior year, someone keyed Roger McAfee's prized Mustang in the teachers' parking lot.

McAfee was so stupid—thinking one of the culprit's friends would turn him in if he kept dealing out homework punishment to the students in his classes.

He didn't stop to think that maybe the culprit didn't have any friends.

# CHAPTER SIX

Heading down the sidewalk by the school, Roger McAfee took out his cell phone. The rain had stopped, and it was getting dark already. The streetlights were on. He noticed that the cop cars were all gone.

Earlier, they'd questioned him—for about a half hour. He'd told them that Damon Shuler had grossly exaggerated the behavior of some of the students in his classes. Roger maintained that he kept the students in line. And, yes, he was friendly with the jocks. Wasn't everyone?

Shuler was the one with the problems. Just one look at the way the kid acted with all his nervous tics and anyone could have figured out he had psychiatric issues. Something like this was bound to happen sooner or later.

He didn't tell the police, but something Damon had

said in his webcast still bothered him. *You didn't come back to high school to educate anybody,* he'd ranted—for everyone to hear. *You came back for another shot of being popular . . .*

The truth was Roger had never been very popular in high school. But when he'd started teaching at Queen Anne High, he'd found it incredibly easy to get the cool kids to admire him. All he had to do was crack a few jokes during classes and cut some football players a little slack as far as their assignments and test scores were concerned. Then he was their buddy. And it wasn't just the guys either. Twenty-five years ago, when he was their age, no girl looked at him twice. But now he had his pick among them. They all had crushes on him—from the most popular cheerleaders to those Jane-Austen-reading, under-the-radar pretty girls.

This was especially gratifying for Roger, whose ex-wife, after four years of marriage, had sneeringly called him "pathetic" when he'd run into her while shopping in Pacific Place a few weeks back. He was forty-two, in debt, and with few friends his own age. He lived in a small, overpriced, scantily furnished one-bedroom apartment in a new building in Queen Anne. Though he taught English lit, he'd long ago lost whatever passion he'd had for reading the classics. So, yes, maybe all that made him kind of pathetic.

But at the high school, he was like a rock star.

That snotty little son of a bitch Damon Shuler had indeed tapped into a little truth. Roger was enjoying his popularity at the school. What was wrong with that? The people who mattered weren't going to believe the ranting and ravings of some insane kid who was about to kill his mother and himself.

Roger told himself he was okay. He'd just come from a meeting with Dunmore, whom the kid had *really* raked over the coals. So Dunmore wasn't about to point any fingers. They'd already been through this before, earlier in the month, when he, Dunmore, and Shuler's parents had a "principal's office" conference regarding how Damon got kicked around. "It doesn't happen on my watch," he'd assured them. "During my class, if some of the kids start in with the name-calling, I always nip it in the bud. I think Damon might be exaggerating."

He'd stuck to the same story with Dunmore just a few minutes ago—pretty much a carbon copy of what he'd told the police. Dunmore hadn't pressed it much beyond that.

Heading toward his car, he focused on his smart phone. His thumbs rapidly moved over the little keypad:

W@ a 4kd ^ dy! M finly fre n on my wa 2 my car. CU sn!

He hit Send, and then shoved his phone into the pocket of his Queen Anne High School Windbreaker—which was identical to the one the coach always wore at their football games. Approaching his Mustang, Roger took out his keys. From this distance, he couldn't quite see where the car had been scratched last month. But as he got closer, there it was. He still hadn't gotten it fixed. The car detail place wanted $460 to make the scratch disappear. He couldn't afford that right now. At least no one had vandalized the car again, not since he'd stopped parking in the teachers' lot.

Roger opened the door and climbed inside. He slid the key into the ignition, but didn't turn it. With a sigh, he sat back and stared out the rain-beaded windshield.

The cops had asked him if Damon Shuler had ever threatened him—or if he'd received any anonymous threats recently. Roger had told them no, and insisted he was very well-liked by the students. He'd didn't think to tell them about the unidentified douche bag who had keyed his car. He'd never associated the incident with Shuler. He'd figured the squirrelly kid would never have had the nerve to do anything like that. But then, until a couple of hours ago, he didn't think Shuler would have been capable of killing his mother and himself in that spectacle of carnage half the school had just witnessed.

Could Shuler have been the one who scratched his Mustang? Did the kid even know what kind of car he drove?

Suddenly someone tapped on the window—right by his ear. Roger sat up with a start. He swiveled toward the door and saw KC Cunningham smirking on the other side of the glass. KC lived with her divorced mother only a few blocks from the school. She'd gone home and changed from her rain-soaked cheerleading uniform to a pair of jeans and a purple sweater. Her close-cropped, blond hair was dry now.

Roger rolled down his window. "You scared the crap out of me," he said, catching his breath. "Talk about a fucked-up day . . ."

She nodded. "So you said in your email. How did the meeting go with Dunmore? Or should I say *Done-Nothing*?" She let out a little laugh. "Hey, it was pretty funny when the Freakazoid went on about that on the webcast. And then—*boom!* I mean, W-T-F. I still can't believe it—"

"The meeting went fine," Roger said, cutting her off. He reached over and unlocked the passenger door. "Hurry up and get in before someone sees you talking to me."

With a sigh, KC rolled her eyes and then flounced around the front of the car to the passenger side.

KC was one of those popular girls who had a crush on him. It was more than a crush now. For Roger, it was a fantasy fulfilled. He was screwing a pretty cheerleader. They'd been secretly meeting for the last three weeks. Her mother was clueless, too busy working—and dating some guy KC didn't like. The sex with KC was pretty fantastic. But he really felt the age difference between them when they were together. Plus she could be a real chatterbox about the most inane things. Sometimes Roger had to bite his lip to keep from telling her to shut the hell up. But then he reminded himself that he was banging a cheerleader, and he suddenly felt better about the whole thing.

KC opened the door and plopped down on the passenger seat. He could tell she was pissed off about something. She let out another sigh and folded her arms. "Are you even going to ask me how it went with the police? Y'know, you're not the only one they talked to. They grilled me for, like, almost a half hour. I'm not sure if that was even legal—questioning someone my age without a parent or a lawyer." She glanced in the rearview mirror and fussed with her hair. "I mean, like it's not my fault he killed his mother and himself . . ."

"So what exactly did you tell the police?" he asked, staring out the windshield—watching for anyone who might spot the two of them sitting in his car together.

"I told them that I used to tease him a little, that's all," she answered.

*Tease him a little?* She was relentless. On social media, she was constantly ridiculing Damon. At school, KC and Reed practically had a whole routine worked out. He'd start in on Damon, and then KC would pretend to rush to his defense: "Don't make fun of my boyfriend! Damon's my stud. We're lovers. I want to spend eternity with him. But first, we're going to get married, and have little freakazoid babies . . ."

Sometimes, it got to be too much—even for Roger. Last week, after he told her to settle down, KC later sulked about it in private: "You yelled at me in front of the whole class . . ."

He shifted around in his seat. "Did you tell the police you teased him in *my* class?"

She frowned at him. "No. I just said I teased him in general. I didn't even mention you. So don't worry. God!"

"I'm just asking," he muttered.

"Maybe I should go home," she said, shaking her head. "I mean, I've been sitting in this car for, like, three minutes, and you haven't even kissed me yet."

He leaned over and kissed her on the mouth.

KC pulled away first, but kept a hand on his thigh. "Hey, you know what the police asked me? Talk about creepy. They asked if Damon Shuler ever threatened me."

"They asked me the same thing," Roger murmured. He wondered if they'd made the exact same inquiries of everyone Shuler had mentioned in his webcast.

Out of the corner of his eye, he saw someone across the street. He realized it was the school nurse, Rachel Porter. "Shit," he whispered. "Get down!"

"What?"

"For God's sake, get down!" He put his hand on top of KC's head and started pushing her down toward the floor.

"Hey, watch it!" she whined, half resisting.

Roger figured she knew the drill. This wasn't the first time she'd had to duck down and hide on the floor of the Mustang. They couldn't afford to take any chances. He glanced at the school nurse across the street. She didn't seem to notice him—at least, not yet.

KC's hand was still on his thigh. Crouched down on the passenger floor, she said something. It didn't make sense. It sounded like she'd said, "Let's dish under the dash."

"What?" he asked, reaching for the key in the ignition.

"I said," she announced more clearly, "what's all this under the—"

Roger heard a strange click as he turned the key.

A tongue of fire shot out from under the steering wheel. KC shrieked in horror.

The blast tore through the car, engulfing it in flames. Roger McAfee's prize Mustang leapt up from the pavement and then came crashing down. The mangled, fiery vehicle toppled over on its side. Acrid, black smoke billowed from the inferno.

The explosion broke windows and set off alarms in the cars parked nearby.

It would be several hours before the police determined there were two bodies in the car, both burnt beyond recognition. They knew one of the corpses was Damon Shuler's English teacher.

It would take another day for them to figure out that the second charred body belonged to KC Cunningham.

For some students in Mr. McAfee's second-period English lit class, it must have seemed rather ironic that KC and Damon had died on the same day. They'd often heard the impish cheerleader say that she wanted to spend eternity with Damon Shuler.

It appeared as if she'd gotten her wish.

# CHAPTER SEVEN

*Thursday—9:22 p.m.*
*Seattle*

"I don't know why the hell they flew me out to Lopez," Luke said on the other end of the phone line. He'd just arrived home—apparently to a swarm of reporters outside his town house. He sounded exhausted and overwrought. "The whole trip was futile. There was hardly anything left to identify. Everything was in ashes. They couldn't even find their bodies . . ."

Andrea heard Luke's voice crack, and he started sobbing. Her heart ached for him.

She sat in the living room of her Ballard apartment, looking out the picture window that had been cracked weeks before. She wished she could be there with Luke right now.

Yet earlier, before he'd left with the police for Lopez Island, Andrea had told him she and Spencer would move out of his town house that afternoon. Luke didn't seem to understand at first—until she'd explained. This was going to be all over the news—and he was a public figure. He'd have reporters following his every move. His divorce from Evelyn still hadn't gone through. People wouldn't understand why he was already living with another woman and her nephew. The media would almost certainly make a big deal out of it. "I just don't want them taking potshots at you—or *us*—not right now," Andrea had told him.

"Fine," he'd murmured, shaking his head in bewilderment. "But *right now*, I don't give a damn what people say. I—I'd really like to see you when I come through the front door tonight. But if you can't be there, okay then . . ."

"It's just temporary," she'd said. "And I really think it's for the best, honey."

What Andrea hadn't told him was that she and Spencer had been through something like this with the press years before. She didn't want anyone resurrecting it tonight.

That afternoon, when they'd gotten back to Luke's, she'd told Spencer they'd be staying in their place in Ballard for a while. They'd packed enough clothes and things for the next few days—and managed to get out of there before the first TV news van pulled up. "Don't you feel like a rat deserting him this way?" Spencer had asked her as they'd driven to Ballard.

"Yes," she'd admitted. But she was doing it to protect the three of them.

Andrea kept telling herself that as they settled back into their old apartment. She found they'd left behind three pairs of shoes on the stairs, the sight of which was somehow reassuring. It made up for the fact that her plants in front were dying, the place smelled musty, and water came out of the taps tinged with rust.

The six o'clock news started with Damon's very public suicide-matricide. They also showed a horde of reporters outside Luke's town house, awaiting the prize-winning playwright's return from Lopez Island.

For Andrea, seeing that media frenzy made her glad she and Spencer had gotten out of there. But she still hated every minute she was away from Luke.

Before the newscast was over, the anchors announced a "breaking story" about another car explosion—this time, near Queen Anne High School. They said the car belonged to a teacher at the school, but couldn't yet confirm if anyone had been inside the car when the blast occurred.

Luke's fears about Damon killing some innocent people in addition to his mother and himself seemed to be coming true.

Andrea listened to him crying on the other end of the line.

"Did you—did you eat anything, honey?" she asked, feeling helpless—and useless.

"Not yet," he replied, his voice gravelly and strained. "I'm not really hungry."

She got to her feet and moved to the window. "You should eat. There's leftover spaghetti sauce in the fridge from the other night. You can heat it up and boil some noodles. Or you can make sort of a poor man's pizza by spreading it over some flatbread, and sprinkling on some Parmesan—"

"Andrea, I'm not hungry," he interrupted. "And you

don't have to mother me. I just called to hear your voice."

She sighed. "Oh, Luke, I'm so sorry I'm not there. I feel awful . . ."

"No, you were right," he murmured. "The reporters are still hovering outside, trying to peek in the windows at me. On my way from the car to the front door, one of them kept hammering away at me, asking who the 'other woman' was that Damon had referred to in the webcast. So it's good you guys are not here. It was a smart call on your part. In fact, I think it might be wise for us not to see each other for a while."

Her heart sank. "For a while?"

"I'm talking just a few days—until the press decides that they're tired of me."

She didn't say anything. Her reflection in the darkened window frowned back at her.

"Andrea, this was your idea, remember?"

She heard him blow his nose. Then he got back on the line. "How's Spencer?"

"Still a little shaken up, but okay," she answered. "He's in his room on his computer—looking for updates."

"So should I cook this poor man's pizza in the microwave or the oven?"

She smiled. "In the oven—at four twenty-five for about ten minutes . . ."

After she hung up, Andrea stared out the living room window for a few more moments. There wasn't a single reporter in sight, just darkness—and her own scared reflection. Still, she couldn't help thinking someone was out there, watching her.

Weeks ago, she'd been pretty sure Evelyn had paid someone to stalk and harass them. But Evelyn was dead. Who could be out there tonight—and why?

"That's over with," she told herself. "Stop worrying . . ."

Maybe she felt vulnerable, or maybe it was just a case of old habits dying hard, but Andrea reached over and pulled shut the drapes.

*Friday, October 9—7:38 a.m.*

Sitting on the stairs near the front door, Andrea slipped on her brown suede loafers. "Spencer!" she called. "Shake a leg, Spence! You're going to be late!"

They'd both checked online, and it looked as if the high school was having a regular schedule today. Andrea was going to drive him.

She was amazed they'd gotten through the night without any calls. And there weren't any reporters or gawkers outside their apartment. Obviously, the press were still in the dark about her and Luke—for now. She couldn't help feeling as if they were living on borrowed time as far as that was concerned.

Luke usually slept until almost nine o'clock, and she would wait until then to call him. She wondered if he'd slept at all. She'd tossed and turned most of the night. In just over a month, she'd become very accustomed to sleeping with him. Everything about yesterday—and last night—was strange.

She heard Spencer barreling down the stairs from the bedroom level—and then down the stairs to the front door. He plopped down on a step above her, unloaded his books, and started to put on his black Chuck Taylor high-tops. "They still haven't identified the second person in the Mustang with McAfee," he said. "The chat online is that it's probably a student . . ."

He tied his laces, and they headed outside—to the chilly, overcast morning. As they hurried toward her parking spot, Andrea opened her purse and started hunting for her keys.

But Spencer suddenly stopped dead. "Oh, shit," he said under his breath.

Andrea frowned at him. "What is it?"

Wordlessly he nodded toward her car.

Andrea stared at her red VW Beetle—and the new, thin, silvery scratch that ran across the passenger door.

It wasn't over with after all.

# CHAPTER EIGHT

*Saturday, October 17—5:27 p.m.*
*Seattle*

"A lot of people here have talked about how beauti-ful she was, but what I remember most about my dear friend Evelyn was her laugh . . ."

Evelyn's chum since college, Cynthia Werth-Hyland, stood at a podium in front of about a hundred people in folding chairs on the terrace of the Ballard Bay Club. It was a gorgeous venue—just off Shilshole Beach with an unencumbered view of the sun setting beyond Puget Sound and the Olympic Mountains. It had just started to get chilly.

Luke sat on the aisle of the first row. The three chairs beside him were empty. He missed Andrea, who had stayed home—in her apartment in Ballard. The re-porters outside Luke's town house had at long last dis-persed, but Andrea and Spencer still hadn't moved back in with him yet.

Since last Thursday, he'd been wandering around in

a daze most of the time. Andrea had helped set up this memorial service. Because of the murders and the suicide, none of the churches wanted to take them. They were able to talk this spot into hosting the memorial by assuring the management it was just a gathering—with no coffins or urns or anything along those lines. The large terrace was off a ballroom, which had white-linen-covered tables and chairs for the guests. They'd hired a caterer, who had set up the hors d'oeuvres buffet and wine bar. The memorial service was by invitation only. "In cases like this, where there's public interest, it's the best way to go," Andrea had explained. "We'll get some funeral crashers. But that comes with the territory. We can have someone at the door taking names. That'll discourage it a bit."

Luke asked how she knew so much about planning a service like this. Andrea said she'd done it all before—when Spencer's parents had died in that car accident.

After all her help making this memorial service happen, Andrea had decided not to attend. It was probably a good call. Most of the attendees were Evelyn's friends and relations. They knew about the separation and the impending divorce. Despite her change in marital status, Evelyn still hadn't altered her will. So, as her surviving spouse, Luke was in line to inherit about four and a half million dollars. He couldn't have cared less about the money. But others cared a lot—and they were bitter.

In advance, Luke had asked certain people to get up and talk. It had been easy to find friends of Evelyn's who were willing. But he'd been hard pressed to come up with people to say something on Damon's behalf.

Damon's godfather had just been up there, telling a cute story about taking Damon to the zoo when he was a kid. The anecdote got some polite chuckles. But Luke knew it must have been tough for people to laugh over the funny things that little boy had said, knowing years later he would kill his mother, himself, and two others. For her speech, Damon's godmother, Evelyn's cousin, chose a poem from William Wordsworth.

Damon's friend Tanya McCallum had volunteered to say something about him. Her turn hadn't come yet. Luke wasn't sure what to expect. The slightly pudgy girl had come to the service dressed in an unflatteringly tight black party dress—and a black hat with a wide brim. The outfit appeared to have been bought at some cheap vintage clothing store. Throughout the Wordsworth poem, she kept sighing loudly as if in pain. It was pretty distracting.

Sitting next to her in the third row, Spencer looked uncomfortable. He'd come, despite his aunt's absence. But Andrea must have briefed him, because earlier when Luke had overheard a friend of Evelyn's ask Spencer how he knew the deceased, he'd answered, "I was in Damon's class at Queen Anne High."

It was a polite group. No one had asked Luke about his girlfriend.

Cynthia Werth-Hyland was telling a story about Evelyn in college. She probably had no idea that Evelyn called her "Mole Face" behind her back.

Luke had once made the mistake of mentioning to his wife that he thought Anne Francis was incredibly sexy in *Forbidden Planet*, and that he liked the beauty mark by her mouth.

"Well, my friend Cyndi has two moles on her face," Evelyn pointed out. "Do you have the hots for her, too? I hope not. I used to sit in our dorm room watching her trim the hair off those things. It was disgusting."

After that, her dear pal Cyndi was "Mole Face"—and not such a dear pal anymore.

Nineteen years ago, when he'd first started dating Evelyn Barrens, he had no idea how jealous and possessive she could be. He'd fallen in love with a beautiful, elegant blonde. She had panache, a snappy wit, and, indeed, a wonderful laugh. It wasn't until things got serious that Luke discovered she was an heiress. For a struggling playwright, this revelation might have been a godsend, but Luke felt uncomfortable about it. When they married—during an impulsive trip to Las Vegas—he made her promise they'd live on their combined incomes, which wasn't bad at all. For his "day job," he wrote press releases for a Seattle-based pharmaceutical company. Evelyn sold ad space for the *Seattle Times*. They had a cute one-bedroom apartment on the second floor of a duplex on Capitol Hill.

It was probably their happiest time together. He'd already written a couple of plays that had done well in Seattle, but had never gone anywhere else. He was struggling to get noticed. At the time, he had no idea she was trying to sabotage his career.

He'd thought it was an accident when she'd erased half of his new play, *Return Again to You*, on his word processor. Still, Luke had managed to finish it, and get several New York agents interested. Evelyn volunteered to FedEx the manuscripts to them. And somehow, those agents never received his play.

Luke didn't realize until years later that she must have tossed out those manuscripts. Evelyn didn't want him to be a success. She'd known even then that if he became an established playwright, she couldn't have him all to herself. When *Return Again to You* became a Broadway sensation, Luke could see she wasn't really happy for him.

Evelyn became pregnant around that same time. She considered having an abortion. But Luke was so thrilled about the prospect of becoming a dad—and so attentive to her—that she reconsidered. Nevertheless, Evelyn had a few suspicious "close calls" while pregnant—including a nasty fall down the stairs from their second-floor apartment. Then there was the time she accidentally took too many sleeping pills, which she shouldn't have been taking in the first place.

Looking back, Luke wondered how he could have been so stupid not to have figured out what she was trying to do.

"Playwright Luke Shuler shows a keen awareness of the neurotic female mind and sensibility," the *USA Today* critic had written in his four-star review of *Return Again to You*. And yet Luke was practically clueless about his own wife.

Despite everything Evelyn had done to prevent it, Damon Barrens Shuler was born healthy.

"I don't want to hear how natural it is, or how I'm going to pass along my immunities to him, or how we're going to bond through breast feeding," she told the nurses at the hospital. "He's getting a bottle. He's ruined my shape enough as it is."

There was another good reason for the bottle method. She didn't have to get up in the middle of the night to feed him. Luke did it most of the time. They went through a series of nannies—none of them under fifty-five, and none lasting very long, because Evelyn didn't get along with any of them.

One of the nannies got fired late in January while Luke was at an out-of-town opening for a new play. Damon was two at the time. The woman called Luke after it happened.

"I came over there at eight in the morning," she said. "And Mrs. Shuler was in the kitchen having coffee. The baby was screaming upstairs. I found him in his crib with a wet diaper on—and nothing else, not even a blanket. He must have been marinating in that wet diaper all night. And all the windows in the nursery were open, Mr. Shuler. I could see my breath when I stepped inside the room. If that poor, sweet baby catches pneumonia, you can blame her. I've never seen anything like it . . ."

Evelyn maintained that the woman was lying—just trying to stir up trouble because she'd been fired. "Maybe if you were home—for a change—you'd see how lousy she was at her job. You have no idea what's happening here. You've been gone for the last two weeks! What kind of husband and father are you anyway? Goddamn you for believing her lies and taking her side in this!"

Luke called a moratorium on his traveling. He hired an au pair—a smart, resourceful fifty-two-year-old widow who agreed to let them install a nanny cam in the nursery.

Evelyn continued to smother Luke with so much affection and attention that it became exasperating. She never left him alone. She was jealous of the time he spent writing and with their son. She was oddly cold toward Damon and talked about sending him to boarding school as soon as he was old enough. She and Luke quarreled about it.

The irony was that little Damon adored her. He was always reaching out to her, smiling at her, trying to catch her eye. After starting school, whenever he came home with a gold star on his paper or a drawing, he'd always go to his mother first to show her what he'd done. Half the time, Evelyn would practically brush him off. Luke could do cartwheels over Damon's smallest accomplishment, and it still didn't seem to fulfill a need in his son. Like a faithful puppy that got kicked around by its owner, Damon kept coming back to his mother for the small crumbs of approval and affection she dished out.

By the time their son was thirteen, Luke had completely fallen out of love with Evelyn—and she knew it.

But he stayed with her for Damon's sake, and threw himself into his work. On the surface, they were an ideal couple. There was even a brief profile of them in *People* magazine's "Sexiest, Happiest Couples" issue. But they both were miserable. While he'd resigned himself to their situation, Evelyn became frustrated, bitter, and a little crazy. Luke wanted to go to couples counseling, but Evelyn refused. "I had my fill of headshrinkers in college, thank you very much," she snapped back at his suggestion. "And by the way, if you think you're going to leave me, you can just forget it. I'll get custody of our son. And I can afford the best, most ruthless divorce attorney in the business. You won't even get visitation rights . . ."

"I never said I was going to leave you, Evelyn," he replied calmly. All her threats weren't going to change the fact that he didn't love her anymore. He wanted to tell her that, but instead, he asked, "What happened in college that you ended up having to get some psychiatric help?"

Evelyn didn't want to talk about it.

"She had sort of a nervous breakdown," Cynthia Werth-Hyland told him over a clandestine brunch at Anthony's Pier 66. Luke had contacted Evelyn's long-time friend and asked if they could meet in private. Thanks to his carefully worded questions, and a couple of glasses of Chardonnay with her salmon cakes, Cynthia was in a talkative mood.

"You mean, she didn't tell you about it? Well, it was all on account of some guy who dumped her. Evelyn was always the one doing the dumping, never the dumpee. Anyway, after he left her, she took an overdose of sleeping pills. They had to pump her stomach. She was a total wreck. She never told you? The guy's name was Josh. In fact, he looked a lot like you. Her mother made her see a shrink. Her father was dead by that time. She saw this doctor for about two months—and then claimed she was just fine, and quit."

Luke was stunned at how much he still didn't know about his wife—after fourteen years of marriage.

By this time, Damon was developing his OCD tics. Luke got him to a psychiatrist, despite Evelyn's protests. He didn't tell her how much he knew about her time in therapy during college. He guessed she had an aversion to it, because her analyst had probably picked up on a lot of issues she wasn't ready to acknowledge.

Unfortunately, Damon was his mother's child—and not very cooperative with the doctors. Evelyn had a toxic influence on their son. She'd even managed to pit Damon against him. Luke found himself on the receiving end of a lot of eye-rolling and backtalk. He figured this came with the territory when raising an adolescent. But his kid radiated utter contempt for him. By the time Damon was in high school, he'd become an arrogant, snobby mama's boy.

Luke still loved his son, but he didn't like him very much.

Ten months ago, Evelyn had started having an affair with a narcissistic, lowlife actor named Troy Slattery. He'd recently been fired from the cast of one of Luke's plays. It was as if she'd picked the most repugnant person she could as her new lover. And she wasn't discreet about it either. Luke figured she was hoping he'd get jealous and rescue her from this sick relationship—then fall in love with her all over again.

Instead, he moved out.

He told Evelyn he wouldn't fight her for custody of Damon. He knew his son wouldn't want to live with him anyway.

As he sat there on the terrace in the front row, listening to "Mole Face" talk about Evelyn's wonderful, infectious laugh, Luke told himself that he should have known it all would come to this. He wondered if things would have been different if he'd stayed.

He hadn't totally given up on Damon. They actually had some nice weekends together—at least, Luke thought so.

Apparently, Evelyn's affair with Troy Slattery lasted only a few weeks. After that, whenever Luke dropped Damon off at the house on Garfield, he'd find Evelyn out there, waiting for them. She'd always have an excuse for talking with Luke or asking him inside: "I still don't know how to operate that thermostat" or "The kitchen light is out, and you're the only one who knows how to take the shade off to change the bulb . . ." She'd always look gorgeous—and just a little sad.

But Luke wasn't interested. By that time, he was comfortably set up in his town house, finishing up a new play, and had already met Andrea.

Still, Evelyn kept up the same routine of subtly flirting with him whenever he dropped off Damon from their alternate weekends together. He was also seeing Evelyn at the school—for impromptu conferences with Damon's principal over the bullying. After these meetings, she'd coyly ask how he was doing. And she'd ask about *Amber* or *Amanda*. She seemed to have a mental block on Andrea's name—like Endora never getting Darrin's name right on *Bewitched*.

Luke had come to see through Evelyn's melancholy vamp act. He also couldn't help wondering if she'd been the one behind Andrea's apartment being vandalized and broken into. Maybe Evelyn had hired someone to do it—or manipulated poor Damon into carrying out her dirty work for her. Luke had confronted her about it. Acting insulted, Evelyn had vehemently denied doing anything to harass *Angela*.

The last time he'd seen Evelyn was three weeks ago, after one of those meetings at the school. At the time, it seemed they'd managed to curtail the physical abuse heaped upon their son—the shoving and tripping. But that didn't stop Damon from being ostracized and teased.

"I really want Damon to get some therapy," he told her as they walked toward the school parking lot. It was a beautiful, balmy September evening. "He needs to talk to a professional about what he's going through— what he's been through. I know you don't like therapists, but I really wish you'd reconsider it, Evelyn."

"All right, I will." Her eyes searched his, and she sighed. "You know, that whole thing with Troy was a huge mistake. You were right about him, of course. What a loser. I mean, the guy had a meth habit, for God's sake." She blushed and gave a little shrug. "I've been seeing this younger guy, very energetic. It's been sort of off and on. It's off right now." She laughed. "I don't think I like being a cougar . . ."

He tried to work up a smile. But all he could think was that Evelyn hadn't changed one bit. He'd been so worried about Damon. And Evelyn wanted to take this moment to flirt and talk about her love life.

"Well, I'm sure you'll find somebody who will suit you," he said. "In the meantime, see if you can't get Damon on board with this idea of seeing a therapist. Okay?"

"Of course, sure," she said. "G'night, Luke."

She touched his arm, and then turned to head toward

her BMW. He watched her. She was wearing black slacks and a pink sweater, which always made her look sensational. She knew it, too.

The next time he saw Evelyn, she was bound and gagged in the backseat of that same BMW—and she would be dead within minutes.

No one talked about that at the memorial service.

Yet it was certainly on everyone's mind. Segments of Damon's webcast had gone viral. For the second time in his life, Luke was featured in a *People* magazine article—this time about his son's suicide, the murders, and the hot topic of bullying in schools.

A single TV news van was parked in front of the Ballard Bay Club to cover the memorial, not much of a media presence compared to last week.

That was because KC Cunningham's funeral was being held across town at the same time. The pretty cheerleader's death—and the scandalous revelation that she'd been having sex with her English teacher—was a bigger, juicier news story. It was all over the Internet that McAfee had nude photos of KC on his home computer. The press was still digging for more lurid details.

The bullied high school boy who had killed his mother and himself was now yesterday's news. Reporters had stopped asking Luke for possible explanations about why his son had gone berserk. They were already on to the next story.

But Luke hadn't stopped asking himself why.

Cynthia Werth-Hyland finished her reminiscence to polite, dignified applause. "Next," Cynthia said, "Damon's best friend at school, Tanya McCallum, will say a few words."

Stepping down from the podium, Cynthia walked over to Luke. He got to his feet, and they hugged. "Thank you, Cyn," he whispered.

He'd phoned her earlier in the week. In fact, he'd called several of Evelyn's friends. He'd asked Cynthia and all the rest of them the same thing: Had Evelyn recently mentioned anything that might explain why Damon had snapped the way he did?

"I'm sorry, Luke, but I haven't talked to Evelyn in weeks," Cynthia had told him. "As for Damon's motives, I thought he was pretty clear about that in the video he made. It was all the bullying he had to put up with at school."

He'd gotten pretty much the same response from the others. But Luke wasn't so sure it was that simple. If it was just about the bullying, why did Damon decide to kill his mother—along with himself? Luke couldn't help wondering if Evelyn had done something to trigger Damon's rage. Or had he found out something about her that had pushed him over the edge?

As Luke sat down again, a chilly breeze came up from the choppy gray water of Puget Sound. He felt it creep into his bones and shuddered.

He watched Damon's friend Tanya totter up the aisle in her thrift store funeral getup. He'd talked to her earlier this week, too. She didn't have anything to tell him—at least nothing new.

Yet Luke couldn't help thinking she knew more than she was letting on.

Maybe Damon's friend wasn't quite as silly as she looked.

# CHAPTER NINE

Spencer held his breath as Tanya stepped up to the podium.

She'd hardly been able to keep it together for the last twenty-five minutes. While the other guests shared their memories of Damon and his mother, she kept gasping and having these mini crying jags. How the hell did she think she was going to get through her speech?

She looked a bit crazy in the wide-brim black hat, the type a widow character might wear in the funeral scene from an old movie. Behind her, the setting sun colored the sky with streaks of orange and pink. Tanya's face was flushed and her eyes were bloodshot from crying. She visibly trembled as she gazed at the other mourners. She grimaced and let out a pained raspy sound—as if she'd just been hit in the stomach. Then she started crying—loud, heavy, inconsolable sobs.

Spencer felt awful for her. He kept waiting for Tanya to compose herself.

But she didn't even wipe her tears—or her runny nose. She opened her mouth like she was about to say something, but she merely let out another wail. She just stood there, having a breakdown in front of everyone. And it looked like she had no intention of stepping away from the podium.

Some people in the audience were squirming in their chairs or clearing their throats. Everyone seemed uncomfortable. She'd been up there blubbering for about three minutes now and hadn't yet said a damn thing.

Luke finally got to his feet—like he might come help her away from the podium. But Tanya shook her head at him, and he returned to his seat.

Then she just kept crying.

Spencer started to wonder if the tears were even real. At this point, it all seemed pretty self-indulgent and theatrical.

"Oh, for God's sake," muttered a woman to her companion in the row behind Spencer. "Somebody give her the hook."

Luke stood up once again and approached her.

Tanya wiped her eyes and shook her head at him again. But he ignored her this time. He started to lead her away from the podium, but she resisted. They had a whispered conference by the podium—in front of the restless guests.

Spencer started tapping his foot—as quietly as possible. He'd spent a lot of time in school this past week with Tanya. Some of that time was spent trying to avoid her. He felt sorry for her. But she could be exasperating, too. She'd sort of latched on to him. Spencer knew she desperately needed a friend, but he didn't want to be her substitute Damon.

One thing they had in common was that they were both appalled at how unremorseful Damon's chief tormentors seemed. Reed and Ron were pretty subdued on Monday, and sported the black ribbons most of the students and faculty wore at school that day. The focus of everyone's bereavement seemed to be the deaths of KC and Mr. McAfee—whose affair hadn't yet become public knowledge. No one talked about Damon as a "victim." No one blamed the bullies for any of this. They blamed the mentally ill kid with all those quirky tics. If Dunmore had taken any kind of disciplinary action with Ron and Reed, no one knew about it.

By Wednesday, Damon's two main tormentors were as loud and as obnoxious as ever, cracking jokes and intimidating freshmen in the hallways. Spencer couldn't help scowling at them every time he saw them—along with certain members of their posse.

"What the fuck is your problem?" Ron bellowed at him. Reed was at his side—the baseball hat on backward, as usual. They were strutting toward him in the corridor, outside Spencer's fourth-period chemistry classroom.

Spencer realized they'd caught him glaring at them.

"What are you looking at?" Reed joined in.

*A couple of worthless assholes*, Spencer wanted to answer. Instead, he shrugged. "Nothing," he muttered, "absolutely nothing."

He started to turn away, but Ron suddenly shoved him. Knocked off balance, Spencer slammed into a locker and dropped his books. It was more startling than painful.

"I've got my eye on you, faggot," Ron growled.

His heart racing, Spencer watched the two of them swagger down the hallway.

"I think we've found our Freakazoid Two," he heard Reed say to his pal, with a moronic little laugh. "I never liked that guy . . ."

Spencer remembered gathering his books from the floor. It had dawned on him at the time that Tanya wasn't the only one who had pegged him as a substitute Damon.

He watched her now, beside the podium, still sobbing. She shook her head at Luke, who tried to lead her back to her seat. She broke away and bolted back to the lectern. If there could have been a collective groan from the audience, it would have been now. But the people at this memorial were far too polite for that.

"I just need to say what no one else has been saying," Tanya announced, finding the words at last. Still, her voice was shaky and shrill.

Standing a few feet away, Luke seemed painfully resigned to let Tanya have her moment.

"Damon Shuler did something horrible," she went on. "Yes, that's true. But he was driven to it by a group of bullies at that school. Don't you people see? He didn't stand a chance. He was a nice guy. If people got to know him, they would have figured that out. He was my best friend. We understood each other. We were together on that—that 'island of misfit toys' that Stephen Chbosky talks about in *Perks of Being a Wallflower* . . ."

Spencer sat up in his chair. After all that blubbering, Tanya was finally having her say—and she was saying it pretty well. She was right. All these polite people needed to hear this.

"Damon was always there for me," she continued, her voice choked with emotion. "He was—well, he truly was the wind beneath my wings . . ."

She took a deep breath and unevenly warbled, "It must have been cold there in my shadow . . ."

His mouth open, Spencer warily watched her and thought, *Oh, no.*

But, yes, Tanya was singing—croaking, really—"Wind Beneath My Wings."

Off to the side, Luke seemed startled. For a moment, he stared at her with utter disbelief—as if she were crazy. Then he quickly put his fist in front of his mouth and looked down at the terrace floor.

Her singing improved by the second verse, and she had a nice voice. But belting the song out a cappella like that was just so awkward.

Tanya started to cry again during the third verse, and her voice kept cracking. But that didn't stop her from finishing the song. Since it was a service, no one applauded, which made things even more cringe-worthy. All Tanya got for her vocalizing were a few people clearing their throats again.

"My God," the woman behind Spencer muttered. "After that, I could sure use a drink."

She wasn't the only one.

Spencer watched the line of people at the wine bar once the speeches on the terrace were over. Luke hadn't given a tribute. He hadn't said anything—except at the end, when he'd thanked everyone for coming and invited them to stay for refreshments. Tanya had bolted to the restroom to check her face. Spencer was standing alone by a long table that had a dozen framed photos of Evelyn and Damon.

Andrea had helped Luke go through his collection of family snapshots. Then she'd scanned, printed, and set them inside various frames she and Luke already had on hand.

"I really hate how perfectly this picture fits in this frame," Andrea had muttered to Spencer last night, sitting at Luke's dinner table—with Luke out of earshot. A beautiful portrait of Luke's estranged wife now occupied an elegant silver frame, covering up a shot of Spencer's dead grandmother—Andrea's mom. "Oh, well, it's only for one day—while we have these on display."

Spencer got another chance to look at Andrea's handiwork while he waited for the line at the bar to dissipate. He really wanted a Coke.

One picture of a toddler-age Damon dressed up like a doctor—complete with a stethoscope around his neck and a white lab coat—was pretty cute, and heartbreaking. Spencer didn't recognize the frame. It must have been one of Luke's.

"We're in Ms. Donahue's chemistry class together," said someone behind him.

Spencer turned around and gaped at Bonnie Middleton. Ron Jarvis's pretty girlfriend had her long chestnut hair pulled back in a ponytail. Yet she looked very grown-up and sophisticated in a square-necked dark blue dress with short sleeves. "Your name's Spencer, isn't it?" she asked.

He nodded. "Spencer Murray. Hi."

"We haven't officially met," she said, clutching her small black handbag at her waist. "I'm Bonnie—"

"Yes, I know," he said, nodding again. "You're Ron's girlfriend."

She shrugged. "Well, you can put that in the past tense. We broke up this week."

"Oh, um, sorry to hear that," he murmured—for lack of anything else to say.

"Why would you be? I'm not." She glanced around the ballroom and sighed. "No, what I'm sorry about is the way everyone treated poor Damon Shuler. I'm sorry that when he killed himself, he had me lumped in there with Ron, Reed, KC, and that whole group. I could have been nicer to him . . ."

Spencer remembered her in the cafeteria when everyone had been watching Damon's live webcast. She'd been the only one at the cool table who seemed upset.

He nervously adjusted his tie and then shoved his hands in his pockets. "I didn't see you out on the terrace . . ."

"I snuck in about twenty minutes ago," she said. "I was at KC's service on Capitol Hill—along with most of the school. But I didn't go to the cemetery. I figured I'd come here instead. I owe Damon at least that much. On my way here, I made up my mind to introduce myself to Damon's father and apologize. I've never been tossed out of a memorial service before. I wonder what it's like." She glanced around the room again. "So, are you here with Tanya?"

He quickly shook his head. "No, we just sort of ended up sitting together."

"It's only that I've seen you and Tanya together a

lot at school this past week. I thought maybe you two were dating or something."

"Oh, God, no," Spencer heard himself say.

"So why are you here? Were you and Damon friends?"

"Well, not exactly . . ." he trailed off.

"There's a story going around school that your aunt has been dating Damon's father. Is that true?"

Spencer hesitated. "Yeah, they've sort of been seeing each other." Andrea wanted him to keep it on the down-low, especially at this event. But he didn't see any other way around it. "Um, she didn't come today, because she figured it would be kind of awkward."

"So you live with your aunt?" Bonnie asked.

"Yeah, my parents died when I was eleven—car accident."

"Oh, I'm sorry. How awful to lose them both at the same time like that . . ."

Spencer wanted to change the subject. He cleared his throat. "My aunt Andrea is a copyeditor. She helped edit *Ask a Tall, Dark Stranger*. It was a big bestseller."

Bonnie nodded. "I've heard of that, but I haven't read it." She seemed to work up a smile. "So, what did you think of Tanya's performance?"

"Um, very unusual," he replied.

"I don't mean to be catty. But let's just say it's a good thing none of the kids from school were here to see it. Tanya would never live it down. By the way, she hates my guts. But then, you probably already knew that. I imagine she's trashed me to you—ad nauseam."

Spencer shrugged. "Well, maybe she's not your

biggest fan because you were going out with Ron. I mean, let's face it, the guy's been kind of a shit to Tanya and Damon—and me."

She nodded glumly. "I'm sorry about that . . ."

"Do you think that's why Damon lumped you in with the others?" Spencer asked. "When he was naming all the people who bullied him, I wondered why he included you. Do you think it was, like, guilt by association—or was there something in particular you did to him?"

Bonnie grimaced a bit and said nothing.

Spencer immediately regretted asking her. But the question had been on his mind ever since he'd watched the cops lead her away from that crowded, muddy playfield last Thursday. Whatever she'd done, she was obviously sorry about it. She'd broken up with Ron, and she was here now, ready to make amends.

"Hey, listen, I'm sorry," he said. "I didn't mean to put you on the spot. It's over and done with . . ."

"It's a perfectly legitimate question," she murmured. "The police asked me the same thing . . ." She suddenly seemed distracted, and then nodded toward the buffet table. "Who's that? Do you know?"

Spencer followed her gaze—toward a thirty-something man with tousled black hair and one of those perfect five o'clock shadows. He wore a black suit with a black shirt and no tie. He was stuffing an appetizer in his mouth.

"You mean the guy dressed like he's in the mafia?" Spencer asked.

"You should have seen the way he was scowling at Damon's father a minute ago. If looks could kill . . ."

Spencer watched the man wolf down another hors d'oeuvre. He saw what Bonnie meant. The man looked dangerous—and he was glaring at Luke as if he wanted to murder him. Across the room, Luke quietly talked with one of the guests.

"I have no idea who that is," Spencer murmured. "I wonder if he was even invited . . ."

"Well, one thing we do know," said Tanya, coming up behind them. "*You* weren't invited, Bonnie."

"No, I guess I wasn't," she conceded. "Hi, Tanya. That's an interesting hat."

"I got it at Goodwill, same with the dress," Tanya replied. "You see, not everyone can afford to buy their bulimia-size designer clothes at Nordstrom."

"Oh, Tanya, give me a break. I borrowed this dress from my mother. And I'm a size six, which doesn't exactly make me bulimic or anorexic."

"Hey, you know," Spencer interjected, trying to break the tension. "We were just wondering who that guy is." He nodded toward the surly stranger by the buffet table.

"That's Troy Slattery," Tanya said. "He's an actor. I saw him a couple of times when I went over to Damon's. For a while, he and Mrs. Shuler had a thing. And you're right. I'd be surprised if he was on the invite list."

Tanya turned and sneered at Bonnie. "The same goes for you. I don't know where you got the nerve to show up here—especially after all the crap you and your friends put Damon through. Aren't you the one who poured a whole container of pencil shavings on the back of Damon's neck while he was dozing in the library? Or was that somebody else?"

Bonnie rolled her eyes. "It was a stupid joke, and when I saw how upset he was about it, I apologized. Plus that was over a year ago."

"Yeah, well, you thought it was pretty funny then," Tanya hissed. "Do you still think it's funny—now that Damon's dead?"

Spencer noticed a few people staring. "Hey, you guys . . ."

"You're not welcome here," Tanya told her, folding her arms. "I'd like you to leave—right now."

"Oh, I'm sorry, Tanya." Putting a hand over her heart, Bonnie gaped at Tanya in mock surprise. "I didn't realize you were hosting this memorial service. If you don't mind, I'm going to say hello to Damon's father before I slip away. Is that all right with you?" She didn't wait for an answer. She turned and started across the room toward Luke.

"Skanky bitch," Tanya muttered. She locked her arm around Spencer's and led him to the bar. It made Spencer uncomfortable. He didn't like it when she hung on him like she was his girlfriend.

"So what were you two talking about?" Tanya asked. "What did she say about me?"

"We really didn't talk much about you, Tanya," he whispered. They passed Troy Slattery. Mrs. Shuler's ex-boyfriend wrapped a couple of appetizers in a napkin and stuffed them into the pocket of his suit jacket. Then he wandered over toward the table full of framed photos.

"God, I hate her," Tanya muttered. "She's, like, the worst one in the bunch."

They got in line for their drinks, and Spencer glanced back at Bonnie. She looked a bit embarrassed as she shook Luke's hand.

"So all she did to Damon was dump some pencil shavings on the back of his head while he was napping in the school library? That was the extent of it?"

"When practically everyone in school is shitting on you, then something like that can be the last straw. Plus she's Ron Jarvis's girlfriend, which is about as low as you can go. Order me a Diet Coke, will you?"

Spencer asked the bartender for a Coke and a Diet Coke. By the time they got their drinks and stepped away from the bar, it looked like Bonnie had finished talking with Luke. She shook his hand again. The smile he gave her seemed reassuring. As Bonnie turned away from him, she pulled a Kleenex from her handbag and wiped her eyes. Then she came toward them.

"How did it go?" Spencer asked.

She still had tears in her eyes, but she smiled. "He was very sweet—and he really didn't have to be. Anyway, listen, Tanya, I didn't mean for things to get all snippy between us. You lost a dear friend, and I'm sorry. If it's any consolation, I feel horrible."

"Well, you should," Tanya replied, sipping her Diet Coke.

Bonnie sighed and turned to Spencer. "It was nice talking with you. I guess I'll see you at school. Take care, Spencer."

Before he could say anything, she brushed past him and headed for the exit.

Spencer watched her hurry out to the hallway.

"Gag me," Tanya said under her breath.

"I think she's kind of nice," Spencer admitted. He took a swig of his Coke.

"It's an act. Watch out for her. If she's being *nice*, she's probably setting you up for something."

Spencer looked over at the table displaying the photos of Damon and his mother. Mrs. Shuler's ex-boyfriend wasn't there anymore. Spencer didn't see him anywhere in the room.

He glanced at the collection of photographs on the table. Something was wrong.

Troy Slattery had disappeared.

And so had the portrait of Evelyn Shuler—in Andrea's silver frame.

# CHAPTER TEN

*Monday, October 19—1:57 p.m.*

Spencer was actually looking forward to chemistry class. He was terrible at it. He figured he'd be lucky if he ended up with a C minus by the end of the term. Plus Reed Logan was in the class, and Spencer wanted to avoid the guy as much as possible.

But Bonnie Middleton was also in that class.

Now that he'd spoken with her at the memorial service, he had an excuse to say hello and talk with her again. She'd broken up with Ron, so there was nothing to prevent him from approaching her. Despite all of Tanya's trash talk about her, Spencer still liked Bonnie. In fact, he hadn't stopped thinking about her since Saturday. He'd hoped to talk to her earlier in the day, but apart from glimpsing her from afar in the lunchroom, that had been a bust. She'd been sitting at the cool table—with the usual crowd, including Ron and Reed. It had been a little disheartening, but then, those people were still her friends. It didn't mean she and Ron were back together.

Heading down the corridor to Ms. Donahue's chemistry class, Spencer kept looking for Bonnie. He didn't notice Reed, leaning against the wall by the classroom doorway, until they were nearly face-to-face. Even then, it was Reed's trademark backward Dodgers cap that caught Spencer's eye first. Then he noticed the smug grin.

"Hey, Spence," Reed said with a strange lisp. "How's it fagging?"

Spencer squinted at him. "That doesn't even make any sense. That's the best you can do?"

He brushed past him into the classroom. He wasn't going to let Reed bother him. He was thinking about how he'd casually wave at Bonnie when he saw her in her chair in the second row.

But she wasn't there. Had she gone home sick? There was still a minute or two before class officially began. She could still show up.

Spencer took his seat and kept his eyes on the door.

Whispering into his phone, Reed strolled in, smirked at him, and subtly flipped him the bird. Spencer wondered if he was talking to his buddy Ron. Maybe they were planning to ambush him between classes somewhere in the hallway or outside after school. *Swell.*

Making matters worse, it looked like Bonnie wasn't coming to class.

The bell rang. Ms. Donahue walked over to the door and closed it. "Put your phone away, Mr. Logan, and lose the cap."

"Later!" Reed said into the phone. Then he slipped

it inside his pocket and made a big deal out of taking off his precious blue cap. He set it on the edge of his desk and then stroked it. For some inexplicable reason, a few people in the class thought this was pretty damn funny. Reed kept up this stupid routine to milk a few more chuckles.

Spencer's hatred for this clown started to boil. He'd read parts of Damon's journal, and knew the extent of Reed and Ron's cruelty toward him. Damon had condemned them both—just minutes before blowing up that BMW with his mother and himself in it. Did Reed have any remorse at all about that? Did he have anything resembling a conscience?

Obviously not.

Spencer slouched lower in his chair. He knew it was mostly his disappointment over Bonnie's absence, but he suddenly couldn't help feeling angry and frustrated about everything.

It had been a shitty weekend when he stopped to analyze it. His aunt was so upset about the disappearance of the silver frame. It wasn't really the expensive frame. It was the photo inside, which had been temporarily covered up by Mrs. Shuler's portrait. Andrea loved that picture of her mother, and it was her only copy.

"God, what was I thinking?" she'd cried, finally breaking down for the first time since Damon's suicide. Up until then, she'd been pretty stoic. But late Saturday afternoon, she sat at the kitchen breakfast bar at the Ballard apartment and cried. Luke wasn't around to see it.

"I should have removed Mom's picture," Andrea

said, weeping into a paper towel. "It would have taken two seconds. Who would be so awful that they'd steal something from a memorial service?"

Spencer told her he was pretty sure—but not certain—the culprit was Mrs. Shuler's ex-boyfriend, Troy Slattery. His aunt was in a horrible mood for the rest of the evening. When Luke called, wanting to get together, she told him she had an awful headache.

On Sunday, Spencer went with Luke to the house on Garfield. The police had already been through it, confiscating Damon's computer—among other items. Mrs. Shuler's lawyers had given the okay for Luke to collect whatever he wanted, since he was her only beneficiary. He was going to pick up some photo albums, books, and a few other items. Luke had invited Andrea and him along and told them to help themselves to whatever they wanted. Andrea had made it pretty clear she wasn't interested in anything that had belonged to Evelyn, and she stayed at home.

But Spencer was curious. The police had given Luke a list of everything they'd bagged and collected as evidence in the case. Spencer saw the list, and Damon's journal wasn't on it. He figured the diary had to be hidden somewhere in Damon's bedroom. He wanted to know what Luke's son had been thinking those last few days before he went on that rampage.

The police had left Damon's bedroom in a shambles. The bed had been stripped, furniture had been pulled out from against the walls, corners of the carpeting had been peeled up, desk drawers were open, books and videos had been removed from the bookshelves. This was Spencer's first look at Damon's sanctum sanctorum. He'd had no idea Damon was such a movie nut. He had about four hundred DVDs, which the police had left in stacks by the bookcase. Damon must have been a classics snob, because only a handful of the movies were from after 1990. Spencer wished he'd known. That would have been something they could have talked about.

Damon had a huge, framed film poster of Orson Welles's *Touch of Evil* above his bed. Spencer had seen the movie a while back. He wondered if the cops knew that a car got blown up in the beginning of that film.

He took some Hitchcock movies and a few other titles. But mostly, he wanted to find that journal. Spencer searched the bedroom for about a half hour— until Luke was ready to leave. He figured Damon must have destroyed the journal before killing himself. Maybe it had been in the BMW—along with his mother and him.

He'd said some pretty harsh things about Tanya in the journal. Perhaps he didn't want it getting around how he really felt about her. But it was a pity, because that diary carried the only firsthand account of the cruelties Reed, Ron, and their friends had inflicted on him. It was too bad no one would know just how awful they'd been to him.

If people knew, maybe then Reed, Ron, and their cronies would actually feel ashamed.

He watched Reed goofing off during chemistry class, soliciting giggles from his misguided admirers.

Every time Ms. Donahue turned her back to the class, he grabbed his hat and put it on again—backward, of course. Then he'd have the hat off his head and on the desk by the time she turned around once more. He was actually pretty good at it—and very, very happy with himself.

Spencer wanted to punch his lights out.

At the bell, he collected his books, got to his feet, and headed for the doorway.

"Hey, Spence, wait up!" Reed called—with that same weird lisp. It must have been his attempt to sound effeminate. "Hey, Spence!"

Stepping out the door, Spencer turned to glance back at him.

"Hey, I was thinking," Reed said, catching up with him in the hallway. He'd dropped the lisp. "You and the Freakazoid were kind of like stepbrothers. Am I right? I mean, isn't your aunt spreading her legs for the dad?" He raised an eyebrow and grinned.

Spencer suddenly lost it. He couldn't hold back. He grabbed Reed by the front of his shirt and slammed him into the lockers. The loud bang got everybody's attention in the corridor.

"What the fuck is your problem?" Spencer growled.

Dumbfounded, Reed gaped at him. He looked terrified.

"Damon Shuler's dead because of you, but you don't really give a shit, do you?" He reached up, grabbed Reed's baseball cap, and hurled it down the corridor. A few people laughed.

"Now, you go crying to Ron about this," Spencer said, tightening his grip on Reed's shirt. He pulled him close, almost raising him off his feet. "I'll take on the two of you. I'll kill you both. The world would be better off without you worthless scumbags . . ."

Spencer shoved him against the lockers again. Reed let out a sharp cry.

A couple of people in the hallway gasped.

"Hey, that's enough, you guys!" Ms. Donahue said, tapping Spencer's shoulder. "Break it up—or finish it in Mr. Dunmore's office."

Spencer realized what he was doing and suddenly felt sick to his stomach. He let go of Reed and hurried down the corridor. Other students got out of his way—except for Tanya, who came up alongside him.

"I saw that," she said, out of breath. He couldn't tell if she gasping to keep up with him—or if she was overly excited. She wore another one of her thrift shop specials, a chartreuse dress with short sleeves. She hugged her books to her chest. "I heard what you said, too. Bravo! You're right, you know. This school—the world—would be better off without them. Reed and Ron—and don't forget that bitch Bonnie Middleton . . ."

Spencer's heart was racing. He really wished Tanya would go away. He wanted everyone to leave him alone. Though he'd be late for his next class, he needed to step outside and get some air.

But before he could slip out a side door, Tanya grabbed his arm. "I think that's an excellent idea, Spencer," she whispered. "They need to pay for what they did to Damon."

Spencer yanked his arm away. "Would you leave me alone? Go on, you'll be late for your next class."

He ducked outside. She didn't follow him, thank God.

He took a few deep breaths and tried to calm down.

But then he remembered telling Bonnie at the memorial service about Luke and his aunt. Had she passed that on to Reed, Ron, and the others? Was that how Reed knew? *Isn't your aunt spreading her legs for the dad?*

He hated to think that maybe Tanya was right about her.

After what they'd done to Damon Shuler, maybe Tanya was right about everything she'd just said.

# CHAPTER ELEVEN

*Five weeks earlier*
*Wednesday, September 16—12:08 p.m.*

Tanya was supposed to meet him by his locker, which had the word *FREAK* scrawled across it in indelible black marker. Damon's locker was the only one that had been defaced in the second floor's west corridor.

Some asshole—probably Ron, Reed, or one of their buddies—had written the epithet on his locker last Friday. Damon had reported the offense to Principal Dunmore right away. It looked like the janitor had tried to clean off the insulting word, because the letters were slightly blurred now. Obviously it needed to be painted over—a couple of coats, at least.

The hallway was clearing out, and only a few stragglers lingered by their lockers. Most everyone had already gone to the cafeteria. Tanya ambled up the corridor in another one of her thrift store ensembles: this time, a tight sleeveless top that showed off her flabby, white arms, and green Bermuda shorts.

"I guess we're just a couple of nonconformists," she'd always say. "You and I, we have to pay a price for being unique . . ."

Damon cringed inside whenever she implied they were two of a kind. He wasn't like her at all. He just wanted to be left alone, but Tanya relished being different.

He often thought people might stop picking on him if he spent less time with Tanya. But the truth was he'd miss her if they quit being friends. Tanya could make an evening of eating Cheetos and barbecue potato chips in front of TV infomercials incredibly fun. If it weren't for her, he might have gone crazy from the loneliness. Still, as much as he liked her, Tanya also annoyed the hell out of him sometimes. She could be bossy and manipulative. Plus, she was such a slob. With just the right clothes, makeup, some hair care, and a healthy diet, she could have made herself a lot more attractive.

"Today from the Gag-Me-Royally Cafeteria, you have a selection of shepherd's pie or beef tacos," Tanya announced, approaching him. "Both were undoubtedly made from the leftover Gag-Me meatloaf we gagged on yesterday!"

"Which was left over from the Gag-Me Salisbury steak we gagged on on Monday," Damon added, rolling his eyes.

Tanya leaned against a locker next to his. "I vote we go to 7-Eleven, buy ourselves a couple of ice cream sandwiches and some Fritos, and make that our lunch. It's a lot safer than what Gag-Me-Royally is offering."

They rarely ate in the cafeteria, where they were sitting ducks for abuse. When the weather allowed, he and Tanya would buy something at the nearby 7-Eleven or the Safeway deli counter, and then sit outside on the playfield's bleachers. No one bothered them there.

"Actually, an ice cream sandwich sounds pretty good right now," he said, leaning against his locker. "Let's eat outside today. Then we can—"

He didn't get to finish. Out of the corner of his eye, he glimpsed someone coming up behind Tanya. If it had been Reed or Ron, he might have noticed sooner, because he was always on his guard when they approached. Damon didn't have time to see who this was. He didn't see the big plastic cup in the guy's hand.

All at once, a rancid-smelling liquid splattered him in the face. The force of it felt like a hard slap. He toppled back and banged into his locker. Tanya let out a startled shriek.

Whatever it was, the stuff got in his eyes, blinding him. Damon felt so helpless. He heard a couple of people in the hallway laughing.

"Oh my God, look at you!" Tanya gasped. "It's all down the front of you . . ."

"What is it?" Damon cried, wiping his eyes. "What—what did they throw on me? I can't tell. God, it stinks . . ."

"Shit, I think it's bong water . . ."

Damon had tried marijuana once—with Tanya. But

he wasn't crazy about the results, especially the feeling that he was losing control. They hadn't used a bong, but he knew what it was. He'd had no idea the water in those pipe contraptions could smell so putrid. It soaked the front of his cherished yellow short-sleeve shirt—the one that made his arms look less spindly.

As soon as he could focus, he saw Tanya gaping at him. "That shit heel!" she growled. "You know what you should do? Right now, you should march into Dunmore's office, stink up the place, and tell him what just happened. He should know the level of crap they've been inflicting on you . . ."

Grimacing from the stench, Damon shook his head at her. Principal Dunmore already knew what was going on. And Damon didn't feel like marching down a flight of stairs and through three corridors, reeking of vile bong water, just to prove a point to the principal.

"Did you see who did it?" Tanya asked. "It happened so fast, I didn't get a chance . . ."

Damon kept shaking his head. He turned away and started to work the combination on his locker. He was trembling.

"What are you doing?" she asked.

He opened his locker and pulled out the gray crew-neck sweatshirt he kept in there for emergencies. "I can't stand this stink for another second," he muttered. "I need to wash off and change . . ."

"But you'll ruin it!" she argued. "You won't make any kind of real impression on Dunmore if you walk into his office all cleaned up . . ."

Damon tried to ignore her. "Let me handle this myself," he muttered, grabbing an old plastic bag out of his locker. He figured he could stuff the rancid-smelling shirt into the bag and present the evidence to Dunmore that way.

Despite the horrible stench emitting from him, Tanya hovered annoyingly close by. "Okay, if you need to wash off before you go see him, if that's the way you want it, fine. I'll go with you to see Dunmore and we'll tell him exactly what happened. I'll make him understand—"

"You don't have to," he said under his breath. Right now, more than anything, he just wanted her to shut up. He kept his head down to avoid looking at her—or anyone else, for that matter. People in the hallway were still snickering at him.

"You need me there when you talk to him," she continued. "I'm a witness . . ."

He shut his locker and headed toward the men's room. "I'm okay on my own."

Tanya followed him. "Well, I'll stand guard outside the restroom while you change. You never know what these creeps are going to pull . . ."

Damon swiveled around. "Goddamn it! Would you just leave me alone?"

Her mouth open, Tanya stopped dead and stared at him.

He turned and ran for the restroom. Ducking inside, he let the door swing shut behind him. Damon didn't see anyone at the urinals or in the stalls. He was alone in there, and for that he was grateful, because he'd already started crying.

The fluorescent overhead light flickered a bit as he moved to the sinks. His every step seemed to echo off the ugly blue-and-gray tiled walls. He set the sweater and empty plastic bag on the counter. Then he peeled off his wet, smelly shirt and threw it in one of the sinks.

At the next sink down the counter, he pushed the faucet cap to dispense some water for a few moments. There were no spigots. Obviously the powers that be at the high school didn't trust the students to turn off a faucet themselves. Bent over the sink, Damon had to pump the faucet cap again and again so he could wash his face. Then he slurped some water to rinse out his mouth.

All the while, he tried to ignore the three words that had been scratched onto the bottom corner of the mirror at the beginning of the school year:

## DAMON FAG SHULER

Principal Dunmore knew about it and promised they'd replace the mirror just as soon as they could. He knew what was happening.

The meetings with Dunmore were practically the only times Damon's parents saw each other. Those conferences were like impromptu family reunions. Within the next day or two, they'd probably have another session with Dunmore—about this bong-water incident.

Shirtless, Damon pumped the faucet cap several times to fill the sink that held his smelly shirt. Then he dispensed some soap into his shaky hand and rubbed it over the material. He knew he was destroying the "evidence," but he couldn't stand the smell. What had just happened had been humiliating enough. He didn't need everyone in the school to know. He imagined this awful stench following him around as he took the soiled shirt to Dunmore's office. It was just the kind of thing that would get around and earn him a new nickname.

Damon heard people talking and laughing in the hallway. He wondered if Tanya was standing guard outside the restroom. He'd probably chased her away. He hadn't meant to snap at her, but she really got on his nerves sometimes.

The last thing he wanted was for someone to come in here and find him half-naked and teary-eyed. Mortified, he couldn't even look at his own pale reflection—any more than he wanted to look at the slur scratched in the corner of the mirror.

He told himself he'd survived worse.

The scariest incident had happened on a rainy Friday last May. Tanya was home sick, so Damon had to eat lunch alone. He picked up a container of milk and two "Marshmallow Munchee" bars (Gag-Me Royally's lame attempt at Rice Krispies treats) in the cafeteria. Then he got the hell out of there. He took refuge in the lobby of the empty auditorium across the courtyard from the cafeteria. He sometimes ate there with Tanya when bad weather prevented them from having lunch on the bleachers. They'd sit on one of the cushioned benches along the lobby wall. Out the window, they'd watch the smokers and stoners across the quad, puffing away.

During lunch hour on that Friday, the motley group of smokers huddled in doorways or wore their hoodies to shield them from the rain. As he nibbled on his Marshmallow Munchee, Damon found himself missing Tanya, who could be pretty funny with her comments about that crowd of burnouts.

Then he noticed two people who didn't belong among them.

The backward blue Dodgers hat was a dead give-away.

Emerging from the group, Reed and Ron strutted up the short walkway toward the building that housed the auditorium.

In a panic, Damon sprung to his feet. He tossed what was left of his lunch into a trash can and ducked into the darkened theater. He figured they'd start searching for him in the rows of vacant seats. So he raced down into the orchestra pit—to a small door that accessed a storage area under the stage. Opening the door, he caught a glimpse of what was inside the tiny crawl space: extra folding chairs and sheet music stands for the orchestra members. He bent down and scurried into the cubby-hole.

With his every movement, he was a still a slave to his OCD, first having to touch and test the door, the latch, and the cold, dirty cement floor. As Damon curled up inside the cramped storage area, he took one last look at the empty auditorium and then shut the small door. There was no inside handle, so he couldn't shut the door completely. It remained open a crack, which was fine by him. The last thing he wanted was to be trapped inside there.

Damon kept perfectly still as he listened to Ron and Reed stomp into the theater. Their all-too-familiar cackling echoed in the near-empty auditorium. One of them shushed the other.

"The freak's in here somewhere," he heard Reed whisper.

"He doesn't have his fag hag to protect him today," Ron said.

He listened to them talk, their voices getting louder and clearer as they came closer to the stage. Damon tried to keep still, but he couldn't stop shaking. The small, dusty crawl space seemed to shrink around him with every passing second. He hated it in there. Yet the alternative seemed too horrible to imagine. Reed and Ron could do whatever they wanted to him here. No teacher was around to stop it. No one would hear him crying out for help.

Suddenly, it got deathly quiet. Someone was in the orchestra pit. Damon could hear the footsteps on the other side of the door. The crack in the small doorway was too slight to peek outside at who it was or what they were doing. Still, Damon leaned closer to the crevice to see what he could.

All at once, the door banged shut—just inches from his face.

He recoiled, banging his head on the low ceiling and knocking into some music stands. They made a loud clatter.

Past that, he heard them snicker.

"I guess the freak's not here," Reed said. But from his sarcastic tone, Reed seemed to know exactly where he was.

Damon held his breath. He heard a chair or a music stand being dragged across the floor. It sounded like Reed or Ron had propped it against the little door to the storage space.

Were they blocking the doorway, maybe wedging a chair against it?

He couldn't tell.

He pushed on the door, but it didn't budge.

"Hey!" he dared to call out. He gave the door another shove. But it didn't do any good.

He heard them laughing. The cackling grew more distant. Damon realized they were leaving him trapped in there.

"Hey, wait a minute!" he yelled, banging on the small door. "Don't go! Come back, please, come back! Don't leave me in here!"

"I guess he isn't around," Reed announced—in that same sarcastic tone.

Ron chuckled. Their voices were fading.

"NO!" Damon screamed, squirming inside the tiny, black crawl space. Suddenly, he couldn't get a breath. He pounded on the door again and again.

When he stopped, it was silent. He couldn't hear them anymore. They were gone.

Struggling within the confines of the tiny space, Damon repositioned himself and then gave the door a kick. But it didn't move.

Damon twisted to one side and reached for his smart phone in the pocket of his cargo pants. He knew the battery was low, but maybe it still had enough juice for one phone call. And at least he'd have some light. The storage space was so dark he couldn't even see his hand in front of his face.

He dug the phone out of his pocket and switched it on. The tiny, dim screen carried a message: LOW BATTERY.

On the keypad, he pulled up Tanya's phone number. He figured she'd get ahold of Dunmore or someone else at the school, and they'd get him out of here.

Damon kept waiting to hear the dial tone. But then a message came up on the little screen: NO SERVICE AVAILABLE. The light was fading.

"Oh God, no," he whimpered.

He knew this theater. He'd sat in the auditorium many a late afternoon, waiting for Tanya in rehearsals for one play or another—always some minuscule part. But to hear her tell it, she had the lead. They didn't have any after-school rehearsals today. As far as Damon knew, no one would be using the auditorium for the entire weekend.

He imagined being trapped in here for the next two days. His parents would have no idea where he was.

He felt doomed. He frantically kicked at the door again. "Help me, please!" he yelled, his voice cracking. "Is anyone there? Can you hear me?"

Damon's neck and shoulders ached from staying hunched inside the cubbyhole. He was convinced he'd suffocate, starve, or go insane before someone found him in there. He kept screaming until his voice was hoarse. He repeatedly tried to push, kick, and pry the small door open—all to no avail.

After a while, the phone light wouldn't go on. He couldn't read the dial on his wristwatch. He had no idea how long he'd been in there.

Were Reed and Ron coming back for him?

Eventually, a custodian heard him banging on the door and crying. A chair had been wedged against the storage area door. Damon had missed two classes. He figured he'd been a prisoner in the tiny space for nearly three hours.

The "family" meeting with Dunmore regarding this incident included Reed, Ron, and their parents. Damon's two tormentors admitted they'd gone looking for him in the theater. "We just wanted to see where he went to eat lunch," Ron said, shrugging. "He's always disappearing around lunch hour."

They said they'd peeked into the auditorium and called out his name, but hadn't actually come inside the theater. Everyone knew they were lying. But Reed and Ron stuck to their story—and their obnoxious parents backed them all the way. It was so close to the end of the school year that Dunmore decided to let Reed and Ron go with just a warning.

A lot of good it had done. In fact, the meeting last May had just made matters worse for Damon when school started again this September. Reed and Ron didn't stop harassing him. They'd just gotten sneakier about it.

Neither of them had so much as uttered a word to him since school had started again. But Damon often caught them scowling at him and whispering to their pals. On occasion, when he dared to make eye contact with Reed or Ron in the hallway, they'd smirk at him. Along with his smug grin, Ron sometimes pointed at him and then drew a line across his own neck. The slit-throat gesture wasn't lost on Damon.

He knew he was as good as dead.

He knew the insults hurled at him and the slurs scribbled on his locker or on bathroom mirrors were just a prelude to something horrible. While biding their time, Ron and Reed had recruited others to do their dirty work. That included the anonymous asshole who had just thrown bong water in his face.

Damon wished like hell he'd gotten a good look at the guy.

Standing over the sink, he wiped off his chest and stomach with a wet paper towel and a little soap. Then he wrung out his shirt. Past the cheap soap scent, it still smelled like bong water.

As Damon stuffed the wet, soiled shirt into the plastic bag, he listened to a steady *drip, drip, drip* in one of the sinks.

He froze. Something was wrong. He didn't hear anyone in the hallway. There wasn't even the faintest sound of people laughing or talking.

Above him, the light flickered again.

"Shush," someone whispered—just outside the bathroom door.

Damon felt his bare skin crawl. He took a step back and bumped into the paper towel dispenser.

All at once, the restroom door swung open. Three guys in black ski masks burst through the doorway and charged toward him. The sudden din sounded like a stampede. The noise reverberated against the tiled walls.

Damon cried out, but before he could do anything, two of the thugs were practically on top of him. They grabbed hold of his arms.

"Guard the door!" one of them grunted.

The third creep pulled back a little, blocking the bathroom door.

Damon tried to scream out again, but one of his attackers slapped a hand over his mouth.

Without his shirt on, Damon felt so scrawny and defenseless. His assailants were practically twice his size. One of them was probably Ron, and the other two, friends of his. Their black ski masks reminded Damon of those cowardly butchers in the ISIS beheading photos. The way they gripped his arms cut off the circulation. They could have easily torn him in two if they wanted.

Still, Damon struggled. No matter how much it hurt, no matter how useless it seemed, he fought back. He tried to bite the big hand clasped over his mouth.

But just then, one of the attackers shifted behind him and took him in a choke hold. The guy squeezed his forearm against Damon's throat. Helpless, Damon couldn't move. His head tipped back and his jaw automatically clenched shut. His assailant started to lift him off the bathroom floor. Damon felt as if he were going to pass out. His feet frantically kicked in the air just inches above the floor tiles.

The second creep fumbled at the front of Damon's jeans, unzipping them and then shucking them down to his ankles.

Damon squirmed. He heard a snipping sound. He managed to focus on the origin of that strange noise. The masked thug in front of him held a pair of scissors, and he kept clicking the blades together as if the shears were a musical instrument.

"Cut off those panties of his," whispered the one behind him. It sounded like Ron trying to disguise his voice. He squeezed tighter with his chokehold. "Don't you move, or he might slice off your pecker."

The pressure against his throat obstructed Damon's windpipe. All the while, the second assailant tugged at the side of his underpants—like he was about to cut them off.

The one who had Damon by the throat loosened his grip for a second. "Did you see who hit you with the bong water?"

Damon gasped for air. "No, I swear, I didn't . . . please . . ."

He snapped Damon's head back. "See that big pipe up near the ceiling?"

Damon saw it—by the flickering fluorescent light, amid several smaller, cobweb-strewn pipes.

"We brought a rope along," he whispered into Damon's ear. "Can you imagine what everyone will say? They'll find you stripped naked and hanging from that pipe. They'll call it a suicide—very kinky, a fitting end for the freak that you are . . ."

The more his masked stranger talked, the more certain Damon was about his identity. It had to be Ron Jarvis.

"None of this happened today," Ron murmured. Damon felt his warm breath in his ear. "You didn't get dowsed with bong water, and nothing went on here in the bathroom. Isn't that right, freak?"

Damon tried to nod, but he couldn't move his neck. "Yes, I—I won't tell a soul," he whimpered.

"No, you don't want to be strung up naked, do you, Damon?"

He heard the scissors snipping.

"No, I don't . . . please . . ."

He felt the grip against his throat slacken. "One word about this to anybody and you're dead. Got that?"

"Yes," he gasped.

Damon had barely gotten the word out when Ron shoved him down onto the grimy tiled floor.

Dazed, he tried to catch his breath. He heard the three scurry out of the bathroom. One of them was snickering. It sounded like Reed.

Damon started to get to his feet, but the room was spinning. He felt cold—and sick to his stomach. He crumpled back down onto the dirty floor. He pulled his pants back up to his waist. Every muscle in his body ached.

Yet, he didn't shed a single tear.

He was telling the truth to those guys. He wouldn't mention a word about this to anyone. He wasn't going to tell Dunmore. He wouldn't say anything to his parents. Tanya would never hear any of the details. None of them could really help him. They were all useless.

He'd already done something to make it right.

Two nights later—on Friday, September 18—he wrote about the incident in his journal. That was his last weekend at his father's town house—before the girl-friend and her nephew moved in. There were certain things he didn't even tell his journal. It turned out to be a smart move on his part.

For several nights, Spencer What's-His-Name slept in the spare bedroom. He might have found the journal and read about the incident in the school restroom—as well as a lot of other personal things. But this house-guest—this intruder into Damon's second bedroom—

had no idea what Damon had done to make everything right.

He'd gone online, established contact with a local dealer, paid with a money order, and received a delivery. It had come to his door in a brown box via USPS just days before the ambush in the school bathroom.

The timing of the delivery couldn't have been more perfect. Damon had been home alone. His mother had been out on an errand at the time.

He'd had no idea it would be so easy to purchase a semiautomatic.

Getting his hands on some dynamite would take a little more planning. But Damon was determined to make it happen. Almost a year of abuse from Reed, Ron, and their buddies had helped strengthen his resolve. What was that old saying? *Whatever doesn't kill you makes you stronger.*

The ones who had made him strong didn't have a clue what was in store for them.

# CHAPTER TWELVE

*Friday, October 23—11:52 a.m.*

Andrea impulsively pulled over in front of the cinderblock storefront. She'd been driving up Aurora Boulevard on her way to Costco when she spotted the ugly yellow sign with black lettering:

**$ = LUCKY DAY LOANS = $**
*Buy & Sell*

GOLD, SILVER, DIAMONDS
COINS, WATCHES, JEWELRY
CAMERAS, COMPUTERS & MORE!

She knew there wasn't a snowball's chance in hell they'd have the silver frame—and the odds were even worse that her mother's photo would still be inside it. But Andrea parked her VW Beetle at the curb and stepped inside the store anyway. It smelled like a basement that had recently flooded—a sharp, dank odor. The oblong windows were high and offered no view outside except for some phone poles. But Andrea could still hear the traffic on Aurora—past a radio playing an evangelical talk show.

Under bright fluorescent lights, piles of junk were stacked on metal shelves. A bin of DVDs and CDs was against one wall. She was the only customer in the place. The clerk stood behind a counter, where the watches, coins, silverware, and jewelry were displayed. He was a paunchy, sixty-something man in a ratty orange cardigan. He glanced up from his book and eyed her suspiciously—as if she'd come in to shoplift.

Andrea worked up a smile for him. "Do you have any frames—silver frames?"

He squinted at her as if she were crazy. "What?" he barked.

"You know, picture frames?" she said—even drawing a square with her fingers. She didn't think it was such an unusual question.

He nodded toward a shelf to her right. "Try over there."

"Thank you," Andrea said. She found a dusty stack of frames—mostly wood or plastic—by some clunky bookends. There was also a vase with a cupid painted on the front. It looked sort of sweet—and pathetic.

A wave of sadness overwhelmed her, and tears welled in her eyes. It wasn't just this depressing, smelly place—or the fact that she was searching for a photograph of her mom that she'd never get back. She was thinking of seven years ago, when she'd hunted through various pawnshops in and around Washington, DC. She'd been looking for her mother's and sister's jewelry. She'd found her sister's scarab bracelet in a Buy & Sell store on Highway 495 in Annandale, Virginia. The police had recovered several other pieces in pawnshops in Falls Church and Arlington. But they'd never found her mother's cocktail ring.

It was just a piece of costume jewelry, maybe worth a hundred dollars at the most, but the slightly gaudy ring had been one of her and her older sister, Vivian's favorite pieces when they were kids playing dress-up with their mother's jewelry. Andrea called it the "fruit salad" ring, because there were five different colored stones in a silver leaf setting. She'd been a little jealous that Vivian ended up with it. Their father didn't try too hard to disguise the fact that Vivian was his favorite. So when their mother died—from an aneurysm at age sixty-eight—their dad gave practically all of her jewelry to Vivian. She also got the china and silverware. At the time, Andrea didn't care that much. She was too devastated by the death of her mother, who didn't seem to have a clear favorite. Andrea was finishing college. Two years older, Vivian was already married, going to a lot of business parties, and doing a lot of entertaining. It made sense that the bulk of their mother's valuables went to her.

But Andrea really wished she'd gotten that silly old ring—for sentimental reasons. Vivian used to joke that she'd leave it to her in her will. It was kind of sad and ironic that the "fruit salad" ring was the one piece never recovered after the murders.

At least she'd inherited a silver frame, in which

she'd put a photo of her mother, looking chic at age thirty in a black sleeveless dress and pearls.

The frame wasn't there amid the junk on the pawn store shelf.

Of course it wasn't.

She thought about buying that pitiful cupid vase— just to give it a home. But her cell phone rang, startling her. She made a mental note to change the "Hello, Good-bye" ringtone, which had gotten pretty old. She fished the phone out of her purse, and glanced at the caller ID: JILL LOGAN. Andrea had no idea who that was, but Jill Logan lived in Seattle. Andrea clicked on the phone. "Hello?" she whispered.

"Andrea Boyle?" the woman asked.

"Yes?"

"This is Jill Stephenson Logan."

Apparently that was supposed to mean something to her. "Yes?" she said again.

"I think you know who I am," the woman hissed.

Andrea didn't know what to say. Just to be polite, she might have pretended the name rang a bell. But this woman sounded so agitated. Every sentence she uttered was almost a confrontation.

"I'm sorry," Andrea said. "Have we met?"

"Don't try to pretend you don't know who my son is."

"I give up," Andrea sighed impatiently. "Who's your son? And who are you? I think you might have the wrong number—"

"I'm Reed Logan's mother, Ms. Boyle."

It took Andrea a moment to remember that name. He was one of the bullies Damon Shuler had mentioned on his webcast before the car explosion. "I—I still don't understand why you're calling me," she said.

"Oh, like you don't know!" the woman snapped. "I'm calling to tell you and your nephew to stop it. Do you hear me? No more! Don't think I'm too afraid to go to the police, because I'll go to them, I will. I'm warning you . . ."

Andrea clutched her phone tighter. "What are you talking about? Stop what?"

There was a click on the other end of the line.

*Friday—12:07 p.m.*

"I swear, I have no idea what she's talking about," Spencer said into his cell phone. He stood in the corridor outside the cafeteria. He'd been on his way to lunch when his aunt had called.

"Well, do you know this Reed?" Andrea asked. "I mean, this is the same kid who was picking on Damon. He isn't a friend of yours, is he?"

"Of course not," Spencer sighed. "In fact—well, I didn't want to tell you, but he's been riding my ass lately—"

"What do you mean?"

"He's been—y'know—trying to push me around," Spencer explained. "I told you I was getting some flak because I'm new."

"And this Reed character is one of the guys picking on you? Spencer, you told me things were getting better."

"Well, things got lousy again," he admitted, leaning against the brick wall. He talked quietly, despite the din from the cafeteria next door. "I guess with Damon dead, they need a new whipping boy. Anyway, on Monday, I kind of screwed up. Reed said some—well, some nasty, offensive shit, and I just lost it. I pushed him against some lockers and told him to lay off."

"Oh, honey, you've got to be careful," she said. "You don't want to get into any kind of trouble. If just one incident gets reported to the police, they'll be all over you. It won't matter who's right or who's wrong—"

"I know," he said, cutting her off. "All I did was shove him, Aunt Dee. Anyway, that was Monday, and since then, they've pretty much left me alone. Plus I've been avoiding them all week. So outside of shoving him—and he really had it coming—I haven't done a thing to Reed Logan. I don't know what his mother's talking about."

There was a long pause on the other end. "Okay, well, just keep doing your best to avoid him and the others. We'll talk tonight . . ."

After he hung up with his aunt, Spencer wandered into the cafeteria. It was always a bit rowdier and louder on Fridays. It was pizza day, and what the school chef considered pizza was a travesty: leathery, tasteless pepperoni with bland, moist cheese and something close to ketchup bleeding through a soggy crust. Spencer had planned on having a salad and breadsticks instead. He'd also planned to avoid Reed and Ron and their tribe. He didn't need his aunt telling him that.

He noticed Bonnie Middleton was at the cool table once again. She'd never really left it. She was still part of that group.

She'd come back to school on Tuesday, and he'd seen her in chemistry class on Wednesday. She'd smiled at him and given him a little wave as he'd taken his seat. But he'd ignored her. Spencer hoped she'd caught the snub. She had it coming for telling Reed and probably half the school about his aunt and Luke. He hated that Tanya was right about her.

Bonnie was looking at him now—with a glum expression. Reed sat across from her. Reed's back was to him, but Spencer recognized him by the stupid backward Dodgers cap. Reed turned and glanced over his shoulder at him.

Spencer headed to the cafeteria line, skipping past the pizza and zeroing in on the breadsticks.

"Hey, Murray!" he heard someone yell. "Spencer Murray . . ."

He turned around and saw Reed Logan coming toward him.

"We've got to talk," Reed said. Then he pointed toward the hallway. "Out there . . ."

Spencer wasn't sure if he was being set up for an ambush or if this had to do with whatever was going on between his aunt and Reed's mother. "What for?" he asked.

Reed sighed and adjusted his cap a bit. "Okay, fine, I'll ask you nicely. Would you mind stepping the fuck outside so we can talk for a minute? *Please*?"

As cool and tough as he was trying to act, Reed seemed desperate, too—maybe even a little scared.

"All right," Spencer replied, still guarded. He headed toward a side door leading to the hallway.

If Reed wanted to talk in private, he was out of luck. Bonnie and a couple of others from the cool table had gotten to their feet and were starting to follow them. Ron wasn't among them. Spencer noticed Tanya—in an ugly denim jumper—emerging from another corner of the cafeteria. She was trying to catch up with them, too. She and the others must have expected to see another confrontation between Reed and him, maybe like the one on Monday afternoon.

"I want you to cut out the shit," Reed muttered as they ducked into the corridor together. "You leave us alone, and I'll leave you alone, okay?"

"I have no idea what the hell you're talking about," Spencer said. He couldn't believe the timing. "My aunt just called me and said your mother was on her case about something. Does this have anything to do with that?"

"So you're pretending you didn't break our living room window or key my mother's car . . ."

"What?" Spencer murmured.

"You haven't been calling my mother, saying shit, and hanging up?"

Wide-eyed, Spencer stared at him and shook his head.

"And you had nothing to do with that dead raccoon on our back porch?"

Spencer let out a stunned, little laugh.

"Yeah, it's pretty goddamn funny, isn't it?"

He shook his head again. "No, it's just that a lot of that stuff happened to my aunt and me."

"Well, you can't prove that I had anything to do with it," Reed shot back.

The two of them saw they had an audience in the

hallway. Reed's voice dropped to a whisper. "That shit going down at your place in Ballard, I'm not responsible for any of it. You have no proof . . ."

Spencer blinked at him. "How did you know about it? I didn't tell anyone."

Reed grabbed his arm and pulled him out the nearby exit. Spencer felt the chilly autumn air hit him. They were with the smokers and potheads in a courtyard area across from the auditorium building. It stunk of cigarette and marijuana smoke.

"You can't pin any of that shit on me," Reed growled. "Don't even try, because it won't stick. I was just an errand boy for the Freakazoid's mother. I was only doing what she paid me to do . . ."

Spencer couldn't believe Reed was admitting all this. "She paid you?"

"That's not the point—"

"How did you break in? When you got in and re-arranged the shoes on our stairs, how did you pull that off?"

"She had someone else do that," Reed answered. "What about you? How'd you break into my house?"

"They got inside your house, too?"

Reed nodded. "They didn't steal anything. They just took a bunch of shit out of the refrigerator and left it on the kitchen counter. Or I should say *you* took that crap out of our refrigerator—"

"It wasn't me," Spencer insisted, shaking his head. "I didn't have a thing to do with it."

"Bullshit," Reed retorted. "It's just the kind of thing somebody from a loony bin might do. And that's where you're from, isn't it?"

Spencer felt like he'd just been sucker-punched in the gut. For a few seconds, he couldn't breathe. He saw that Bonnie, Tanya, and a few others from the cafeteria had merged with the smoker crowd. They'd obviously heard what Reed had just said.

"Shut up," he said quietly.

"You and the Freakazoid were a perfect pair," Reed went on. He was playing to the audience now. "He was crazy, and you're crazy. They sprung you out of a loony bin in Virginia before you came here. Are you going to deny it?"

It was all Spencer could do to keep from punching Reed in the face. He knew if he did, the *reason* he belted him would be all over the school. He took a deep breath. "Leave me the hell alone," he said finally. Then he turned away.

"That's what I'm telling you, asshole!" Reed yelled. "Leave me and my family alone!"

Spencer weaved around the smokers and headed toward the sidewalk.

Bonnie Middleton caught up with him. "What was Reed talking about back there?" she asked, folding her arms in front of her. She shivered from the cold. "Is it true what he said?"

Spencer stopped and turned toward her. "Why don't you ask him? He's your good buddy. Last weekend at the memorial, I told you in confidence about my aunt and Damon's father. And two days later, that weasel back there asked me if it's true my aunt's 'spreading her legs' for Damon's dad. Who else did you tell besides him? I mean, really, why the hell would I confide in you?"

"Spencer, I didn't mention it to anyone," she said.

"Yeah, right . . ." He started walking again. He had no idea where he was going. He just needed to get away from all those people before he hit somebody—or started crying.

"Remember, I told you—it was *the word going around school*," Bonnie said, keeping up alongside him. "I heard about your aunt and Mr. Shuler from Reed last week, for God's sake. You just confirmed it on Saturday. I didn't talk about it with anybody . . ."

"Fine," he grunted. "That's terrific. Why don't you go back to your friends?"

"I'm just trying to help you," she said.

"You can help me by leaving me alone," he said, picking up the pace.

She stopped abruptly, and for that Spencer was grateful.

He kept on walking. He didn't want her to see the tears in his eyes.

It was always easy to spot Reed Logan in the crowded corridor. All she had to do was look for the backward blue cap. After his run-in with Spencer, he hadn't gone back to the cafeteria. But Bonnie found him heading toward his locker on the second floor. He was by himself, talking on his phone. He didn't seem to notice her.

As Bonnie approached him, she heard him mutter: "Anyway, I don't think we'll have any more problems—at least not from him . . ." He grimaced. "Yeah, well . . . I understand. I'll come right home after school . . . I told you I would, okay? Jesus. G'bye . . ." He clicked off the phone and started to tuck it into the pocket of his jeans.

"What's going on?" Bonnie asked him.

He swiveled around. "Shit, were you listening in?"

"Hardly," she replied, frowning at him. "What's going on between you and Spencer Murray? It sounded like you were accusing him of harassing your family . . ."

"The guy stepped out of line, and it's been taken care of," Reed replied. "End of story." He headed to his locker and started working the combination.

Bonnie followed him. "Last week, when you mentioned that Spencer's aunt was seeing Damon's father, how did you know about that? Who told you?"

He opened up his locker and pulled out a jacket. "I just knew."

"You mean the same way you *just know* about Spencer spending time in a—an institution? Is it true?"

With a sigh, he took his cell phone out of his pocket, switched it on, and showed it to her. "I got this text at five o'clock this morning," Reed said. "And don't ask me who sent it, because I'll be fucked if I know."

Bonnie gazed at the illuminated little screen:

Tel Spencer Murray 2 stop buging u & yr family or Ls
every1 wl know bout him. He wz n an Nsane Asylum in VA.
By d wa, Spencer Murray isn't evn hs real nme.

"It's got to be true," she heard Reed say. "Did you see the way the crazy bastard looked when I mentioned it?"

\*    \*    \*

"Did he say how he found out?" Andrea asked, with the cell phone to her ear. She sat in her car with the motor off—in the Costco parking lot.

Jill Stephenson Logan's strange call had unnerved her. Maybe it had made her a bit paranoid, too, because Andrea was pretty certain a maroon Impala had been following her since she'd left the pawnshop ten minutes ago. She thought she'd lost the other vehicle here in the vast parking lot. Just to be sure, she'd stayed inside her VW and scanned the lot for the Impala. There had been no sign of it. Spencer's call had come just as she'd been ready to climb out of the car.

Andrea was still trying to process everything he'd just told her. Someone was doing to Reed and his family what Reed had done to her and Spencer—at the behest of Evelyn Shuler. Andrea couldn't fathom it. Evelyn had hired the bully who had been tormenting her son to carry out her dirty deeds. Then again, she probably figured he was an ideal candidate for the job. But all the while, he was still picking on Damon.

And Evelyn knew about it.

Luke's estranged wife had paid Reed Logan to harass her and Spencer. Had she also paid the boy to torment her own son? Every time her son was bullied, it was an excuse for Evelyn to call Luke or have a meeting with Luke and the school principal.

In one of the manuscripts she'd edited, Andrea had read about Munchausen syndrome by proxy. Was this Evelyn's spin on that? The constant bullying of her son kept her connected to Luke. Andrea couldn't imagine a mother so horrible. And yet it seemed possible. There was a bizarre, twisted logic in it.

She wondered if Damon had found out about what his mother had done. Was that why he'd snapped? Is that why he'd tied her up, thrown her in the back of the BMW, and forced her to die with him in that horrific explosion?

Right now, it was just conjecture, but Andrea needed to discuss it with Luke tonight—and then maybe the police.

Yesterday, she and Spencer had loaded up the VW and moved back into Luke's town house. It hadn't taken much persuading on Luke's part. He'd said the last two weeks alone had practically been unbearable. "I don't think things will start to feel okay again until you guys move back in with me."

She wondered how *okay* he'd feel when she told him this news about his late wife. And Luke still had no idea that Spencer had spent time in a mental institution—five years, in fact.

Andrea wondered how much Reed Logan knew.

"He didn't say who told him or how he found out," Spencer said on the other end of the line. "He knows I was in a place in Virginia. I can't be sure what else he knows. But it's only a matter of time before everyone else finds out about it—before they know my whole history." She heard him starting to cry.

"It's going to be okay, Spencer, I promise," she said. "We'll work it out tonight. The worst thing that'll happen is maybe you'll have to switch schools."

"To where no one knows me—or what I did?" he asked in a shaky, broken voice. "How soon before they find out about me at the next school—or the school after that? And Luke still doesn't know. What do you think will happen after you tell him? And you'll have to tell him now. You can't let him hear about it from Reed Logan or Reed's mother or somebody else . . ."

"We'll be okay, honey," Andrea said into the phone, trying to believe it herself. She shifted restlessly behind the wheel.

"Luke's such a nice guy," Spencer went on. "I know you love him. And I'm screwing that up for you."

"Listen, you just said it yourself. Luke's a nice guy. It's not going to be easy, but he'll understand. And if he doesn't, well, then we just weren't meant to be." She sighed. "And don't worry about Reed Logan. He's in no position to threaten you. We've got him on destruction of private property, vandalism, and God knows what else. He has more to lose than you do if he starts shooting off his mouth about you. Just give him and his buddies a wide berth for the rest of the afternoon. Luke's got rehearsals tonight. So it's just you and me for dinner. We'll figure all this out tonight. I'm here at Costco. How about if I get you that lasagna you like?"

There was a silence on the other end. "Yeah, that sounds good," Spencer said, finally.

After Andrea clicked off with him, she sat in the car for another few minutes.

They'd just moved back in with Luke. She'd even bought some perennials yesterday to plant outside his town house over the weekend. But after hearing what she had to tell him, he might just ask them to move out again.

She remembered how she and Spencer had wanted to start fresh in Seattle. They were going to blend in and stay out of trouble. But then she fell in love with Luke—

and they inherited all this baggage. Still, that was no excuse for keeping Luke in the dark about Spencer's past.

She had been Spencer's guardian since his release from Northern Virginia Behavioral Health Center five months ago. In Virginia, he'd seen a therapist three times a week, and in Seattle, he met every other week with a woman named Diane Leppert, whom he really liked. Starting someplace new where no one knew them seemed like a good idea. But Andrea was still adjusting to a new city—and to Spencer. Sometimes, he felt like a total stranger.

She knew he must have felt the same way about her.

Andrea remembered six years ago, when she got the call at two o'clock in the morning. A cop told her that her sister and brother-in-law had been shot by an intruder. She learned that eleven-year-old Spencer and another boy, who was spending the night, had survived by hiding under his bunk bed.

The news absolutely devastated Andrea's widower father—losing his favorite daughter like that. But at least he had his grandson, whom he adored. At first, he was so grateful that Spencer had been spared.

But her father stopped communicating with Spencer when the boy was admitted to the institution. He moved away to Scottsdale and remarried. Andrea kept in touch by phoning him once or twice a month, but their relationship was strained. She had a feeling he wouldn't miss her if she didn't call. She'd long ago given up asking if he wanted to talk with Spencer.

She wondered how Luke would react when she told him the truth. She thought about a new way to approach the subject: *You know how Spencer sees a ther-*

*apist every two weeks? Well, there's more to it than I let on . . .*

She felt the knot forming in her stomach already.

Grabbing her purse, Andrea climbed out of the car. Before she shut the door, she spotted a woman emerge from a row of cars across the way. She was about forty-five, tall and big-boned. In a pale blue pullover and jeans, she walked at a brisk, determined clip. Her long black Morticia Addams hair fluttered behind her. She zeroed in on Andrea. "I want you to know I'm watching you!" she declared in a shrill tone.

Andrea automatically stepped back. "Let me guess, Jill Logan?" she said, frowning. "Do you drive a maroon Impala?"

"You already know what kind of car I drive," Reed's mother retorted. "You saw it—or your nephew did—when you scratched it the other night."

"You mean, like how your son scratched my car twice—and broke my headlight?" Andrea stepped aside to show Reed's mother the scrape across her Volkswagen's driver-side door. "This is his handiwork from two weeks ago. And just for the record, Mrs. Logan, I didn't key your car and neither did my nephew. We didn't break any of your windows or leave any dead animals outside your door. We aren't responsible for any of the acts being done to you and your family—"

"Then how did you know about those things? Huh? Answer that!"

"Because your son just accused my nephew, Spencer, of doing them," she answered. "Spencer called me three minutes ago. Are you and your son tag-teaming us or something?"

"One more incident and we're going to the police," Jill Logan warned.

Andrea threw her hands up in resignation. "Go ahead. I hope you find out who's responsible. I sympathize with you. I was at my wits' end when your son was doing those things to us. Tell me, how long have you known that Evelyn Shuler was paying Reed to pick on Damon—and harass us?"

"Oh, now really," Mrs. Logan scowled. "Are you saying you're not the one who emailed me about it night before last? And you're not the one who's been calling and leaving all sorts of filthy, threatening messages?"

Andrea shook her head. "That's just crazy—"

"Then it must be your nephew. Talk about crazy. I understand he spent time in a mental institution. How do you know for sure he's not the one—"

"Because I know," Andrea said, cutting her off. "Neither one of us would lower ourselves. Why on earth would we? If either Spencer or I had known any time before today that your son was behind all that vicious harassment, we would have gone directly to the police. And we still might. Reed admitted his guilt to Spencer only a half hour ago, and you just confirmed it for me. Neither Spencer nor I have broken any laws. But Reed could be in a lot of trouble for what he's done. So quit threatening me, Mrs. Logan, and tell your son to back off. No one at the school needs to know about Spencer's past. If that gets out, I won't have to guess twice who's to blame—your son. You tell that little criminal to leave my nephew alone."

She slammed her car door. The VW let out a beep as she locked it with the device. She pointed to the scratch on the side of the vehicle. "And I'm sending you a bill for that."

Her heart beating wildly, Andrea hurried toward the Costco entrance. She didn't look back.

She figured for now maybe Spencer's secret was safe—and Reed would leave him alone. But all she'd done was put a Band-Aid on a gushing wound.

# CHAPTER THIRTEEN

*Friday—9:12 p.m.*

"Hi, Jill, this is Andrea Boyle," she said into her cell phone. She was sitting in one of the four bar-stool chairs at the tall, round glass-top café table in Luke's kitchen. It was one of those updated kitchens with stainless steel appliances and granite countertops. Andrea could see her own reflection in the sliding glass door. She had her hair in a ponytail and wore a long-sleeve white T-shirt with striped flannel drawstring pants.

She was tired. She'd been acting upbeat and optimistic for Spencer's sake most of the evening. She'd tried to assure him that nothing was going to happen over the weekend. He seemed half-convinced. She knew he wasn't quite himself. He'd knocked off only a third of his Dinner-for-Two Lasagna, which under normal circumstances he inhaled in its entirety. Afterward, he'd ducked into Luke's study to watch *St.*

*Vincent* for about the fifth time. He always turned to a Bill Murray DVD to take his mind off his worries.

Over dinner, she'd reminded him that Reed and his mother were in no position to make life any more difficult for him. But it had dawned on her that maybe it would be better for everyone if she tried to make friends with Jill Logan. Maybe if they worked together, they could figure out who was behind all of this. And maybe, just maybe, Reed Logan would stop being such a little shit to her nephew.

"Listen, Jill, I'm sorry we got off on the wrong foot earlier today," she said into the phone. "Please, believe me, I understand your frustration. I was just about at the end of my rope back in late August when Spencer and I were getting practically the same treatment from your son. And I realize now that he was simply doing what Evelyn Shuler was paying him to do. I—I don't plan on holding him accountable . . ."

Andrea realized she was babbling, and she hadn't heard a peep from Mrs. Logan yet—outside of her first hello.

"Are you there?" she asked. "Jill?"

"I'm here," she said at last. "I'm just wondering if you're recording this."

"No, I'm not, I promise you," Andrea replied. "I think we're better off working together to figure out who's behind everything that's been happening to you and your family. Obviously, they're trying to pit you against Spencer and me. I mean, think about it. They're giving Reed all this information about Spencer, things he'd rather not have getting around the school. And they're telling you about how Evelyn Shuler paid Reed to harass us. They're stirring up this hornet's nest, and I don't know why. Do you?"

"I have no idea," she said tonelessly.

Andrea could tell Reed's mother still didn't trust her.

"Listen," she said, hunched over Luke's breakfast table, "if anything else happens there at your house, could you call and let me know? I think you should also call the police and report it. Whoever is behind this, they seem to be—"

"You know what I think?" Jill Logan interrupted. "I think you or your lunatic nephew—or both of you—are behind these vicious attacks, and now you're trying to throw me off—"

"I assure you—"

"I don't have anything to say to you," she cut in. "Please, stop calling me, and stop this harassment."

Andrea heard a click on the other end. Then the line went dead.

"Nice talking to you, too," she muttered.

She clicked off the line and sighed. She realized she'd never get Jill Logan's cooperation. Moreover, Jill would never give a straight answer to a question that had been plaguing Andrea since this afternoon: If Evelyn had paid Reed to key her Volkswagen, why did he scratch it a second time—the night after Evelyn had died?

Someone else must have pulled off that encore prank—maybe the same person who was now harassing the Logan family.

Spencer said Reed had told him he wasn't the one who had broken into their apartment and rearranged the shoes on the stairs. So Evelyn had another errand boy besides Reed on her payroll.

Andrea wondered about Evelyn's former boyfriend, Troy Slattery. Spencer said Troy was shooting eye-daggers at Luke throughout the memorial reception. He was also pretty sure Troy was the one who had stolen the silver frame. But by early September, Evelyn had already long since split with Troy and was campaigning to win back Luke. At least, that was the impression she got from Luke when he returned from a meeting with the principal one week into the start of the school year. Why would Troy Slattery be doing Evelyn any favors after she'd dumped him? And with Evelyn dead, why would he be harassing Reed Logan's family? What did Troy possibly hope to gain?

Her cell phone rang, and she wondered if Jill Logan had had a change of heart. She snatched it off the glass-top table and clicked it on. "Hello?"

"Hi, hon," Luke said. "Guess who's stuck here in Rewrite Hell for at least another hour and a half. I'm sorry . . ."

"It's all right. Don't worry about it," Andrea said. "Did you get something to eat?"

"Yeah, we ordered out—Thai food. I feel like a jerk doing this to you on your second night back. Anyway, don't wait up for me."

"Is it okay if I do wait up?" she asked.

"Yeah, that would be nice."

After she hung up with Luke, Andrea felt relieved. The knots in her stomach went away. She'd put off the talk until tomorrow—or maybe Sunday. There was no reason for urgency. Reed Logan wasn't going to start spreading the word about Spencer's medical history before they were back in school on Monday—if even then.

So, the dreaded talk could wait.

After all, Andrea told herself, nothing was going to happen over the weekend.

*Saturday, October 24—1:21 a.m.*

Reed Logan woke up to the sound of the alarm.

He sat up in bed with a start—to a dark bedroom. It wasn't morning yet.

Every time it happened, he was so disoriented. He saw the blinking red light on the alarm unit on the nightstand—alongside the clock, his cell phone, and his Dodgers hat. He quickly reached over and switched off the alarm. He relished the silence—after that incessant ringing. He prayed it hadn't awoken his parents, especially his mother.

With trepidation, he listened for the sound of footsteps in the hallway. He didn't hear anything—just the usual house-settling noises.

Reed slid his hand down under the covers. His underpants were wet.

"Goddamn it," he muttered.

He'd had nearly an entire week of dry nights and had felt confident enough to go to bed last night wearing regular Jockey briefs instead of his usual boys' extra large GoodNites. He was trying to wean himself out of nighttime diapers before college.

He switched on the light. His bedroom walls were cluttered with sports pennants, some pilfered street signs, and a framed *300* movie poster with Gerard Butler leading the Spartan troops into battle. Above his bed was a rack of samurai swords that were knockoffs, but looked pretty real. The place was kind of a mess. His mother was on his ass to straighten it up.

His mother had been on his ass about a lot of things since two nights ago—when she'd gotten that text saying Mrs. Shuler had paid him to put the screws on that twitchy, neurotic kid of hers. Mrs. Shuler had said she wanted to toughen him up. It had been pretty bizarre, sitting in Dunmore's office, getting reamed for picking on the Freakazoid while both sets of parents were there. But he didn't give her away. He'd gotten a two-hundred-dollar bonus and a blow job for keeping quiet about that.

He'd been all too happy to take on more work for her with that harassment job at the apartment in Ballard. He had no idea who the people were—just that he had to screw with them. He didn't put it together until later that the victims were the new kid in their class, Spencer Murray, and his aunt. By that time, around early September, Evelyn didn't seem to need him anymore. In fact, she didn't want anything to do with him. He called, but she stopped picking up. He took out his frustrations on the Freakazoid.

At the time of Evelyn Shuler's death, Reed hadn't seen or spoken with her in well over a month. So far, no one had linked the two of them. In fact, he didn't really give it too much thought until some asshole keyed his mother's Impala while it was parked in their driveway on Monday night. Spencer Murray had shoved him against the lockers that same afternoon. Reed figured that was too much of a coincidence. They'd found the dead raccoon by the kitchen door the next day. Then there were the phone calls—and the text to his mother two nights ago, blowing the whistle on him as Evelyn Shuler's errand boy. Fortunately, they didn't tell her about the sex with Evelyn. Maybe they didn't know.

Just the same, his mother went absolutely ballistic on him.

That incident on Thursday with somebody breaking in and emptying a shelf out of the refrigerator had really freaked her out. He'd found it pretty disturbing, too. Then he'd gotten the anonymous text, blaming Spencer Whatever-His-Real-Last-Name-Was for everything and revealing that he'd been in a nuthouse.

They'd had one night after another of disturbing occurrences. But so far, they'd gotten through Friday night without an incident—until just now. And he really couldn't blame pissing in his bed on Spencer What's-His-Name.

Reed checked the towel covering the moisture-sensor pad on his mattress. It was wet. He wondered if any urine had gotten on the sheets. He was in luck. It hadn't soaked down to the fitted sheet and the flat sheet was merely damp in one spot. He wouldn't have to change the sheets tonight. He'd dodged a bullet.

Reed carefully carried the soggy towel toward his bathroom, which was right off his bedroom. He'd clean up the mess—and his mother wouldn't be any the wiser. He was just switching on the bathroom light when he thought he heard something. It lasted only a couple of seconds, and sounded like someone dragging a chair across the floor downstairs.

Biting his lip, he listened and waited. Nothing.

Reed told himself it was probably just the ice machine in the refrigerator. If his parents had gotten up, he'd have heard them. Stepping back, he glanced over toward his closed bedroom door—with the Nerf basketball net mounted on it. He didn't see any light under the door. That was always a telltale sign that he'd woken one of them.

"Relax," he whispered to himself. Ducking into the bathroom again, he threw the wet towel into the tub. Then he peeled off his soaked underpants and tossed them on top of the towel. Naked, he stepped into the tub, shut the map-of-the-world shower curtain, and grabbed the handheld shower off the pole. He'd been through this hundreds of times before. He didn't need to wash his whole body—just from the waist down. Irish Spring took care of the urine smell. He lathered himself up and then ran the bar of soap over the towel and his Jockey briefs.

The pipes let out a squeak as he turned off the water. He opened the shower curtain and reached for a towel on the rack. He started to dry himself.

After the roar of the shower, it suddenly seemed so quiet—until he heard the footsteps.

Had the shower woken up his mother or father?

Wrapping the towel around him, Reed crept into the bedroom and made his way to the door. The crack at the threshold was still dark. The hallway light wasn't on. Yet, again, he still heard footsteps and the creaking floorboards.

Was somebody coming up the stairs?

If one of his parents had awoken and gone down to

the first floor, they would have turned on the upstairs hallway light.

They still hadn't figured out how anyone could have broken in the day before yesterday—only to empty a shelf from the fridge. As far as his parents could tell, nothing had been stolen from the house. His mother had pitched all the food—not just the stuff that had gone bad, but anything with a broken seal and all the leftovers still inside the refrigerator. The incident had shown them how vulnerable they were to an intruder.

Somebody from the security company was supposed to come over later today to change the locks and the alarm code. But for now, they were still vulnerable.

Wet and shivering, Reed clutched the towel around his waist and leaned close to the door. His face was right beside the Nerf basketball hoop.

The footsteps were in the hallway now.

A part of him wanted to believe it was his mom or dad. He quickly tiptoed to his dresser, took out a pair of GoodNites, and struggled to put them on. He didn't want to be naked right now. He couldn't stop shaking.

From the squeaking floorboards, it sounded like whoever it was had moved away from his room— toward his parents' bedroom down the hall.

Relieved, Reed let out a sigh. It must have been his mother or father getting up in the middle of the night for a snack or something. And he hadn't been busted for peeing in his sleep again. Whoever it was, Mom or Dad, it sounded like they were going back to bed.

"Reed?" his father said, sounding startled. "Reed, is that you?"

It took Reed a moment to realize his father wasn't calling to him. He was talking to somebody in their bedroom.

"What's going on?" his father asked. "Who are you?"

His ear to the door, Reed heard someone whisper a response, but he couldn't make out what they said.

"Jill, honey—"

"Who's this?" his mother asked. "What in God's name . . ."

"Shut the fuck up," someone barked.

"Oh, my God!" his father cried. "No, no—wait!"

Reed jumped at the single blast of gunfire.

His mother screamed.

The second shot cut her off. Reed heard his mother sigh—and then nothing.

He knew it was her last breath. He knew both his parents were dead.

Horror-struck, he couldn't move. Trembling against the door, he felt his legs start to give out from under him. He held on to the doorknob to keep from crumpling to the floor. With tears in his eyes, he glanced back toward his nightstand—at his phone. He gazed at the samurai swords above his bed. But he couldn't get to them.

He'd always thought that in a crisis like this, he would keep his cool and spring into action. With sheer determination and guts, he'd overcome a gunman threatening him and his family or friends.

Yet, now, he was paralyzed, utterly helpless.

He heard the footsteps once more—coming closer. It sounded like two people. One of them whispered to the other. This time, Reed could make out the faint murmuring: "His room's down the hall. I checked it out during the visit on Thursday. There's no lock on the door . . ."

He heard a strange cackle.

"We're coming for you, Reed," one of the intruders called softly to him.

He was just on the other side of the door.

Reed recognized the voice.

He didn't think he had anything left, but he still wet himself.

# CHAPTER FOURTEEN

*Saturday—2:10 a.m.*

Bonnie Middleton found the bestseller *Ask a Tall Dark Stranger* listed on Amazon.com. A "sneak peek" option allowed her to read the first few pages for free. The acknowledgments were on the third page, and the aunt's full name was right there: . . . *And many thanks to Andrea Boyle, who helped make a silk purse out of a sow's ear.*

Spencer had said at the memorial service that she was an editor. And this was the only Andrea the author mentioned.

Sitting at her desktop computer in her small pink-and-white bedroom, Bonnie clicked out of Amazon.com, and opened Google. In front of her was a framed poster—Robert Doisneau's famous black-and-white shot of a Parisian couple kissing. Bonnie was wearing blue flannel pajamas.

She was a night owl, and searching for information on Google at two in the morning somehow always seemed more important than sleep. Taylor Swift was on the radio—at a low volume. At this time of night, when she was the only one awake in the house, Bonnie didn't like to use earphones. They blocked the outside noise. Maybe she was slightly paranoid, but she wanted to hear if someone was trying to break into the house.

The Middletons lived in one of those beautiful old stately Tudor-style homes on Queen Anne Hill—with a gorgeous view of the city and water from practically every window but hers. When they'd moved in five years ago, Bonnie had campaigned for this small, rather isolated bedroom with a bath at the top of the back stairs. Her dad said it had probably been a maid's quarters for the house's first occupants. Bonnie had enjoyed the idea of living in a servant's quarters—like Audrey Hepburn in *Sabrina*. She'd also wanted privacy. Her two younger brothers' rooms, a guest room, and the master bedroom were down the hall in practically another part of the house.

Bonnie remembered inviting Tanya McCallum over to see the new house—her room especially. She and Tanya had been best friends in sixth grade. Bonnie hadn't had much of a choice in the matter. She didn't have many friends at the time, and Tanya, living two doors down with her divorcée mom, had glommed on to her. Though Bonnie hadn't particularly liked Tanya, they'd spent a lot of time together—until the Middletons moved into the Tudor-style house on the Hill, nearly a mile away. A mile wasn't really so far away for good friends. But Bonnie used the move as an excuse to see Tanya less and less.

Tanya had made it over to the "new" house only a few times. During that first visit, Tanya kept saying the place was too big—especially for a family with three kids. "Aren't you afraid you'll get robbed or something?" she'd asked. "And your room's totally cut off from the rest of the house. If somebody broke in and came up the back stairs, you'd be the first person they'd murder . . ."

For some reason, Bonnie had never forgotten that. So she never put on earphones when she was up late at night.

And for reasons all too apparent, Tanya had never forgotten that the two of them had once been "best friends"—until Bonnie pulled away. So in Tanya's mind, she was evil incarnate. It didn't help matters that for a while now, Bonnie had been dating Ron Jarvis, who teased and tortured poor Tanya every chance he got.

She didn't feel too good about herself for that. But she'd gotten swept up by the notion of dating the star quarterback. Plus Ron was so cute—especially when he wore his glasses, which deceptively gave him a "sensitive jock" look. They were one of the most popular couples at school. Ron was sexy, and a good kisser. She convinced herself that she was lucky to be his girlfriend.

But Damon Shuler's suicide made her realize that not only was she dating a bully, but she'd become kind of a bully herself. She felt horrible for dumping that container of pencil shavings on Damon's head while he was asleep at one of the library reading tables last spring. She'd meant it as a stupid, harmless joke.

Of course, to hear Tanya tell it, she may as well have poured acid on the back of Damon's head instead of pencil shavings.

Still, it had been a lousy thing to do. Damon was too easy a target. Picking on him in a different, clever way won her points with Ron and his crowd. But she'd simply gone for the cheap laugh.

In the wake of Damon's suicide, it didn't seem so funny anymore. If she could only take that moment back, she would have.

Instead, she broke up with Ron and started to pull away from the others—a little bit at a time. She continued to eat lunch with them. On the surface, they were still nice to her, but she knew her days at the cool table in the cafeteria were numbered. It was just as well. Except for a handful of fellow cheerleaders she genuinely liked, the others were pretty phony.

For example, KC Cunningham had been enormously popular, but her closest friends didn't seem to miss her much. They acted all heartbroken when the local TV stations interviewed them on the news. But no one was really that close to her. No one had known about KC's affair with their English lit teacher. As one cheerleader friend put it, "It's hard to imagine that KC managed to keep it a secret while she was screwing Mr. McAfee. I mean, how could she have not tweeted about it?" No one ever got KC's full attention. She was always on her phone, most of the time posting on Instagram, Twitter, and Facebook—usually selfies.

While Bonnie still had a place at the elite table, she

tried to be the group's voice of conscience. She figured if she reminded them that bullying was extremely uncool, maybe she could help save other kids from going through what had destroyed Damon Shuler. This, of course, made her a total drag to Ron, Reed, and their pals.

Now that Damon was dead, the group seemed determined to make Spencer Murray's life miserable.

Bonnie wanted to help him. And it wasn't merely because she was trying to make up for what happened to Damon or because she felt sorry for Spencer. She also had a little crush on him.

According to the anonymous text sent to Reed Logan, "Spencer Murray" wasn't even his real name. And he'd spent time in a mental institution somewhere in Virginia. Bonnie wondered if her taste in guys was really that horrible—first a bullying creep and now someone certifiably crazy.

It wasn't likely she'd discover in one Google search Spencer's real name or the circumstances of his institutionalization. But it was worth a shot. Bonnie stared at the keywords beneath the Google banner: Spencer, Andrea Boyle, Virginia. She hit the Enter key and watched the first page of search results come up.

All the results on page one were obituaries that contained the keywords. If she wanted to read up on the death of ninety-year-old Andrea Spencer from Falls Church, Virginia, she was in luck. It was like that for every search result on the page—each time a different combination of those names.

On page two, the third result listed caught her eye:

<u>Fairfax Couple Slain in House Robbery</u>
articles.washingtonpost.com/ . . . /07132009p . . .
Washington Post
July 13, 2009—Fairfax, **Virginia** . . . the Rowes' eleven-year-old
son, **Spencer**, hid under his bed along with a friend . . . the
victim's sister, **Andrea Boyle**, of Washington, DC, identified
the bodies . . .

Bonnie remembered Spencer telling her at Damon's
memorial that his parents had died in a car accident.
But it was understandable that he wouldn't want to say
they'd been murdered. It was also understandable that
a kid who had lived through something so horrible
might end up needing psychiatric help. According to
the article, Spencer and his friend, who was spending
the night, were in his bedroom when they heard the
gunshots in his parents' room just down the hall.

The article didn't have a picture of Spencer Rowe.
But the *Post* had run a photo of his parents, which must
have been taken at some semiformal party. Smiling,
they both had their arms around each other. Even in the
blurry black-and-white photo, Bonnie could tell Lawrence
and Vivian Rowe were an attractive couple. Both were
only thirty-seven years old at the time of their deaths.

She kept thinking of what Spencer was going through
now—with those jerks picking on him at school. Hadn't
the poor guy been through enough?

She wondered if the police had ever caught the
killer, who made off with some jewelry and the money
from Lawrence Rowe's wallet. She shifted around in
her desk chair and typed in the search box: Lawrence
Rowe, Vivian Rowe, Fairfax Murders.

Bonnie looked at the first result listed, and wondered if she was reading it right.

"Oh, my God," she murmured. She clicked on the link to an article in *The Washington Post*, dated July 15, 2009. She read the headline:

### 11-YEAR-OLD BOY CONFESSES
### TO PARENTS' MURDERS
Juvenile in Fairfax Double Homicide Admits
Robbery Was Staged; Claims Friend, 13, Helped
"Pull the Trigger" in Killings

There was a photo of the once-happy family posing in front of the Jefferson Memorial. Spencer's face was blacked out. All Bonnie could see was his skinny little body in jeans and a Redskins sweatshirt. It took her a moment to realize the newspaper was protecting the identity of a murder suspect who was underage. Obviously, that was why the article didn't mention the name of Spencer's thirteen-year-old friend. In the article, they kept referring to him as "the other boy" or "the older boy."

Bonnie read through five more articles before "the older boy" was named. Apparently, Garrett Holmes Beale denied any wrongdoing at first. However, a few pieces of Vivian Rowe's jewelry—the pieces that hadn't yet been sold off to pawnshops—were found in a stack of folded sweaters in Garrett's bedroom closet.

Bonnie got the impression that Garrett Beale's lawyers put up quite a defense. But the thirteen-year-old was eventually found guilty of second-degree murder—along with Spencer. Because both boys were underage, the press coverage was a bit limited. From what Bonnie could tell, the trial had been conducted behind closed doors.

According to the articles, Garrett had been spending the night at Spencer's home in the Mantua section of Fairfax. While Spencer's parents were at a dinner party, the boys had found a gun Lawrence Rowe kept hidden in the master bedroom. Mr. and Mrs. Rowe returned home before the boys had had a chance to put the gun back in its hiding place. Guests at the dinner party testified that Larry Rowe had seemed intoxicated. When he discovered the boys had found his gun, he flew into a rage. He hit Spencer and threatened Garrett. Spencer shot his father. Then, with "the older boy" manipulating the gun, they shot the mother, too. It was Garrett's idea to make the whole incident look like a house burglary gone wrong.

The boys served their sentences at separate state-run psychiatric facilities. Apparently, the court saw fit to keep the two young killers apart during their rehabilitation. Bonnie wanted to think Garrett Beale was the guiltier party, using his influence on a younger, impressionable kid. But Garrett was paroled in January 2015, several months before Spencer.

The most current article about Garrett was dated April 14, 2015. Bonnie winced at the headline:

### HOUSE FIRE KILLS ARLINGTON FAMILY
Three Dead; Arson Investigation Pending
Teenage Son Had "Troubled Past"

The story carried a head shot of Garrett, which looked like a driver's license photo—or maybe it had been taken in the psychiatric hospital or a juvenile detention facility. He was handsome, with messy blond hair and a sexy smile. Bonnie hated herself for finding him attractive. The photo caption read: "Garrett Beale, seventeen, died along with his parents, Clinton and Denise Beale, in their Arlington home. Garrett had recently been paroled after serving nearly five years for his involvement in the shooting deaths of a Fairfax couple."

There were no articles about Spencer Rowe after his release from Northern Virginia Behavioral Health Center ten months later.

Hunched in front of her laptop, Bonnie read until four in the morning. Yet she had a feeling she wasn't getting the entire story. She still didn't know Spencer well enough to ask him what had really happened.

She shut down her laptop and switched off the radio. Crawling into her twin bed with the Eiffel-Tower-print spread, Bonnie switched off the light. She lay there in the darkness and wondered just how much Reed Logan knew about Spencer.

There was a football game tomorrow afternoon. She'd probably see Reed there. She'd ask him then. Maybe he'd gotten another text from that anonymous source.

If she missed Reed at the game, she could always talk to him on Monday.

*Sunday, October 25—4:14 p.m.*

Scott Logan was ticked off.

He'd schlepped all the way down from Bellingham on the Greyhound for a Sunday dinner at home. Scott was a sophomore at Western Washington University. He hadn't been able to come down for the entire weekend, but his parents had talked him into coming for a belated birthday dinner for his father. It would be just the four of them, and his mother was cooking a prime rib. So it was sort of a big deal.

When he'd talked to his parents on Thursday, Scott had told them which bus he'd be on. He'd bought his father *The Magnificent Seven* on Blu-ray. After two hours on the damn bus, he'd arrived at the station only to find no one had come to pick him up. He'd called home, but no one had answered.

So Scott took a taxi. He figured it wouldn't be unreasonable for him to hit up his parents to reimburse him for the cab fare. Or maybe it was stupid-ass Reed who was supposed to pick him up. Whatever, somebody had dropped the ball.

It was just starting to get dark when the taxi dropped him off. And yet he didn't see any lights on inside their modern craftsman two-story home. It didn't make any sense, because his dad's BMW and his mother's maroon Impala were in the driveway.

That was when it finally dawned on him something could be wrong.

Scott took out his house key and started to unlock the front door. But it was already unlocked—and yawned open with just a little push. Stepping into the shadowy front hall, he hit a wall of stench. It smelled like rotten fruit or meat gone bad.

"What the fuck?" he muttered, leaving the front door open behind him—in hopes of airing out the place a little. "Mom?" he called out. He set the Blu-ray and his father's birthday card down on the hallway table. "Dad? Reed? Where is everybody?"

He walked toward the kitchen near the back of the house, and the rancid odor got stronger. Grimacing, he fanned the air in front of his face. At the kitchen entry, he stopped dead. "Jesus," he said under his breath.

The place was a mess. He saw the source of the foul smell. Someone had emptied out the refrigerator. They'd even taken out the shelves. Cans of beer and soda were on the floor—amid a puddle of spilled milk and rotting vegetables. The raw prime rib roast was on the counter—with a couple of flies buzzing around it. Beside the big slab of meat were some of his dad's power tools and an extension cord.

The refrigerator hummed. It was a stainless steel side-by-side model.

Scott started to gag as he stepped closer to it, and he put a hand over his nose and mouth. He saw that some-one had screwed a lock onto the refrigerator. The metal hasp ran across both doors. In lieu of a combina-tion or key lock, a thick-handled ladle and a spatula had been rammed through the lock's shackle to keep the hasp in place.

As he wiggled and tugged at both utensils, Scott thought the makeshift lock had been screwed on there to keep someone from getting into the refrigerator.

But he was wrong.

Scott finally managed to wrench out the ladle and the spatula. He dropped them on the floor. He lifted the latch and then opened the door. The inside light went on.

"Oh, Jesus, no," he cried, stepping back into the puddle of milk.

His kid brother was curled up inside the refrigerator—almost fetal-like. Reed wasn't wearing anything except his special underpants. His body was so pale that it had a slight blue tinge. His eyes were open in a dead stare, and his swollen tongue drooped over his lower lip. Someone had tied his hands together and bound his ankles.

When he made the 911 call, Scott Logan was weeping and barely making any sense.

And he hadn't even gone upstairs yet.

# CHAPTER FIFTEEN

*Monday, October 26—8:22 a.m.*

When the bus dropped him off at school, Spencer prayed Reed Logan wouldn't be there today. Was it too much to ask that he'd gotten sick—or maybe been run over by a truck?

Before he'd left the house this morning, his aunt had told him that Luke still didn't know about what happened with his parents. She'd planned to have "the talk" with Luke last night. "You saw how stressed he was over the play rehearsals," she'd whispered to Spencer in the kitchen—while Luke had slept in. "He's staying home today, and I'll tell him this afternoon. Meanwhile, try to avoid Reed Logan . . ."

Spencer noticed two TV news vans parked outside the school. Reporters were stopping students and interviewing them. He figured they were probably taping some follow-up feature on Damon's suicide—or maybe KC and Mr. McAfee's last rendezvous. Slinging his backpack over his shoulder, Spencer hurried past the TV news cameras and into the building. Other students were doing their damnedest to get on camera, but not him.

Heading down the crowded, noisy hallway toward his locker, he kept a lookout for Reed—as well as Ron or any of their pals.

"Spencer!" Tanya's shrill voice was unmistakable. It rang out over all the chatter and locker-slamming. She clutched her phone and threaded through the crowd toward him. Today she wore a somewhat conventional sweater and jeans ensemble.

Stopping at his locker, he tried to work up a smile for her.

"Spencer, have you heard?" she asked excitedly. She grabbed his arm, and her voice dropped to a whisper. "It was on the news this morning, and it's all over the Internet. Reed Logan's dead . . ."

"What?" he asked, not sure he'd heard her right.

Tanya nodded. "His brother found him last night. Someone locked him inside the refrigerator in their kitchen—and he suffocated. The police think it happened late Friday night. Mr. and Mrs. Logan are dead, too—shot in their bedroom. Can you believe it?"

Bewildered, Spencer stared at her.

Tanya wasn't smiling. But she certainly was keyed up about telling him—and didn't seem the least bit sorry. He now realized the TV newspeople outside had come to get reactions from Reed's classmates about his death. He looked at the others in the hallway, checking the news on their mobile devices. They all knew.

But Spencer was still trying to put it together. "Do

the police know who did it?" He couldn't understand why Reed had been locked inside a refrigerator. What was the point to killing him that way? Spencer remembered just minutes ago cynically wishing Reed were dead.

"Mrs. Logan's jewelry was missing, along with some expensive techno toys and the money from Mr. Logan's wallet," Tanya explained.

Spencer felt sick. He was thinking it seemed awfully similar to the scene staged in his parents' bedroom—with his mother's jewels and his father's wallet money missing.

"You didn't do it, did you?" Tanya asked.

He scowled at her. "Why would you even ask that?"

She laughed nervously. "Hey, I'm kidding. It's just that we talked about him the other day, saying everyone would be better off if he was dead. I'm not going to be a hypocrite and shed any crocodile tears for Reed Logan. He was a total prick to me. He was awful to Damon, too—and to you. I mean, really, think about it. Are you truly sorry he's gone?"

Spencer couldn't answer her. His life at school would sure be easier now. And yes, Reed was a jerk. But did he deserve to die? Did his parents deserve to die? No.

The first bell rang.

"Well, I've got to get to that snooze-fest known as world history," Tanya said—with an eye roll. She smiled at him. "See you at lunch, okay?"

Spencer couldn't believe she could act so cutesy right now. Then again, she'd had a little time to get used to the idea of Reed's death. It was all still a shock to him.

He squinted at her. "Do you—" he hesitated. "Do you have any idea who might have done this?"

She shrugged—almost evasively.

It was a strange response. "You mean you might know?" Spencer asked. "Did you have anything to do with it?"

She laughed again. "God, no! But hey, you know it's not exactly like I lost a good friend." She rubbed his shoulder. "See you in the cafeteria."

He watched Tanya saunter down the hallway. She seemed so content and self-satisfied—as if she'd just won a gold star for something.

Spencer pulled out his phone, and went online to confirm what Tanya had just told him. He still couldn't fathom it. He was barely aware of the hallway empty-ing out—or the second bell ringing to signify that first period had begun.

He speed-dialed Andrea, but got her voice mail. She was probably in the shower. It was hardly the thing to leave on a recording, but he told her about Reed and his parents. He said he'd try her again later.

He wasn't sure what else he could do—except go to his first class. He hurried to his locker to grab his trig book. As he worked the combination, he tried to think of what excuse he'd use for being late.

But then he opened his locker—and everything stopped for a moment.

Something hung from one of the hooks, something that hadn't been there before.

It was a blue Dodgers baseball cap.

\* \* \*

It started to drizzle as Spencer waited for Andrea to show up. With his backpack slung over his shoulder, he stood on the street corner—by the teachers' parking lot. He stepped under the protection of a big elm, its leaves a hodgepodge of autumn colors. He'd been waiting for fifteen minutes, and still no sign of his aunt's VW.

They'd talked at lunchtime. The news about Reed and his parents had obviously upset her. She'd said she would pick him up after school. Spencer hadn't told her about finding Reed's trademark cap in his locker. In fact, he hadn't told anyone yet. He still wasn't sure what he was going to do about it.

At first, Spencer had wondered if someone was playing a sick joke on him. Was it really Reed's cap? He couldn't be sure. It had to have belonged to someone. It wasn't new. The inside band had dark spots from sweat.

Part of him wanted to go to the police with it, but then he'd only bring attention to himself as a potential suspect. He couldn't leave the cap there in his locker because the school held random locker inspections. He almost wanted to destroy it. But that would be just plain stupid. So Spencer carefully slipped the cap into an old plastic Gap bag he'd had at the bottom of his locker. Then he stashed the bag in his backpack, which he held on to for the rest of the day.

At lunch, he managed to avoid Tanya. Everyone was still talking about the murders of Reed and his parents. Spencer listened and said nothing. He was the only person there with a souvenir of the killings. He couldn't be sure if the cap was the genuine article. Maybe someone was trying to screw with his head? Or were they trying to frame him for the homicides on Friday night?

He figured he'd ask his aunt what to do. But where was she? He'd been waiting in the rain for almost twenty minutes now.

"Hi, Spencer."

He turned around to see Bonnie shyly smiling at him. "I thought that was you," she said, stepping under the tree with him. "Are you waiting for a ride?"

"Yeah," he nodded—more times than necessary. His hand automatically reached back to make sure his backpack hadn't opened up. This was probably the twentieth time he'd checked his backpack today—like it might suddenly and magically pop open.

"Pretty weird day," she remarked, hugging her books to her chest.

"Really weird," he replied. "Um, are you waiting for a ride, too?"

"No, I'm walking home. It's only a mile. They called off cheerleading practice. Anyway, I spotted you over here and thought I'd come say hello."

He nodded again. "Thanks. Um, hello . . ."

"I'm glad you're talking to me. At least that's an improvement over last time."

Spencer shrugged. "Um, listen, I know Reed was your friend, so I—I want to say, sorry for your loss."

"That's very nice of you, considering what a rat he was to you." Bonnie plucked a brown leaf from one of the tree's lower branches. "Like I was trying to tell you on Friday, Reed and I weren't really all that close."

Spencer said nothing. She seemed so guarded and

nervous. He remembered seeing that same apprehension in people he met who knew about his time at Northern Virginia Behavioral Health Center.

She knew that he'd been institutionalized. Did she know why?

His phone rang. He pulled it from his jacket pocket and checked the caller ID. It was his aunt. "Excuse me," he said, clicking on the line. "Hi, Aunt Dee. What's going on?"

"I'm sorry, Spencer, I couldn't get away," she said, sounding a bit stiff. "Is it possible for you to take a bus or a cab home?"

"No sweat," he said. "Is everything all right? You sound weird."

"Everything's fine. Come right home, okay?"

"Sure," he said. Then he turned away so Bonnie couldn't hear him. "Did you—talk to Luke? Does he know?"

"We'll discuss it when you get here. Hurry on home, all right?"

"Yeah, sure," he said, puzzled. "See you in a bit."

"See you," she said. There was a click on the other end.

Spencer switched off his phone and turned to Bonnie again. "My ride bailed on me," he explained, trying to smile. "That was my aunt. She wants me to grab the next bus home. Anyway, it was nice talking to you."

"You, too," Bonnie replied, tossing the leaf aside.

He started toward the bus stop on the other end of the street.

"Spencer?" she called.

He swiveled around. "Yes?"

"Listen, if you want, you can walk with me to my house. Like I said, it's only a mile. Then I'll drive you wherever you want. It'll probably be faster for you than taking the bus."

He studied her pretty face. He could almost see how conflicted she was, working up the courage to offer a ride to a crazy person, acting as if she wasn't scared to be alone with him. Or was he just projecting his own stuff onto her? That was what his therapist called it, *projecting*.

"I'm okay with the bus," he said. "But thanks just the same. See you tomorrow." He waved, then turned and started walking again.

As much as he wanted to, Spencer didn't look back over his shoulder.


Walking home in the light rain, Bonnie told herself it was for the best.

Until she knew more about him, she really needed to exercise caution. She couldn't let Spencer's sad, puppy dog eyes fool her. The fact that he was being bullied didn't make him any less dangerous. Last Thursday she'd seen how he'd snapped, pinning Reed against the lockers and threatening him. And the next night, Reed and his parents were murdered. How could she be so certain Spencer wasn't the killer? After all, he'd killed before.

But Bonnie knew she still didn't have the full story there. Plus Spencer had been only eleven years old at the time. There was every indication that he'd fallen under the influence of the older boy, Garrett. He'd spent nearly six years in a psychiatric hospital and juvenile detention. They wouldn't have let him go if he was still a danger to himself or other people. He deserved a second chance.

Still, she needed to give him a wide berth until she knew more about him. It was dumb to have put herself in a situation in which she'd be alone with him for an extended period of time—even just an hour. Bonnie reminded herself once again that she didn't exactly have a terrific track record as far as judging guys at face value.

Apparently, Ron had gotten the news about Reed and his parents before leaving for school, and had stayed home. She'd called him at lunchtime and left a message: "If you get really blue, and you need someone to talk to, give me a call, okay?" Just because she didn't want to be his girlfriend anymore, it didn't mean she had to cut him out of her life completely. Ron hadn't called back. She really didn't expect him to.

Bonnie felt the light rain on her face. She glanced back over her shoulder. She couldn't see Spencer anymore. He must have turned the corner.

Her phone rang, and she dug it out of the pocket of her hooded sweater. She automatically thought of Spencer—even though she was pretty sure he didn't even have her phone number. The caller ID showed: UNKNOWN CALLER.

Bonnie clicked on the phone anyway. "Hello?"

She heard someone sigh on the other end.

"Hello?" she asked again, glancing around to make sure no one was on their phone across the street playing a joke on her.

"Bonnie?" the caller whispered, almost singing her

name—like it was part of a rhyme or something. She couldn't make out if the caller was a male or female.

"Who is this?" she asked, stopping in her tracks. A shudder passed through her.

"Bonnie . . ." the caller repeated in that same lyrical tone. "You're next . . . you're next . . . you bitch . . ."

There was a click, and the line went dead.


The bus dropped him off three blocks from Luke's town house on Olympic Drive. His head down, Spencer walked in the drizzle. He wished he'd taken up Bonnie Middleton on her offer. As undecided as he was about her, it certainly would have been better than walking home alone. Then again, this wasn't really his home. And he wasn't quite alone. He had Reed Logan's prized baseball cap with him. And he still had no idea what to do with it. Just having the damn thing in his possession made him feel guilty, trapped, and doomed.

Spencer still had his head down as he turned the corner and started toward Luke's town house—a Spanish-style two-story with an attached garage, a small yard, and a common wall with another town house just like it. Apparently, the neighbors were in Europe for a few months. Spencer hadn't met them yet.

He stared at the fallen brown leaves scattered along the sidewalk in front of him. He had no idea what was waiting for him at Luke's place. His aunt had sounded so strange on the phone. He had an awful feeling that she'd told Luke the truth—and he hadn't taken it well at all.

Spencer glanced up as he approached Luke's place.

Two cars were parked in front of the town house. One of them, a police car, blocked the driveway. Spencer abruptly stopped and stood on the sidewalk, frozen for a moment. His first thought was that his aunt and Luke had been killed—and the police had discovered their bodies. Was that why Aunt Dee had sounded so strange on the phone? Had someone been holding a gun to her head the whole time they'd been talking?

His heart racing, Spencer hurried toward the town house. He told himself there would be more police cars here if anyone had been murdered. Certainly, there would have been an ambulance.

Still, the police were here, and they had to have a reason. Had someone phoned the police with a tip about the baseball hat?

Near the front walkway, he passed the parked squad car. A cop sat at the wheel with his window open. Spencer heard him muttering into a mobile device.

He made a beeline to the front door. It wasn't locked.

Spencer was shaking and out of breath as he stepped into the front hallway. He saw four people standing in Luke's living room—almost as if they were waiting for him. He heard some static-laced gibberish on a speaker phone.

It took him a moment to focus on everyone in the room. He saw a thirty-something East Indian woman in a tan pantsuit. Her black hair fell down to her shoulders. Next to her was a guy in his mid-twenties with light brown hair and a ruddy complexion. He wore a badge on the lapel of his blue suit jacket, but he looked like a computer geek. Luke stood by the coffee table with his arms folded and a cold, somber expression on his face. And there was Aunt Dee in a black pullover and jeans. As her eyes met his, she looked so sorry and sad.

"Spencer, honey," she said in a strained voice. She nodded at the other woman. "This is Detective Talwar, and she'd like to talk with you . . ."

# CHAPTER SIXTEEN

*Monday—3:57 p.m.*

Spencer looked as if he'd stepped into a trap. Wide-eyed, he stood in the foyer, staring at the four of them. He reached back to check his backpack—as if making sure he still had it on him.

Andrea couldn't help remembering that hot July afternoon six years ago when her traumatized young nephew was staying with her in Washington, DC, after the violent deaths of his parents. He'd told her that the robbery story was all a lie. He'd admitted he and his friend, Garrett, had shot Viv and Larry. Andrea phoned her father, asking for him to recommend a good criminal lawyer. When her father wanted to know why she needed an attorney, she told him, "Because Spencer's in trouble."

He'd gotten a lawyer friend to come over to Andrea's place and talk with them. It turned out to be the last thing Martin A. Boyle ever did for his grandson. He never uttered a word to the boy again.

The balding, forty-something attorney had been caught on his day off. So for the interview with Spencer, he had on a sweater and khakis. He recommended that they phone the police at once. Andrea remembered waiting for the police to arrive—with the lawyer and eleven-year-old Spencer sitting in the living room of her Forest Hills apartment. The police buzzed the intercom and a minute later, knocked on her door. Spencer started trembling. He looked so frightened and helpless—as if he were about to be hauled in front of a firing squad. It was almost impossible to think of him killing her sister and Larry. Andrea recalled wanting to hold and hug him—and assure him that everything would be all right.

That was how she felt now.

Spencer looked so bewildered and scared. He closed the front door and then stepped toward them in the living room. "Hello," he said, nervously nodding at the tall, handsome Indian woman.

"Hello, Spencer," she said with a perfunctory smile. "I'm Detective Maya Talwar, and this is Deputy Ken Marston."

He reached out to shake her hand, but when the detective didn't respond, Spencer awkwardly backed away.

Andrea knew just how he was feeling. Detective Talwar had done the same damn thing to her. Since the moment the detective and her assistant had—without warning—shown up at Luke's door, Andrea hadn't been able to breathe right.

That had been almost two hours ago. Andrea had tried to be cooperative and accommodating. She'd gotten coffee for Detective Talwar and a Diet Coke for the deputy.

Though the sweet smell of her patchouli perfume filled the living room, Detective Talwar barely cracked a smile. She and Deputy Marston sat in matching easy chairs across from Andrea and Luke on the couch. Detective Talwar didn't waste any time explaining in her crisp East Indian accent the reason for their visit. The police had examined Jill Logan's phone records and found a call to Andrea at 12:03 p.m. on the day before the Logans were killed. Another call was recorded that same day at 9:12 p.m., from Andrea to Mrs. Logan.

While the deputy took notes, Andrea told them practically the whole story. The only detail she omitted was that the Logans knew about Spencer's time at the psychiatric institution. Even without that vital, potentially explosive piece of the puzzle, her account seemed to be a disturbing revelation for Luke—especially the fact that Reed had been paid by his late, estranged wife to bully Damon.

"Are you sure about this?" he asked, squinting at her. "I can't believe it . . ."

"Well, neither Reed nor his mother would deny it," Andrea explained. "And Reed sort of inadvertently admitted to Spencer that Evelyn had paid him to harass us. He's the one who keyed my car, broke the window, and left that dead squirrel on our front stoop—practically the same things that started to happen to the Logans last week."

Luke frowned at her. "And you've known about this since Friday? For God's sake, why didn't you tell me?"

Andrea squirmed on the other end of the sofa. "You

were so busy with rewrites. I didn't want to bother you. I thought I could work it out with Mrs. Logan . . ."

"That's crazy," Luke muttered. "You should have said something. I mean, if Damon found out Evelyn was paying someone to abuse him, then that would explain why he became so unhinged. I can't believe you've kept this to yourself. My God, what else haven't you told me?"

Andrea felt her stomach lurch. Should she tell him now—right here, in front of the police? They probably already knew about Spencer's history.

His head down, the deputy furiously scribbled notes while Detective Talwar glowered at the two of them with disapproval. "Ms. Boyle, you mentioned earlier that someone was harassing the Logans in the same manner in which you were harassed at your Ballard apartment. And you say someone broke into the Logans' house on Thursday afternoon and emptied out a shelf in their refrigerator?"

"That's right," Andrea said.

"We don't have a record of this incident at the Logans' on Thursday," Detective Talwar said, frowning. "We don't have an account of any disturbances at the Logan house."

"Well, I'm not surprised," Andrea said. "I think Mrs. Logan was afraid if they reported it and pointed a finger at us, we'd tell the police Reed had done the same things to us in August. The ironic thing is, Spencer and I had no idea Reed was the one who had harassed us—not until he confronted Spencer at school on Friday afternoon."

Andrea couldn't tell if she was getting through to

the detective. "That's why I phoned Jill Logan on Friday night," she continued. "I urged her to call the police the next time they had an incident at their house. I thought that, together, we could figure out who was behind all this."

"Why so generous and understanding?" the detective asked, her head cocked to one side.

"Pardon me?" Andrea asked.

"Once you found out that Reed was the one who had caused you so much heartache back in August, why didn't you just go to the police yourself?"

Luke turned toward her. "I don't understand that either," he said. "This kid made your life miserable for nearly a month. He made Damon's life miserable. You knew about this on Friday, and you didn't tell the police. You didn't even tell me . . ."

Crossing her arms in front of her, Andrea sighed. "Well, I put myself in Jill Logan's place. She was trying to protect her son. I knew what she was going through."

"All right," Detective Talwar said. "Let's go back to this confrontation at school between Reed Logan and your nephew on Friday. By the way, when does Spencer usually return home from school?"

Andrea glanced at her wristwatch and realized she was supposed to have picked up Spencer fifteen minutes ago. The detective allowed her to phone him. When Andrea spoke to him, it was obvious he knew something was wrong. But the poor kid had no idea what was in store for him.

While waiting for Spencer to arrive, Detective Talwar asked—just as a formality—where they were between eleven on Friday night and four in the morning on Saturday. Deputy Marston stopped scribbling and looked up from his notepad.

Luke explained that after returning home from play rehearsals at eleven-thirty, he'd gone to bed at one. He'd noticed Spencer had turned off the light in his room at around the same time. Andrea confirmed that. She'd fallen asleep shortly after one-thirty.

But she lied to the detective and her deputy. She told them she'd stayed up until three-thirty in the morning, working on a manuscript.

It was a little white lie, and no one would know the difference. Luke had been asleep. He couldn't refute her. Andrea knew she was taking a slight chance, but she didn't want anyone thinking Spencer might have gotten up at one-thirty in the morning to sneak out of the house to murder the Jordans. She knew he couldn't have killed Reed and his parents. So if Spencer needed an alibi, she was providing one for him.

When Spencer had finally come through the door, he'd looked so nervous. Once they'd gotten past the somber introductions, Detective Talwar suggested that he sit down.

Spencer nodded obediently. He took off his backpack and his jacket. Sitting in the middle of the couch, he set the pack on the floor—by his feet. He clutched his hands together in front of him.

Andrea sat back down again—along with everyone else. She resisted the impulse to put her arm around Spencer. "Detective Talwar is investigating the deaths of Reed Logan and his parents," she said. "I've told her everything we know . . ."

"Specifically, I want to ask about your altercations at school with Reed," Detective Talwar explained, studying him up and down. "But before we get started on that, I need to clear up something. You're registered at the high school as Spencer Murray, but you are, in fact, Spencer *Rowe*. Is that correct?"

Spencer nodded once again.

"Spencer legally changed his name a few months ago," Andrea said, taking hold of his arm. She could feel him trembling. "I have all the paperwork if you want to see it, Detective Talwar."

She glanced past Spencer—at Luke. He was staring back at her with a slight frown on his face. She couldn't quite read his expression.

Talwar nodded at the deputy and held out her hand. He gave her the notepad. She flipped back a few pages. "And you are the same Spencer Rowe—from Fairfax, Virginia—who shot and killed both his parents back in 2009. Is that correct?"

"Yes," Spencer murmured.

"Is it true you lied about the murders at first and tried to make it look like a robbery?"

"He was barely eleven at the time," Andrea interjected. "Is this really necessary?"

Spencer turned to Luke on his right. "I—I'm sorry, Luke," he murmured.

Luke gave a somber nod—more an acknowledgment than any indication of forgiveness. If he was angry, he wasn't showing it yet.

Andrea stroked Spencer's arm, but she was looking at Luke as well. Her eyes searched his. "I didn't want you to find out about it like this."

Luke cleared his throat and turned toward Detective Talwar. "I think Andrea has a point," he said calmly. "This line of questioning doesn't seem necessary. Spencer has paid his debt to society. He spent five years in hospitals and juvenile detention centers. He's been rehabilitated. He's a good kid. I don't see what his past record has to do with the murders on Friday night."

Andrea stared at him. "You know?" she whispered.

He glanced at her for only a moment. Then he turned to the detective again. "If it's any help, Detective Talwar, I got an anonymous text Thursday night. It's not the first one I've gotten since my son's death. But this one said, in effect, 'I think you know some of these people,' and there was a link to a *Washington Post* story from September 2009. It was an article about Spencer's confession to the murders in Fairfax."

"My God," Andrea said under her breath. Somebody had gotten to Luke before her.

"Anyway, I think Andrea is right," he went on. "Someone out there is trying to stir up trouble for us. There's every indication this person might have known my wife—at least, if it's the same person Evelyn hired to break into Andrea and Spencer's apartment in Ballard. If it's true she paid Reed Logan to do her dirty work for her, then maybe she paid this other person, too."

"That's an interesting theory," Detective Talwar said, a bit condescendingly. "But right now, I'd like to focus on young Mr. *Rowe* here. And I'll determine what line of questioning is necessary."

"I was just going to say that I'd be happy to give

you complete access to my wife's financial records and personal notes—if that's any help," Luke said. "I want to cooperate in your investigation. But I'm not going to sit here and keep still while you ride rough-shod over this boy."

Talwar handed the notepad back to her deputy, and then she got to her feet. She gave a phony smile. "I think we'd be better off conducting the rest of this interview with Spencer at the precinct station."

"Well, I'm coming along with you," Andrea said, standing up.

"That's not really necessary," Talwar said. "We can arrange for his transportation back here."

"No, it's necessary," Andrea replied. "He's not yet eighteen. He shouldn't be questioned by the police without a legal guardian or a lawyer present. And I'm his legal guardian."

Spencer and Luke got to their feet. As he put his jacket back on, Spencer looked down at his backpack. He seemed uncertain about what to do with it.

Andrea took hold of his arm again. "You can leave your bag here," she said. Then she looked at the detective. "Do you want us in the police car with you—or can we follow you in my car?"

"We'll drive you," the policewoman said.

"Then I'll follow you there—and drive you back," Luke volunteered.

Spencer opened the front door for the detective and her deputy. Andrea grabbed a heavy sweater from the closet. Luke put on his jacket.

Once she saw Talwar was out of earshot, she touched Luke's shoulder. "Thank you for this," she whispered.

"I hate that you found out about Spencer that way. And you've known since Thursday? My God, why didn't you tell me?"

"I wanted to ask you the exact same thing," he replied in a cold tone. "You should have let me know a long time ago, Andrea."

He pulled away from her and then stepped outside. He looked down at the ground while waiting to lock the door after her.

With tears in her eyes, Andrea stood in the foyer for a moment. She felt sick, disgusted with herself. But there was no time to analyze it—or beg Luke's forgiveness. She knew she had to hold it together for Spencer.

He was waiting out there in the rain, by the open door to the unmarked police car. He looked so scared.

Taking a deep breath, Andrea stepped outside so she could accompany her nephew to the police station.

She'd always hoped she would never have to do that again.

# CHAPTER SEVENTEEN

*Monday—8:17 p.m.*

Going out to dinner with her family had turned out to be a good choice. In the first place, it beat being alone in the house so soon after that disturbing phone call—and Reed's murder. It also got her out of her sad, frightened mood for a short while.

Bonnie figured the caller might have been Ron, trying to freak her out—Ron or one of his friends. It was just the kind of tasteless thing one of them would do to blow off some steam. If Reed weren't dead, he'd have been in on it, too. She'd probably opened a can of worms by leaving Ron that sympathetic voice mail message. Now he was trying to get back at her or reconnect with her or something. Whatever, he hadn't called again—and for that, she was grateful.

The Middletons went to T. S. McHugh's, an Irish pub–style restaurant her parents liked. Her folks were in their mid-forties, but still youthful looking—though her dad was starting to go bald on top. Dressed in their best J. Crew casuals, her parents had their cocktails and chatted with the waitstaff while her brothers gorged on bread and butter. By the time her cheeseburger arrived, Bonnie was surprised that she had an appetite. And she actually found herself smiling when her kid brothers started carrying on—and Billy got Tim laughing so hard that root beer came out of his nose.

But on the way home, Tim had joked about finding a dead body in the refrigerator. Her mom had snapped at him, "I don't think that's at all funny, mister." It had made for a tense car ride during those last few blocks home. She could tell her parents were a bit on edge anyway. The Logans lived less than a mile away. A lot of families in the Queen Anne neighborhood would be double-locking their doors tonight. Bonnie had decided not to add to her parents' anxieties by telling them about the phone call.

Once home, her father bolted and chain-locked the front door. Billy announced that he'd be sleeping with his baseball bat at his bedside. Bonnie's mother told the boys she wanted to talk to them. Bonnie went into the kitchen to get a bottled water. She knew it was silly, but she hesitated in front of the refrigerator. She was queasy about opening the door.

She could hear her mom speaking to her brothers in a serious, hushed tone. Meanwhile, her father checked the back door and a couple of ground-floor windows—to make sure they were secured.

Bonnie took a deep breath and opened the fridge. No surprises, thank God. She grabbed her bottled water and turned toward the back stairs.

"Thanks for the dinner out, Pop," she said over her shoulder.

"Oh, you bet, sweetie," he said, interrupting his security check to come give her a kiss on the forehead. "How are you holding up? Are you okay?"

"I'm fine, really," she assured him. She switched on the second floor hallway light and headed up the stairs.

"Bonnie!" Tim yelled.

She paused and watched him charge up the steps. He was eleven years old, gawky and cute. He stopped two steps below her. "I'm really sorry I made that stupid joke in the car," he said quietly. "I forgot he was your friend."

She smiled and mussed his hair. "It's okay," she said. "Don't sweat it."

"I don't have any dead friends," he mumbled. "Must be weird."

Bonnie nodded. "Sure is."

She watched him retreat down the stairs. It dawned on her that when Spencer had murdered his parents, he'd been the same age as her brother.

She continued up to the second floor, then headed into her bedroom and switched on the light. Bonnie planned to check the local news at ten and eleven o'clock. She didn't want to be ghoulish, but they might have some updates that weren't on the Internet. After taking her phone out of her pocket, she shucked off her jacket and tossed it over the back of her desk chair. She switched on the phone, but then something on her bed caught her eye.

What looked like a small mound of pale brown dust

was in the center of her bed—on the Eiffel-Tower-print spread. Bonnie put down the phone and stepped closer. Now she could clearly see it wasn't dust or dirt.

It was a little mound of pencil shavings.


Spencer quietly locked the door to Luke's guest room.

He wasn't sure how much longer he and his aunt would be welcome here. Luke had really stuck up for him with the cops, and he'd waited for them at the police station the whole time they were there. But he'd given Andrea the silent treatment on the way back home—except for when they'd swung by Dick's Drive-In, and he'd asked what she wanted so he could order for her.

Spencer could hear them talking downstairs. He couldn't make out the words, but it sounded like they were arguing.

He tossed his jacket on the bed—and then more carefully, set the backpack beside it.

He was exhausted and also slightly ill from gobbling down his Dick's burger and fries as if it were his last meal.

They'd been in that windowless conference room at the police station for over three hours—with Detective Talwar asking the same questions over and over. Her perfume filled the room and became a little sickening after a while. There was a long mirror on the wall, which no doubt allowed some cop—or a whole pack of them—to look in on what was happening. Andrea and he sat on one side of the table, and Talwar and the deputy on the other. A digital recorder between them got everything down. Luke waited in the precinct lobby.

All the while, Spencer kept thinking he should tell them about finding Reed's baseball cap in his locker. But the detective and her deputy were already treating him like he was guilty. It made no sense to give them another reason to think he'd killed Reed and his parents. Besides, as crazy as it sounded, he loathed the idea of mentioning anything that meant more questions and more time in that awful, stuffy little room. All he wanted to do was go home.

Spencer was so grateful when Detective Talwar announced they were free to go. But he couldn't feel any sense of relief. It was obvious they weren't satisfied with his answers. Maybe it was because he'd been through all this before, but he was scared. He knew that as far as the police were concerned, he was still a suspect in the murders—maybe even their number-one suspect.

And he really couldn't blame them.

He unzipped his backpack and gently removed the plastic bag with the baseball cap inside it. He kept thinking there could be DNA on it, maybe even some blood.

He stood still and listened for a moment to make certain neither Andrea nor Luke was coming upstairs. Then he crept to the closet and slid the bag under a couple of his sweaters on the upper shelf.

Spencer could still hear them murmuring downstairs. Luke started to raise his voice, but Andrea must have shushed him, because he got quiet again.

Spencer realized he'd have to adjust to the idea that

Luke knew the truth about him now. If Luke had indeed known since Thursday, he'd done a pretty decent job of not treating him any differently. Back in DC, when people found out about what had happened to his parents, they usually didn't want a damn thing to do with him—or they got nervous around him, like he was a dangerous character. Of course, no one knew the full story—except his therapist here, Diane Leppert.

Luke knew he was seeing a shrink every two weeks. He'd been cool with that, maybe because his own son was pretty screwed up and could have used some therapy himself. But Luke didn't know *why* he was seeing someone, not until a couple of days ago.

Spencer couldn't help worrying that he'd ruined things for his aunt. She'd done so much for him—when most anyone else in her situation would hate him. The Internet was full of incredible, inspirational stories about compassion and forgiveness: "Mother of Slain Girl Forgives Killer," or "Paralyzed Victim in School Massacre Embraces Shooter's Parents." But what his aunt had done for him went far beyond forgiveness. He knew her life would be a lot easier if he were dead.

He'd admitted that to his therapist. "Why would you think that?" Diane had told him. She was fifty-something, a bit stocky, sort of motherly and very down to earth. "You're her family. She loves you. When you love someone, you sacrifice for them. You two are there for each other. I mean, if she needed a kidney, you'd give her one of yours, wouldn't you? You'd take a bullet for her, wouldn't you? So please, Spencer, don't give me this 'She's better off without me' malarkey."

He always felt good after his sessions with Diane.

But his next appointment with her wasn't for another week. And the way things were going, he could be in jail by then.

Maybe he could talk with Diane on the phone. Maybe then he'd feel better and this nagging, stomach-churning dread would go away. Diane had given him a number he could call in case of an emergency. This pretty much counted as an emergency, didn't it?

Spencer found the number in his wallet. He took his cell phone out of his jacket and called her. He got a recording: "You've reached the behavioral health office of Diane Leppert, therapist. If this is an emergency—or if you feel you may do harm to yourself or someone else—hang up and dial nine-one-one. Otherwise, you may leave a message, and your call will be returned during normal business hours. Be sure to include your name and contact information. Thank you."

He couldn't help feeling slightly betrayed. She'd led him to believe this was some kind of hotline just for him. Spencer suddenly felt so alone. He listened to the beep on the other end. "Hi, Diane," he said, trying to keep from sobbing—only it didn't work. "Um, it's Spencer. Something's happened. I'm in trouble. I really need to talk with you—and not to this dumb machine thing. I'm sorry. But could you—could you please call me when you get this? Thanks."

He hung up, wiped the tears from his eyes and ran his shirtsleeve under his nose. As soon as he composed himself, he could hear his aunt and Luke downstairs again. Their voices were still slightly muffled.

But he realized his aunt was crying, too.

*   *   *

"You lied to the police," Luke said.

"What are you talking about?" Andrea asked in a quiet voice. She had a Kleenex in her hand.

They were sitting at the table in Luke's dining room—the most sparsely furnished room in his town house. Except for the cherry veneer table and the matching ladder-back chairs, there was nothing else. The shelves of the built-in breakfront were bare. And there was no centerpiece on the table. They rarely used the dining room, but it was the farthest spot from Spencer's room in the town house. So that was where they sat with their drinks, having "the talk" Andrea had dreaded for so long.

"In there," Luke said, nodding toward the living room, "you told the detective that you were awake until three-thirty in the morning on Saturday. You were lying. I woke up around two-fifteen, and you were sound asleep beside me."

She took a sip of her bourbon and 7UP. "I just didn't want her thinking that Spencer snuck out of the house while we were asleep—"

"I know," he interrupted. "But how can you be so certain he didn't?"

"Because I know him," she answered.

"How can you say that when up until six months ago he'd been in an institution? You don't really know him, Andrea. Please, don't get me wrong. I think he's a terrific kid, and I like him a hell of a lot. I thought I knew him, too. But it turns out that I don't really know him at all."

Shifting around in her chair, she watched Luke sip his scotch on the rocks.

The last few hours at the police station had been grueling. But Luke had put on a good show of support earlier while they'd been grilled by the police. So it was extra-defeating to hear him now questioning Spencer's innocence.

"I mean, how can you be so sure he doesn't have a gun hidden in his room?" Luke asked.

*Or some dynamite?* Andrea wondered. She knew he was thinking about his own son, and how he hadn't really known him either. But he had a point.

The truth was she couldn't be absolutely positive about Spencer's innocence.

Neither one of them said anything for a few moments. With his elbows on the table, Luke leaned forward and rubbed his eyes. "Goddamn it," he muttered, breaking the silence. "This is killing me, because I really care about him. And I care about you."

"But suddenly it's a little scary to sleep under the same roof as him, is that it?"

He frowned at her. "And it wasn't a little scary for you at first?"

Andrea nodded in resignation. "All right, so what do you want to do? Do you want us to move out?"

"I think it's too soon for me to make a decision. I'm still angry, but I'm not ready to send you guys back to your place in Ballard—not after what happened to the Logans, and not when someone was able to break into your place last August." He got to his feet. "I'll sleep in my study tonight."

She looked up at him. "Luke, I'm sorry."

"So am I," he replied. Then he took his drink and walked into the kitchen.

She watched him in there, checking the locks on the back door.

"I don't know what the hell you're talking about," Ron said.

"No, of course you don't," Bonnie said into the phone. She realized he was telling the truth. Ron wasn't the one who had called her, and he hadn't left the pencil shavings on her bed either. She'd been way off on her initial assumption. But now she had a pretty good idea who was behind this strange campaign.

"Are you being sarcastic?" he asked. "I never could tell with you . . ."

"No, I mean it," she said. "Listen, I'm sorry to bother you, Ron—especially now."

"You called me this morning, and you're calling me again tonight. Is this your way of trying to get back together or something?"

"No, not at all," she said. "I just felt bad for you because Reed was one of your best friends . . ." That was true, but still, Ron had often referred to Reed behind his back as "that weasel," which made Bonnie wonder how he described her to his other friends. "Anyway, I just wanted to offer my condolences, Ron. Don't try to read too much else into it. Listen, I need to scram. I have another call to make. Are you coming to school tomorrow?"

"Probably," he grunted.

"Well, then I'll see you there. Okay?"

"Yeah, sure. Bye," he muttered. Then he hung up.

Bonnie clicked off. Sitting at her desk, she stared down into her trash can. She was gazing at the pencil shavings she'd cleaned off her bedspread. She'd had to use a lint roller to finish the job. Maybe she was imagining it, but her bedroom still seemed to have that slightly acrid smell of freshly sharpened pencils.

When she'd seen those shavings, she should have known right then who had left them as a calling card.

Hell, Tanya was more upset about the pencil sharpener prank in the library than Damon had ever been. Tanya had never forgiven her for that. Tanya hated her. And she knew how to break into this house undetected.

The second time Tanya had come over, which had been years ago, no one else had been home that afternoon. The two of them had played in the backyard, and gotten locked out of the house. This was before either one of them had a cell phone. They'd made several attempts to get in—and finally tried a basement window on the side of the house, near the back, behind some bushes. With a little push, the lock gave, and she was able to flip up the hinged window. Bonnie had easily climbed down into the furnace room. But it was the creepiest spot in the house, dark and dank with unpainted, peeling plaster walls. At the time, the area had been crammed with boxes of junk they didn't know what to do with after the move. Bonnie remembered how anxious she'd felt—alone in the new house, in the bowels of that gloomy basement. Even with her friend hovering on the other side of the window, she'd raced upstairs as quickly as she could.

Since then, her father had installed some metal shelves along one wall to make a storage area across from the ugly monster of a furnace. But the room was still gloomy, and the lock on that window still didn't work. Billy and Tim had used it to get inside the house just a few weeks back.

And Bonnie was pretty certain her former friend, Tanya, had used that basement window to gain entry into the house earlier tonight.

It had been so long since she'd called her, Bonnie had to look up the McCallums' number. Fortunately, Tanya and her mother still had the same old landline. Bonnie dialed the number and counted two ringtones before someone picked up on the other end. "Hello?"

She recognized Tanya's voice. "Hi, Tanya, it's Bonnie."

"I know," she said curtly. "We have caller ID. What do you want?"

"I wanted to let you know I got your message. I got both of them."

"What are you talking about?"

"You left me two messages, one on my phone and one on my bed," Bonnie explained. "I know it was you. Who else could it be? I mean, you're still totally obsessed with that little joke I played on Damon in the school library. If I could take it back, I would. It was a stupid thing to do. But it was like—six months ago, Tanya. And I think—"

"Wait a minute," Tanya interrupted. "What are you prattling on about? You sound like a crazy person . . ."

"So you're going to pretend you don't know anything about the pile of pencil shavings on my bed?"

Tanya let out a surprised laugh, but it sounded forced. "Wow, that's perfect!"

Bonnie started pacing around her bedroom. "I know it was you who left them there, and I know it was you who called me, talking in that creepy, puppetlike voice. You're not fooling anybody, Tanya. No one else would know how to break into this house. But you saw me do it a few years ago. You know how it's done."

"Listen, I have better things to do with my time, okay? I happen to have spent most of this afternoon and tonight rehearsing for the school play. We're doing *The Pajama Game*. We all went out for pizza afterward—until about a half hour ago. If you don't believe me, you can ask anyone who's in the play. So I was nowhere near your house tonight."

Bonnie stopped pacing. "How did you know someone broke into my house *tonight*? I never said when it happened."

"Yes, you did," Tanya argued.

"No, I didn't," Bonnie insisted. She'd caught her.

"Well, you implied it."

"You might not have pulled the job yourself," Bonnie said. "And you might have your alibi. But you put somebody up to it—or at the very least, you were in on it. I'm on to you, Tanya."

"Oh, I'm really scared, I'm shaking," Tanya replied. "Listen, if you ever find out who actually pulled these stunts, let me know—so I can send them a thank-you note. You're crazy. It's what happens to bulimic bitches. They go insane. Don't call me anymore."

Bonnie heard a click on the other end.

She had no idea where Tanya came up with this bulimia nonsense. If there were any basis for it, Bonnie might have been hurt or offended, but the accusation seemed like a diversionary tactic. Tanya knew she'd screwed up—giving her alibi just a bit too prematurely. So maybe she was with her theater group friends tonight. But she definitely knew about the break-in and the pencil shavings.

Bonnie wondered if Tanya had paid some stranger to do the job for her. She couldn't think of anyone at school who might have pulled this prank for her. Tanya didn't have any real friends at school now that Damon was dead.

The only person she ever hung out with was Spencer.

Bonnie once again glanced down into her trash basket at the pencil shavings. A shudder passed through her. She remembered that eerie, singsong voice on the phone: *Bonnie . . . you're next . . . you're next . . . you bitch . . .*

*Tuesday, October 27—1:20 a.m.*
*Duvall, Washington*

They took a turn off Northeast Big Rock Road onto a tree-lined gravel drive. The Toyota Corolla's headlights pierced the blackness around them. Jostled by potholes in the crude road, the young man in the passenger seat braced his hand against the dash. His driver was still doing thirty-five. It sounded like a hailstorm as gravel ricocheted against the underside of the car.

The high beams swept across a sign on the side of the road:

## LYNNE/DAVIS LANDSCAPING
TREE FARM—GARDENING & LAWN SERVICE

His driver finally slowed down as they approached a turnaround—with two trailers, a large greenhouse, and a lot with row after row of Christmas trees. The place looked deserted. There wasn't a light anywhere. Tall trees surrounded the property.

This was a dry run.

They would be back here tomorrow at this same time—with Bonnie Middleton in the trunk.

They'd already conducted their dry run in the Middletons' house earlier in the evening—and left her a little souvenir. The young man in the passenger seat had drawn a layout of the house, and they'd figured out their every move. Like the job they did on the Logans, they'd surprise them in their sleep. But the Middletons' house wasn't quite as isolated as the Logans'. Some pain-in-the-ass neighbor was bound to hear the gunshots at one in the morning. A couple of shots might be ignored. But in this case, there would be a minimum of four. So they'd decided to tie up Bonnie, the parents, and the boys. They'd chloroform Bonnie. As for the others, they'd keep them bound and gagged in their respective bedrooms. Before taking Bonnie out to the car, they'd go from room to room and slit each one's throat. They'd choreographed the whole thing in the bedrooms earlier tonight.

The young man had figured out that the drive from

the Middletons' Queen Anne neighborhood to this spot outside Duvall had taken about a half hour. If by chance the chloroform wore off, Bonnie might kick and fuss in the trunk for a while, but she'd still be bound and gagged. Besides, in the last ten minutes of this dry run, they'd seen only three other cars between Route 203 and here.

The owners of this place didn't live on the premises. It seemed locked up pretty tight, with a tall chain-link fence around the Christmas tree lot. Both trailer doors had a shield-shaped decal from some twenty-four-hour-security place, but there were no cameras on-site.

They drove around to the other side of the greenhouse. The headlights shone on a big yellow contraption on wheels—with a trailer hitch. The thing sort of looked like a dinosaur—with its bulky, low body, a long, high neck, and the head tilted down.

"You ready to give it a try?" the driver asked, switching off the engine.

The headlights remained on.

The driver reached under the front seat and pulled out a large key ring with at least a hundred keys on it. Meanwhile, the young man got out of the car, opened the back door, and grabbed a bundle of logs from the floor. He hauled them over to the big yellow machine and set them by the conveyor belt that went into a big drum—part of the contraption's body. He listened to the keys jangle in his partner's hand.

The driver hovered over the operating panel, trying to find a key that would start the engine. "I'm narrowing it down," the driver said. "Go back to the car. Pop the trunk, and get our friend."

Retreating to the Corolla, the young man opened the driver's door and pulled the lever to unlock the trunk. He wanted this run-through to be as close to the real thing as possible. They needed a stand-in for Bonnie.

All it took was a pound of ground beef and some strychnine. They put the dead raccoon inside a gray, heavy-duty, extra-large trash bag and then dumped it in a big, oblong freezer. They didn't want it decaying.

Though the thing was huge—at least thirty-five pounds—they'd had an easier time fitting it into cold storage than they had with Reed. This thing had been dead. In Reed's case, they'd knocked him out, but had to bend his arms and legs at just the right angles to cram him inside the Frigidaire. So after all that maneuvering with the still-breathing Reed, it had been a snap tossing the dead raccoon inside its cold coffin.

They'd taken the raccoon out of the freezer last night—so it would thaw. They wanted its body temperature and density consistent with a live human being's. After all, this creature was a stand-in for someone who would be unconscious, but very much alive.

As he opened the trunk, the young man got a waft of rotting meat. Even with the plastic bag around the defrosted thing, some of the smell was escaping. The trunk was going to stink for a while. It would be a very unpleasant journey for Bonnie Middleton if she happened to regain consciousness in there tomorrow night.

Grabbing the plastic bag by its drawstrings, he hoisted it out of the trunk and then dropped it to the ground. He guessed Bonnie was about three times the weight of this thing—maybe more. It would take the two of them to carry her.

They had only one bundle of logs to go with the raccoon. With Bonnie, there would be three bundles. He wanted just the right proportion of wood pulp with the blood and ground flesh. He wanted to see it spray out of the mouth of that huge dinosaur-like machine.

With a grunt, he lifted the heavy-duty trash bag and carried it toward the conveyor belt. Just then, he heard the engine start to churn. His partner had found the right skeleton key among the ones on the ring.

Now they knew how to switch on the big wood chipper.

And all they had to do was feed it.

# CHAPTER EIGHTEEN

*Tuesday, October 27—12:09 p.m.*

"Hi, Diane, it's Spencer," he said into the phone. He sat on a bench in front of an upright piano in a little, windowless room. The walls were gray—with an egg-carton surface to keep the noise in. Though it was somewhat muted, he could still hear some guy next door singing, "Hey there, you with the stars in your eyes . . ." Spencer had discovered these individual rehearsal rooms off a narrow hallway of the third floor in the school's music-arts wing. It was a good place to escape—especially during lunch hour, when hardly anyone was here. He didn't feel like people today—and he didn't feel like lunch either: liver and onions. Most of all, he wanted complete privacy to call his therapist.

He'd gotten her answering machine again, but it was okay this time. "Thanks for calling me back," he said for the recording. "Sorry I couldn't pick up. I was in chemistry class. I'm really glad you can see me. To-night at seven sounds great. I'll be there. Thanks again, Diane."

He clicked off, and then shoved the phone into the pocket of his chinos. He tinkered around on the piano a little. His mom and dad had made him take lessons from age eight to ten. He'd never been very good at it. But in the hospital, the therapists encouraged him to take up some kind of hobby. Even if he was mediocre at it, playing the piano seemed a better option than painting, sculpting—or making baskets, which, believe it or not, was actually on their occupational therapy ac-tivity list. He still didn't think he was very good. That was why this little room with no one else around was the perfect place for him to tinker on the keys.

He'd only been at it for a couple of minutes when the door squeaked open a crack. There was a little port-hole window in the door, but Spencer couldn't quite make out who was on the other side of it. He stopped playing and stood up.

Bonnie poked her head in. She was wearing jeans with a clingy burgundy sweater. Her dark hair was down around her shoulders. "Please, don't stop," she said. "That was really pretty. You're good . . ."

Spencer shrugged. "It was just 'Heart and Soul.'"

"Well, it was nice." She stepped into the little room. "Listen, I'm not stalking you. I—" She hesitated and let out a little laugh. "I'll bet no one actually says that unless they're a stalker. The truth is I was looking for a chance to talk with you, and I followed you here, which I guess means I was, like, stalking you." She rolled her eyes and laughed again. "I'm sorry . . ."

"What did you want to talk to me about?" Spencer asked. As much as he liked Bonnie, he still didn't completely trust her. Was this awkward-cutesy thing just an act?

Bonnie suddenly seemed serious. "I've seen you and Tanya McCallum together from time to time," she said. "And—well, you heard her the other day, telling that story about how I emptied out a pencil sharpener on the back of Damon's head while he was napping at one of the library's reading desks . . ."

Sitting back down on the piano bench, Spencer nodded. "Yeah, I remember . . ."

"Well, to hear Tanya tell it, I might as well have burnt down an orphanage and eaten the only surviving child. Anyway, the point is, someone broke into my house last night and dumped a pile of pencil shavings on my bed." Her voice cracked a little. Spencer could tell she was genuinely upset. "And earlier—yesterday afternoon, practically right after I said goodbye to you, I got this bizarre call from someone with a blocked number, and they told me in this weird voice, 'You're next, bitch . . .'"

Spencer frowned. "What does any of this have to do with me?"

"I wondered if maybe Tanya put you up to it," Bonnie said.

"I don't know a thing about it."

"Are you sure? She's not paying you—or blackmailing you to do this stuff?"

"Blackmailing?" Spencer shook his head. "No, I swear . . ."

"Well, Tanya's involved in this somehow," Bonnie

said. "The pencil shavings on my bed were her idea—only she must have gotten someone else to break into my house and plant them there . . ."

Spencer thought about Reed Logan. "Has anyone smashed a window in your house or keyed the family car?" he asked. "Have you found any dead animals—squirrels, cats, or raccoons—at your door?"

She frowned at him. "I don't understand . . ."

"Last week, Reed told me someone broke into his house and emptied a shelf in the family refrigerator. And a couple of days later, Reed suffocated inside that same refrigerator. Don't you see what's happening? "

With a baffled look, Bonnie shook her head.

"They sent him a message before they killed him. With that small pile of pencil shavings, I'm pretty sure they're sending you a message, too."

She laughed nervously. "What—are you saying I'm going to end up buried under a pile of pencil shavings or something?"

"I don't know. But you got a phone call saying you're next. Someone broke into your house—"

"Yes, I figured it was Tanya. That's why I'm trying not to take it too seriously."

"Well, you should," Spencer warned her. "You should take it very seriously. I think you're right that Tanya's in on it. I have a feeling she was somehow involved in what happened to Reed, too."

"But Tanya's all talk. She's harmless. You don't really think I'm in danger, do you?"

"It's not just you," Spencer said. "When they killed Reed, they killed everyone else in the house."

Wide-eyed, Bonnie stared at him.

"You should tell your parents what's happened. Get the police in on it. Do whatever you can to protect your family and yourself."

Bonnie folded her arms in front of her like she was suddenly cold. She took a step back and bumped against the egg-carton wall. For a moment, neither of them said anything. Spencer could still hear the guy singing and playing the piano next door.

"When you talk to the police, could you leave me out of it?" he asked. "I don't want to get involved any deeper in this. Somebody's trying to set me up for Reed's murder, and the police already suspect me. Plus they know about my past. That stuff you overheard Reed say about me the other day is true."

He felt so vulnerable and exposed divulging this to her. He knew he probably shouldn't have. He waited for some kind of reaction.

"I know," she said finally. "I looked up your aunt on Google and found the story about you and—and your parents."

Spencer glanced down at the tiled floor. His hands gripped the sides of the piano bench. "I guess you think I'm some kind of monster or something," he muttered. "Don't you think you're taking an awfully big risk being alone in here with me?"

"Everybody deserves a second chance," she said. "Besides, I got the impression the older boy was mostly responsible for what happened."

"It was my finger on the trigger," Spencer muttered.

"Do you want to talk about it?"

Though he appreciated how she tried to be understanding, Spencer frowned and shook his head. "Are *you* going to talk about it?"

"You mean, spread it around school? No, your secret's safe with me."

"Thank you."

Bonnie opened the door as if she were about to step outside, but then she hesitated. She glanced back at him. "By the way, I think you were right earlier when you said someone was trying to set you up. Reed got an anonymous text about you being in the sanitarium. And the texter said you were to blame for bothering Reed and his family."

"How do you know this?" Spencer asked, standing up.

"I asked Reed if what he'd said about you was true, and he showed me the text."

Spencer wondered why the police hadn't questioned him about that. Maybe they didn't know. Had Reed's killer stolen or destroyed his cell phone?

"Well, I—I better call my mom and tell her about the phone call and the break-in," Bonnie said, opening the door wider. She had a perplexed look on her face. "Maybe when I tell her, it'll sink in just how serious this is. I still don't want to believe it. Anyway, thanks for your help. You might have even saved my life."

"Hey, Bonnie," he said—before she ducked out. "Did you mean that about people deserving a second chance?"

She nodded. "Yes."

"And after reading about me, you don't think I'm—horrible?"

Bonnie shook her head. "No," she replied, "not at all."

Then she stepped out to the hallway.

"Anyway, I'll be helping Tanya with her play rehearsal after school."

"Well, okay," Andrea said into the phone. She was sitting at the tall glass-top breakfast table. She'd been struggling through all the grammatical problems with a four-star general's autobiography when Spencer had called. The last time Spencer had mentioned Tanya, he'd said she'd gotten on his nerves. Andrea didn't quite understand why he wanted to hang out with her this afternoon.

"How late do you think you'll be?" she asked.

"Well, that's the other thing. I called Diane, and she agreed to see me tonight at seven. So I'm just going to catch a bus up to Capitol Hill. I'll grab some dinner before I see her. That Greek place, Vios, is right near her office."

Andrea was glad he'd get some time in with his therapist. After the terrible day he'd had yesterday, he probably needed a professional's shoulder to cry on. "What time do you think you'll be done? I'll come pick you up."

"That's okay. I'll catch the bus back."

She nervously drummed her fingers on the table. She didn't like the idea of him wandering around in a different part of town after dark—not with some killer on the loose. "No, listen," she said. "Fifteen or twenty minutes before you think you'll be done, why don't you call me? I'll be there by the time you guys wrap it up."

"The bus is fine, Aunt Dee, really. Hey, I got to go. I'll be late for English. Take care." He hung up.

As Andrea clicked off the line, she couldn't help wondering how much of what Spencer had just told her was the truth.

She could almost hear Luke again: *I think he's a terrific kid, and I like him a hell of a lot. I thought I knew him, too. But it turns out that I don't really know him at all.*

True to his word, Luke had slept in his study last night—if he'd slept at all. She certainly hadn't. Her eyes were sore and her bones felt brittle from fatigue and stress. Five cups of coffee this morning had only given her heartburn. She and Luke had barely talked before he'd taken off for the theater. He'd kept things polite and distant. He hadn't tried to conceal his disappointment in her.

After putting up with a clingy, demanding, neurotic wife, he'd probably thought he'd found a real prize with her—until yesterday. Poor Luke, it wasn't just Spencer who suddenly seemed like a stranger to him.

*How can you be sure he doesn't have a gun hidden in his room?*

Andrea climbed off the bar stool. She stood in the kitchen for a moment—long enough to realize she'd never searched Spencer's room before. Had she been foolish to blindly trust him ever since he'd moved in with her after his release from the hospital?

She headed upstairs to his bedroom. Spencer still hadn't put his personal stamp on it yet. His room in the

Ballard apartment had Bill Murray movie posters on the walls. But this was still Luke's guest room. On the walls were a big framed map of the world and a pair of framed prints—old posters from the Seattle World's Fair of 1962. It was all very neutral. Except for some books, DVDs, and a fortune-telling Magic 8 Ball on one of the built-in bookshelves, there was nothing of Spencer's in this room. The majority of personal effects belonged to Damon.

She knew it was silly, but she grabbed the 8 Ball off the shelf and turned it upside down. "Should I even be in here?" she asked aloud.

She gave the ball a little shake, then turned it over and read the response: *It Is Decidedly So.*

Did she really think Spencer had somehow managed to get his hands on a gun—a kid with a murder conviction and five years in state-run mental hospitals and juvenile detention centers?

Of course he could have found a gun.

*It Is Decidedly So.*

The closest thing Luke had to a gun was a fake revolver from one of his stage plays, which he kept as a paperweight on the desk in his study.

With a sigh, Andrea started looking through the desk drawers. It was almost like searching through a vacant hotel room's desk. Except for a couple of receipts, a Seattle's Best Coffee punch card, a few Bic ballpoint pens, and a notepad that had *Luke Shuler* by a cartoon smiling sun (obviously a freebie from a soliciting charity), she didn't find anything in the top center drawer. It seemed as if neither Damon nor Spencer had used the desk much. The rest of the drawers were empty—except for the bottom left drawer. She found a big manila envelope—stuffed with old birthday cards and photos Spencer had saved. She didn't know he had them. The pictures were of his parents and him. She didn't keep any pictures of Vivian and Larry on display. She'd figured it would be too painful for Spencer. Plus she didn't want to explain to visitors who they were and what had happened to them.

It was strange, how Spencer had these snapshots hidden—like contraband. Stranger still, he had several photos of himself in recent years—from rare upbeat moments during his time in those state-run facilities. Andrea had also taken dozens of photos of him in the last six months—especially when they'd first moved to Seattle. But none of the photos in this envelope were from after 2009. It was as if his life had stopped that year—as if that kid in those pictures had died along with his parents.

Andrea put the photos back and checked under the bed.

She'd read up on the Logan family murders. The newspaper articles mentioned that money, jewels, and certain techno gadgets were missing from the Logans' house. In the back of her mind she wondered if she'd find something like that in this room.

She'd seen several different photos of Reed Logan in the media accounts of the murders, and in most of them he was wearing a blue baseball cap—backward. She'd always thought that the backward-cap look was the trademark of a cocky jerk or a bully—not all the time, but often enough. In Reed's case, he appeared smug and obnoxious in the photos. He looked like the bully he was.

Andrea didn't see anything under the bed. The dresser was full of clothes—nothing new, nothing she hadn't put in the washer and dryer for Spencer dozens of times. He had some receipts, coupons, and cards in the top drawer—but no jewelry, gadgets, or pawn tickets.

She didn't have to remind herself that it was the other boy, Garrett Beale, who had pawned her sister's jewelry. She knew Spencer had fallen under his spell. She knew if that boy hadn't been spending the night, none of it would have happened. While her father had washed his hands of the case, Andrea had pushed Spencer's lawyer to focus the blame where it belonged—on this manipulative thirteen-year-old. Garrett's parents were quite rich. They'd tried to bribe and intimidate her into changing her tack. But Andrea couldn't be swayed. She'd done everything she could to help Spencer.

Her life had sort of gone on hold during his incarceration. Anyone would have thought she'd have used those years to focus on herself, but it wasn't until Spencer's release from the hospital that she'd resolved to move on with her life—or *their* lives, rather.

But now they were back to square one. It was 2009 all over again—with a multiple murder, the police questioning Spencer's every move, and her wondering if everything that came out of his mouth was a lie.

She believed that he'd indeed made an appointment with his therapist at seven tonight. He knew she could check up on that. But he didn't like Tanya. So why in the world would he give her three hours of his time after school? What was he really up to?

Andrea started going through the closet—through the pockets of his pants and inside his shoes. There was nothing. The shelves were uncluttered—just two neat stacks of sweaters.

Under the bottom sweater in the second stack, Andrea discovered an old, beat-up navy blue bag from the Gap.

She reached inside it and took out what Spencer had hidden in there.

It was an old blue baseball cap—the kind a bully might have worn backward.


"Mom?" she called as she came through the front door. The family SUV wasn't in the driveway—a definite sign that her mother wasn't home. But Bonnie called out anyway. "Mom, are you around?" She just needed to make sure. She really wasn't sure of anything today.

Bonnie had phoned her mother during lunch period, after talking with Spencer. But she'd gotten her voice mail. She'd left a message: "Hi, I wanted to talk to you about something that happened yesterday. I should have told you last night. I'm sorry to sound so weird, but could you call me back when you get this? It's important, okay? Thanks, Mom. Love you."

Her mother hadn't called back. By two o'clock, Bonnie had tried calling again—and gotten her mother's voice mail once more. She'd pictured her mother, dead in a pool of blood on the kitchen floor. She'd skipped her last class and hurried home—convinced the house would be surrounded by cops and squad cars, and cordoned off with yellow police tape.

She was out of breath as she staggered into the foyer. There was a small crystal chandelier overhead and a Persian rug on the hardwood floor. Bonnie frantically glanced around. From this spot she could see part of the living room, kitchen, and dining room. Nothing was out of place, no sign of a struggle, no blood. She told herself she was overreacting. Everything Spencer had told her was just a theory—pure speculation.

She started to close the door behind her, but then figured she should keep it open for a quicker escape. Besides, there was a better chance of someone hearing her scream if the door was open.

"You're being ridiculous," she muttered to herself. Taking a deep breath, Bonnie closed the door. With a bit of trepidation, she started toward the kitchen. There were some unwashed dishes in the sink, but nothing unusual. She stared at the refrigerator for a moment before finally opening the door. No one was stuffed inside there. "See, stupid?" she said under her breath. "Quit doing this to yourself."

Still, she took a big knife from the butcher-block knife holder on the counter. Then she went from room to closet to room, checking the entire first floor. Climbing up the front stairs, she continued her search on the second floor, the butcher knife poised the whole time. At the end of the hallway, her room was last. Would there be another pile of pencil shavings on her bed—or something far worse?

There was nothing. The room was just as she'd left it this morning. The bed was made, nothing was out of place. The bathroom was a bit messy, but that was all her doing. Bonnie stepped back into her bedroom and sank down on her bed. She set the knife beside her.

She still couldn't breathe easy. She hadn't gone up to the attic. And she hadn't checked the basement, where they had the window with the faulty lock.

Sometimes, all it took was a scary book or movie to remind Bonnie about that window and how vulnerable they all were. She'd had a few restless, nervous nights knowing she was the only one awake in the house. She'd think about that basement window and imagine some faceless stranger quietly crawling through it. From the basement he'd creep up to the first floor— and then up the back stairs. *You'd be the first person he'd kill . . .*

Her former friend, Tanya, had been the one who had warned her of that.

A chill raced through her.

Bonnie grabbed the knife and got to her feet. She headed down the back stairs to the kitchen—and then into the pantry. As she opened the basement door, the hinges squeaked. She switched on the light at the top of the wood-plank staircase. The house had a laundry hamper chute on the second floor, and the soiled clothes came out at the foot of the basement stairs. Heading down the creaky steps, Bonnie stared at the pile of clothes and towels. She kept expecting to see blood on something in that heap—though it made absolutely no sense. The house was empty. Nothing had happened.

She was alone here. She had to remind herself it was the middle of the afternoon.

As she neared the bottom of the stairs, Bonnie paused and glanced at the laundry room. No one was hiding behind the dryer. It was the usual mess of clothes, towels, and sheets—piled up on the floor by the washer, in baskets and hanging on the clothesline. A travel poster of Venice, which her mother still hadn't visited, was on the wall. From this spot on the stairs, Bonnie had a partial view of the basement bathroom— with just a toilet and a forever-dirty sink. No one used that bathroom except her brothers and their friends when they congregated in the playroom, which ex- plained why it was always so disgusting in there.

Bonnie could also see part of the darkened play- room. The cheaply paneled area was her brothers' do- main. It had an older model big-screen TV, a sectional sofa, Billy's drum set, and a StairMaster no one had used in eons.

Her father's workroom and the furnace room were beyond that—behind a door that was always closed. It wasn't just her, everyone thought that part of the house was creepy. Even with the lights on, those back rooms seemed perpetually dark and sinister. Her mother once admitted that during their first year in the house, she wouldn't go down there to use the washer or dryer un- less someone else was home.

Bonnie heard a mechanical click and then a hum- ming sound. She told herself it was just the furnace starting up—or maybe the whirring noise had come from outside. Either way, she didn't want to go any far- ther into the basement. And for a moment, she couldn't move at all. She kept a tight grip on the knife, and held on to the banister with her other hand.

Then she thought she heard a door yawn open.

Bonnie turned and rushed back up the stairs. Stumbling into the pantry, she swiveled around and slammed the door shut. The knife accidentally flew out of her hand and just missed landing on her foot. Her heart was beating wildly. She expected to hear someone clamoring up the stairs in pursuit. But it was quiet.

Catching her breath, Bonnie picked up the knife and moved over to the kitchen phone. She set the knife on the counter—within reaching distance. She tried phoning her mother again. It was almost past three. Why hadn't she called back yet?

Her mother's voice mail picked up again. "Damn it," Bonnie muttered, hanging up. Something was wrong. Hadn't she made it clear in her message two and a half hours ago that it was pretty urgent?

Bonnie glanced over at the closed basement door.

She couldn't stand another minute alone in this house. It might be crazy, but sitting on the front stoop—until her mother, brothers, or father got home—somehow seemed safer. She should have stayed at school this afternoon, but she'd been worried about her mom.

Bonnie set the knife in the sink. She checked her pockets for her phone and her house key, and then hurried to the front door.

Once outside, she closed the door behind her.

She couldn't just wait there, not without checking something out. So she headed along the side of the house toward the backyard. The basement window with the broken lock was behind some low shrubs and a big rhododendron bush. Under the shadow of a tall ever-green, Bonnie threaded through the shrubbery to the window. The ground was still a bit muddy from yester-day's rain. She was ruining her beige sneakers.

She stopped and gazed down at the window, the top of which hit her at knee level. The window was open just a hairline crack. But it could have been that way for a long, long time.

Then Bonnie noticed the cluster of footprints in the muddy ground.

Someone had climbed through this window last night.

Or had they just climbed through it within the last hour?

Bonnie turned and ran, nearly tripping over the shrubs. She staggered out to the driveway—only to see the family's SUV coming right at her. She froze. The tires screeched. She let out a little shriek and put a shaky hand on the front hood. Her whole body felt wobbly. Past the windshield, she could see her mother in the driver's seat.

Her mom opened the door and jumped out of the car. "My God, Bonnie, you almost gave me a heart at-tack!" She rushed toward her. "Are you all right? What's going on?"

Bonnie started crying. "Where were you? I phoned you. Practically three hours ago, I phoned . . ."

"My cell battery conked out," her mother said, rub-bing her shoulder. "Honey, what's going on? What happened?"

Bonnie swallowed hard. "We—we need to call the police . . ."

# CHAPTER NINETEEN

*Tuesday—6:08 p.m.*

He hadn't been completely honest with his aunt about what he was doing after school. Spencer wasn't *helping* Tanya with her play rehearsals. He was watching her rehearse—only Tanya didn't know it. At least, he didn't think she knew. He'd found a seat in the shadowy balcony of the auditorium. No one down on the stage seemed to notice him. Still, he remained slouched down in the seat most of the time—just in case.

Having listened to Tanya go on and on these past few weeks about her part in *The Pajama Game*, he'd thought she was the star of the show. But it looked like she had about three lines, playing a factory worker.

That was what this surveillance was all about: finding out just how honest Tanya had been with him.

Yesterday, he'd asked her right out if she'd had anything to do with the deaths of the Logans, and she'd responded with an unconvincing, "God, no!"

Spencer was pretty certain she was in cahoots with someone. But as far as he knew, Tanya didn't have any friends. Seeing how she got along with her fellow cast members and the stage crew confirmed that. When she wasn't needed, which was often, Tanya sat alone in the theater's first or second row. No one talked with her.

Spencer wanted to see if she met up with someone during or after the rehearsal. So far—except for her texting somebody at one point, she'd kept to herself.

Last Friday, when Reed had said Spencer had been "sprung out of a loony bin in Virginia," a handful of people had heard it—including Bonnie and Tanya. Bonnie had immediately asked him if it was true. The others didn't know him well enough to approach him and bring it up. But Tanya hadn't asked him a thing about it. Was that because she already knew? Was she the one who had sent the text to Reed?

Tanya had been Damon's best friend. And three of the people Damon had condemned in his webcast suicide were now dead. KC Cunningham and Mr. McAfee had perished in a car explosion within hours after Damon's suicide. But it was Reed's bizarre murder last weekend that seemed to start a precedent.

Spencer had read parts of Damon's journal. He remembered Damon's account of how Reed and Ron had locked him in a storage space under the stage: *I could hardly move,* Damon had written. *I couldn't breathe. It was so dark in there. I thought I was going to die in there . . .*

From where he sat, Spencer could see the little door

in the orchestra pit. It was along a wood panel under the stage where the cast was now rehearsing another musical number. That was where Damon had been trapped for two or three hours—until a janitor had come by and rescued him.

But no one had rescued Reed Logan. He'd suffocated to death inside the refrigerator in his home. Spencer imagined what it must have been like for the poor bastard—trapped in that dark space, unable to move or breathe.

There was nothing bizarre or random about Reed's murder. It was the perfect retribution. And Tanya had almost certainly been in on it. She didn't seem a bit sorry that Reed had died. And who else was left to punish Damon's abusers?

Now they were targeting Bonnie Middleton, who had made the mistake of emptying out the contents of a pencil sharpener onto Damon's head as he'd slept in the library. Damon had mentioned Bonnie in his webcast tirade. Spencer wondered just how angry and hurt Damon had actually been over that stupid prank—and how much Tanya had goaded him about it, fanning the flames so he'd hate her former best friend as fervently as she did.

Spencer wasn't sure what they had planned for Bonnie, but he figured it would involve pencils, lead, a woodcutter, or something along those lines. Bonnie probably hadn't been too far off wondering aloud if she'd "end up buried under a pile of pencil shavings."

He hoped she'd warned her parents and notified the police by now.

And he hoped something would happen with Tanya—so this long, dreary surveillance might prove worth his while. He couldn't hang around here much longer. He needed to be at Diane's office by seven, and he had to transfer buses to get there.

Before seeing Diane, he always thought about what he wanted to tell her. Tonight, he wanted to talk about Bonnie, Reed's murder, and the police questioning him—along with all the memories that questioning had dredged up.

He remembered how he'd met Garrett Beale in the summer of 2009. He and his parents had moved from Silver Spring, Maryland, to Fairfax, Virginia, just days after he'd finished sixth grade in early May. Some summer vacation. If it hadn't been for his Aunt Dee, he would have gone crazy. She'd helped them move, and that first month, she'd taken him into DC a few times to do touristy stuff, which he loved. They'd always been close. But then she was his aunt. It wasn't like having a friend his own age. He didn't know anybody in Fairfax.

His parents were pretty much in the same boat. So they wasted no time joining the local country club, Westchester Hills. It was a ten-minute bike ride away for Spencer. He figured their pool would be his summer salvation. This one looked better than the community pool in Silver Spring. It had a waterslide, three different diving boards, and a snack shack serving burgers, hot dogs, and soft drinks. But after the first half hour of his first visit there, Spencer started to get bored. Going alone just wasn't much fun. Plus he felt self-conscious about his pale, skinny, prepubescent body.

Still, it beat sitting around the new house, and he enjoyed looking at the girls in their swimsuits.

One girl in particular caught his eye—a long-limbed brunette in a yellow bikini. Spencer figured she was older, maybe even in high school. He felt like a little pervert as he watched Miss Yellow Bikini practice diving—over and over again. And each time she got out of the pool her bikini top and bottom slipped a little.

Suddenly someone came up on the other side of him, blocking out the sun. "Check out the tits on her . . ."

Just as Spencer turned in the lounge chair, the sun-blocker shook out his wet long hair—all over him. Then he laughed. He was a big kid, slightly pear-shaped, with green trunks that rode low on his wide hips. Spencer couldn't believe this total stranger was suddenly clowning around with him like they were best friends. The kid pulled up another lounge chair and sat down beside him. Spencer guessed he was a couple of years older. He had armpit hair. He said his name, but Spencer didn't catch it.

In the course of the next hour, Mr. Green Trunks pushed Spencer into the pool twice, flicked him in the ear countless times, held his head underwater for at least half a minute, splashed him so many times that Spencer's eyes burned from the chlorine, and then when Spencer bought a hot dog at the snack shack and took one bite, the jerk stole it from him and wolfed it down. Green Trunks seemed to think all of these stunts were hysterical and they were on their way to becoming bosom buddies—even though Spencer hadn't concealed his annoyance with the guy. He must have said, "Cut it out!" to him about twenty times.

Just to avoid him, Spencer didn't go back to the pool for a week—even though it had been perfect swimming weather. When he finally returned, he was relieved to find that the kid was nowhere in sight. Spencer had been lounging in a sunny spot for about ten minutes when something stung his earlobe.

It was Green Trunks, hovering over him, flicking his ear, and cackling.

"Hey, you know, that hurts," Spencer said, sitting up.

"Oh, quit being such a pussy!" Green Trunks said, pulling a lounge chair close to Spencer's. His trunks were riding even lower this afternoon, so half his butt crack was showing. "There's nothing here but a bunch of dogs today. Where the hell have you been for the last few days?"

Spencer grabbed his bottle of SPF30 sunscreen and started rubbing it on himself. "Hey, you know," he said, mustering up the courage to go on, "no offense, but I really don't feel like hanging out with you."

"Well, who pissed in your Cheerios?"

"I'm sorry, but all you did last week was pick on me," Spencer said, his heart racing. He didn't like confrontations. Plus Green Trunks was intolerable enough when he thought they were *friends*. How abusive would he get once he knew Spencer didn't like him? "I mean, I don't exactly enjoy having my head pushed underwater and almost drowning. You almost broke my neck doing that, and I got water up my nose. And news flash: that ear-swatting thing you keep doing hurts."

"Does it hurt as bad as this?" Green Trunks asked, punching him on the side of the shoulder. He knew what he was doing, too, because the prominent knuckle slammed against a nerve, sending a jolt of pain down Spencer's arm.

He dropped the bottle of sunscreen. Wincing, he rubbed his shoulder. "God, what the hell's wrong with you?"

Sitting back in the lounge chair, Green Trunks laughed. His fleshy stomach jiggled. He closed his eyes. "Oh, you're such a wimp. It doesn't hurt that much!"

Green Trunks didn't see another guy coming up beside him. The new arrival was about thirteen or fourteen, and good-looking with a wiry, muscular build. He wore sunglasses and blue striped surfer shorts.

"Does it hurt as much as this?" the new guy asked. With a loud smack, he slapped his open hand across Green Trunks' jelly belly.

Green Trunks let out a yelp. He sat up and grabbed his gut as if he'd just been shot there.

"Or does this hurt more?" asked the new guy, flicking his finger against the other boy's ear.

"Ouch! Cut it out!" he cried, covering his ear. "Goddamn it . . ." He almost tripped climbing off the lounge chair to get away.

Spencer caught a glimpse of his stomach—with a red mark from the other boy's hand. He usually didn't get a kick out of other people's misery, but he couldn't help smiling a little.

"Now you know how it feels," the new arrival said.

"Buzz off, Duncan. You loser . . ."

"Psycho," Green Trunks muttered. Rubbing his stomach, he wandered away. He glanced over his shoulder at them. "You two deserve each other . . ."

The lean, older boy settled in Green Trunks' lounge chair. Spencer was in awe of him—and a bit jealous of his tan and his adult hairy legs. The guy was shorter than Green Trunks, but in far better shape and utterly fearless. The way he reclined in the lounge chair, he was a like young lion stretching out and resting after a victory in battle. "I was watching you and Duncan last week," the boy said. "The first time he pushed you into the pool you should have climbed right out and slugged him. Duncan can dish it out, but he can't take it. Anyway, he won't bug you again."

"Well, thanks," Spencer said.

"You're new here, aren't you?"

Before Spencer could answer, someone stepped in front of them, blocking the sun. It was the yellow-bikini girl. "Hi, Garrett," she said, giving him a nervous smile.

"Hey, yeah, hi, Courtney," he said, lazily reaching over and mussing Spencer's hair. "This is my new buddy . . ." He lowered his sunglasses to squint at him. "Hey, what's your name, anyway?"

"Spencer Rowe," he said. Then he nodded at Miss Yellow Bikini. "Hi . . ."

"Listen, Courtney," Garrett said, pushing his sunglasses over his eyes again. "Why don't you grab us some hamburgers and Cokes at the snack shack? Get something for yourself, too. Have them charge it to Clinton Beale." He touched Spencer's arm. "Hey, do you want cheese on your burger, Spence-o?"

Spencer had made his first friend in Fairfax. He felt so lucky that this cool thirteen-year-old had taken him under his wing. He couldn't help wondering why Garrett didn't have a whole bunch of friends his own age. He was certainly popular with the girls. Garrett went through them pretty fast. Every few days a different one would hang around with them at the pool.

Spencer had been moderately popular in Silver Spring, but he felt privileged to be hanging around with Garrett. His new friend lived in a beautiful, big house, and he had a wide assortment of techno toys and games. He also had a faithful German shepherd named Al, who was all banged up. Garrett said he'd gotten him that way from a rescue shelter. Suddenly Spencer wanted to get a dog, too—one he could rescue. Everything Garrett did, he wanted to do. He even started dressing like Garrett and combing his hair like him.

One thing he didn't want to emulate was the way Garrett treated other people. He'd be so charming and polite, but Spencer realized after a while that it was all an act. Garrett rarely had a kind word to say about the girls who flocked to him at the pool. He was always criticizing them behind their backs. This one stuffed her bra; that one had a flat ass. But they seemed to adore him—for a while, at least. Garrett had certain adults bamboozled, too. He'd go into a store and ooze friendliness to the salesperson while ripping them off. He was always stealing potato chips and candy bars from the snack shack. And the older woman who worked there fawned over him. Spencer always left her a big tip in the jar, hoping to make up for his friend. A part of him found Garrett's recklessness sort of exciting. But Garrett had a cruel streak, too. Spencer was constantly telling him, "That's not nice, don't do that . . ."

"Oh, you're no fun at all, Spence-o," he'd say.

About a month after they started hanging out, Spencer went to the pool by himself for a change. Garrett had been busy that hot July afternoon. Spencer was in their usual spot, drying off after a dip in the pool, when Green Trunks Duncan came by. This was the first time Duncan had approached him since Garrett had chased him away weeks before. From his lounge chair, Spencer lowered his sunglasses and frowned at him. He felt a lot more confident dealing with Duncan now. Plus a little bit of Garrett's cockiness had rubbed off onto him.

"Where's your douche bag buddy?" Duncan asked with a sneer.

"Huh, I'd like to see you call him that to his face."

"You know, you must be dumber than you look if you haven't caught on to him yet. The guy's a total psycho."

"I'd like to see you call him that to his face, too." Spencer waved him away. "Why don't you go bother someone else?"

But Duncan pulled up a chair and sat down beside him. "I used to be just like you. Garret and me were practically best friends last summer."

"Yeah, right," Spencer muttered. "Garrett would never have anything to do with you. You're the one who's a psycho."

"We were here almost every day—this same spot," Duncan said. "Then I started putting it together what a creep he is. That's why Garrett doesn't have any friends his own age. That's why he can't keep a girlfriend. Ever notice how the ones hanging around him are new or just passing through? They're like you—either new or too stupid to know the truth about him."

Spencer rolled his eyes. "So what's this big, scary *truth*?"

"It's that he's crazy—I mean, like evil crazy," Duncan said. He nudged Spencer in the arm. "Have you had him over to your house yet? Because if you have, I'll bet you'll find something's missing. The guy's a klepto—as well as a sadist. Back when we were hanging out together, he had this dog, this golden retriever, Rollo, and he was always beating the shit out of that thing. He *experimented* on it, even burnt off a big patch of its hair once. The poor dog finally croaked . . ."

Spencer thought about Garrett's German shepherd, Al, and how banged up he was. He quickly shook his head. "That's bullshit. He gets abused dogs from shelters. He rescues them. You don't know what you're talking about."

"I hear he's been through, like, five dogs in the last few years. He picks them up at rescue shelters, all right—different rescue shelters in different counties. That way, they can't know he just got another dog like a few months back that's already dead, because he killed it. He acts like they've run away, but the Beales' gardener found one in their garbage, wrapped in a beach towel . . ."

"That's such a crock," Spencer insisted. "You're making this up. Don't you think his parents would catch on?"

"They're a couple of stupid rich people. They're hardly ever at home, and they spoil the shit out of him. He gets away with murder—literally."

Spencer refused to believe him. After all, he had to consider the source of this "truth." The guy was a major loser, whom Garrett had humiliated. If they'd actually been friends once, he was probably pissed that Garrett had dumped him. But Spencer doubted they'd ever been friends at all. Plus Garrett had been over at the house twice now, and nothing had gone missing.

Spencer's parents had been invited to a dinner party the following evening. Ordinarily, his Aunt Dee would come over and they'd order pizza or go out for dinner someplace fun. But she'd had a date that night. So Spencer had asked if Garrett could sleep over. He was at that age when he was too old for them to hire a sitter, but being alone in a big new house for the evening could be pretty scary. His mother thought Garrett was a charmer, and since he was older, he could look after Spencer. His dad agreed—based on the fact that Garrett's father was a big shot at the country club.

Before taking off for their fancy dinner party, Spencer's parents gave him thirty dollars to order a pizza. His dad said he didn't want them going out or having anyone else over. Garrett was all smiles and very polite. But as they stood at the front window and watched the car backing out of the driveway, he turned to Spencer. "God, I didn't realize what Nazis your parents are. We're supposed to stay locked in the house all night? What—we're not supposed to have any fun? Fuck that . . ."

Spencer thought he had a pretty good point. But outside of skateboarding down the sloped driveway and around the block for a couple of hours, they didn't go anywhere. They finally ordered the pizza and decided to watch *Se7en*, which was available on demand. Spencer made the mistake of mentioning that even if the movie got really scary, they wouldn't have to worry, because he knew where his dad kept a gun.

"What type of gun is it?" Garrett asked, obviously fascinated. "Does it have bullets or a clip? Is it even loaded?" When not laughing or cheering during violent points in the movie, he'd ask again about the gun: "Okay, just tell me this much. Is the gun upstairs or somewhere here on this floor? It's upstairs, isn't it?"

Spencer had experienced some uncomfortable moments with Garrett before—usually when he thought his friend was going to get them in trouble. He was feeling that way now. He thought of Duncan's farfetched accusations the day before. He hadn't said anything to Garrett about it. He couldn't help wondering if there was a grain of truth in what Duncan had said.

"So, um, how's Al doing?" Spencer casually asked during one of the talky at-home scenes with Brad Pitt and Gwyneth Paltrow.

Garrett tossed a wedge of pizza crust into the empty delivery box in front of them, and then he leaned back on the sofa. "Beats me," he sighed. "The son of a bitch ran away yesterday. I let him out to crap in the backyard and he ran off. Stupid-ass mutt . . ."

"Wow," Spencer murmured.

"Yeah, it sucks."

"You want to hear something weird?" Spencer said, trying to sound nonchalant. "That—uh, that Duncan guy came up and talked to me when I was at the pool yesterday . . ."

"Did he hit you or anything?" Garrett asked—very concerned. "Because if he did . . ."

"No, but he said something pretty screwy about you and your dogs," Spencer replied. He wasn't sure he should even bring it up—especially after Garrett had been ready to stand up for him just a moment ago. "Duncan said—and I'm sure he's such a liar—he said you've owned several dogs and you killed them all. But that's only after you kicked them around for a while. And once they were dead, you always told people that they ran away . . ."

His brow furrowed, Garrett looked hurt. "How can you even repeat that to me—when Al just ran away last night? I mean, this is killing me. What a mound of horseshit! You should have punched his lights out for saying that. Did you believe him? Did you even believe it for a minute?"

Wide-eyed, Spencer quickly shook his head. "God, no . . ."

"I've had a total of three dogs in my life," Garrett said solemnly, "First Ernie, then Rollo, and Al. I loved each one of them. Ernie got hit by a car, Rollo died of cancer, and Al ran away. Each time, it's been awful. You just don't know. I'm still hoping someone finds Al and returns him to us. I almost didn't come over here tonight. I didn't want to miss Al in case he comes back. When I think that he might be out there some-where—frightened, lost, or hurt . . ."

"God, I'm so sorry," Spencer murmured.

With a sigh, Garrett reached over and patted his shoulder.

Spencer looked at the TV screen for a few moments.

He wondered if Garrett might start crying. He stole another glance at him.

The light from the TV flickered across Garrett's handsome face as he watched the movie. He was dry-eyed—and grinning.

Spencer didn't know what he was smiling about. He didn't have much time to think about it, because after a minute Garrett asked once again where his dad kept the gun.

He should have figured out right then that something awful was going to happen before the evening was over. He should have realized there was a lot of truth in what Green Trunks had said about Garrett Beale.


Sitting in the shadowy balcony of the school auditorium, Spencer kept thinking—if only he'd been alone that night, his parents would still be alive.

Tanya had been ensconced in a seat in the second row for the last twenty minutes while some guy on stage sang, "Hey there, you with the stars in your eyes." Spencer realized he'd been practicing it earlier, during lunch hour, in the little music room next door to him.

It looked like Tanya got a phone call in the middle of his song.

Taking out her phone, she got to her feet and moved toward the far left aisle of the auditorium. It was obvious she didn't want anyone to hear what she had to discuss with the caller.

Grabbing his backpack, Spencer quickly got up and hurried across the row of seats to the balcony's left exit. He raced down the stairs, trying like hell not to make too much noise. He hoped to get as close as possible to Tanya so he could hear her end of this secret phone conversation. He pushed open the door to the lobby, ran down the corridor and tried a door into the left side of the theater's main level.

Tanya stood in the side aisle, about thirty feet away. She had the phone to her ear. She glanced toward him.

Spencer ducked back, but held the door open a crack so he could still spy on her. It didn't do much good. He had no idea what she was saying. He couldn't read her lips.

But from her slightly hunched-over stance and the way she was talking, Spencer could tell she didn't want anyone overhearing her conversation.

"It's not going to happen tonight," said the person on the other end of the phone. "There's a cop car outside her place right now. And three minutes ago, I picked this up on the scanner. They're placing extra patrols on the block—with instructions to keep an eye on this house in particular. We can't hope to get to her for at least another couple of days. Right now, it's too risky."

"Crap," Tanya grumbled.

"It's okay. I have a better idea. It involves your new boyfriend."

"What is it?"

"The less you know about it for now, the better. Anyway, I'm headed over to the town house to check up on him and his aunt."

"Why don't you come here to the theater instead?" Tanya asked.

"You mean to see you?"

"I mean," Tanya said, "if you're looking for Spencer, he's here. He's watching me right now."


The connection to the Capitol Hill bus was in a dicey part of downtown. An emaciated thirty-something woman sitting on the bus bench was picking things out of her long, limp brown hair. Two seedy guys with backpacks were having a loud conversation in which every other word out of their mouths was *fuck*—or a derivative thereof. Someone with a shopping cart full of crap was asleep in the doorway behind him. Across the street, a crazy man in tattered clothes was screaming at everyone—and every car that passed him.

Spencer kept his hand over the wallet in his back pocket. He had to come back this way to get home. He wondered how much worse this spot would be in about ninety minutes—when the next shift of creeps took over, and there would be fewer actual bus passengers.

Andrea had called him while he'd been on the Queen Anne bus. She'd sounded weird. He'd asked if anything was wrong, if she and Luke were splitting up. "Not yet, thank God," Andrea had said. "But he's working late again tonight, which is just as well, because I need to talk with you when you get back."

"Talk to me about what?" he'd asked.

"Just—things," she'd answered cryptically.

Spencer thought about the last time she'd sounded so weird on the phone. It had been yesterday afternoon, and he'd come home to find the police waiting to question him.

She'd made another pitch to pick him up at the therapist's office, and again, he'd said no thanks. He always liked some alone time after his sessions with Diane Leppert—to think about what they'd discussed and make some resolutions. It was the best part of his therapy session.

Now, Spencer wished he'd taken his aunt up on her offer.

Two women were arguing with each other just a few feet away from him. The altercation seemed on the brink of becoming violent. Spencer prayed that the bus would arrive soon—and that the two women wouldn't be boarding it.

Watching Tanya rehearse had been a waste of time. He didn't have a clue who had phoned her or what had been discussed. It could have been her mother for all he knew. She'd still been rehearsing when he'd left.

Spencer glanced at his wristwatch. His bus should have arrived five minutes ago. He stepped off the curb to look down the street for it. But there was no sign of the number 10.

Across the street, not far from the crazy guy, Spencer saw a black Toyota Corolla parked in the alley. The headlights had just gone off. But no one had climbed out of the car yet. Earlier, he'd spotted a black Corolla halfway down the block from the school bus stop. He probably wouldn't have noticed it, except the Corolla had pulled into a no-parking zone and switched off its lights. No one had emerged from that vehicle either. Could it be the same car—doing the exact same thing again? Was someone following him?

He couldn't help wondering if it was the police,

keeping a tail on him. Or was he just paranoid? How many black Toyota Corollas were in this city anyway?

His phone rang. Spencer took his hand away from his wallet for a moment so he could check who was calling him: MIDDLETON, B—206-555-0829.

He clicked his phone on. "Hello?"

"Hi, Spencer, it's Bonnie," she said. "Did I get you at an okay time?"

She was practically whispering, and he covered his free ear to block out the street traffic noise—along with the "Fucking This, Fucking That" backpack guys and the two women screaming at each other. "Yeah, I'm just downtown, waiting for a bus," he said into the phone. "How are you? Did you talk to your parents? Did you call the police?"

There was a pause. "Bonnie?"

"In answer to your questions: fine, yes, and yes," she said. "The cops said dozens of kids from school have been getting these weird threatening calls and texts—and not just the kids in our class. I guess all the parents are freaking out. One guy alone, calling himself the Ice Tray Killer, sent out like twenty creepy texts. And there have been a lot of other sick pranks along those lines. So I guess I'm not the only one getting spooked out. But the police were concerned about the break-in, and they're beefing up patrols on our block. So I think we're okay for tonight. Anyway, thanks for convincing me to tell my folks and the police. I feel a lot safer now."

Spencer wondered once again if that had really been Reed's Dodgers cap in his locker. Or had someone planted a random cap there just to screw around with his head?

"Are you still there?" Bonnie asked.

"Yes," he said. The two screaming women had moved on. But he kept his hand over one ear.

"I told the police about Tanya—and the pencil shavings and how she was the only one who knew about our basement window with the bad lock. They said they'd talk to her. That ought to go over well with her. Huh, like she doesn't already hate me enough . . ."

"You did the right thing," Spencer said.

"They asked me about you."

Spencer felt his stomach clench. "Did you tell them we talked? I asked you not to—"

"The police were the ones who brought you up," Bonnie explained. "They asked how well I knew you. I told them we've talked a couple of times, and that you seemed like a nice guy."

"Is that it?"

"No, they also asked how you got along with Reed, and I was honest. I told them he was kind of a jerk to you. They already knew about your *Fight Club* moment with him on Thursday, and again in the smoking pit outside the lunchroom on Friday. They wanted to know what I saw and heard. Anyway, they got around to asking if I was aware you'd spent some time in a—an institution. I didn't want to lie. But here's where I might have botched things up for you. I said that someone had texted Reed about your stint in the institution, and that Reed was kind of rubbing your face in it. I'm sorry. I'm afraid I might have given them a motive for why you'd want him dead . . ."

"No, it's okay," Spencer assured her. "That's stuff

they already knew. You didn't make things any worse for me, really. And I'm glad you didn't have to lie on my account. I wouldn't want you to get in trouble if the cops found out . . ."

With the phone to his ear, he glanced over at the black Corolla, still parked near the mouth of the alley.

"I was right," he heard Bonnie say. "You are a nice guy. Listen, my mom's calling me to dinner. I better go."

"Okay," he said. "Thanks a lot for calling."

"See you at school tomorrow—if I don't get killed tonight," she said.

She hung up before Spencer could tell her she shouldn't joke like that.

As he clicked off the phone, he saw the number 10 bus coming up the street. He glanced back over at the black Corolla. It was still parked near the mouth of the alley.

And the driver was still inside.


Spencer watched the raindrops accumulate against the window of the bus as it headed up Olive Way on Capitol Hill. He'd wanted to sit in the very back to make sure the black Corolla didn't follow the bus. But, unfortunately, the two backpack guys had hopped on before him and taken the backseat: ". . . And he came out of the fucking store, and I knew the stupid fuck was so fucking high, and I figured, like, fuck it . . ." Spencer wondered what swearwords they used when they were actually upset about something.

With his backpack in his lap, he sat near the rear

door and tried to block out their conversation. He had another ten minutes before his stop—and then three blocks of walking in the rain to Diane Leppert's office.

She was the only other person who knew the whole story about what had happened that July night, six years ago—a night that hadn't stopped haunting him.

If only he hadn't mentioned to Garrett that his father had a gun.

He remembered Garrett wouldn't stop asking where the gun was. He just wouldn't let up.

"Listen, I'm not really sure where he keeps the stupid gun," Spencer lied. They were spread out on the sofa—with the empty pizza box and Coke cans on the coffee table in front of them. "He keeps changing the hiding place."

"Well, earlier, you acted like you knew where it was. Where was it the last time you checked? I'll bet it's in their bedroom . . ."

Spencer kept changing the subject. Fortunately, Garrett got more and more interested in *Se7en*. But once the end credits began to roll, he started in about the gun again. He was determined to find it. He wore Spencer down.

"Okay, you were right earlier," he sighed. "It's in my mom and dad's bedroom. But that's off-limits."

Garrett hopped off the sofa. "I'll bet I can find it."

"Oh, c'mon, please, don't go up there," Spencer said. But Garrett was already rushing up the stairs. Spencer hurried after him. "Hey, y'know, it's past eleven. My folks might be back any minute. We're not supposed to go in their bedroom. My dad will kill us if he finds out!"

"Why? What is it—a sex dungeon or something?" Garrett laughed. He headed into the master bedroom. "Is this the fornication station?"

As Spencer stepped in after him, he saw that Garrett was already opening the drawer of the nightstand on the right side of his parents' bed.

"Listen, Garrett, we really can't be in here. Plus it's dangerous. What if the gun goes off accidentally?"

"I just want to look at it, that's all," Garrett said, peeking under the bed. "It's not like I'm going to shoot you with it. Tell me if I'm getting hot or cold."

Spencer watched him check the other nightstand. He cringed when Garrett opened the closet door. "I'll bet it's in here," Garrett said.

"It isn't," Spencer sighed. "Listen, do you promise just to look at it—for like, thirty seconds?"

Garrett smiled and nodded eagerly. "Yeah, that's all I want to do."

"And then we're going to put it away, right?"

"Of course."

Spencer took a deep breath, marched over to his father's dresser, and opened the bottom drawer. He pulled the Glock 19 out from under a pile of folded casual shirts. With his fingertips, he held it by the barrel and reluctantly passed it to Garrett. "Thirty seconds, starting now," he said. "One, two . . ."

"Shit, it's loaded," Garrett said, examining it. "I can tell. This mother could do some damage." He pointed the gun at Spencer. "You know, you really piss me off sometimes. *Bang!*"

Spencer flinched.

Garrett laughed. "Hey, relax, the trigger safety's on."

"You have fifteen more seconds," Spencer said, nervously tapping his foot.

Garrett stuck the Glock in the waist of his cargo shorts, and then whipped it out as if in a gunfight. He repeated the move.

"Okay, time's up." Spencer held out his shaky hand. "C'mon, my mom and dad could be back any minute."

"I want to see how I look with it," Garrett said, heading out of the bedroom.

Spencer followed him down the hallway to his own room. He didn't understand it. His parents had two different mirrors in their bedroom, but Garrett had to pose in front of the full-length mirror on the back of Spencer's door. "Just like James Bond," Garrett said. He pointed the Glock at the mirror and pretended to fire. "Die, you son of a bitch! *Bang!* Fuck me? No, fuck you! *Bang!*"

"C'mon, Garrett, hand it over. Please? Thirty seconds, that was the agreement."

But his friend kept up his charade in front of the mirror—waving the gun, screaming at his reflection, and imitating heavy metal music. Past all of it, Spencer heard the front door open downstairs.

"Oh, God, that's them! Give it to me!" He tried to grab the gun.

But Garrett wouldn't surrender it. He opened his mouth to laugh, but no sound came out. "Oh, Jesus," he finally whispered. "Your old man's gonna shit . . ." He backed away and hurled the gun under Spencer's bunk bed.

"Damn it," Spencer hissed. "Why'd you do that?"

"To hide it . . ."

Spencer dropped to his knees. Now he had to crawl under the bed to retrieve the stupid gun—and his parents were already in the house. He could hear the footsteps downstairs, and his mother talking quietly.

"Spencer!" his dad yelled. He sounded angry. "Spencer, get down here!"

He couldn't see the gun under his bed. He straightened up and then hurried to the top of the stairs. "How was the party?" he called, a little out of breath.

"Come down here!" his father replied.

Biting his lip, he crept back to the master bedroom doorway. He saw his father's dresser drawer was still open. He padded across the room and shut it. Then he hurried back toward the hallway, stopping only to switch off the light.

Stifling a laugh, Garrett waited for him near the top of the stairs. He didn't seem to realize how serious this was.

Spencer started down the steps, with Garrett behind him.

"Oh, for God's sake, it's no biggie," Spencer's mother was saying in a hushed tone. "You always get this way when you've had too much to drink . . ."

"Shut up," his father grumbled. "And don't touch that. Don't touch a thing."

"I can't deal with you when you're like this. I'm taking a sleeping pill."

From the front hallway, Spencer could hear them in the family room, where he and Garrett had been watching the movie. They'd left the TV on. He headed toward the back of the house while Garrett remained by the stairs.

In the family room, Spencer found his father standing between the TV and the sofa. He'd loosened his tie, and his face was a little flushed—the usual sign that he was drunk. It was an on-again, off-again problem. He tended to get pretty smashed at parties, which irritated the hell out of Spencer's mother. When he was drunk, he'd get angry and abusive. Although he never hit either one of them, he was still pretty scary. Spencer's mother was in the kitchen area, which was separated from the family room by a counter. She looked pretty in a red, sleeveless party dress. She was downing some pills with a glass of water.

"What the hell is this?" his father asked, nodding at the coffee table in front of the sofa. "We treated you guys to pizza. Are we supposed to clean up after you, too?"

Spencer stole a look toward the front hallway, where he knew Garrett could hear every word. Anyone listening could have figured out his dad was hammered. He was so embarrassed. He glanced at the source of all the trouble: an empty pizza box, some dirty napkins, and a couple empty Coke cans. "Sorry," Spencer mumbled. "We were gonna clean it up. We just didn't think you'd be home this early . . ."

"And the TV's on—with no one watching it. How'd you like to pay the Dominion Virginia Power bill?"

"I'm sorry."

His father scowled at him. "Well, don't just stand there like an idiot. Clean up this goddamn mess."

Spencer's mother clicked her tongue against her teeth. "Larry, you're being an ogre . . ."

Spencer started to gather up the box, napkins, and Coke cans. "Mom, it's okay."

"It's not okay!" his father snapped. "Where's this friend of yours? Is he still here?"

Spencer dumped the cans in the recycling bin under the sink. "He's in the other room," Spencer whispered. "Dad, can we please leave him out of it? This was all my fault . . ." He started to crunch up the pizza box to fit it inside the garbage can.

"You two need to hit the sack right now," his father said as he headed to the liquor cabinet. "I want you two in your beds, no video games, no chitchat, nothing. You're going to need your sleep because you're both doing yard work in the morning to pay me back for the pizza. Maybe then, you can learn a little gratitude." He dropped some ice in a glass.

"Oh, Larry, ease up," his mother muttered.

He glared at Spencer. "Upstairs, the two of you!" he barked. "Go on. And I don't want to hear a peep out of either one of you ungrateful brats."

A half hour later, they were in their bunks in Spencer's room: Spencer in the bottom bunk, and Garrett on top. The lights were off. Spencer's father had just been in to check on them. Spencer could still pick up the faint odor of alcohol that had been on his breath. "You two slackers get ready for a seven o'clock wake-up call," he'd said before closing the door.

They'd remained quiet and listened to him lumber down the hallway to the master bedroom. Then, past the low hum of the house's air-conditioning, they'd heard the other door shut.

"Your old man's a real prick, isn't he?" Garrett whispered.

Spencer stared up at the slats holding the mattress overhead. "He gets that way after a few drinks," he said. "Really, he's not so bad."

"Well, I'm not doing any yard work for that asshole tomorrow," Garrett hissed. "You can bet on it. I can't believe the way he talked to you downstairs. You deserve better, Spence-o. How about him carrying on like he treated us to a weekend in Las Vegas or something? Big spender! It was thirty bucks for a pizza. Get over it, numb nuts."

Spencer shushed him. "He might hear you . . ."

He was still on edge, wondering if his father would discover the gun was missing. These next few minutes before his father went to bed were crucial. Chances were pretty good his dad wouldn't go into that drawer any time tonight or tomorrow. Most of the shirts in there were for fall or winter.

Spencer decided to wait a few more minutes—until his father was asleep. Then he'd crawl under his bunk and retrieve the gun. He wanted easy access to it tomorrow—for a quick transfer back inside his father's drawer. He'd stash the Glock in his closet until he found the right opportunity to move it. His father would never know.

"Listen, we won't have to do any yard work," he assured Garrett. "My dad's not even going to remember this tomorrow morning. He'll be too hungover."

"I don't know how you put up with it. Earlier, when I heard him talking to you like that downstairs, I really wanted to come in there and slug him." Spencer heard

Garrett stir around under the covers. "I can't believe we're in bed already—and on a Saturday night, too. It's not even midnight . . ."

Spencer felt so humiliated. He hated his father for embarrassing him in front of his only friend. No way would Garrett ever agree to spend the night again. Would he even sit with him at the country club pool after this?

He sighed. "I'm really sorry. This has been a pretty shitty sleepover for you . . ."

"Oh, I've had worse. We had a few laughs. Plus I got to handle a gun."

"That reminds me," Spencer murmured, switching on the little reading light on the wall. Then he threw back the covers and climbed out of the bed. He wore a T-shirt with pajama shorts. Getting down on the floor, he crawled under his bunk to retrieve the gun. But he couldn't see it. A panic swept through him. He'd been in the bathroom earlier, getting ready for bed. He'd left Garrett alone in here. Had Garrett taken the Glock? If so, he'd never give it back—not without a huge argument.

"What are you doing?" Garrett asked.

"I'm looking for the gun," Spencer whispered. "It's not here . . ."

The bunk bed set squeaked a little as Garrett came down the ladder. "I heard it hit something when I tossed it under there," he said. "Try in the corner, against the wall."

To his utter relief, Spencer spotted the Glock there in the shadows, amid the dust bunnies. He grabbed it and scrambled out from under the bunk. He found Garrett standing over him with his arms folded. Leaning against the bunk ladder, he was wearing white briefs and nothing else.

Spencer couldn't help envying him. For some reason, he wasn't able to fall asleep without a T-shirt on. It felt more comfortable, and he figured if something happened and he had to run out of the house in the middle of the night, he wouldn't be practically naked. That thought didn't seem to occur to Garrett. Spencer wished he was more like him. He wished he weren't scared and uncomfortable most of the time.

"You found it," Garrett said.

"Yeah, thanks," Spencer said, wiping the dust off the gun with the bottom of his T-shirt. He took the Glock to his closet, then on his tiptoes reached up and stashed it under some folded sweaters.

As he closed the closet door, he caught Garrett watching his every move. A part of him wondered if his friend might get up in the middle of the night to fool around with the gun again. "Let's just leave it there tonight, okay?" he said.

Garrett grinned. "Well, if I hear your old man coming, I may just grab it and shoot the son of a bitch. I'd be doing you a favor. We could tell everyone we thought he was a burglar."

"That's not funny," Spencer murmured.

"Neither is your old man," Garrett said. "He's an embarrassment. Good thing you're not a bit like him." Moving over to the desk, he picked up the alarm clock and glanced at it. "On weekends, I don't usually go to bed until one or two in the morning."

Spencer sat down on his bed. "So what would you be doing if you'd stayed home tonight—and weren't stuck here?"

"Oh, I'd probably be making out with that Molly chick from the pool." He laughed and then shrugged. "Or maybe I'd just be in my room alone, jacking off." With his fist, he made a pumping motion in front of his crotch.

Spencer chuckled nervously.

"I forget, you're, like, eleven, right? Have you even jacked off yet?"

"I don't think so," Spencer said, feeling a little pang in his stomach.

Garrett snickered. "Well, you'd know it if you did. Take my word for it. Do you even know about sex?"

He nodded. "Yeah, a friend of mine in Silver Spring told me."

That was only a few months before. George Camper had told him how babies were made. For a week afterward, Spencer couldn't look his parents in the eyes. He couldn't imagine them doing that in order to have children. Being an only child, he figured they'd done it only once, which made them a lot less perverted than George's parents, because he had six brothers and sisters. They'd have to have done it seven times.

"So now you're an expert, huh?" Garrett said, leaning back on the desk.

Spencer frowned. "Well, there's some stuff I don't know, I guess."

"Like what?"

"Like, what's sixty-nine?"

Garrett drew the number in the air. "That's the head, that's the body," he explained. "So the girl is blowing the guy while he eats her out."

Spencer nodded. But he still wasn't sure he understood. It sounded like a guy was getting a blow job while he and the girl were at a restaurant. He wondered where in the restaurant they did sixty-nine.

Garrett scratched his bare stomach. "At the beginning of summer, I got a blow job from this chick from Pittsburgh I met at the pool. She was really hot." He grinned at Spencer. "You don't know what I'm talking about, do you? I mean, you probably don't even have pubic hair yet, do you?"

"I have a little," Spencer lied.

"Oh, yeah?" Garrett took a step toward him. "Let's see . . ."

"No! God, are you kidding me?" Spencer squirmed back in the bunk. He tried to laugh and act like it was funny, but he felt really uncomfortable.

"Chicken," Garrett teased.

The house's air-conditioning system kicked in again with a roar. Then it got quiet again.

"I'll show you mine," Garrett said, his thumb on the elastic waistband of his briefs.

"Ah, no thanks," Spencer said—with another skittish laugh. At the same time, he was kind of curious. But he never would have admitted it. He could see Garrett's tan line.

"I can show you how to jerk off," Garrett whispered, pulling down his underpants. He stood in front of him naked.

Spencer caught a glimpse of Garrett's cock, which

was, of course, bigger than his—and crowned with a patch of dark pubic hair. In comparison, Spencer felt like such a *baby*, so inferior. He immediately looked away—toward his bedroom door.

It was opening.

"What the hell is going on in here?" his father bellowed.

"Shit," Garrett muttered, struggling to pull his underpants back up.

"We're not doing anything!" Spencer said.

His father charged into the room with his robe billowing open. He wore a pair of blue boxers under the robe. His face was flushed, and he looked furious. Spencer watched in horror as his father slapped Garrett across the face.

"God, Dad, no!"

Garrett reeled back, knocking over the desk chair and falling to the floor with a loud thud. "Fuck!" he yelled, his hand over his jaw. He still hadn't pulled his briefs up all the way. Now he tugged at the waistband and glowered up at Spencer's father.

"Get dressed," he growled, standing over Garrett with his fists clenched. "You aren't staying here. I don't want you anywhere near my son—"

"Dad, nothing happened!"

His father swiveled around and pointed a finger at him. "You shut up. I'll deal with you later."

He turned toward Garrett again. "You heard me. Get up and put your clothes on. I'm driving you home."

"You can't drive me home," Garrett said defiantly. "You're too drunk to drive."

His father took a step toward Garrett. It looked like he was about to lunge at him again.

Half sitting up on the floor by the desk, Garrett reached for the fallen chair.

"Dad, please!" Spencer cried, jumping up from the bed. He grabbed his father's arm. "Garrett didn't mean it. Please, I'm sorry . . ."

His father kept staring at Garrett, who glared right back at him. "You're going to call your father. Tell him to come pick you up. And when he gets here, your father's going to hear a thing or two about his smart-ass, deviant son. I'm giving you three minutes to get dressed and pack your bag. Tell your father to hurry up. I don't want to have you in my house any longer than necessary."

Spencer's father marched out of the bedroom.

Spencer gently closed the door after him. His heart was pounding. He thought he was going to be sick. He turned toward Garrett, who was getting to his feet. "God, I'm so sorry," he whispered. "Are you okay? My dad—he's never hit me or my mother. I can't believe he did that . . ."

He touched his friend's shoulder, and Garrett angrily recoiled. "He isn't telling my father a goddamn thing," he hissed. He rubbed his left jaw. "I'll kill him first—or you will. We have his gun. We should kill the motherfucker . . ."

"Y'know, if we get dressed, and we—we wait for my dad to calm down, we can explain how nothing happened. And if you apologize to him—"

"Me apologize to him? Are you crazy? He's the one who hit me." Garrett bent down and swiped his cargo shorts off the floor. He started to put them on. "And you want to 'explain how nothing happened'? He's already made up his mind about what we were doing. He's not going to believe us—and neither will my father. And my old man hates gays. If he hears about this, he'll kill me. He'll kill me or he'll kick me out of the house and send me to one of those conversion places where they give you electric shock. And I'm not even a homo. I wouldn't be surprised if your dad does the same thing to you. He's a real bastard . . ." Garrett put on his T-shirt.

Spencer started to get dressed, too. He'd seen a TV news show about places like that. They seemed almost worse than prison. How could he convince his father it was all a big misunderstanding? He hated to think that Garrett was probably right. This wasn't something that would blow over once his father sobered up.

"Why does your mother let him treat you like that?" Garrett asked. "What's wrong with her? She must have heard what was going on in here. Doesn't she give a crap about you? Where is she?"

"She took a sleeping pill," Spencer answered meekly.

"When we kill your old man, we'll be doing her a favor, too."

"C'mon, Garrett, quit talking like that."

"I'm not just talking," he said. "I'm serious. We've got the gun. I'm not getting kicked out of the house and disinherited and Christ only knows what else because of your douche bag old man. Plus that asshole hit me. We're killing him. I can tell the police that it was self-defense." He turned toward the closet.

"No, I'll do it!" Spencer heard himself say. "He's my father. I'm the one who should do it." Spencer reached the closet before Garrett and grabbed the Glock from under the sweaters on the shelf. He clutched the gun close to his chest.

"You mean it?" Garrett asked. "Because if you don't shoot him, you might as well shoot yourself. Are you really gonna kill him?"

"Yeah," Spencer nodded.

He felt horrible, lying to his friend. But he was terrified that Garrett meant every word he'd just said. If Garrett had the Glock, someone would certainly get killed with it. The only solution Spencer could think of was giving the gun to his dad and confessing that they'd taken it out of his drawer. He'd stress that it was the only thing they'd done wrong. Nothing had happened between him and Garrett. He'd throw himself on his father's mercy—and endure his wrath. Even though his dad was drunk, it would be better for everyone if he had the gun—and not Garrett. His friend was too much of a loose cannon.

"Take the safety off," Garrett whispered, reaching over and adjusting something on the trigger. He put his arm around Spencer's shoulder. "I'm proud of you, man. You're standing up for yourself—and me. No one's going to blame you. He's drunk. He hit me for absolutely no reason . . ."

Garrett started guiding him toward his bedroom door—and then down the hallway. Spencer clutched the gun. It felt heavy in his small hand. Garrett stroked him on the back. "You can do this," he murmured, again and again. His warm breath swirled in Spencer's ear. "Kill the bastard. He's making your life miserable. You do this for me—*you do this for us*—and I'll owe you, man. I'll get you anything you want . . ."

Approaching the master bedroom, Spencer could see a light was on. Shadows moved on the wall as his father got dressed.

He was mesmerized by Garrett's words and the intense connection he felt to him. A part of him almost wanted to go through with his plan—anything for his friend. If he didn't go through with it, Garrett would never forgive him.

And his friend was right. His dad was a real bastard sometimes.

But then, did Garrett really think his mom would go along with this? What was supposed to happen to her?

As he crossed the threshold to his parents' room, Spencer was shaking. He was careful to keep the gun pointed at the floor. He dreaded what he was about to do. It didn't matter that it was the right thing. His father would still be furious at him. His friend would be furious at him. He thought of what Garrett had said: ". . . If you don't shoot him, you might as well shoot yourself."

His father's back was to them. He'd put on a pair of khakis and an undershirt. He was still barefoot. Looking dazed and half-asleep, Spencer's mother was sitting up in bed. She wore a light yellow nightgown. The closet door was open, and the light was on in there. His father had also switched on his nightstand lamp, but the room was still shadowy.

Spencer's mouth went dry as he started to speak. "Dad . . ."

"Hey, asshole," Garrett interrupted, his voice raised. "Look at this. Look at what we found . . ."

Spencer's father turned toward them, looking startled. His pants weren't completely fastened in front yet. "What the hell?"

"Shoot him!" Garrett yelled—practically in Spencer's ear. "Kill that motherfucker!"

Spencer froze. He still had the Glock pointed toward the floor.

Staring at it, his father seemed to realize what was happening. He shook his head. But he didn't appear frightened at all. "Goddamn it!" he growled, stomping toward them. "What do you think you're doing?" He looked as if he was ready to tear into both of them.

It all happened so fast.

Spencer felt Garrett behind him, grabbing his arm and lifting it up so that the gun was pointed at his father. His dad came at them with his fist clenched. Spencer was terrified. He just wanted to stop him. He didn't want to kill him.

He didn't even remember pulling the trigger.

The shot rang out, and he screamed. He saw the explosion of blood under his father's chin. He watched him stagger back and grab his throat with both hands. His dad had a strange, bewildered grimace on his face. His father kept blinking as he gaped at him—like he couldn't fathom how his own son had just shot him in the throat.

He collapsed on the floor in front of the bed.

His mother's shrieking filled the room. Still sitting in the bed, she held the sheets up to her neck.

"Shoot her," Garrett hissed, tightening his grip on Spencer's arm. "Do it, do it!"

"Oh, God, no!" she begged. "Spencer, wait—"

Spencer recoiled as the gun went off again. This time, Garrett's finger was over his. It was as if he were Garrett's puppet.

The first shot must have missed because his mother was still screaming.

"No!" he yelled.

But Garrett now had both arms around him and pressed his finger again.

Another shot rang out. It silenced her screams. Spencer saw the blood on the white sheet over his mother's chest. Horrified, he watched her flop back in the bed, suddenly lifeless.

Stunned, he stood in the doorway, looking at the carnage in his parents' bedroom. Garrett slowly let go of his arms, and the gun dropped to the floor with a clatter. Spencer could hear his friend breathing heavily.

"We're going to have to change our story," he said.

After that, everything was just a blur. But he remembered how Garrett kept his cool. His friend was the one who came up with the idea about an intruder shooting his parents while the two of them hid under the bunk bed. Garrett took money from Spencer's father's wallet—along with his father's Rolex and some jewelry from his mom's drawer. He'd made Spencer strip down to underpants—in case blood had spattered his clothes. The jewelry, the money, Spencer's clothes, and the Glock 19—all went into Garrett's overnight bag.

Sick to his stomach, Spencer threw up in the bathroom. Meanwhile his friend went downstairs and staged a break-in by opening a kitchen window and pushing out the screen. Afterwards, he bragged to Spencer that he'd worn his mother's dishwashing gloves to do it—so as not to leave fingerprints. He claimed he'd gotten some of his ideas from the *CSI* shows, but Spencer wondered how much he was operating on sheer killer instinct.

He went over the intruder story with Spencer twice—so there would be no contradictions in their versions of what had happened. Then he'd coached him on what to say to the 911 operator. Spencer was his puppet. Garrett was so clever. It was his idea to leave the knapsack full of evidence half-open on Spencer's desk chair—so it would look like they had nothing to hide. And by some miracle, it worked. The police never examined it.

Later, Spencer wondered if his friend had left the bag out in the open like that just to push the envelope a little. It probably gave him a thrill to see the police checking over the rooms—coming so dangerously close to uncovering Garrett's ruse.

But as clever as Garrett was, he was still just a thirteen-year-old kid. By the following day, the police were already seeing through the boys' deception. The next afternoon, Garrett sold most of Spencer's mother's jewelry to a landscaper at the club, who had gotten him some drugs once. That same night, Spencer broke down and confessed everything to his aunt.

The one thing he didn't admit to her was that Garrett had been naked when his father had walked in on them. He convinced himself that it was an unnecessary detail—and besides, it was embarrassing. He merely said they'd been "horsing around" and making too much noise. Ironically, without any kind of collaboration, Garrett's confession had left out that same detail. In his version, they'd just been "goofing off" when a drunken Mr. Rowe had stormed into the bedroom and attacked him. His account of that night had him begging Spencer not to shoot anyone, and the gun going off when he'd tried to stop him. In Garrett's version, the break-in story had been Spencer's idea. He'd merely helped Spencer stage the scene.

At the hearing, the lawyer Spencer's aunt had hired was able to discredit Garrett's claims.

Just when Spencer didn't think he had a friend in the world, his aunt had come to his rescue. If she hadn't stepped in and worked so tirelessly with the lawyer, the Beales' attorneys would have piled all the blame for the murders on him. Andrea had made certain Garrett was held accountable for his part in what had happened that night.

Both boys were found guilty of second-degree murder. They were sentenced to a minimum of four years in a juvenile correctional facility—following extensive psychological evaluations. They split them up: Garrett was sent to a place in Richmond, and Spencer to the Behavioral Health Center in Arlington.

Earlier this year, when he'd learned about the house fire that had killed Garrett and his parents, Spencer couldn't help thinking that his ex-friend had probably started it. That would have been so like him—playing with fire.

If his theory was true, it meant that they'd both ended up killing their parents.

Even with Garrett sharing the blame and after years of counseling, Spencer still felt culpable for his mother's and father's deaths. And all that while, he missed them, too. He missed them terribly.

His Seattle therapist, Diane Leppert, was helping him learn to forgive himself and move on. They'd made some progress, but still had a long way to go.

The Metro bus let him out on Nineteenth Avenue, by St. Joseph's Church, three blocks from Diane's office. This was mostly a residential area—with a few quaint, specialty shops and a couple of restaurants along Nineteenth. Diane's office was above a candle and soap store.

Putting the hood of his sweatshirt over his head, Spencer walked briskly in the rain. He decided to tell Diane about Reed's baseball cap. He'd ask her what to do. He had the list in his head of other things he needed to tell her: Reed's murder, the police questioning, Luke finding out the truth about him, and his conflicted feelings for Bonnie. He kept thinking he was forgetting something. Was it even something he was supposed to discuss with Diane?

Reaching the old, beige brick building, Spencer passed by the darkened storefront of Blissful Scents, and pushed open the second door. It was mostly glass with a dark wood frame. The street number and the second floor businesses were listed on the window:

~**1711**~

M. FREEMAN, LAC LMP—ACUPUNCTURE
D. LEPPERT, PHD—THERAPIST
C. LAHART, BS, DC—CHIROPRACTOR
G. MARTINSEN, LLC—HYPNOTHERAPY

As soon as Spencer entered the tiny lobby, he got a whiff of the aromatic candles and soaps from the boutique next door. He pulled back his hood and started up the worn maroon-carpeted stairs to the second floor. On the landing at the top of the stairs, he suddenly remembered what had been on his mind earlier.

All his daydreaming on the bus had made him forget about the black Toyota Corolla that may or may not have been following him. He'd forgotten to look for it when he'd gotten off at his stop.

Spencer glanced out the rain-beaded window on the stairway landing. He didn't see the car on the dark, wet street below.

He turned and started down the hallway toward Diane's office. Maybe he'd tell her about the car, too.

# CHAPTER TWENTY

*Tuesday—7:04 p.m.*

Spencer hadn't been in Diane's office for five minutes when he broke down crying. He couldn't help it. He'd started telling her about everything that had happened in the last few days, and he lost it. He kept wiping his nose on his sleeve—until Diane nodded at the Kleenex box on the table beside him. He took out a tissue. Practically every flat surface in her office had a box of tissues on it, but he'd never needed one until now.

They sat across from each other in matching easy chairs. Diane was in her late fifties with a handsome, careworn face and short-cropped, sandy-colored hair. Spencer imagined his mom—if she were alive now—might have looked like a younger version of his therapist. Diane always wore "librarian" glasses on a chain around her neck, and she favored suits. Tonight she had on a dark blue suit with a lavender blouse.

Spencer's hooded sweatshirt was draped over the chair arm, and his backpack was at his feet. His paperback copy of *The Grapes of Wrath* for English class was underneath it. He'd been reading it in the waiting room before his appointment.

He wiped his eyes and blew his nose, but then didn't know what to do with the soiled Kleenex. He didn't see a wastebasket anywhere, so he stuffed the tissue in the pocket of his jeans.

For their sessions, Diane always kept the lights dim in her office. Spencer never got a good look at anything—including the titles of the books on her bookshelves and the fancy script on the framed diplomas on her wall. She had a few beautiful glass pieces that caught the light—including a green pyramid on her desk, a multicolored vase on the shelf, and a purple Saturn sculpture about the size of a softball on the table beside her chair. Diane absently stroked it from time to time while she talked to him. There was only one window in the room—by her desk. From where Spencer sat, it offered a view of the treetops and the church steeple. It was still raining out.

He plucked another tissue from the box and wiped his nose. "I'm sorry," he muttered. "I can't believe I'm bawling like this . . ."

"It's okay," Diane said. "It sounds like a hell of a week you've had. Keep going. Unload . . ."

She'd gotten that term from him, because he so often said to her, "I need to unload this on you . . ."

He liked Diane, and opened up to her more easily than he had to any other therapist before. Maybe that was because he'd felt everything he said to the doctors in Virginia might be used against him. But after *unloading* on Diane, he always felt better.

Diane was the only one who knew about Garrett getting naked in Spencer's room the night of the murders. During the police questioning, the trial, and all the sessions with all those doctors at the institution, Spencer had kept that essential detail a secret. If Garrett had ever admitted it to anyone, Spencer certainly never heard about it. But he'd told Diane during their third session.

She'd seemed totally unfazed. She'd just nodded.

"You act like it's not important," Spencer remembered saying. "I mean, I haven't been able to tell anyone else about it. You're the first . . ."

"Well, it does give me some insights," she'd said. "It explains your friend's desire for wanting your parents out of the picture. He didn't want his father finding out that he'd exposed himself to another boy. But you—you never wanted to kill your parents. You weren't the one caught with his pants down. You weren't a willing participant in anything that happened that night. Still, it's perfectly understandable why you wouldn't want that portion of the evening available for public consumption. It's embarrassing. You were eleven years old, and you were involved in a double murder. You didn't want your sexuality questioned on top of everything else. And let's face it, that part of the night would have been the lurid detail a lot of people would have focused on . . ."

They'd talked about it for the rest of the session.

She pointed out that once he'd decided to omit that detail from his confession, he'd been trapped into keeping it secret from then on. Maybe he didn't want anyone thinking his relationship with Garrett was sexual, which up to that point, it hadn't been. If anything, it was more of a case of misguided hero worship on Spencer's part.

"I keep thinking had my dad not walked in, Garrett might have taken it further than just 'I'll show you mine if you show me yours,'" Spencer had admitted.

"I wouldn't doubt it," she'd said. "From everything you've told me about him and what I've read on the case, I think he would have taken it a lot further than you were willing to go. The scary thing is, I don't believe he was acting out of curiosity or attraction or anything really sexual. In my opinion, as far as your late friend, Garrett, is concerned, it was all about control, power, and manipulation. I keep thinking about him and his poor, doomed pets. That's all classic sociopathic behavior."

She'd reminded Spencer that despite Garrett's influence, he'd never stolen anything or intentionally hurt anybody. And he'd been forever telling his friend, "That's not nice."

"You held your moral ground with him," she'd said. "You didn't give in to him. Your parents would still be alive if he hadn't been there behind you that night with his hands on the gun. I think you got a raw deal, Spencer. I think the only thing you're guilty of is picking the wrong friend."

Spencer remembered walking away from that session

feeling for the first time in years that maybe he wasn't some kind of monster. He'd even gotten a little choked up about it.

But today was the first time he'd actually cried in Diane's office.

Now he pulled himself together and *unloaded* on her about all the traumatic events from the past week.

Diane seemed to have an answer for everything—or in some cases, a question. On the subject of Luke and his Aunt Dee possibly breaking up: "That was your aunt's decision not to tell him about your history. That's between her and Luke. Let them work it out. With everything that's happened, do you really want to take that on as your responsibility, too?"

On the murders of Reed and his parents: "You need to be totally honest with your aunt and the police. Anything you hide from them is liable to come up later and bite you on the fanny. This business with the baseball cap is very disconcerting. Either someone's playing a sick joke on you or it's a setup. Either way, tell your aunt about it and talk to the police. Nip this in the bud. I'm going to be at my place on Vashon Island from tomorrow through Sunday. But I'll be checking my messages and emails. If the police want to talk to me, I'll vouch for your character. Give them my number."

Sometimes, her answers weren't what he wanted to hear. On the topic of Bonnie Middleton: "It's obvious you like her a lot and you're attracted to her. But you're right to be a little wary of her. If she's been running around with that crowd, she could be the one who's setting you up . . ."

Spencer shifted in the easy chair. "I'm not sure

that's true, because she's broken away from that group. Plus she seems pretty nice—"

"Just a second," Diane interrupted, turning toward the door to her waiting room. She got to her feet. "Excuse me."

She glanced at her watch and then moved to the door. "Is anyone out there?" she called, her hand on the knob. She waited a moment and then opened the door. "That's strange," she murmured. She stepped into the anteroom, and Spencer heard a door shut. A moment later, she came back into the office and closed the door behind her. "Weird. I thought I heard someone. And I could have sworn that door to the hallway was closed before."

Spencer shrugged. "I must not have closed it all the way."

She smiled and nodded. "Maybe that's it. Sorry for the interruption." She sat down again. "Anyway, I think it's terrific you like this girl. But proceed with caution, okay? I'm not sure she can be trusted. The same goes for that Tanya. If I were you, I'd watch my back with both of them. Right now, you need to put your trust in your aunt—and me."

One of the things he liked about Diane was that she didn't hesitate to tell him what she thought. She was so unlike those doctors at the institution who would answer his questions with another question, like, "What are your feelings on that?" Diane was more direct—and almost always had an answer for him. Sometimes it just wasn't the answer he wanted.

At the end of the session, he wasn't quite as buoyant as he usually was after talking with Diane. He had a feeling the police were going to jump all over him once he told them about the baseball cap—and how long he'd had it. His aunt certainly wouldn't be happy that he hadn't told her about it sooner.

Walking down the hallway toward the stairs, he noticed that the frosted windows in the doors of the other offices were dark. Diane and he were the only ones left in the building. No wonder she'd been concerned when she'd thought she heard someone in her waiting room. Spencer figured if she was leaving soon, maybe he should walk her to her car—just to be on the safe side.

He went back to her office door and saw the light was off in the waiting room. He tried the knob: locked. There was a second door in her office. Maybe she'd already gone out that way. Maybe the building was completely deserted—except for him.

He turned and started toward the stairs. But he heard a door hinge squeak. He stopped and swiveled around. "Diane?"

Spencer gazed at the empty hallway. There was an alcove at the far end—on the right. He didn't see anyone. He waited for another sound, but there was nothing.

He suddenly wanted to get out of there. He backed away toward the stairs and then hurried down to the little lobby. Heading toward the door, Spencer glanced over his shoulder at a shadowy nook on the other side of the stairs. He didn't see anyone, but couldn't be certain that somebody wasn't hiding there.

"You're freaking yourself out," he muttered. Then again, he had every reason to be scared.

Spencer grabbed the doorknob and gave it a pull. The door didn't budge.

For a moment, he thought he was locked inside this empty building, which might not actually be empty.

He'd never been here this late. The door had always opened easily when he'd left on previous visits. Then he noticed the second lock on the door—just below eye level. It was a little brass box with a small knob. He twisted the knob and then tugged at the door again. The door opened, and he ran outside.

The cold air and rain actually felt refreshing.

Catching his breath, Spencer started toward the bus stop—three blocks away. He pulled his sweatshirt hood over his head and adjusted the shoulder straps to his backpack. He glanced around, keeping his eye out for that black Toyota Corolla.

He thought about Bonnie again, and wondered if she was all right. She was the only person at school he considered an ally, and he wanted to trust her. He hoped Diane was wrong about her. He really liked her.

But then, he had a history of liking the wrong person.

Diane switched off the light in the waiting room and locked the outside door. She jotted a few notes about her session with Spencer. She'd been following the story about the murders of the Queen Anne family, but had no idea the police had questioned Spencer about the murders until his phone message yesterday. She had a feeling she'd be hearing from Spencer or the police while she was at her house on Vashon Island this week.

She was turning off the lights when she found Spencer's copy of *The Grapes of Wrath* beside the chair. His name was in it—along with some notes in the margins and yellow-highlighted sections. The poor kid, along with everything else that was going wrong, he'd be without his book for school. The last thing she wanted to do tonight was drive to Queen Anne and return it to him. But Spencer probably needed it before Monday. And he probably needed some help talking to his aunt—and to the police. Diane had a feeling she'd be stuck there for hours. She hadn't even had dinner yet.

She thought she heard the front door shut downstairs. It was supposed to be locked after seven-thirty, but sometimes it didn't close all the way. She wondered if it was Spencer, coming back for his book.

With the paperback in her hand, Diane opened the door to the waiting room—and then the door to the hallway. She heard footsteps on the stairs.

"Spencer?" she called. "You forgot your book."

The footsteps stopped. There was silence.

"Spencer? Is that you?"

No answer.

Suddenly uneasy, Diane ducked back into the waiting room. She locked the door and retreated inside her darkened office. She wondered if it was a burglar or a vagrant. They'd had a break-in about two months ago—some idiot thinking these were medical offices full of drugs. And last month, they'd found a homeless man sleeping under the stairs.

She could hear the footsteps again—this time, in the corridor.

Could it possibly be Spencer? Maybe he just hadn't heard her call to him. He could have been plugged into his smart phone music like every other kid out there. She didn't want to call the police if it was him.

She had a small canister of mace in her purse, which was on her desk.

She tossed Spencer's book onto the easy chair and hurried to her desk. But she heard something that made her stop in her tracks. It was the sound of keys jangling—a lot of keys. Someone was trying to unlock the door to the waiting room. She knew it couldn't be the custodian. He worked only on weekends.

Diane was about to switch on her desk lamp when she heard the lock click on the outside door. A moment later, a thin line of light appeared at the threshold of her office door. Whoever it was, they'd gotten into the waiting room and turned on the light.

She watched the doorknob twitch.

Grabbing the purse from her desk, she rifled through it for the little canister of mace. "Who's there?" she yelled in her most forceful voice.

She heard the keys rattling again. Then the lock clicked. "I've called the police!" she lied.

The door opened, and Diane froze.

With the light behind him, it looked like Spencer—in his hooded sweatshirt. He paused in the doorway and tossed a big ring full of keys on the sofa in the waiting room. They hit the cushion with a clatter.

"Spencer?" she asked, uncertain.

"You said he left one of his books?" It wasn't Spencer's voice.

Diane still had a hand in her purse, groping for the mace canister. "Who are you?"

"He left something behind. Good," the stranger said, stepping into her office.

Now she could see him better. She noticed he was wearing surgical gloves. She could see his eyes. He was looking down at her easy chair—and Spencer's copy of *The Grapes of Wrath*. "Now the police will find it here—when they find you."

"What?" Diane asked. She still had one hand in her purse. Her fingertips brushed against something that felt like the little canister.

He darted toward the chair. She thought he was going for the book. But he swiped the glass Saturn sphere off the side table. Holding it up in the air, he rushed toward her.

"No, wait!" Diane screamed, dropping the purse. The little canister of mace spilled out and rolled along the carpet. She put her hands up to fend him off. But she was too late.

He slammed the glass sphere against her skull.

There was a loud crack.

But it wasn't the glass.

# CHAPTER TWENTY-ONE

*Tuesday—8:26 p.m.*

With the collar of her trench coat turned up, Andrea stood outside Vios, a Greek restaurant on Nineteenth Avenue. The raindrops on the flat metal awning above competed a bit with her cell phone conversation. "Spencer's getting gyros to go," she told Luke. "Did you have dinner yet? Can we order something for you?"

Andrea had loathed the idea of Spencer wandering around Capitol Hill alone at night—especially with everything that was happening lately. So when he'd missed his bus and called her, she was all too happy to come pick him up. And she was so relieved to learn that he'd found that Dodgers cap in his school locker. Without any prompting, he'd brought it up soon after climbing into her car at the bus stop. When she'd first found the cap hidden in Spencer's closet, Andrea couldn't help imagining the worst. Now there was an explanation.

She understood why he'd been reluctant to tell the police about it yesterday. Like him, she'd reached a point in that police interrogation room where she would have said or suppressed anything if it meant getting out of there any sooner.

Spencer had explained about the rash of macabre pranks going around school. So Andrea clung to the hope that maybe the Dodgers cap in his locker was just a sick joke. But she had a feeling it was something far more malignant than that. Either way, they'd have to let the police know. There would probably be another round of questions. But on the plus side, they had a little time to brace themselves for it. Spencer said that Diane had volunteered to talk to the police and vouch for his character. Now at least they had someone else in their corner.

Andrea needed to let Luke know about this latest development. No surprises this time. She didn't want him coming home from late rehearsals to find a police car in his driveway.

Spencer hadn't eaten yet. So, while he ordered gyros to go, she stepped out of the noisy restaurant to phone Luke. He said he'd be heading home in about twenty minutes. He'd already had dinner with the director and some cast members.

Andrea watched the rain drip off the metal awning. "Listen, there's been a potential new wrinkle in what the police were investigating yesterday," she said into the phone. "It could be nothing, or it could be pretty

serious. Anyway, do you want to hear about it now—
or when you get home?"

"Oh, Jesus," he muttered. "What is it?"

She told him about Spencer's discovery in his school
locker yesterday—and all the possible implications. He
was silent on the other end. When she finished talking,
she heard him sigh.

"Let's not call the police until I get home, okay?" he
said at last.

"All right, sounds good to me," she said. "I'm sorry
about this, Luke."

"It's not your fault. See you in a bit."

She heard a click.

Andrea slipped the phone into the pocket of her
trench coat and then walked to the far end of the building, where the restaurant's awning still shielded her
from the downpour. She gazed up at the church tower
against the rainy night sky. She still didn't know how
things stood with Luke and her. Would he be spending
the night on the couch in his study again? Or maybe
they'd all be spending the night at the police station.

"Aunt Dee?"

She glanced back at Spencer, who was standing outside the restaurant door with a big white bag in his
hands. "Sorry it took so long," he said. "Did you get
ahold of Luke?"

She nodded. "How about you?" she asked. "Did you
talk to Diane?"

He shook his head. "She wasn't picking up. But I
left a message."

Andrea managed a smile. "I'm sure she'll call back,"
she said. "C'mon, your dinner's going to get cold."

In the rain, they hurried across the street to where she'd parked the VW.

It still had the scratch on the driver's door.

### Tuesday—8:50 p.m.

He'd been sitting behind the wheel of the parked Mazda CX-9 for the last half hour. He held his breath and felt his heart pounding every time a cop car drove by. It was scary, but kind of exciting, too. It gave him a rush and got him pumped up for what he was about to do.

He'd stolen the Mazda early this afternoon. He'd taken it from one of those cut-rate parking lots near the airport. He figured it might be hours or even days before the owner missed it. Still, he was on his guard.

Raindrops covered the windshield and tapped on the car roof. It was cold in the car, and twice now he'd turned on the engine to get a blast of heat and defog the windows.

He was parked on a four-lane, one-way street, half a block down from the theater where Luke Shuler was working on his new play. They were rehearsing late again. The man had been here before—twice in the last week, observing and plotting. He'd sat in a café on the corner, watching the theater from there.

Last night, Luke hadn't come to rehearsals.

So he'd driven to Luke's town house and spotted the squad cars parked in front of it. He'd figured they were questioning him in connection with the Logan family murders. At the time, he couldn't help smiling and wondering how that bastard felt with the cops breathing down his neck.

Now he was waiting for Luke to come out the theater's side door and head to his green Mini Cooper, parked across the street.

Only he would never make it to the car.

As soon as he saw Luke and had a good shot, he'd step on the gas—pedal to the metal—and plow right into him. If everything went his way, the son of a bitch wouldn't die immediately. He'd linger in agony for a while.

The man at the wheel glanced at his wristwatch. It felt as if he'd been waiting there an eternity. His hands were sweating against the steering wheel.

Then, at last, it looked like the theater's side door was opening.

Starting up the car, he switched on the wipers to get a better look across the way. He turned on the heat to defog the windshield and rolled down his window to hasten the process.

He spotted Luke among a group of people emerging from the side door. Luke held a big black umbrella, which he shared with a thin woman who looked like somebody's grandmother. She must have been a character actress—or maybe some rich-bitch contributor to the theater group. "Well, Grandma, you better get your ass out of the way," the man in the driver's seat muttered.

He didn't give a damn about collateral damage. If he had to mow down some old hag, he wouldn't hesitate—as long as it meant killing Luke Shuler.

The wipers let out a groan as they moved across the windshield—almost like the distant sound of someone wailing in pain.

On the sidewalk in front of the theater, Luke led the older woman to a BMW parked at the curb. He held the umbrella up while she climbed into the car. Then he waved to her as she drove off. It looked like he was about to cross the rain-slick street.

The man in the Mazda CX-9 went to switch on his headlights, but decided against it. He'd do it at the last second. He didn't want Luke to see him coming, not until it was too late to jump out of the way.

Some cute actress type with a red umbrella stopped Luke and chatted with him on the sidewalk for a couple of minutes.

"C'mon, c'mon, you fucker," growled the man at the wheel. He shifted to Drive, but kept his foot on the brake.

Luke finally started to back away from the girl. He waved at her, then turned and stepped over a puddle by the curb. There was a lull in traffic. Luke started across the empty four-lane road.

The driver slowly pulled away from the curb. He waited until Luke was in the middle lane. Then he stepped on the gas. The tires screeched and the car swerved as he sped up the street.

The red umbrella woman screamed. Luke froze.

The driver switched on the brights, knowing he'd just blinded his target for a few seconds.

Squinting in the bright glare, Luke dropped his umbrella. He put a hand up to shield his eyes. He seemed panic-stricken. He looked so silly—almost comical—

with that terrified expression on his face. The man at the wheel had to laugh, and he pressed harder on the accelerator.

Luke tried to leap out of the way, but he was too late.

The loud, heavy thud against the Mazda's front bumper didn't slow down its driver—not even when Luke bounced off the hood and smashed into the windshield. A crack splintered across the glass. Blood mixed with raindrops. Luke's broken body rolled off the passenger side of the car.

It all happened in an instant. The girl with the red umbrella was still screaming.

The driver pressed harder on the gas. The Mazda skidded slightly and then got some traction. He sped through a traffic light and stole a glance in his rearview mirror. He had to slow down for a moment to take it all in.

Traffic had come to a standstill behind him. The other cars' headlights illuminated the lifeless thing in the middle of the rain-soaked street. Beside Luke's body, the wind caught his open umbrella. It seemed to skip across the pavement on its own.

The man in the Mazda smiled and drove on.

# CHAPTER TWENTY-TWO

***Wednesday, October 28—12:53 a.m.***

They couldn't find the car.

Andrea and Spencer wandered around the "Kangaroo" level of the hospital's underground parking garage in search of her red VW. The cavernous concrete space was well lit, but still seemed eerie. Despite the late hour, the parking level was at least three-quarters full. Yet there wasn't another person in sight. Andrea had tried clicking the locking device on her key ring so that she could track the car's locale from the beep. But there was a strange echo in the garage, which distorted the sound.

"This is ridiculous," Spencer muttered. "I think we've covered this whole floor . . ."

She knew they were on the right level. The buttons on the elevator each had a different animal and color: white elephant for level A; blue lion for level B; orange kangaroo for level C; and so on. Andrea remembered their level was orange kangaroo, but had absolutely no recall as to which direction they'd gone to reach the elevators.

When they'd arrived at the hospital over three hours ago, making mental notes about where they'd parked the car hadn't really occurred to Andrea. At the time, all she could think about was Luke—and trying not to get into an accident on the way to the hospital.

She'd wondered why he hadn't beaten them home earlier. She'd called him twice, and instead of his regular message, she'd gotten a generic recording: "The cellular customer you're trying to reach is unavailable right now . . ." Something had to be wrong with his phone—or with him. By nine-forty, she was about to call the theater when Jim Munchel, the play's assistant director, phoned.

"Luke's been in an accident," he said. "They took him to Harborview . . ."

The ER waiting area was crowded and chaotic. Two cops were there, getting statements from some of Luke's theater associates who had witnessed the hit-and-run.

"All we know is that he's alive and they've moved him into the OR," Jim told her. He was a handsome, brown-haired, bearded man in his late thirties. He told her that from the erratic way the car had been moving, it looked like a drunk driver had hit Luke. Because of the rain and how fast the hit-and-run had happened, no one had gotten a look at the license plate number.

Andrea couldn't help thinking the hit-and-run was no random accident. "It's got to be connected to everything else that's happened recently," she told the sturdy-looking young policewoman who had interviewed Jim. The cop had a smooth ebony complexion and short-cropped hair. Her partner—with his eighties-throwback sideburns and mustache—looked like a young Burt Reynolds. While Andrea tried to explain to them about the previous night's marathon interview with Detective Talwar, they kept getting interrupted by a skinny, demented-looking, thirty-something woman. She had a tattoo on her neck and a gash on her forehead, and she wanted them to arrest her boyfriend.

Spencer told them about finding Reed's baseball cap in his school locker. He said he had it at home in a plastic bag—in case they needed it as evidence. He admitted that he'd been too scared to tell Detective Talwar about it yesterday.

The policewoman muttered something to her partner and then headed outside. The other officer frowned at Andrea and Spencer. "Is there anything else you didn't tell Detective Talwar yesterday?"

"No," Andrea said. She was too concerned about Luke to let this cop intimidate her. She got up and checked with the receptionist again—to see if they had an update on Luke. They didn't.

Over the next half hour, most of Luke's theater friends left, but Jim stayed. Andrea kept waiting for a doctor to come around the corner with news about Luke. She spotted the policewoman walking in through the smudged sliding-glass doors. Scratching the back of her neck, she approached them. "Well, I spoke with Detective Talwar," she said. "About the Dodgers cap, it looks like your nephew has some comedians at his high school. Someone must have left that cap in your locker as a joke. Detective Talwar said they found Reed Logan's Dodgers cap in his bedroom when they responded to the nine-one-one call from his older brother."

Andrea felt a tiny bit of relief at that news. She patted Spencer's arm. "When we get home tonight, you can throw that damn thing out."

The police didn't hang around for very long after that.

It was another two hours before a tall, forty-something man with a full head of blond hair emerged from around the corner. He was wearing green scrubs. As he conferred with the receptionist, Andrea prayed this was their doctor. By this time, she'd had a few false alarms. Just for luck, she didn't get up from her chair as he came toward them—not until he addressed her.

"Ms. Boyle?" he said.

She, Spencer, and Jim all jumped to their feet. "Yes?" she said.

He nodded. "I'm Luke's surgeon, Dr. Cegielski. Can I talk with you alone?"

"Of course," she said, suddenly a little short of breath. She followed him to a quiet corner of the room, where someone had tacked on the wall a skeleton decoration for Halloween. Andrea couldn't read from the doctor's expression what kind of news he had for her: good or terrible. "Is he going to be okay?" she asked with a tremor in her voice.

The doctor sighed. "We had to remove his spleen."

Andrea numbly stared at him.

He began to list all the injuries Luke had sustained—including a pelvic fracture, three broken ribs, a tibia fracture, a broken arm, multiple sprains, cuts, and lacerations. "He was very, very lucky there was no serious head trauma or spinal injury. But he's still in critical condition. We've moved him to the ICU."

"Can I see him?" Andrea asked.

He shook his head. "I'm sorry. I recommend you go home, get some sleep, and come back tomorrow afternoon. He won't be ready for visitors any time before then."

That had been nearly a half hour ago. She'd thanked the doctor. Then she and Spencer had said goodbye to Jim. They'd both become so bewildered and turned around that they'd had a tough time locating the elevator to the parking garage.

And now they couldn't find the damn car.

"Wait, is that it?" Spencer said, nodding to a gap between two parked SUVs against a far wall.

Andrea pointed the key fob in that direction and pressed the unlock button. They heard a beep and saw a subtle flash of light between the two SUVs. "Hallelujah," Andrea muttered, and they headed toward the car. Their footsteps echoed within the vast concrete space.

Andrea heard a mechanical whoosh sound, and glanced over her shoulder. A tall, thin balding man in a leather jacket stepped off the elevator. He had his hands in his jacket pockets. He seemed to be staring at them.

Andrea picked up the pace and nudged Spencer. "C'mon, let's go . . ."

He glanced back and hesitated. "Who's that?" he whispered. "Do you know him?"

"No, and at one in the morning, I don't want an introduction," she said under her breath. "C'mon."

The man was coming toward them. He walked at a brisk clip—as if he were about to break into a sprint at any minute.

She and Spencer hurried to her Volkswagen Beetle, sandwiched between the two SUVs. "Get in, get in," she whispered, opening her door.

"It's locked!" he hissed, frantically tugging at the passenger door handle. "You have to hit the thing again!"

The stranger seemed to be zeroing in on them.

Andrea pressed the device again, and heard the lock click. She jumped in behind the wheel while Spencer scurried into the passenger side. She flicked the universal door lock on her armrest and then jammed the key into the ignition.

"Wait," Spencer said, putting his hand on her arm.

Breathless, she paused and looked up at the man about twenty feet away. He pulled a key out of his pocket as he trotted to a Honda Civic parked in the last spot of the row directly in front of them. She and Spencer silently watched him start up the car, pull out of the space, and drive up the ramp.

Spencer burst out laughing.

Andrea began to laugh as well. But then something caught in her throat, and the tears started to come. Clutching the steering wheel, she leaned forward and sobbed.

She felt Spencer's hand on her shoulder. "Luke's going to be okay," she heard him say. "Really, Aunt Dee, he'll be all right. It's all going to be okay."

She wished to God she could believe him.

\* \* \*

"Okay, this is from something called Healthlink Forum," Spencer said, looking at Andrea's smart phone. He was slouched in the passenger seat.

At the wheel, Andrea nodded, but she kept her eyes on the road ahead. The rain had stopped. They were about three blocks from the town house. Reaching for the dash, she blindly felt around for the volume knob and turned down "Under the Boardwalk" on her oldies station. "Okay, go on . . ."

"It says, 'People can live a long life without a spleen . . .'"

She nodded. "That's the good news. I thought so. But there's a big *but* coming up, isn't there?"

"It's a *however,*" Spencer replied glumly. He went back to reading off the smart phone's screen. " 'However, because the spleen helps the body fight bacteria, living without this organ can make someone very susceptible to dangerous infections, including pneumonia, meningitis, and influenza.'"

Biting her lip, Andrea tried to hold back her tears. She was thinking about Luke and the weeks ahead for him just learning to walk again—and the months of recovery after that. And yet, his life would never be the same. He'd been so healthy and resilient. She knew many introverted writers who loathed having to promote their work, travel, and interact with their reading public. But Luke seemed to thrive on it. Now he'd have to be careful about traveling and getting together with people. He'd have to avoid crowds and take all sorts of precautions.

Why did this happen? Until just a few hours ago, she'd thought someone might be targeting her or Spencer, implicating them in the Logan family murders. But now this person seemed to be going after Luke. Why? What did Luke do? What had any of them done to deserve this?

She pulled into the driveway, parked, and turned off the ignition. She gazed at the Spanish-style town house. The garden she'd started in front sort of put her own stamp on it. They'd left some lights on. At least they wouldn't have to walk into a dark house.

She and Spencer climbed out of the VW and started up the walk to the front door. "I think I'll ditch school tomorrow and go to the hospital with you—if that's okay," he said.

Andrea took the house key out of her purse and then checked her watch. If he went to bed right now, he'd need to be up for school in five and a half hours. "It's okay with me," she said with a sigh as she unlocked the door.

Andrea took a step inside, but hesitated. The house was quiet. The alarm should have been beeping. She realized they'd left in such a hurry that she'd forgotten to set it.

"What's wrong?" Spencer asked, unzipping his hooded sweatshirt.

"Nothing—"

All at once, the silence was broken. Glass shattered somewhere upstairs.

Andrea froze. At first, she thought someone had thrown a rock through a window again. But this seemed to come from inside. Then she heard the rumble of foot-steps directly above them.

The hair stood up on the back of her neck. "Oh,

Jesus, someone's in the house," she whispered, grabbing Spencer's arm.

Andrea frantically pulled him toward the door.

He resisted. "I have a gun!" he yelled.

All she could think was the intruder had nowhere to go. He'd have to come down the stairs right in front of them. There was a back door in the kitchen, but no back stairway. Spencer didn't seem to realize the stranger upstairs—unlike them—probably really did have a gun.

The floorboards creaked. It sounded like the prowler was at the top of the steps.

"Spencer, for God's sake . . ." She flung the door open and dragged him outside.

Andrea shut the door after them. She remembered Spencer still had her smart phone. "Call nine-one-one!" she said, pulling him down the walkway toward her car. She expected someone to come charging out the front door at any minute.

With a shaky hand, she dug her car key out of her purse and pressed the unlocking device. The car beeped and the headlights flashed. "Get in!" she hissed. "Hurry . . ."

With the phone in his hand, Spencer paused to look back at the house.

Andrea wasn't sure, but she thought she heard a door slam. Had the intruder run out the back way?

She ducked into the car and Spencer got into the passenger seat. Andrea locked the car doors, and put the key in the ignition.

"It's ringing," Spencer said.

She grabbed the phone out of his hand. "Thanks," she said, catching her breath. They both watched the town house. None of the outside lights were on. Anyone could have been hiding in those shadows—those pockets of blackness behind the trees and shrubs. There was a fence in back. Andrea kept expecting to see someone emerge from the bushes alongside the house.

"Seattle Police Emergency," the 911 operator finally answered.

"Yes, someone broke into my house at nine-one-five Olympic Drive in Queen Anne," Andrea said.

"Is the perpetrator still on the premises, ma'am?"

Andrea tried to steady her voice. "He could be," she said. "I'm afraid to go back inside. I'm in my car in the driveway—with my nephew. Could you—could you send someone right away?"

They found the shattered glass—a bottle of witch hazel that had fallen from the open medicine chest and smashed in the bathroom sink. Except for the open kitchen door, there was no other evidence that anyone had broken into the town house. The police did a room-to-room check with him and his aunt, and they couldn't find anything missing or damaged.

One of the cops suggested the intruder had been looking for drugs in the medicine chest. He said that some thieves had police scanners. When an accident got reported, the thief would go to the victim's address—counting on the probability that no one would be home. He suggested that something like that may have happened here. The cop said it was very unlikely the culprit would be returning anytime soon, but they'd keep an eye on the house tonight.

Spencer figured that was something he had in common with Bonnie. Both of them had the cops watching their homes tonight. She'd probably fallen asleep hours ago.

He thought of Diane's warning not to trust Bonnie. But he was pretty disappointed in his therapist. She'd acted as if she would be there for him at a moment's notice if he needed someone to vouch for him with the police. Well, he'd phoned her earlier tonight, much earlier, and she still hadn't called back.

He glanced at the digital clock on his nightstand: 3:18 a.m. He'd heard his aunt get up to use the washroom about ten minutes ago. Neither one of them were able to sleep.

He didn't buy the cop's theory about tonight's break-in. This wasn't random. It was personal. If someone had been looking for drugs here, that was merely secondary.

Spencer wondered if their intruder had broken in to search for the baseball cap. Maybe he—or she—had been worried their DNA was on it or something. And now they wanted it back.

He threw off the covers and crept out of bed. Padding over to the closet, he turned on the light and lifted the pile of sweaters. The cap was still there—in the plastic bag. He carefully took it out.

He saw how the brim was sweat-stained and worn in spots. This wasn't a hat someone had bought recently for some stupid prank. Someone wore this—and for a long time.

Detective Talwar probably had a pat answer for that. She'd say the prankster probably bought it used—or stole it. Why would someone buy a brand-new hat just to play a prank?

Besides, Detective Talwar said they'd found Reed's Dodgers cap in his bedroom—at the same time they'd found him and his parents dead.

Spencer slipped the hat back inside the Gap bag and set it on the closet shelf. No sense in hiding it under the sweaters anymore. Everyone knew he had it.

He switched off the closet light, and crawled back under the covers.

He thought about Reed and that stupid cap. It had been his trademark. He wore it to school every day, and took it off only when a teacher insisted he do so. Those were the only times Spencer ever saw him without that damn Dodgers cap on. He'd overheard someone say that Reed had worn the cap all summer long, too. The brim on it would have been in terrible shape. In fact, the whole hat would have been tattered and frayed. With that much use, it would have been falling apart—unless, of course, Reed had two identical caps.

Now the police had one of them, and he had the other.

Spencer turned over on his side, but his eyes were wide open.

He was convinced the Dodgers cap hadn't been planted in his locker as a joke. It was a trophy from a kill.

And the killer wanted him to have it.

# CHAPTER TWENTY-THREE

*Thursday, October 29—4:22 p.m.*

"I'm understudying the part of the secretary, Mabel, which is practically one of the leads," Tanya said. "If Elizabeth Noll gets sick or anything, I have to take over for her. I have to know the music and choreography for all her scenes as well as my own."

Sitting across from her in the intensive care unit's waiting room, Andrea had stopped really listening about ten minutes ago. She worked up a smile. "Well, it's really nice of you to give up valuable rehearsal time to come here, Tanya. I'm just sorry you can't see Luke. But as I said, because of his condition, they've put restrictions on the number of visitors . . ."

When Andrea had taken Spencer to see Luke a half hour ago, they'd had to wear surgical masks, smocks, and gloves as a precaution against infections. It was Spencer's first look at Luke since the accident, and he was visibly taken aback. Andrea thought Luke's appearance had improved a little since yesterday. At least, some of the swelling had gone down. Nearly half of him was covered in bandages and splints. He had a tube in his nose, and a machine hooked up to a line into his banged-up, purplish arm. His face was bruised and still slightly bloated. The painkillers they'd given him had slurred his speech, and he seemed out of it. Yet, when he saw Spencer, he worked up a smile and muttered, "Hey, Spencer. Sorry I can't get up . . ."

Andrea knew how Spencer felt to see sturdy, robust Luke suddenly so broken and frail. Spencer made some awkward small talk, but almost seemed relieved when a nurse came in and had them clear out so that she could change the dressings on Luke's wounds.

They silently shed the smocks, masks, and gloves, and then tossed them into a laundry bin. Then they headed back toward the small waiting room with its two beige couches, each flanked by end tables with a fake plant and a Kleenex box.

When they'd gone in to see Luke, the TV bracketed to the wall had been showing an old episode of *Two and a Half Men*. But on their return, they found the TV tuned in to *The Ellen Show*, and Tanya McCallum sitting on one of the couches, the remote control in her hand. Andrea immediately knew it was her from what Spencer had told her about Tanya's odd taste in thrift-store attire. Today she was wearing aqua slacks and a yellow peasant blouse from the 1970s.

Apparently, Tanya had told the hospital receptionist that she was practically family, and she'd insisted she be given a pass to the ICU wing. It baffled Andrea that without any clearance, they'd allowed this teenager, who looked and dressed like a crazy person, to visit someone in Intensive Care who was sort of a public figure. Spencer had said Tanya was pretty damn pushy and bossy. Maybe that explained it.

For the last fifteen minutes, Tanya had been talking about her part in the school play and how she was missing rehearsals right now. Now she was jabbering about all the other people in the play—as if Andrea already knew them or was supposed to care.

Spencer finally cleared his throat and asked her, "Don't you want to know how Luke's doing? You haven't even asked about him."

Andrea wanted to cheer him for shutting Tanya up for a second.

"Well, why do you think I'm here?" she asked. "Did they let you see him? How does he look?"

"Have you seen *Misery*?" Spencer asked. "Because that's how he looks—like James Caan in *Misery* when he woke up in bed after the car crash—all banged up and practically dead. Only Luke looks worse."

Tanya let out a long, dramatic sigh. "That's so awful. Who would do a thing like this?"

"You mean, you really don't have any idea?" Spencer pressed.

"What's that supposed to mean?"

"It's a legitimate question," Andrea chimed in. "You've known Mr. Shuler longer than we have, Tanya. If this hit-and-run is connected in any way with what's been going on at the school—well, you've been there a lot longer than Spencer. You were friends with Damon, and familiar with the people who bullied him. You'd have a better idea than either of us who might have done something like this."

Tanya squirmed. "Listen, I don't know why you think I have some inside scoop about who's behind this accident—or the stuff going on at school . . ."

"And you don't have, like, even a vague notion of who might have killed Reed Logan and his parents?" Spencer asked.

"God, you're almost as bad as the police, questioning me the night before last," Tanya said. "Okay, I didn't like Reed. He was a total creep to me. But I didn't kill him, and I have no idea who did. And as for Damon's father, I'm a huge fan of his. Why do you think I skipped rehearsals to come here? I have no idea who would want to hurt him. Damon's father didn't have any enemies."

"How can you say that?" Spencer asked. "I mean, for starters, there's that Troy or Trey guy we saw at the memorial service, the actor who dated Mrs. Shuler. Just looking at him, it was obvious to me he hates Luke's guts . . ."

"You mean Troy Slattery?" she asked. "Well, I really don't know how he feels about Luke. I've never met him."

"But at the memorial, you said you met him twice at Damon's mother's place . . ."

She shrugged. "Okay, but that doesn't mean I *know* him."

Andrea wondered if Tanya was really involved in all of this—or was she just one of those people who always acted like she knew everyone and everything when she really didn't. "Tanya, did Damon ever talk about this Troy person with you?" she asked.

"Well, maybe, I guess," she muttered. "But it's not like they were together a long time. Troy and Mrs. Shuler were seeing each other for, like, only two months or so."

It occurred to Andrea that Tanya could be protecting her fellow actor, Troy Slattery. Someone close to Evelyn had to be behind all this. No one else would have that inside information about Reed having worked for her. Troy seemed the most likely candidate.

Andrea had wondered if he was Evelyn's errand boy, the one who had broken into the apartment in Ballard. But then she'd figured Evelyn had broken up with him by that time. So why would Troy be doing Evelyn any favors?

Now it occurred to her. Maybe he'd hoped to win Evelyn back. It would explain why he'd stolen Evelyn's photo in the silver frame.

"Excuse me," Andrea said, working up a polite smile for Tanya. "I need to use the restroom."

As she started down the hallway, she heard Tanya muttering to Spencer: "Why are you and your aunt giving me such a hard time?"

Since yesterday morning, Andrea had checked twice with the police about their follow-up investigation into the hit-and-run. So far, they had no suspects. However, they'd found the Mazda CX-9 that had barreled into Luke. The vehicle had a cracked windshield and Luke's blood on the hood. The rain hadn't completely washed it away. The car had been stolen from the E-Z Park & Fly lot by Sea-Tac Airport, and been abandoned in the lot of a defunct Ethiopian restaurant called Empress of the Nile near the Central District.

Andrea fished her smart phone out of her purse, but then noticed the signs posted in the corridor: NO CELL PHONE USE—with the circle and slash symbol over an image of a cell phone. She spotted an exit sign over a doorway just down the hall. Hurrying to the door, she pushed it open and found herself in a gray cinderblock stairwell. She didn't see any signs about cell phone restrictions in the stairwell. Slipping off her shoe, she set it in the doorway to keep the door from shutting all the way. She didn't want to chance getting locked out of the ICU.

She Googled "Troy Slattery, actor" and found him listed on the Internet Movie Database as appearing in *Fifty Shades of Grey*. Andrea found his name listed sixth from the bottom of the complete cast list:

Second Man in Airport     Troy Slattery *(uncredited)*

There were no other film credits. The other search results linked to cast lists of several plays performed in Seattle. She tried Google Image and found two photos in the second row that must have been publicity shots. He had a dark, dangerous look to him, broodingly handsome with sexy eyes and a five o'clock shadow. She tried the links, but the pictures were from playbills—without any contact information.

Andrea glanced over her shoulder to make sure her shoe was still in the doorway. On her phone's call history, she found the number for Jim Munchel, Luke's assistant director and friend.

He answered after the third ring: "Hi, Andrea. How's Luke doing?"

"Better, I think," she said. "They're keeping him in the ICU at least until Saturday. Listen, I'm wondering if you have an address for an actor Luke worked with, Troy Slattery."

"Troy Slattery?" he asked, sounding baffled. "Why would you need his address?"

"Ah, he sent Luke flowers," she lied. "I thought I'd shoot off a thank-you note to him."

"That's one for Ripley's," Jim said.

Andrea looked back at the door again. "What do you mean?"

"I can't believe Troy would do something that thoughtful for anyone—least of all, Luke."

"Well, I know Troy and Evelyn had a thing, but—"

"If there was a card with the flowers, I'm sure he wrote something snide on it," Jim said. "Troy was a real hothead—and total screwup. Luke tried to give him a chance, and he shit all over it. On top of that, he had a major drug problem—crystal meth. Luke finally had to fire him. It was a real mess . . ."

"Well, maybe Troy got his act together and was trying to make amends," she said. "Anyway, do you have an address for him?"

"Just a sec. Let me see if I have anything current here. I don't think he's worked for a couple of months . . ."

The address was on East Capitol Hill.

Andrea checked Mapquest.com and saw that Troy lived less than a mile from Empress of the Nile in the

Central District. If he was the one who had mowed down Luke, he'd had an easy walk home after ditching the car.

She checked how far Troy's Twenty-fourth Street address was from the hospital. That was walking distance, too.

"Aunt Dee?"

She swiveled around and gaped at Spencer in the corridor. He stared at her through the crack in the doorway. "I've been looking all over for you," he murmured.

"I just needed to make a call," she said.

He held the door open for her while she put her shoe back on. "I thought something might have happened to you. The nurse said Luke wants to see you."

She nodded and then slipped her phone back inside her purse. "Thanks," she said, stepping back into the corridor. She was about to start down the hallway, but Spencer took hold of her arm.

"Listen, Luke only asked for you," he whispered. "I feel kind of useless around here. Would you mind if I grab a bus with Tanya back to Queen Anne?"

Andrea sighed. "You'd be doing me a huge favor if you got her out of here. But I really don't like the idea of you being alone—not after that break-in the other night."

"Well, visiting hours are over at eight," Spencer said. "You'll get home at—what—eight-thirty? I'll be okay until then . . ."

Andrea gave him thirty dollars so he could order a pizza. She made him promise he'd call her when he got back to Luke's—and that he'd double-lock the doors. Spencer kept assuring her that he'd be fine. Still, she felt uneasy sending him off with Tanya.

Before entering Luke's private room, Andrea donned the required surgical mask, smock, and gloves. If he'd been cognizant enough to ask for her a few minutes ago, he seemed pretty out of it now. The TV bracketed to the wall was showing Marlon Brando up on the tenement roof with his pigeons and Eva Marie Saint. Leonard Bernstein's love theme was reaching a crescendo. But Luke was oblivious—and he loved *On the Waterfront*. He was either drugged up or in great pain.

Andrea ducked into his bathroom, where she ran a washcloth under the cold water and wrung it out. She gently dabbed Luke's bruised forehead with the cool, damp washcloth.

"You're mothering me again," he muttered with his eyes closed.

"Oh, shut up," she said.

She saw a flicker of a smile on his battered face. "It's okay, I like it."

As she laid the cool washcloth on his head, Andrea thought about Troy Slattery—less than a mile away.

From what Luke had told her, Troy was practically living with Evelyn last May, when Damon was getting bullied at school. Had the two of them formed some kind of bond? Was Troy going after everyone on Damon's hate list? Was Tanya involved, too?

"You don't need to stay, honey," Luke mumbled. "Go home, get some rest. Come back tomorrow. I've got *Waterfront* here to keep me entertained—and I can hardly keep awake for that. I'm so tired . . ."

"Are you awake enough to answer a question?" she asked, hovering over him.

With his eyes closed, he groaned something that sounded like an affirmative.

"Do you think it's possible that Troy Slattery was the one who did this to you?"

His eyes opened, and he seemed to focus on her for a second. "Yes," Luke whispered. "I wouldn't put it past the son of a bitch."

# CHAPTER TWENTY-FOUR

*Thursday—5:22 p.m.*

The bus from Harborview was crammed with rush hour commuters and hospital employees. Despite Tanya's protests that she didn't want to sit next to some stranger, Spencer gave up his seat to an old, frail-looking Asian woman.

As he stood in the aisle, holding on to a bar, he had a few minutes to think about Tanya. He couldn't quite picture her killing anyone, but he could definitely see her working with the killer—or killers. She was the only one alive with an axe to grind for Damon's tormentors. Maybe she'd convinced herself that she was on a noble mission to rid the school of bullies. Or perhaps she had a crush on someone who was manipulating her. Spencer certainly knew what that was like. There wasn't much difference between hero worship and a crush.

Someone like Troy Slattery could easily have her

under his thumb—if he just pretended to like her. She'd probably do just about anything for a guy like that as long as he paid attention to her. Maybe Slattery wasn't telling her everything about what he was doing. If he'd plowed into Luke with that stolen car, he didn't necessarily have to tell Tanya about it.

Spencer tried to put out of his mind that image of Luke in the hospital bed, so battered and broken. It hurt just to look at him.

Tanya had repeatedly contradicted herself when he and Aunt Dee had questioned her in the ICU waiting room. Spencer wondered if she knew about the baseball cap he'd found in his locker. She often came up and talked with him while he was at his locker. She could have seen him working the combination at any time. If she hadn't planted the cap herself, she might have furnished his locker combination to someone who did plant it. And she was the only one who knew about that broken window lock in Bonnie's house.

Spencer hadn't talked with Bonnie much today. It was sort of intentional. She was still sitting at the cool table at lunch. So he'd decided to heed Diane's warning about her and give her a wide berth. Bonnie had approached him in the hallway after chemistry class to tell him how sorry she was to hear about Luke.

"I guess my timing kind of sucks here," she'd added. "But I'm wondering if you want to come with me to a Halloween party at Amanda Brooks's house on Friday night."

"Um, I'm not sure I can get away," Spencer had replied. "Could I let you know later?"

"Sure. Listen, are you mad at me or something?"

"No, I'm just—I need to get to history class."

Spencer had felt bad giving her the brush-off. But for now he'd follow Diane's advice.

He'd realized he must have left his copy of *The Grapes of Wrath* at Diane's office. He'd left her two more messages, but still hadn't heard back from her. He was pretty disappointed in Diane, especially since she'd acted as if he could really count on her.

The bus passed his stop. He got off with Tanya at the top of Queen Anne Hill and offered to walk her home. He wanted to see where she lived. And he wanted to ask her something that had been bothering him for a couple of days now.

It was dark and chilly. The wind kicked up, scattering fallen leaves in their path as they walked through an older neighborhood—with some new construction amid the homes that probably went up long before World War II. Tanya's shoulder occasionally brushed against his. Spencer wasn't sure if it was flirtatious or not. But he used the opportunity to nudge her. "So how come you haven't asked me about my time in the institution?"

"What?" she asked, stopping in her tracks. "You were in an institution? You mean, like a nuthouse? Are you kidding me?"

"You were right there when Reed threw it in my face last week," Spencer reminded her. "I've been wondering why you haven't asked me about it."

She shrugged and started walking again. "I—I don't know what you're talking about."

"You were standing, like, six feet away when he said it."

"Well, I stopped listening to whatever Reed said ages ago. Is it really true?"

"Yes, it is. Before I came here, I was in an institution—or like you said, *a nuthouse*. It was in Milwaukee."

"I thought it was in Virginia," she said. She had barely gotten the words out when she seemed to realize she'd been tricked. She rolled her eyes. "Okay, so I knew—so I heard him. I didn't ask you about it, because I didn't want to be rude."

There she was, caught in another lie. Spencer wondered if he could believe anything that came out of her mouth. "That was a whole week ago," he said. "Weren't you at all curious? Didn't you want to find out whether or not it was true?"

"I figured you'd tell me if you wanted me to know."

"And so you just put it out of your head, is that it? Tanya, no one does that. If you find out someone was institutionalized—someone you see practically every day—you'll want to know why they were institutionalized and how long, stuff like that."

Tanya sighed. "God, what is with you and your aunt this afternoon? All these questions, trying to trip me up, you're *badgering* me."

"It's because you're not being honest with us," Spencer said. "I think you know who's responsible for Reed's murder. That same person was harassing Bonnie Middleton and may have even tried to kill Luke—only they're not telling you about it—"

"That's crazy," Tanya said, walking faster. "Maybe it's not a nice word to use, considering your background, but it's true."

"Tanya, you act like you care about me," Spencer continued. "Well, did you know this same person tried to frame me for Reed's murder? Is it this Troy guy? Are you trying to protect him?"

She stopped and turned toward him. "I told you, I hardly know him! Goddamn it, stop picking on me!"

She hurried ahead of him and then turned up a walkway to a dilapidated bungalow with ugly purple shutters. The lawn was neglected. Spencer's dad used to complain about a house like this one on their block in Silver Spring. He said it was an *eyesore*, and it brought down property values. Spencer couldn't help feeling a little sorry for Tanya, living in a dump like this. It was just her and her divorced mother. People on the block probably hated them.

Tanya paused halfway to her front door and called back to him. "Thanks a lot for walking me home!" Her tone dripped with sarcasm.

"Tanya?" he said, reaching the end of the walkway.

"What?" she answered impatiently.

"It's out there now," he said. "And I'm the one who brought it up. So you aren't being rude. I mean, it just proves my point. You haven't even asked. Aren't you at all curious why I was in an institution?"

Ignoring him, she moved on to her front door, unlocked it, and opened it. She turned back to glare at him. "I already know!" she yelled. "It's because you murdered your parents, you sick bastard! And here I was, trying to be nice to you . . ."

She ducked inside her house and slammed the door.

Spencer felt like someone had just hit him in the gut. He'd heard that before—several times in the hospital and the juvenile detention facility. But hearing Tanya say it—and with such venom—caught him by surprise.

He wondered if she'd known all along—if she'd been the one sending those texts to Luke and Reed. Or had she found out the same way Bonnie had, by looking it up on the Internet after overhearing Reed taunt him about it last week?

The front of the sad, ramshackle house was unlit. Spencer couldn't see anything in the windows. But he noticed a construction site next door. He wasn't sure if Tanya was there in the dark, watching him from one of the windows.

He pretended to continue down the block. Passing the construction site, he spotted a gap in the chain-link fence and slipped through it. The house was just an unfinished shell right now, but there were stairs going up to a second floor. It looked like he would have a view into the windows of that side of Tanya's house, and most of them were lit, too. He made his way across the muddy ground and onto some gravel. Then he hoisted himself up through the opening for a front window. He guessed this dark and creepy area would be someone's living room someday. Right now it smelled like mud and sawdust.

Spencer moved to the stairs, which didn't have a railing. He carefully crept up to the second floor. There was no actual floor, just boards and planks laid out over beams. He precariously made his way to a window across from the McCallums' bungalow. He peered down into their living room.

Tanya had told him that two years ago, her mother

had fallen off a small stepladder at work. Ever since, she'd been milking the minor injury and living on disability, spending most of her day on the couch in front of the Game Show Network on TV. It looked like Tanya had at least been honest about that. Spencer could see the back of a woman with brassy red hair, lying on the sofa with a bed pillow behind her. She was wearing a robe. A TV table near her was covered with a couple of dirty cereal bowls, a bag of Hershey's miniatures, three glasses, and some candy wrappers. He could see the flickering light from an old-model TV set, and he heard muffled chatter. From the tone, it sounded like a game show announcer.

Suddenly a light went on in a room directly across from him. Spencer ducked to one side of the window opening. He realized he was right across from Tanya's bedroom. She had Broadway posters on her wall: *Rent, A Chorus Line,* and *Dreamgirls.* The place was a mess—with an unmade single bed and clothes scattered everywhere.

Spencer watched as Tanya took her cell phone out of her coat pocket. Then she shucked off the coat and threw it on her bed. She looked nervous and agitated. Pacing back and forth, she punched some numbers on the phone. Tanya started talking, but her words were muffled and indistinguishable.

Spencer wondered if she was talking to Troy Slattery.

He knew it couldn't be anyone from school. Her only friend at school had been Damon.

He had no idea who she could be talking to. But he was pretty certain she was talking about him.

*  *  *

"It's not fair," Tanya said into the phone. "I'm help-ing you. I'm protecting you. And I'm the one getting grilled by the police—not to mention Spencer and his aunt. You should have heard them ganging up on me at the hospital. I'm tired of being your decoy."

"But I need you. This is for you, too, Tanya. And everything is falling into place perfectly. I want you to do me a favor. Tell Spencer tomorrow that you planned to take him out to dinner to make up for tonight's little misunderstanding—but you have to meet someone in-stead. Then make a date for Saturday night."

"I don't understand," Tanya said, pacing around her messy bedroom. "Who am I meeting? Is it you? Am I finally going to see you again?"

"You aren't meeting anybody, but we want your boyfriend to think you are. We want him tailing you. And I know you like the attention. I know you have a little crush on him. So wear something pretty for him tomorrow night. Stay home, or maybe take a walk . . ."

"I don't get it," Tanya said.

"You don't have to. We just need you to go on being a decoy a little while longer."

"What are you talking about, *we*?"

"I mean you and me," the person on the other end explained.

Tanya suspected he was working with someone else—besides her. She'd been feeling that way for a while now—even before everyone saw the webcast of Damon and his mother in that fiery car explosion. The news reports about the Logan family said the murders had the earmarks of a two-person job. So she wasn't the only one thinking he had a secret partner.

If only she could look him in the eye and ask him. Then she'd be able to tell if he was lying. But she hadn't seen him in three weeks. It had just been texts and phone calls.

"Are you sure by *we,* you don't mean you and somebody else—some secret partner?" she pressed.

"You're my partner, my only partner. And you're essential."

"I'm your decoy, that's all," she said, frowning at her reflection in the dresser mirror. She could hear the TV downstairs—too loud, as usual. "What makes you so sure Spencer will follow me around tomorrow night? This story about meeting someone, what makes you so sure he'll swallow the bait?"

"Because he didn't even have any bait tonight, and he's on your tail." The person on the other end of the line chuckled. "Don't look, but he's spying on you right now from that unfinished house next door."

Tanya automatically glanced out her window at the skeleton of a house less than twenty feet away. But all she could see past the window openings was blackness. She shuddered.

"I'm watching him watch you," he said on the other end of the line. "You probably thought you were all alone. But the two men in your life are both very close to you right now, Tanya. You just can't see us in the dark."

# CHAPTER TWENTY-FIVE

*Thursday—5:43 p.m.*

Andrea sat at the wheel of her VW, staring at the big, cedar-shingle house across the street. It needed a fresh coat of paint. The front porch light was on, and she could see three separate entrances—green doors, each with a letter on it: *A, B,* and *C.* Andrea counted four mailboxes by the porch steps. Troy Slattery lived in Apartment *D.* Andrea wondered where it was.

She'd left Luke midway through *On the Waterfront.* He'd kept nodding off, and had finally insisted she go home. She didn't tell him she intended to pay a visit to the man she thought may have tried to kill him.

She probably should have called the police—or Detective Talwar. But she didn't have any proof that Troy had driven the Mazda in the hit-and-run. She just knew he hated Luke, and she had some theories. So far, Detective Talwar didn't take much stock in any of her theories. In fact, Andrea was pretty certain the only reason Talwar had paid any attention to her at all was because the police considered Spencer a suspect in the Logan family murders. They didn't want to hear about the possibility of an elaborate conspiracy that involved someone who knew Evelyn Shuler. They were dealing with all sorts of false alarms, threats, and high school pranks. How could she have expected them to follow up on everything she'd told them when most of it was conjecture?

At least Detective Talwar had reviewed Evelyn's bank account. There were no checks written to Reed Logan. Nor were there any check or credit card payments to a private detective agency. That might have debunked Andrea's assumption that Evelyn had hired that private investigator to look into her past. However, Evelyn's bank record showed several large withdrawals over the summer. So she could have paid the detective, Reed, and this other person—the one who broke into their Ballard apartment—with cash or money orders.

Andrea was convinced the other person was Evelyn's onetime lover, Troy.

She wasn't sure if Troy knew what she looked like. And she still hadn't quite figured out how to approach him.

She spotted a stout, sixty-something woman with glasses emerging from apartment A. The woman held a plastic trash bag that seemed about to burst at the seams. She waddled down the porch steps and hauled the bag to a Dumpster on the side of the apartment house.

Andrea climbed out of the car and hurried across the

street. She caught up with the woman just as she closed the Dumpster lid. "Hi, I'm sorry to bother you," she said. "I'm looking for Troy Slattery in Apartment *D*."

"You missed him," the woman answered. "I saw him leave about a half hour ago. But I'm sure one of his roommates is down there . . ."

"Down where?" Andrea asked.

"The basement apartment," the woman explained. "It's around back."

"Do you know if Troy was home last night?"

The woman shrugged. "Beats me. Why don't you ask one of his roommates? And while you're at it, maybe you can ask them to turn down that damn heavy metal music. I can't hear myself think some of the time." She wandered back toward the front porch.

"I'll do that. Thank you!"

Andrea followed a narrow sidewalk to the back of the apartment house. Down four steps was another green door, this one with a *D* on it. Andrea didn't hear any heavy metal music as she rang the doorbell.

There was no answer. She rang the bell again.

"Yeah, come in, it's not locked!" she heard a woman yell.

Biting her lip, Andrea opened the door and stepped into the apartment, which smelled of stale marijuana smoke. She found herself in a hallway across from an untidy living room. It was a strange mix of banged-up furniture and expensive-looking toys—like the big flat-screen TV, which played the news on mute to the unoccupied room. The sofa in front of it was losing its stuffing and looked as if it might have been picked up off a curb somewhere. She wondered if the TV—along with the stereo equipment—had been stolen off a truck or from someone's house. She scanned the room for her mother's silver frame.

"Who's there?" the woman called—from the other end of the long hallway.

"I'm here to see Troy!" Andrea replied, raising her voice. "I'm a friend of Evelyn Shuler's!"

"I can't hear you! Come down to the end of the hall!"

Starting down the long, narrow corridor, Andrea got a peek into the other rooms. The place was a pigsty. In the bedroom at the end of the hallway, she found a half-dressed, goth-looking young woman sitting at a dressing table. The place was a shambles and stank of cigarette smoke. The girl was on her smart phone. She nodded at Andrea in the mirror. "Yeah, okay, I gotta go," she muttered. "I have some friend of Troy's here . . ." She cackled. "No kidding. Okay, later . . ." She still seemed focused on her phone, but sort of turned in Andrea's direction. "So, Troy's not home. I'm not sure when he's going to be back . . ."

"Well, I was hoping to track him down," Andrea said. "I'm a friend of Evelyn Shuler's . . ."

"Isn't that the lady who got blown up?" the girl asked, finally looking up from her phone.

"That's right," Andrea said, still standing in the doorway. "Evelyn owed Troy some money. A while back, she asked me to make sure he got it—and, well, I got sidetracked. Anyway, it's not much money, but it's the principle of the thing. I was supposed to meet Troy Tuesday night, but somehow I missed him."

"Are you the one Troy was meeting at the airport?"

the young woman asked. She put down her phone and lit a cigarette.

Andrea nodded. The Mazda CX-9 had been stolen from an airport parking lot on Tuesday. "So he mentioned it to you?"

"Yeah, he said something about running an errand and that he'd finally have some rent money—which he owes me." She exhaled a cloud of smoke. "Anyway, he was gone until two in the morning and didn't come back any richer."

"Maybe we got our times mixed up," Andrea said. "I was supposed to meet him around eight-fifteen." She figured that was about a half hour before Luke was hit. She wondered if Troy had an alibi.

The girl shrugged. "Well, he left here sometime in the afternoon. How much money are you giving him?"

"Like I say, it's not much," Andrea replied. "It's for a favor he did. Evelyn wanted him to break into this apartment in Ballard. It was part of a prank she was pulling on a friend of hers. Do you know anything about that?"

The girl shook her head and puffed on her cigarette. "No, but it sounds like something Troy would do . . ."

Another door in the bedroom, which Andrea thought led to a bathroom, suddenly swung open. She realized the door was to a connecting bedroom. A sinewy, twenty-something man with a shaved-to-stubble head stood in the doorway. He wore a dingy, yellowing T-shirt and gray sweat shorts. His muscular arms were covered with tattoos. "Who's this bitch?" he grumbled.

"A friend of Troy's," the girl said. "She has money for him."

"Yeah?" He stared at Andrea. "How much?"

She tried to think of how much cash she had on her—and how much she could spare. She gave a nervous shrug. "Just fifty dollars."

He turned to glare at the girl. "Where's my fucking omelet? You said you were going to make me an omelet, like, a half hour ago."

She stubbed out her cigarette and got to her feet. "Okay, okay, don't have a cow," she muttered. She plucked a kimono from a pile of clothes on her bed. Throwing it on, she brushed past Andrea as she headed out the door.

"It just so happens Troy owes me fifty bucks," the man said, scratching his chest.

"That's quite a coincidence," Andrea said, backing out of the doorway. She didn't want to be alone in the room with this guy. He looked dangerous, like someone who had done time in a maximum-security penitentiary. What with the haircut, those tattoos, and his build, she could almost picture him pumping up in the prison gym.

He chuckled. "You're a hell of a lot better-looking than most of the skanks he brings through here."

"Well, thanks," she said, trying to work up a smile. Her back was against the wall in the corridor. "Ah, I was asking your friend if Troy ever pulled a break-in job for Evelyn Shuler. It was a joke on a friend of hers in Ballard. This would have been in August, around—"

"You said you got fifty bucks on you?" he interrupted.

"Yes, but I'm supposed to give it directly to Troy."

She glanced down the long hallway—to the door out-side.

"Why don't you come in here?" He nodded toward his bedroom.

"No thanks. Listen, I should go. I have someone outside, waiting for me. I don't want to keep him . . ."

"I don't give a shit about that," the man said, slowly moving toward her. He looked her up and down. "Troy owes me. And if you're a friend of his, I'm going to collect—one way or another."

Andrea started to back down the hallway. "Actu-ally, it's my brother who's waiting for me," she said. Her heart was pounding. "He gets real impatient. I don't want to make him mad. He's a—parole officer, and you probably know what hotheads some of them can be . . ."

He abruptly stopped outside the girl's bedroom door.

"Thanks for your time," Andrea said, short of breath.

His eyes narrowed at her. Andrea couldn't tell if he believed her or not.

She turned and hurried to the door, careful not to break into a sprint. She didn't want him running after her. She ducked outside and closed the door behind her.

Scurrying up the steps, she ran toward her car and fumbled for the key. But then she realized if he fol-lowed her, she'd lead him directly to her VW. He'd get to her before she even managed to pull away from the curb.

Andrea raced past her VW and several more cars. Then she crossed the street and ducked behind an

SUV. Catching her breath, she peeked over the vehicle's roof at the apartment house down the block. No one had come out after her—at least, she didn't see anybody. She really couldn't tell whether or not anyone was in the shadows, behind the shrubs or that Dumpster.

She decided to stay there for another few minutes until she knew she was safe—or at least, until she stopped shaking.

Sitting in the parked VW with the key in the ignition, Andrea squinted at the headlights of a passing car. She knew she was pushing her luck a little, but she'd decided to stick around just a while longer to see if Troy showed up. But her windshield kept fogging. Every few minutes, she wiped off the condensation with a Kleenex.

Her venture hadn't been totally in vain. She had Troy going to the airport, where the Mazda was stolen on Tuesday. He'd returned home at two in the morning, which meant he could have been the one who broke into the town house. His roommate had said that breaking and entering "sounds like something Troy would do." He'd also returned home without money he thought he'd have. Was that because he'd been interrupted at the town house before he'd been able to steal anything?

It still wasn't enough to prove that Troy had run down Luke with the stolen car Tuesday night. She didn't know where to take it from here—outside of questioning Troy directly. She needed a professional investigator, some-

one who could determine exactly where Troy Slattery
was Tuesday night, and whether he had a criminal record, or a history of breaking and entering. But she
couldn't afford a private investigator. She didn't have
money like Evelyn.

"The private investigator . . ." Andrea murmured.

The man who had questioned her friend Sylvia
Goethals in Washington, DC, back in August knew
about Spencer, the trial, and everything. How long had
he known? And if he had been working for Evelyn,
when did he share that information with her? Was she
still seeing Troy at the time?

The VW's windows were starting to fog again. Andrea was still a bit shaky from her experience with
Troy's roommate. She took out her smart phone, and
looked up Sylvia's number. As she clicked on it and
listened to the ringtones, she prayed her friend was
back from India.

Sylvia answered on the third ring. "Hey, Andrea."

"You're back!"

"Yes, I got in night before last. I'm still jet-lagged.
In fact, I was just about to turn in."

"Well, I don't want to keep you, but I was wondering if you still have that private detective's business
card . . ."

It took Sylvia only a minute to find the card in her
desk drawer. The detective's name was Hugh Badger
Lyman. He had a Web site—and a phone number with
a Seattle area code.

Andrea switched on the VW's interior light and jotted everything down on the back of an envelope that
had been in her purse.

She thanked her friend, clicked off the line, and tried the number for Hugh Badger Lyman.

It rang once. Then a recording came on: *"We're sorry, you've reached a number that has been disconnected or is no longer in service. If you feel you've reached this recording in error, please check the number and try your call again."*

Andrea clicked off and punched in the number once more. She got the recording again. She figured she must have copied the number down wrong. She didn't want to bother Sylvia again, so she switched to the Internet and tried the Web site, www.hblymaninvestigations.com.

The site came up—with a rather unimaginative illustration of an eye looking through a magnifying glass:

## H. B. LYMAN INVESTIGATIONS
*Discreet & Dependable*
*Serving the Seattle area since 1996*
Specializing in Background Checks,
Employee Screening,
Theft, Surveillance, Vehicle Tracking & Infidelity.

The phone number listed matched what she'd scribbled down on the back of the envelope. His office hours were from 10 a.m. until 6 p.m. weekdays. The office address was on Eastlake Avenue, not far away.

Andrea noticed a contact option. She clicked on it and was about to write an email, but hesitated. She wondered if Hugh Badger Lyman would be willing to meet with someone he'd been investigating to answer questions about his client—even if that client was now dead.

Andrea decided a surprise attack was best. She'd swing by his office on Eastlake tomorrow afternoon on her way back from the hospital.

Her phone rang, startling her. She realized it was probably Spencer, calling to say he was home. She clicked on the phone. "Hello?"

She didn't hear anything on the other end. It was probably a telemarketer. There were always a couple of dead seconds before they started their sales pitch. Andrea quickly hung up and then checked the caller ID: UNKNOWN CALLER.

Checking her watch, she decided to give Spencer ten more minutes before calling to make sure he was okay. He should have been home by now.

Starting up the car, she switched on the window defogger.

Her phone rang once more, UNKNOWN CALLER again. Annoyed, she clicked it on and sighed. "Yes, who's calling please?"

There was another pause and then a gravelly voice crept over the line: "By the time I'm done, I'll get a lot more than fifty bucks out of you, bitch."

He hung up.

Panic-stricken, Andrea clicked off. She quickly checked the armrest to make sure all the car doors were locked. The call was either from Troy or his friend. Had Troy returned home in the last fifteen minutes? If he had, it must have been while her car windows were fogged. Troy's roommates could have described her to him. But how did he get her cell number?

Then she remembered Luke had a listing of phone numbers by the landline in his kitchen. Their intruder on Tuesday night could have seen it.

She swiped her hand over the still-foggy windshield.

Andrea spotted someone standing in front of the apartment house. The porch light was in back of him, so that she could only see a tall, lean silhouette. She couldn't tell who it was, but he seemed to be staring at her.

He held something in his hand. Was it a phone?

She turned the key in the ignition. The car made a grating screech, and she realized the engine was already running.

The man hadn't moved.

Flustered, she switched on her headlights and shifted gears.

The headlights didn't make any difference. She still couldn't see his face. She couldn't tell if it was Troy or his roommate—or just some stranger.

The tires squealed as Andrea peeled away from the curb. Her phone and purse slid off the passenger seat and toppled to the floor. She sped past the apartment house. The stranger in front of it was just a blur.

After half a block, Andrea forced herself to ease up on the accelerator. But she still clutched the steering wheel tightly. And her stomach was still in knots.

She glanced in her rearview mirror and saw him standing in the middle of the road—a tall, dark figure.

He raised his hand and gave a little wave.

# CHAPTER TWENTY-SIX

*Friday, October 30—12:06 p.m.*

"Anyway, I'm sorry I snapped at you last night," Tanya said. "It was rude. But you have to admit, you were kind of picking on me."

Spencer didn't think he had to admit anything like that. "I was just trying to get a straight answer out of you," he said.

He stood by his locker, where Tanya had approached him shortly after the lunch bell. The hallway was crowded. Some of the students had dressed for Halloween, and that included Tanya. It was kind of hard to take her apology seriously when she was dressed as Waldo from *Where's Waldo?* She wore round glasses, a beanie cap, and a red-and-white striped sweater. Spencer had sported the same outfit for Halloween when he was eight. It seemed lost on everyone now. Most of the kids were dressed like zombies.

Last night, he'd watched Tanya until seven o'clock.

She'd made only that one brief phone call. Then she'd lowered her blinds. When she'd raised them again a few minutes later, she'd had on a baggy jersey and sweatpants. Spencer had figured she wasn't going out again in those clothes. So he'd headed home, beating his Aunt Dee there by about an hour.

"Well, let's just put it all behind us," Tanya said, leaning against the lockers. "In fact, I wanted to take you out and treat you to dinner tonight—only I'm meeting someone. So I was wondering if I could take you out for an apology dinner tomorrow night."

Spencer wasn't dying to spend his Saturday night with Tanya. He didn't mind spying on her, but having to interact with her and listen to her was another story. "Well, that's really nice of you," he said. "I'll get back to you about it later, okay?"

Behind her round glasses, she looked a bit crest-fallen. "Like I said, I'd take you out tonight, only I'm meeting this person."

Nodding, he shut his locker. "That's cool. Who are you getting together with?"

She shrugged. "Oh, you don't know him. Anyway, let me know if tomorrow night works for you."

Spencer watched her walk away—with a little bounce in her step.

All at once, someone slammed into him. Spencer crashed against the lockers, banging his shoulder. He cried out in pain. Before he could figure out what was happening, a hand grabbed his arm and roughly spun him around.

Ron Jarvis's face was just inches from his. He pressed his forearm on Spencer's chest, pinning him against the lockers. Spencer could hardly breathe. He was so startled, he didn't try to struggle or fight back.

Everyone in the hallway stopped to watch them.

"You stay away from me and my family, or I'll fucking destroy you," Ron growled. "One more call or text, and I'm coming after you. Do you understand me, psycho?"

"It—it's not me," Spencer started to say.

"I don't want to hear one word from you," Ron said. "I know it's you doing this shit. Don't pretend it isn't. Don't say anything, or I swear to God, I'm going to swat that innocent look off your face."

Ron punched the locker—right beside Spencer's head. He jumped. The sound was deafening.

His ear was still ringing as Ron turned and stomped down the corridor.


"I've got to be honest, I'm really disappointed," Spencer murmured into the phone. He'd gotten Diane's voice mail again. He stood in the hallway outside of the cafeteria. He wanted to talk to Bonnie, but she was at the cool table once again—along with Ron. He didn't dare go anywhere near him.

"This is my fourth message, Diane," he continued. "I don't get it. You acted like you'd be there for me if I needed you. Anyway, I'm in trouble again—big-time. I think somebody else is going to get killed. I don't know what to do. Please, please, call me back. Okay? Thanks."

Spencer clicked off the phone.

He thought about calling Andrea. But what could she do? She had enough on her mind with Luke in the

hospital. Plus she was suddenly worried about Troy
Slattery coming after them. She'd told him last night to
call her or the police if he spotted Troy anywhere near
him today. And she didn't want him alone in the town
house anymore—not even during the daytime.

He wondered if Troy Slattery was the one who had
called and texted Ron.

Spencer stuck his phone in his back pocket. He peeked
into the cafeteria again. Bonnie had finished eating,
but was still chatting with her cheerleader friends. All
of them wore their skimpy cheer uniforms, a Friday
tradition. The people at the elite table were too cool to
dress up for Halloween. Ron was sitting at the other
end, talking to some of his buddies. He was smiling
and laughing. Whatever had been boiling up inside
him he must have gotten out of his system.

Meanwhile, Spencer still had a slight ringing in his
ear, and he was pretty sure his shoulder would have a
huge bruise on it tonight.

He scanned the room for Tanya in her glasses, beanie,
and red-and-white striped jersey. *Where's Tanya?* He
didn't see her anywhere. He figured she probably
knew who was harassing Ron Jarvis. He could ask her,
but what were his chances of getting a straight answer?

Bonnie got up from the table and collected her
lunch tray. She cleaned it off at the recycling station,
and set it with the other dirty trays. As she headed toward the doors to the corridor, she took out her phone.

"Bonnie?" he called, feeling a bit like a stalker.

She looked at him and shut off her phone. "Hi," she
said, stepping into the corridor. "Are we on for tonight?"

He stared at her and blinked. "What?"

"The Halloween party at Amanda Brooks's house, you said you'd let me know today if you could go. I asked you after chemistry class yesterday . . ."

"Oh, that," he murmured. "Um, I don't think so. Something's come up . . ."

"Well, that's okay, it's no biggie—"

"No, I mean something has really come up. Did Ron say anything to you about some calls and texts that he's been getting?"

Bonnie shrugged. "Ron doesn't say much to me at all nowadays."

"Well, it's happening to him now—what happened to Reed Logan before he was killed, what happened to you—until the police started patrolling your house. I think he's getting harassed, and someone has him believing I'm the one behind it all. He just threatened to *destroy* me if I bothered him and his family again."

"What?"

"He confronted me about a half hour ago in the hallway," Spencer explained. "I can't approach him. He'll pummel me. You need to talk to him, tell him it isn't me, and tell him how serious this is . . ."

"Don't you realize that over half the people Damon called out as bullies in his webcast are now *dead*?" Bonnie said. "First Mr. McAfee and KC, and then Reed—all killed within less than a month. I'd be dead, too—if Spencer hadn't warned me and we'd gotten the police to patrol our block."

"You're seeing a lot of that squirrelly Spencer dude lately, aren't you?" Ron asked. "Is he your new boyfriend or something?"

Bonnie just rolled her eyes. She'd caught Ron outside the varsity locker room on his way out to football practice. Carrying his helmet, he wore his football gear. They stood in the hallway—beside a large trophy case.

Nothing she'd told him so far seemed to leave an impression.

"Well?" Ron said, leaning close to her. "Is he the reason you broke up with me?"

"No, I already explained that to you—weeks ago. I didn't like who I was when I was with you."

He laughed. "What the hell is that supposed to mean? And why are you here talking to me now? Are you trying to get back together?"

"No, Ron, I'm trying to warn you that you're in serious danger." She grabbed his jersey sleeve. "Spencer said you mentioned you'd gotten some phone calls and texts. Was someone threatening you—or your family?"

"It's nothing I haven't already handled," Ron said. "It's taken care of. Now you're making me late for practice."

He turned away and moved down the corridor, his cleats clicking on the floor. He hit the lever across the door, pushed it open, and started outside to the playfield.

Bonnie stood there, watching the door slowly close behind him.

She'd been through all this before, when she'd talked with Reed in the hallway—after his skirmish with Spencer. He'd said practically the same thing: *The guy stepped out of line, and it's been taken care of. End of story.*

It was the last time she ever talked with Reed.

He was dead twelve hours later.

# CHAPTER TWENTY-SEVEN

*Friday—4:57 p.m.*

She stood in the narrow hallway outside a door that had a faux wood plaque on it with white lettering: 304—H. B. LYMAN INVESTIGATIONS.

Andrea had planned to pay a surprise visit to the private detective. But the surprise was on her. The office was closed—and the door was locked.

She'd thought her timing was perfect, too. Luke had wanted to take a nap, so she wasn't needed at the hospital for a while. And Spencer had texted earlier, saying he was attending Tanya's play rehearsals again, and he'd been invited to go out for pizza with the cast afterward. Would she mind?

She didn't mind—especially since he'd be safe with a bunch of people. She'd come here directly from the hospital, and couldn't help thinking about Troy Slattery while in the Blue Lion level of the hospital's underground parking garage. She hadn't been able to shake the sensation that he was lurking somewhere nearby, watching her every move. On her way to the Eastlake neighborhood, she'd checked the rearview mirror again and again.

Andrea noticed that down the hall from H. B. Lyman's office, a door was propped open. She walked down the corridor and poked her head in the doorway. She saw a chubby sixty-something, pale-blond receptionist on her computer at her desk. The sofa and chair in the waiting room were empty. On the door it said: 301—KATE GERA, ATTORNEY AT LAW.

"May I help you?" the woman asked, glancing up from her computer screen. "Did you have an appointment to see Kate?"

"No, actually I'm looking for H. B. Lyman—in three-oh-four," Andrea said, hovering in the doorway. "I knocked and no one answered. And his phone service seems to be cut off."

"You mean Hugh? Are you a friend of his?"

"No, but he was working on a case for a friend of mine."

"Oh, well, I'm sorry, but Hugh died. He was killed in an automobile accident about six or seven weeks ago."

Andrea just stared at her.

"The office has been locked up for over a month now," the secretary explained. "His assistant, Dana, took all the files and cleared out the place."

She stepped into the waiting room. "Do you know where I can find this Dana? It's really important I talk to someone about this case . . ."

"Well, you won't have to go too far," the woman

said. "Dana works the day shift at the convenience store down the block, Eastlake Foods. In fact, the shift's almost over. You can catch Dana there if you hurry . . ."

The corner market looked like a 7-Eleven—only with a huge beer and wine section. It also had a popcorn machine that made the place smell like a movie theater lobby. The only person working the counter was a short, odd-looking middle-aged man with receding gray hair. His left hand was deformed or had somehow been mangled—with a normal thumb, but four nubs instead of fingers.

"Help you?" he said, counting singles at the register.

"Hi, yes," Andrea said. "Is Dana working today?"

"I'm Dana," he said.

Andrea had been expecting a woman. "Oh, hi . . ."

He smiled at her. His teeth were yellow. "I know who you are," he said. "You're Andrea Boyle, aren't you?"

"You were the last person Hugh investigated," Dana said.

His coworker had come back from a break and now worked the register. Dana was sitting on a box in the middle aisle, punching price stickers on the tops of the Campbell's soup cans in a case.

Andrea stood over him. Something about his quiet, soft-spoken manner was slightly creepy. It didn't help that this total stranger knew who she was. But she had to admire how he didn't let his damaged hand slow him down any.

"Hugh was still researching the case when he went head-to-head with that Burlington Northern train," he said, focusing on his work.

"What happened exactly?" Andrea asked. "Do they know?"

"They think he was trying to beat the freight train at the crossing," Dana explained in his quiet voice. "It was one of those crossings that didn't have a gate. I think it has one now, though. That was just like Hugh, always in a hurry. He drove like a maniac. Sometimes he'd drive all night, pumped full of uppers, to get to his destination. Anyway, they found drugs and a high level of alcohol in his system. Really a shame, too, because he'd been off the booze for eleven months. He'd been so good up until that point." He started to stack the soup cans on the shelf. "Anyway, you're Hugh's only open file."

"I don't suppose you're at liberty to say who hired him to investigate me, are you?" Andrea asked.

"Well, I'm probably breaking a bunch of confidentiality laws by telling you, but I figure what the heck? I mean, what are they going to do—fire me? Besides, the person who hired us is dead, so I don't see how it's going to do anybody any harm. You know that guy you've been seeing? It was his wife—or his *estranged* wife I should say, Evelyn Shuler."

Even though the man wasn't looking at her, Andrea nodded. The news wasn't much of a surprise. "Can you tell me if Evelyn ever paid Hugh to—to break into my apartment?"

Dana stopped stocking the shelf to look up at her. His eyes narrowed. "Hugh would never do anything like that. He was a good guy. He was decent enough to hire me when nobody else would. Now that he's dead, I'm stuck here." He went back to placing soup cans on the shelf.

"I'm sorry," Andrea murmured. "It was a dumb question."

"It's okay, you didn't know him—not like he knew you."

"The receptionist at the law office down the hall from your old office said you came and collected all of Hugh's files." Andrea nervously cleared her throat. "Was mine among them?"

He nodded. "Yeah, old Hugh didn't trust computers. So we had backup paperwork for everything. I shredded it all . . ."

"Oh," Andrea said, disappointed.

He glanced up and smiled at her with those yellow teeth again. "Except yours. Like I said, it was the only open case. So I took it home. I live just three blocks away. My shift's over in a few minutes. Would you like to come over and see your file?"


Dana's apartment was above a dilapidated, vacant store with a FOR LEASE sign in the darkened front window. It looked like the store had been vacant for a long time. The painted sign on the window was faded and chipped:

**UNIQUE ANTIQUES**
VINTAGE COLLECTIBLES

The building sat alone, a dumpy little shack on prime real estate one block from Lake Union. Andrea followed Dana up a stairway on the side of the building and into the kitchen entrance of his apartment. The appliances were avocado green, and the table was a scratched-up yellow dinette set from the fifties. Though tidy, the place was still a bit gloomy—and it smelled.

The smell got stronger as they moved down the hall to the living room. He switched on the light. A canary, hamster, squirrel, and several other small critters were in cages scattered around the room. A ferret had free rein over the place, which might have explained the scratch marks on the old sofa. The animals banged around in their cages, making a slightly unnerving tinny sound.

"Hey, kids, Daddy's home!" he called. The tinny sound escalated, and the canary chirped.

He turned to her and smiled. "You know, I haven't had a pretty woman here in a long, long time. I should have bought some nice wine while we were at the store. Would you like a Coke? Or I have a gallon of ginger ale that's open."

"No, thanks," she said, trying to smile back.

"I'm guessing you probably just want to get your file and be on your way," he said.

"Oh, it's not that, really. I have a friend in the hospital, and I want to get back to him."

"Yes, I read about Luke's accident. That's really terrible. I hope they get the guy who hit him."

"Me, too," Andrea murmured. She felt so uncomfortable. She didn't know a thing about this man who knew her so well. She wished she'd phoned Spencer or Luke to tell them where she was. Doing it now would just seem rude. She reminded herself that Dana's co-worker had seen them leave the store together. He wasn't about to try anything.

"Well, the files are over here," he said, moving down the hallway.

Andrea followed him. She could see the darkened bedroom ahead. With a rumble, the ferret scurried past her on the floor, and she almost jumped out of her skin.

Dana stopped just short of the bedroom door and reached for a pole, which leaned against the wall in the corner. The pole had a hook on the end of it.

"I didn't think I'd ever really need this stuff, so I stored it up here." He raised the pole to a trapdoor in the ceiling. "Better stand back." He maneuvered the hook into a latch, gave it a tug, and the door creaked open at a downward angle. With his bad hand, he grabbed a wooden stair-ladder attached to the back of the door and unfolded it.

Andrea gazed up at the blackness beyond the opening in the ceiling.

He flicked a light switch by his bedroom door.

Now she could see the old, cobweb-laced rafters. It still looked dark up there.

"I really need to change that bulb one of these days," Dana said. "Something with a higher wattage." He ducked into his bedroom for a moment. Andrea stood by the ladder. She heard that tinny sound of the cages rattling in the next room.

He came back with a flashlight. "You'll probably need this," he said, handing her the flashlight.

"Wait. You want me to go up there?"

"Well, I can't really manage it too easily," he said, showing her his mangled hand, "especially getting down while carrying something. You should have seen me taking it up there. I have the files in a box, and I put the box in a shopping bag, and I got it up there with the bag handles in my teeth—like some retriever dog." He smiled at her. "Are you really going to make me find a shopping bag and go through that again?"

"Of course not," she replied, switching on the flashlight.

"If you're worried about rats up there, I'm pretty sure I don't have any," he said. "This close to the lake, I'm lucky I don't have a problem . . ."

The ferret circled around his legs, and he picked it up. "It's probably thanks to Boris, here."

"Yes, probably," she murmured. Then with trepidation, she ascended the stair-ladder to the dark, dismal attic. It smelled musty. Near the top rung, she saw something close by that made her gasp. She shined the flashlight on the lone figure, and realized it was a headless dress mannequin. Beside it was a beat-up rocking horse for a child.

"A lot of the stuff up there belonged to the people who lived here before me," Dana called, from the bottom of the stair-ladder. "They owned the antique store downstairs, really more like a junk store . . ."

Andrea glanced down at him. Gazing back up at her, he held the ferret in his arms and stroked it. "Look for a Macy's box that says 'Work Shit' on it."

She reluctantly stepped up into the cluttered attic. She half-expected the trapdoor to shut behind her.

Then he'd turn off the light, and she'd be trapped up here—like one of his caged pets.

Andrea told herself she was being silly. The man had been perfectly nice to her so far. And she had her phone with her. Still, she couldn't shake her wariness.

She saw a couple of ornate, ugly floor lamps, a steamer trunk, and a portable stereo—among other items. Everything up there seemed broken and beat-up.

"All the boxes are over to the left of the opening," she heard her host say. "Are you okay up there?"

"So far," she nervously called back.

"Want me to come up there and help you?"

"No, that's okay," Andrea replied. She directed the flashlight to the left of the attic opening, and saw the stack of boxes.

"I'm just not very good at carrying things up and down ladders," he said. She couldn't see him. Right now, he was merely a voice coming from below. "You know that silent movie actor Harold Lloyd, the one who was always hanging from building ledges and pulling stunts like that?"

"I think so," Andrea answered, making her way to the boxes. She remembered seeing a photo of Harold Lloyd precariously dangling from the minute hand of a tower clock. If she recalled correctly, he wore little round glasses.

"Well, did you know that he lost the thumb and index finger of his right hand in an accident?" Dana said. "And yet he did all those stunts for the movies, hanging at some incredible height. I wish I was as good as him. I lost my fingers on this hand the day after my nineteenth birthday. A grenade took them off in the Battle of Khe Sanh. It's weird to think that was forty-five years ago . . ."

Andrea shone the light on the Macy's box—with "Work Shit" scribbled on it in black Magic Marker. But she was thinking of nineteen-year-old Dana in Vietnam. She'd been to the Vietnam War Memorial several times and looked at the rows of names with reverence and heartbreak. She wondered how many people walked into that convenience store and treated him like some nobody. She was no better. Until a moment ago, she'd thought he was creepy.

"Did you find it yet?" he called.

"Yes, thank you," she replied, moving toward the box.

"I have to admit," he said. "I kind of have an ulterior motive for getting you up there . . ."

Andrea hesitated. She suddenly felt wary again. "What's that?"

"I don't think I'll have another visitor for at least a few weeks," he said. "I'm kind of a loner. Could you do me a big favor? There are a couple of boxes up there marked "Christmas Shit." Can you bring them down? Hugh used to help me out every year, hauling them down and taking them back up for me. Do you mind?"

"Of course not," she called back. Andrea felt herself tearing up, but she fought it. She spotted the two big brown boxes with "Xmas Shit" scrawled across them.

She stuck the flashlight handle in her armpit and then picked up the Macy's box. It wasn't exactly light-weight. She imagined Dana carrying it up here with the bag handles in his teeth. Carefully, she made her way down the ladder.

Lowering his ferret to the floor, Dana took the box from her midway down. "You know, Hugh was right about you. After all the snooping and research he did, he came to the conclusion—in fact, we both did—that you're a pretty nice lady."

Andrea smiled at him. "Thanks." She was about to start up the ladder again for his "Christmas Shit," but she hesitated. "Did Evelyn ever say what she was hoping to find in this investigation?"

Clutching the box, he looked up at her and winced. "She wanted us to find out how promiscuous you were," he muttered, obviously embarrassed. He cleared his throat. "But then after we found out about your nephew and the murders, Mrs. Shuler wanted to know more about that. She wanted details. She thought we could come up with something that would make you look bad. And when we couldn't, she paid Hugh off. But on his own, he kept looking into what happened with your nephew and the other kid—the one who died in the fire."

"Why would he do that?" Andrea asked.

"Because—Hugh said—after the murders, the trial, and the fire, something just didn't feel right to him about it."

Andrea gazed down at him—and then at the box marked "Work Shit" in his hands.

"I don't think Hugh ever found out," he said. "He met up with that freight train before he finished the investigation."

# CHAPTER TWENTY-EIGHT

*Friday—6:22 p.m.*

"I texted Ron after his practice, and he agreed to come to Amanda's party tonight," Bonnie told him over the phone. "Maybe before he gets too drunk, I can pull him aside and get through to him just how serious all this is."

"You've got to," Spencer urged her. He stood in the doorway alcove of a closed gift shop. A Halloween display was in the store window, and fake cobwebs draped the doorway. He was across the street from a Thai restaurant where Tanya and her fellow cast members were eating dinner. A few of them had dressed up for Halloween. The restaurant was in an old craftsman-style house, with empty tables on the front patio.

"I don't think anything's going to happen to Ron's family while he's out," Bonnie said. "At least, I've been assuming that's the case with me, too. I just can't see them going after my folks and my brothers when I'm not even here." She paused. "What's Tanya doing?"

"She's been with the *Pajama Game* cast ever since three-thirty," he said. "She hasn't called anyone—unless it was during one of her two trips to the bathroom. They're all having Thai food now."

After they'd gone into the restaurant, Spencer had grabbed a slice of pizza at a spot next door, and used their restroom. He knew it was going to be a long night ahead. He should have asked Tanya when exactly she was meeting this mystery person, but he'd had to act like he wasn't interested. He wondered if they were having this rendezvous to finalize plans for Ron's murder. Were they carrying it out tonight?

"The last thing I feel like doing tonight is going to a party," Bonnie said.

"When is it?" he asked.

"I'm getting together with Emily Goodwin, and we're heading over there at eight o'clock. We're zombie nurses. If I can't convince Ron just how serious this is, I'll talk to one of the guys on the team and see if they can't get him to spend the night at their house."

"Good, that's smart," Spencer said. "Listen, you might not think it's any of my business, but if Ron tries to get you alone somewhere away from the party, don't go with him. Okay?"

"Spencer, I'm not getting back together with him."

"I know, but you don't want to be caught somewhere alone with him. I mean, they might try killing the two of you at once. It would be just too good to resist . . ."

"I really wish you hadn't said that," Bonnie replied

with a nervous laugh. "You think they'd pass up the chance to bury me in pencil shavings or whatever—just so they could get two of us at once?"

"Maybe," Spencer said into the phone. "Either way, why take a chance?"

"What do you suppose they've cooked up for Ron?"

"I don't know—maybe the same thing they did to Reed. Or maybe they'll kill him in a bathroom. Ron and some of his buddies attacked Damon in a restroom at school earlier this year."

"Ron didn't tell me about that," she said.

"I wouldn't have known myself if I hadn't gotten a look at Damon's journal."

"You have his diary?"

"No, the first week I stayed at Luke's, I found Damon's journal," Spencer explained. "It was there right under the mattress I was sleeping on. I know it's a creepy thing to do, reading someone else's private journal, but I was bored. I couldn't resist checking it out."

"Oh, please, I would have done the same thing," Bonnie said. "So what happened to this journal?"

"I have no idea. It wasn't in his room at his mother's house. I looked. And it wasn't on the list of stuff the police took as evidence. I'm thinking Damon must have destroyed it before he killed himself."

"That's weird," she murmured.

"What do you mean?"

"Well, covering your tracks like that before committing suicide. It's almost as if he knew there was going to be something else."

"I still don't understand," Spencer said.

"It's as if Damon knew killing himself wasn't going to be the end of it. Maybe he knew there'd be something to follow it up—like these murders. Maybe he even arranged them. Was there a hint of anything like that in his journal?"

"I don't know for sure," Spencer admitted. "I read some chunks and skimmed over the rest. But I didn't see anything in there where he was planning to kill himself—or anyone else."

"Did he mention having another friend besides Tanya?"

"No," Spencer answered, staring at the Thai restaurant across the street. "But if there was someone else, I might just get a chance to see him tonight."

The clock on the old, avocado-colored range still worked, and read six-thirty. Andrea had promised Luke she'd be back to see him at the hospital by now. Instead she was sitting at Dana's fifties dinette table with Hugh Badger Lyman's file in front of her. It was in a folder among a stack of other "Work Shit" in the Macy's box.

Andrea sipped a Coke, which Dana had opened for her. He sat across from her with a glass of ginger ale and a box of Ritz crackers. Andrea was a little more relaxed now—except every so often when Boris, the ferret, brushed against her ankles.

It was far more unsettling to see how Evelyn's private detective had collected and composed a profile on a dozen different men she'd dated in the last five years.

"I can't believe you have Bob Gold in here, Dana," she said. "We only had three dates—the third one at a restaurant in Dupont Circle, where he told me he still wasn't over his ex-girlfriend."

"They're married now," Dana said, munching on a Ritz cracker. "He spoke very highly of you."

"That's nice." She leaned toward him. "Listen, speaking of boyfriends, did you ever meet Evelyn's boyfriend, Troy Slattery? Did Hugh mention him?"

"I never met him—or her. I just faxed things to her and talked to her on the phone a couple of times. But I remember Hugh was over there at the house on Garfield once and he said she was hanging around with this 'good-looking, actor-type creep.'"

"That sounds like him," Andrea said, nodding pensively. It confirmed that Troy certainly had access to the private detective's information about her and Spencer. And if Evelyn wasn't very discreet, Damon might have had access to some of Hugh's findings, too.

She studied three yellow sheets from a legal pad—full of notes Hugh had jotted down while interviewing a paralegal at the firm that had defended Garrett Beale six years ago. Apparently, they'd hired their own private detective to dig up dirt on her—without much luck. They'd hoped to use something from her past to persuade her to back off so Garrett wouldn't be prosecuted for Vivian's and Larry's murders. They'd even procured records of the two speeding tickets she'd gotten, her Forest Hills apartment rental contract, and her college transcripts. God only knew how they got their hands on all the information.

"The fact that these attorneys were so thorough saved Hugh a lot of time researching you," Dana explained.

Andrea found rap sheets—with mug shots—for two teenage boys she didn't recognize. "Who are these two?" she asked.

"Hugh talked to some surviving members of the Beale family for any inside information they might have about the murders or the fire that killed Garrett and his parents. He also talked to some of the boys who knew Garrett at the juvenile detention facilities—those two in particular. They were Garrett's best buddies. 'The Three Musketeers,' one of the other kids called them."

Andrea studied the rap sheets. Kirk Mowery was fair-haired and baby-faced. The other boy, Richard Phelps, had long dark hair that fell into his eyes and a mole on his cheek. From their birthdates, both boys would be nineteen now. Between the two of them, they'd been charged with breaking and entering, arson, destruction of private property, automobile theft, and a number of other crimes. On Richard's rap sheet, the detective had a Post-it:

*MIA—4/15—Dead? Runaway or connected to fire?*

"Both Kirk and Richard were released months before Garrett," she heard Dana explain. "They managed to stay out of trouble and kept in touch with their pal behind bars. About two months before Garrett was sprung, his parents' house was robbed while the parents were away on vacation. They never caught the thieves. But Hugh always wondered if Kirk and Richard had anything to do with it."

"What's this Post-it note about?" Andrea asked.

"Well, Garrett was paroled in January of this year, and three months later, he died in the house fire with his parents." Dana was holding a half-eaten Ritz cracker and got some crumbs on Richard's rap sheet as he pointed to the Post-it. "April 2015, that's when the fire happened, and that's also when Richard Phelps disappeared without a trace. Richard's history is there on another page. It explains his fascination with fire— starting when he torched a neighbor's garage at the age of ten. He also set fire to a car, a Christmas nativity display outside his local church, and a greenhouse. The greenhouse incident was the only charge they made stick. He was thirteen at the time and got off with community service work. He wound up in juvie for breaking into a teacher's house, trashing the place, and attacking her. The teacher called nine-one-one, and the cops arrived before Richard could make his escape. It didn't come up at the hearing, but Hugh said the cops found a box of strike-anywhere matches and a can of lighter fluid in the pocket of Richard's jacket . . ."

"So Hugh figured Richard must have had something to do with the fire that killed Garrett and his parents?" Andrea asked.

Dana nodded over his ginger ale. "Like maybe he came back to rob them again and ended up torching the house. The police looked into it, too, but they didn't have much hard evidence. There was hardly anything left of the place—or the three corpses in it. They had to identify them all from dental records. The police knew about the Three Musketeers business, and when Richard went missing around the time of the fire, they questioned Kirk Mowery. But apparently he didn't know a damn thing and had a solid alibi for the night of the fire. Hugh questioned him, too. In fact, it was his last interview on the case . . ."

Andrea looked at Kirk's rap sheet again. He had sort of an angelic face, which belied the fact that he'd been arrested at age fourteen for stealing a car.

"Hugh got Kirk to admit that he was pretty sure his pal Richard was responsible for the fire," Dana said. "He swore up and down that he never heard from Richard after that."

With a sigh, Andrea set the two boys' rap sheets on top of the file folder. "I'm sorry, but what does this have to do with me—or Spencer? He didn't know these boys. He was at a different facility—and he wasn't released until *after* the fire."

Dana shrugged and his mouth twisted into a frown. "Well, Evelyn Shuler was curious about the fire and wondered if it could be pinned on you somehow. I hate to say this, but she was really out to get you . . ."

# CHAPTER TWENTY-NINE

*Friday—9:17 p.m.*

"The Monster Mash" blared over the sound system in Amanda's parents' family room. It was the fourth time someone had played the song since Bonnie had arrived at the party. The place was packed. Amanda's parents were out of town, and word must have gotten around, because a lot of people Bonnie didn't know had shown up. She was pretty sure Amanda didn't know them either. But they'd knocked off a keg of beer, and so far, nothing had gotten broken and no one had thrown up.

Some of the party had spilled outside to the backyard. Bonnie wandered out there to get some air and look for Ron. He'd arrived about a half hour ago—already buzzed. His Groucho Marx look had obviously been thrown together at the last minute: burnt-cork blackened eyebrows and a mustache—along with his own glasses and a suit jacket and tie. He carried around a big cigar in one hand and a beer in the other. He looked pretty cute—and knew it. For a while now, some girl from another school dressed like Princess Leia had been all over him. Bonnie had wanted to catch him alone—before he got too drunk.

Leia must have gone inside for another wine cooler, because Bonnie spotted Ron standing near the fire pit on the patio. And he was by himself.

Rubbing her bare arms from the chill, Bonnie approached him. "Hey, Ron, I've been hoping to talk to you . . ."

"You look pretty sexy in your zombie flight-attendant outfit," he smiled.

"Thanks, but I'm supposed to be a zombie nurse, and I'm freezing." She moved close to the fire pit.

Ron took off his suit jacket and put it over her shoulders. It felt so warm and big—and it smelled like him. She'd forgotten that he could be pretty nice sometimes. "Thank you," she said. "Listen, those calls and texts you've gotten—"

"Hey, no sweat," he interrupted. "I hear everybody's been getting them. It's all a big joke. Anyway, I got a tip from somebody about who's been calling me, and I took care of it."

"It's not Spencer Murray," she said. "That's what I've been trying to tell you. Somebody was doing the same thing to Reed before he and his parents were killed. And it wasn't Spencer then either."

"You have the hots for him, don't you?" he asked. He took a swig of beer.

"That's not the point. Ron, please listen to me.

Reed, KC, Mr. McAfee, you, me—we were all mentioned in Damon's speech before he killed himself. Someone started to threaten me, too. Remember when I asked if it was you? Well, I took it seriously, and I think the police patrols on my block have kept this killer away. Reed wasn't as lucky. You have to take these threats seriously. You and your family could be in danger . . ."

"My folks talked to the police," he said. A bit of his burnt-cork mustache had rubbed off of his upper lip. "The cops are the ones who told us that everybody was getting punked with texts and calls like this. It's just people blowing off steam after what happened to Reed. Throw Halloween into the mix and everything's up for grabs. The thing is, I don't mind somebody having a little fun with me—just so long as it's a buddy. But I don't take that shit from creeps I don't like. So be sure to tell that to your new boyfriend."

"What's this?" someone asked. "Who are you?"

Bonnie turned to see the girl had returned with her wine cooler.

"I'm the ex-girlfriend," Bonnie said. "And could you please give us just another couple of minutes, Princess?"

The girl frowned at her, then turned and walked away.

With a sigh, Bonnie took off Ron's jacket and handed it back to him. "Do me a favor. Spend the night at someone else's house tonight, one of the guys on the team. And call your parents and make sure they set the alarm before going to bed . . ."

"Maybe I'll spend the night with Princess Leia—in

a galaxy far, far away," Ron said with a smirk. He took another gulp of beer, draining the bottle.

"That's fine with me," Bonnie said. "Just be careful. I'm worried about you . . ."

"Well, worry about your new boyfriend," Ron growled, suddenly turning ugly. "CUZ I'M GONNA KICK HIS ASS!" At least twenty people at the party must have heard him. And if that wasn't enough, he hurled his empty beer bottle at a tree. It made a loud pop as it smashed to bits. A few girls screamed, and there was some snickering, too. "TELL SPENCER MURRAY HE'S A DEAD MAN!"

Bonnie turned and started toward the house. She brushed past Princess Leia. "He's all yours," she muttered. "May the Force be with you . . ."

She retreated inside the house to search for one of Ron's teammates to make sure he didn't try to drive home later tonight.

Bonnie hoped Ron's parents and kid sister would be okay. She clung to her theory that whoever was behind these killings had no interest in harming anyone's family. She'd convinced herself that Reed's parents hadn't been targeted in the murders. They'd just been in the house at the time, innocent bystanders.

She thought her family was safe so long as she wasn't home. But what if she was wrong? What if she came home from this party and found them all dead?

She wondered how much longer those extra police patrols might be covering her block.

Bonnie threaded her way through the noisy, sweaty crowd jammed in Amanda's family room.

Once she found someone to make sure Ron would

be okay, she'd start looking for somebody else to take her home—just as soon as possible.

"Anyway, we're all at this movie now—at the Uptown," Spencer said into his cell phone. "I should be back by eleven."

"Why are you whispering?" Andrea asked.

"Oh, I'm in the restroom—in a stall," he said. "I just don't want to be one of those d-bags who come into a public restroom on his cell phone, talking while other guys are there trying to pee."

There was a silence on the other end of the line.

Spencer wondered if she knew he was lying.

He was actually on the second floor of the half-finished house next door to Tanya's place. He could hear the TV blaring in the McCallums' living room downstairs. Tanya was upstairs in her bedroom. She'd taken off the *Where's Waldo?* beanie and glasses, and was now reading a *People* magazine on her bed.

After leaving the Thai restaurant, the cast members had split up into twos or threes and gone their separate ways. Tanya was the only one who had wandered off by herself. She'd gone across the street to the Queen Anne Book Company. Spencer had figured this might be her rendezvous spot. He'd remained outside the bookshop, occasionally peeking through the window to see if Tanya was with anyone. At one point, he'd thought she'd spotted him, but it had been a false alarm. She'd left the bookshop when it closed at eight. From there, he'd followed her home.

Tanya still had her shoes on—and hadn't yet changed

into her usual at-home sweats. So it was possible she still planned on going out. Spencer decided to hang around for at least another hour.

He'd just bought himself some more time with the lie to his aunt about going to a movie.

"What movie are you seeing?" she finally asked.

He hesitated. "Um, I'm not sure. It hasn't started yet. Tanya just sort of dragged me in."

More silence.

"Aunt Dee?" he said.

"Well, when's the movie over? I'll come pick you up. I don't like you being out alone at eleven o'clock—not with everything that's happened."

"I'll be okay, Aunt Dee," he whispered. "There'll be a lot of people out late tonight because of Halloween tomorrow."

Across the way, Tanya suddenly looked up from her magazine—almost directly out her window at him. He stepped back from the window opening. He wondered if somehow, past the TV noise downstairs, she'd heard him.

"How much money do you have on you?" his aunt asked.

"I—I think I have about ten left," he murmured, hiding on one side of the opening. "Why do you ask?" It was chilly, and he could see his breath as he talked. He wondered if Tanya had noticed it across the way—the white vapor in the black window opening.

"Well, when the movie ends, call a cab and have them pick you up at the theater. Okay?"

"Okay, I'll do that. Take care," he whispered quickly. Then he clicked off.

Spencer shoved the phone into his jacket pocket. He waited another minute and inched toward the window again. The board beneath his feet groaned. He peeked past the edge of the opening.

Just then, Tanya pulled down her shade.


Andrea didn't want to think that Spencer was lying to her.

But he was certainly spending a lot of time with someone he obviously didn't like very much. Was he really with Tanya—or was he with someone else?

She sat in a bar stool chair at the tall glass-top table in Luke's kitchen. She'd changed into jeans and a "Virginia is for Lovers" sweatshirt Spencer had given her. Andrea could see herself in the darkened sliding-glass door. She contemplated closing the drapes, but wanted to see outside in case someone came up to the town house. She had her smart phone on the table—along with a Lean Cuisine meatloaf dinner she hadn't finished, a half-drained glass of pinot noir, and Hugh Badger Lyman's file on her.

One page was full of facts—everything anybody would want to know about her: her current address and phone number, her driver's license number, and her VW Beetle's plate number, among other statistics. She'd wondered how Troy Slattery had known her phone number last night—and her car. It was obvious now. He'd seen her file.

So much of what was inside the folder had to do with Spencer—and the murders. Once again, she remembered what Luke had said just a few days ago when she'd insisted that Spencer couldn't have killed Reed Logan and his parents: *How can you say that when up until six months ago he'd been in an institution? You don't really know him, Andrea . . .*

She glanced at some of the photocopies of the news clippings about the murders. She felt a pang of sadness looking at the newspaper photos of Viv and Larry. But she felt terrible for Spencer, too. His life was ruined, and his parents were dead—all because he'd made friends with the wrong person.

For all she knew, Spencer could be out there doing something horrible right now. Maybe he'd made friends with the wrong person again.

She'd have a talk with him when he got home tonight. Until then, she couldn't do anything—except try to convince herself that he'd be at the movies for the next two hours.

She studied the rap sheets for Garrett's friends, Kirk Mowery and Richard Phelps. Spencer wasn't like either of these boys. The friends he made in the hospital and the detention center were all scared, screwed-up younger kids he tried to help. Until Garrett had come along, Spencer had never been in trouble before. These friends of Garrett's at the Richmond facility were almost hardened criminals by the time they were fifteen.

On the back of Richard's rap sheet, Hugh Badger Lyman had stuck a Post-it:

*Check on Doreen Carter—Girlfriend?*

Sifting through the file, she searched for a document, another Post-it, or a piece of notebook paper with that name on it again—anything that might explain Doreen Carter's significance in all this. But there was nothing else about her.

Andrea figured Hugh's assistant might know who this woman was. She'd written Dana's home phone number on the file folder. She called him.

He picked up after two rings. "Hello?"

"Hi, Dana, this is Andrea. I hope I didn't wake you . . ."

"No, I was just going through my Christmas stuff—thanks to you. What's up?"

"Well, I found a note Hugh wrote to himself—or maybe to you," Andrea explained. "It says, 'Check on Doreen Carter'—and then, 'Girlfriend' with a question mark after it. Does that name sound familiar to you?"

"No, not at all," Dana replied. "Where did you find this?"

"It was in the file, on a Post-it on the back of Richard Phelps's rap sheet. Did Richard have a girlfriend named Doreen? Or was this someone who was supposed to know me?"

"Beats me," he answered. "Like I said, that name doesn't ring a bell. Hugh was looking at the file a couple of days before he died. He must have scribbled the note to himself then, otherwise I'd have noticed. Sorry I can't be more help."

"That's okay," Andrea said. "Sorry to bother you. Thanks again for everything you did for me today . . ."

After she hung up, Andrea went into Luke's study and sat down in front of his computer. She connected to Google and typed in the name: Doreen Carter.

The search results came up. "Oh, crap," she muttered.

It was a common name, and the entire first page of results focused on a member of the House of Representatives in Georgia. She tried: "Doreen Carter, Richard Phelps," and got obituaries for people with those name combinations—along with stories about President Jimmy Carter, and more articles about Georgia state politics. She found the same results when she paired "Doreen Carter" with Garrett Beale, Kirk Mowery, and Spencer Rowe.

She was on page three of the search results for "Doreen Carter, Virginia," when she heard her phone ring. She ran back into the kitchen, snatched up the phone and looked at the caller ID: CALLER UNKNOWN.

Andrea immediately put the phone back down. She watched as it rang and vibrated a little on the glass-top table. It was just after ten o'clock—too late for a telemarketer. She had a pretty good idea who the caller was.

After one more ring, the call went to voice mail. They didn't leave a message.

She glanced out the sliding glass door and wondered if the caller was out there in the darkness, watching her. Moving over to the door, she checked the lock again and then closed the curtains.

The phone rang once more—again, UNKNOWN CALLER. She stood over the phone for a moment, then finally grabbed it and clicked on. "Troy?" she said, breathlessly. "Troy Slattery?"

There was no response. But she could tell the caller was still on the line.

"I know this is you," she said. Yet she really wasn't so sure now.

"Hello?" He had a strange, singsong voice—almost like something out of a cartoon.

"Who is this?" Andrea asked.

There was a sigh, and then that puppet-like voice again. "Do you know what your nephew's doing right now?"

"Who the hell are you?"

He shushed her.

Bewildered, Andrea fell silent.

"Spencer's being a bad boy again," he whispered. "You'll see . . ."

Then he hung up.


As he staggered down the residential street in search of his Miata convertible, Ron Jarvis didn't think he was that drunk.

He was just ticked off.

He'd told several people at the party that he was going to kick Spencer Murray's ass. He'd been talking about it with somebody in Amanda's kitchen when he smashed another beer bottle—this time on the counter. A piece of glass flew up and cut Kate Coupland on the cheek. It wasn't like she needed stitches or a transfusion or anything. She just bled a little. But Amanda had a cow and tossed him out on his ass.

One of his teammates, Mike Walter, had volunteered earlier to be his designated driver, and he'd said something about having him sleep over at his place tonight. But Ron had kept it noncommittal, thinking he might go home with Princess Leia. They'd even made out a little, but she'd gotten all pissy because his burnt-cork mustache had rubbed off onto her face and her white costume. Plus, she wouldn't stop asking him about Bonnie. When she'd referred to Bonnie as "that skank," he'd said she was hardly one to talk—and that had killed it. She'd blown him off.

When he'd left the party, Ron had spotted her hanging all over some guy dressed like Spiderman.

*Well, screw her*, he thought.

As he made his way to his car, Ron figured missing out on a night in heaven with Princess Leia was no great loss. He didn't want to admit it, not even to himself, but he still wasn't over Bonnie.

He spotted his green Miata and took a few fortifying, deep breaths. It was only a couple of miles to his house, but the cops were out in full force tonight looking to catch drunk partiers. He figured he'd be okay driving—especially if he kept the window open and the radio blasting.

He clicked the unlock button, and watched the Miata's parking lights flicker. Opening the door, he climbed behind the wheel and then froze.

"What the fuck?" he muttered, staring at the thing dangling from his rearview mirror.

It was a GI Joe doll, hanging from a shoestring around its neck. The doll's fatigue trousers had been shucked down to its boots, and the shirt was bunched up under its chin. The doll was naked from the chest down to its ankles.

"What the fuck?" he repeated, angry now.

Was this somebody's idea of a joke? What was it supposed to mean anyway?

He wondered how someone had gotten into his car. Had he forgotten to lock it? He couldn't remember.

Ron quickly checked the back. He was relieved to see his blue and gray varsity letter jacket where he'd left it.

He turned and started to yank the doll off his rearview mirror. But then he realized the damn thing was tightly tied to the bar connecting the mirror to the windshield. He didn't want to tear down the whole rearview mirror. So he tried to loosen the knot around the bar. He kept picking and pulling at the stupid shoelace. It was frustrating as hell and seemed to take forever. "Goddamn it," he muttered, again and again—until he finally untied the knot.

Ron hurled the doll outside, slammed his door shut, and started up the car. Then he peeled down the street.

He forgot to keep a lookout for cops. And after all that attention he'd just paid to his rearview mirror, he didn't bother to look in it now.

If he had, Ron might have seen the car following him.


The driver of the Toyota Corolla kept one hand on the wheel and the other held his phone. He watched the Miata about half a block ahead of him.

"I believe our boy is DUI, and on his way home," he told his friend on the phone. "What's the situation there?"

"Lights out," whispered his cohort. "It looks like his parents and kid sister have all gone beddie-bye."

The driver of the Corolla glanced at his wristwatch: 10:38. "I don't think he's going to take a side trip. He needs to go to bed. He's got a big game tomorrow. I wonder if he's worried about having to play with a hangover. I doubt it. Do you think they'll cancel the game on account of him?"

"Do you really think they'll find him that quickly?" his friend asked.

"Oh, yeah," he said. "I'll bet they'll find him tomorrow morning. If they don't cancel the game, they'll at least give the scumbag a minute of silence . . ."

He followed the Miata as Ron took a turn on Queen Anne Avenue. There were four more turns until Ron would reach his house.

"Be ready for him in about five minutes," said the man in the Corolla.

"I'm here," his friend said, "just waiting . . ."


He was convinced someone in the apartment house across from Kerry Park was going to call the police on him. He skulked around on their front lawn—behind trees and some shrubs.

The park was halfway up Queen Anne Hill and offered a spectacular view of downtown Seattle and Elliott Bay—with the Space Needle up close and taking center stage. Surrounded by bushes, the lookout point had a tall abstract metal sculpture, several park benches, and a coin-operated telescope. Only a few couples and one slightly noisy foursome were checking out the view at this late hour.

And then there was Tanya, sitting alone on one of the park benches.

Spencer's phone vibrated. He dug it out of his jacket pocket, checked the caller ID, and clicked the phone on. "Hello?"

"Hi," Bonnie said. "Are you still on surveillance duty?"

"Yeah," he replied in a hushed voice. He glanced over his shoulder to make sure no one from the apartment building had come out to chase him away. "About forty-five minutes ago, Tanya got dressed up—in almost normal clothes. She even put on lipstick. Then she walked to Kerry Park. She's been sitting on a bench here for about a half hour now. She's checked her phone a few times, but hasn't called anybody. I wonder if she's being stood up. Anyway, I'll stick around here. I have about another hour until I'm supposed to be home." He glanced back toward the apartment building again. "How are you? Did you talk to Ron?"

"Like talking to a brick wall," she replied. "I finally gave up and left the party. But Mike Walter said he'd drive him back to his place and they'd crash there. Ron's parents talked to the police about the texts and the calls."

"Did they think I was behind them? Did they blame me?" Spencer asked.

"I'm guessing no. Otherwise the police would be on your case right now, don't you think?"

"Or they'd be watching me," Spencer said. He

thought about the Toyota Corolla that might have been following him the other night.

"Well, anyway, I'm home in my room now," Bonnie sighed. "At the party, I started worrying about my family, so I came back here. It's weird. When I'm not with them, I'm worried about them. And when I'm here, I think I might be putting them all at risk just by being under the same roof as them. I saw a patrol car cruise by about ten minutes ago, and that makes me feel a little better. So I think we've done as much as we can for Ron, short of calling the police ourselves." She paused. "Spencer? Are you still there?"

"Yeah," he whispered, eyeing Tanya across the way. "And I guess I'm going to be here a while."

"Well, call me if anything happens. And if nothing happens, call me when you get home. Either way, call me. I'll be up late."

"I will," he said.

"You know, Ron's really jealous of you."

"Why's that?"

"He thinks we're—a couple," she said. She gave a nervous, little laugh. "Isn't that crazy?"

"Yeah, it's crazy," he murmured, not knowing what else to say.

"Well, call me later, okay?"

"Okay, bye," he said. Then he clicked off.

Spencer slipped the phone back inside his jacket pocket. He gazed at Tanya, still sitting alone on the park bench with the illuminated cityscape in front of her. He had a feeling her friend wasn't going to show up.

Spencer also had another feeling, one that tore at his

gut. He was almost certain something awful was going to happen tonight.

Ron let out a long sigh as he turned into the driveway. The drive home had sobered him up a bit. He'd been worried about a cop pulling him over.

It looked like everyone had gone to bed. But his parents had left the front light on.

Pulling into the carport beside the garage, he parked the Miata and then checked his reflection in the rearview mirror. Most of the burnt-cork, drawn-on eyebrows and mustache had smeared off. He looked like shit. He figured if he took an aspirin and a glass of OJ before bed tonight, maybe he'd be okay for the game tomorrow.

Ron switched off the headlights. As he climbed out of the car, a shadow swept over him. He turned around to see someone in a ski mask, holding what looked like a blackjack above his head.

"Payback time," the man said under his breath.

"What?" Ron gasped.

It happened so fast. Maybe it was because he was drunk and tired, but Ron barely had time to react. He saw the short, leather-covered club coming down at him. He dropped his car keys and started to put up his hand. But he was too late.

"No—"

It was all he could say before the stranger slammed the blackjack over his head.

Ron let out a feeble moan and flopped down on the driveway with a thud.

The stranger picked up the keys. While he was bent over, he whispered in Ron's ear. "I said, it's payback time, you sad, stupid son of a bitch."

It was fascinating how the blackjack worked.

Here was a guy who was used to having these two-hundred-and-fifty-pound giants slamming into him, trying to crush him every Saturday afternoon during football season. And he went down with one forceful blow from this little weapon. And the frail, stricken sound he'd made—like an old man getting punched in the gut—was so pitiful. It had all been so easy.

But now the stranger in the ski mask had to pick up Ron and drag his one hundred and eighty pounds of dead weight into the Miata's passenger seat. He managed to haul him around to the other side of the car and got the door open.

Suddenly a patch of light appeared on the front lawn. Someone on the second floor must have switched on a light.

He froze. He was pretty sure they couldn't see the carport from the window. But what was keeping them from coming down to investigate the noise?

He'd discussed with his partner the possibility of this very thing happening. The Corolla was parked across the street, one house down. They'd decided that if anyone came out of the house during the abduction phase, then that was it for the whole family. They'd kill whoever tried to come to Ron's rescue, drag the body into the backyard, and then kill everyone inside the house. After that, they could transport Ron to the designated spot and take their time proceeding as planned.

For a minute, he didn't move. He just stood over Ron's near-lifeless body and waited for the next light to go on—or the sound of a door opening. But everything remained quiet.

He took a deep breath and hoisted Ron onto the passenger seat. Ron moaned a little in protest, but he was still out of it. He didn't move at all as he was buckled into the seat. The man in the mask quietly closed the door, hurried around to the other side and climbed behind the wheel. He started up the Miata and backed out of the driveway.

He kept the lights off until he was halfway down the block. He pulled the ski mask up to his forehead. His face felt sweaty and flushed.

His head tipped to one side, Ron groaned in the passenger seat.

The driver checked the rearview mirror and spotted the Corolla following them.

Ron's phone started ringing. But Ron didn't stir. It was most likely one of his parents calling, wondering why their sonny boy had come home, only to pull out of the driveway again. Where was their precious Ronny going at this hour when he had a big game tomorrow?

They had no idea they'd never see him alive again.

The driver glanced in the rearview mirror once more. Something in the back caught his eye. It was Ron's varsity letter jacket.

The driver smiled.

They'd have a souvenir from tonight—or, more accurately, Spencer would.

# CHAPTER THIRTY

*Friday—11:08 p.m.*

Tanya walked home from the park, knowing Spencer was tailing her. Two blocks of her trek were practically straight uphill. She had to stop and catch her breath a few times. All the while, she could sense him behind her, stopping, too—watching her every move.

Tanya knew she was a decoy. She was setting up Spencer for something, but she wasn't quite sure what it was. She felt bad about that. She liked Spencer. It was all she could do to keep from turning around and calling to him. She'd been tempted to do that at least a dozen times tonight.

If only he emerged from those shadows, then she'd warn him that someone was out to get him. She just couldn't say who.

Even if she told him, he wouldn't believe her.

She kind of liked all the secret attention from her

handsome stalker. Being watched all the time, she felt like a real actress—giving an ongoing performance. But it would have been so much nicer walking alongside of him, maybe even holding hands.

Instead, she had to settle for this. And she had to do what she was told.

As Tanya turned down her block, she took out her phone.

Spencer wondered if Tanya was calling her mystery man.

But then his phone vibrated in his jacket pocket, and he realized she'd dialed his number. A quarter of a block ahead of him, she paused on the sidewalk for a moment. Spencer quickly ducked behind a tree. He clicked on the phone: "Yeah, hello?" he murmured.

"Hi," she said. "You sound funny. You're whispering. Were you asleep?"

"No, I just don't want to wake up my aunt," he whispered.

"Oh, so you're home?"

"Yeah," he lied. "Watching TV . . ."

"I thought you were trying to be quiet for your aunt," she said.

"I've got the volume down and the subtitles on," he said, peeking around the tree at her.

She'd started walking again—at a very leisurely pace. "Well, I just called to confirm that I'm taking you out for an apology dinner tomorrow night."

"Um, sure," Spencer said. "Did everything go okay tonight with your meeting?"

"Oh, it got canceled."

"Sorry to hear that," he said, watching her walk farther away.

"The night wasn't a total loss. I had Thai food with some of the cast. Then I went to the bookstore. Then I went home, but got kind of restless and ended up taking a late night stroll to Kerry Park, down the hill. It's such a beautiful night. I'm just getting back home now."

Spencer didn't say anything. He realized she'd just told him everything she'd done tonight. Had he actually caught her being totally honest with him for a change? Or was there some other reason she felt compelled to give him a blow-by-blow of her evening activities?

"Well, so then we have a date for tomorrow?" she asked.

"You bet," he said. "Good night, Tanya."

"Spencer?"

"Yeah?" He could see her at her front walkway, beside the neglected front yard. She was looking back in his direction. He stayed behind the tree. He didn't dare move a muscle.

"Nothing," she muttered. "Good night."

He heard a click on the other end. Then he watched Tanya with her head down, walking toward that decrepit bungalow.

Ron wasn't sure what was happening. He couldn't feel his arms. He was cold, and his head throbbed so badly he thought he was going to be sick.

Someone was dragging him across the ground. They had him by his feet. It sounded like two guys. He could hear them breathing heavily, but nothing else—no traffic noise, not even the wind. It was deathly quiet. Where was he? He couldn't quite focus. It wasn't just because he didn't have his glasses on. This had something to do with his head. He remembered drinking at the party—and then that guy hitting him in the carport.

He realized his jeans were bunched down around his ankles—like that GI Joe doll he'd found hanging from its neck on his rearview mirror earlier tonight. His vision started to right itself, and he saw all the trees above him. They'd taken him to some woods. But who were they?

A panic swept through him. Ron tried to struggle, but he couldn't move his hands. They were dragging against the ground—numb and cold, cut up from sticks and rocks on this wooded trail. His wrists were tied behind him.

"What are you doing?" he yelled, trying to get a look at the two guys pulling him down the pathway.

He rolled to one side and then another, catching a glimpse of them. Both of his abductors wore dark clothes and black ski masks. They didn't say anything—to him or each other. They were like a couple of furniture movers—all business, hauling something away in a hurry.

Ron tilted his head back and saw they were coming to a bald spot in the forest. He noticed a tree at the edge of the little clearing. A rope with a noose dangled from a low-hanging branch. Beneath it was an old milk crate, turned upside down.

Ron remembered the GI Joe doll again.

"No!" he cried. "Help me! SOMEBODY HELP ME! HELP—"

All at once, one of them had his hand on his throat, choking him. Ron flailed, but the guy had him pinned down. He kept moving his head from side to side as the masked stranger tried to stuff a rag into his mouth. All his struggling didn't do any good. And now they'd silenced him.

They stood him up, and he rammed his whole body into one of them. The guy fell onto the dirt. "Shit!" he grumbled.

But as Ron tried to escape, he stumbled over his pants, tangled around his feet. He fell to the cold, hard ground. Curled up on his side, he heard the other guy snickering.

Ron didn't see him take a step back and kick him in the kidney.

He felt it. The rag almost popped out of his mouth. He would have screamed if he'd had any breath left in him. The pain in his gut was excruciating—as if the organs in there had been mashed up.

He couldn't resist or struggle as they stood him up again and led him to the makeshift gallows. They lifted him onto the milk crate and put the noose around his neck. "Get on your tiptoes, Ron," one of them said.

He thought he recognized the voice, but told himself it couldn't be.

He tried to thrash around, but the noose started to choke him. His abductor was right. He had to stay on his tiptoes to keep the rope slack—and to get a breath.

Ron kept thinking this had to be a joke or something. He couldn't die here.

"How does it feel, Ron?" one of them asked.

He knew that voice. He wanted to scream at him to take off that mask so he could see his face.

The other one pulled a pair of scissors out of his jacket pocket. He clicked the blades together as if the shears were a musical instrument. "I'm going to cut off these panties now," he announced. "Don't you move, Ron, or I might slice off your pecker."

Ron remembered attacking Damon Shuler in the restroom, keeping him in a chokehold while his buddy, Max, threatened to cut off the freak's underpants. They told him they were going to string him up from one of the pipes near the ceiling and make it look like a kinky suicide. They'd worn black masks—like these two wore.

But that had all been a joke. They'd just been messing with Damon, trying to scare him.

This was real.

The one with the scissors started to cut at his underwear—at the side of his hip, from the bottom up. He stopped just before the elastic waistband. "Y'know, you were right," he said to his friend. "This milk crate's the perfect height . . ."

Trembling, Ron stood on his tiptoes. Tears started to stream down his face. He kept thinking that if they just took the gag out of his mouth, he'd tell them he was sorry.

But the one whose voice he knew started kicking at the milk crate.

Ron desperately struggled to keep his toes on top of the crate. He wanted to scream at him: *Stop! Show me your face!* He felt the milk crate moving away with every kick.

In his head, Ron could almost hear himself screaming: *Let me see your face!*

But all at once, the crate flew out from beneath him.

And all Ron heard was his neck snapping.

He repositioned the milk crate and climbed up on it so he could cut the ropes off Ron's wrists. He touched Ron's hand first. It was still warm. Careful not to nick him, he cut away the rope with the same scissors his friend had used to cut Ron's underpants. As the rope fell to the ground, his partner retrieved it and stashed it in his jacket pocket.

They both still wore their executioners' masks.

Even with Ron dead, he wanted some kind of anonymity while this close to him. Ron's crimson face was just inches from his. He pulled the gag from Ron's mouth. The football player's body swayed in the air, and the tree limb sagged slightly from his dead weight. Ron's eyes remained open in a blank, dead stare. The stench around him was awful.

His friend took off his ski mask and grinned up at him. His handsome face was flushed. "What did I tell you about him crapping himself?"

He nodded. His partner had done so much of the planning with him. They were so careful, down to the last detail. If the police traced the milk crate, they'd find it was stolen from outside a 7-Eleven three blocks from Ron's house.

Ron's Miata would remain parked nearby.

His friend had left the Corolla farther down the woodland trail—at the end of a gravel drive so there would be no tire marks. They weren't worried about their shoe prints. The shoes came from a Goodwill store on Capitol Hill.

With Ron nearly naked from the waist down, people would wonder about this bizarre suicide in the woods. He asked his friend if the police would notice the red marks on Ron's wrists. Would they see the bump on his head from the blackjack?

"So what if they do?" his pal had answered.

The police wouldn't think it was suicide for long.

The two of them had set it up that way. And they'd set it up so Spencer *Rowe* would be the central suspect in Ron Jarvis's murder. Several students had witnessed an altercation between the two of them at school today. And less than an hour ago, Ron was telling everyone at the party that he would kick Spencer's ass.

If the coroner got the time of death right, Spencer would have no alibi for tonight. Right now, he was outside Tanya McCallum's house, hiding in the shadows, watching her. He was alone. Tanya had been instructed to phone Spencer and tell him exactly what she'd done tonight. So his claims he'd spent the night tailing her would carry no weight with the police.

They had just one more thing to do to put the final nail in Spencer's coffin—and it involved Ron's precious letter jacket.

He climbed down from the crate and pulled off his ski mask. The cool air felt good against his face. He gave the milk crate another kick—turning it on its side. It lay there on the ground in the shadow of Ron's dangling corpse.

He couldn't help feeling a little disappointed now that it was over. It was that way with the others, too. The planning, the masterminding—that was the best part. He liked feeling in control.

But some things he had no control over. His friend was certain a jogger or some hikers would find Ron's body here in the woods near Discovery Park by noon tomorrow. But then, he'd also been sure someone would stumble upon Spencer's dead therapist within twenty-four hours—and that had been three days ago. She must not have had any appointments for the rest of the week. Her body would have started to decay by now. Did fragrances from the candle and soap shop below her office help camouflage the smell? He couldn't be sure, and hated that uncertainty.

After one last look at their handiwork, he and his partner started toward the gravel drive where the Corolla was parked.

As they neared the car, his friend put a hand on his shoulder and squeezed it. "Hey, I want you to look over here at what I did in the wee hours this morning while you were asleep."

"What are you talking about?" he asked—with a mystified smile.

"It's just over here, c'mon," he said, taking him by the arm. His friend led him into the woods. Twigs snapped beneath their feet.

Not far from the gravel drive, he spotted what looked like a shallow trench. "What's this?" he asked.

His partner chuckled. "Oh, God, I just hate to tell you this," he said, taking something from his pocket. "But I really don't need you anymore."

"What?" It took him a moment to realize his friend was holding a gun—and that he was standing in front of his own grave.

At that same moment, a loud, single shot echoed in the woods.


His aunt flung the door open. "What happened to you?" she asked.

She must have been waiting and watching from the front window, because Spencer hadn't even reached the front stoop yet.

"You said you'd be home by eleven," she continued. "And I thought we agreed you'd take a cab . . ."

Spencer glanced at his watch. "It's only half-past."

"What happened to the cab?" she pressed.

"I decided to walk Tanya home," he said.

She glanced down at his muddy shoes. "Where does she live? In a swamp?"

Stepping through the front door, he started to take off his dirty Converse All Stars. "Sorry I'm late," he muttered.

"Well, I don't mean to jump on your case, but I've been worried," she said, shutting the door behind him. She locked it and put the chain on. "So how was the movie?"

"Good," he said, leaving his soiled shoes by the door.

"What did you end up seeing?"

"Um, the new Adam Sandler," he said, figuring she wouldn't be interested in any more details. His Aunt Andrea wasn't an Adam Sandler fan.

"Really?" she said, folding her arms. "I had no idea he was in the Iranian film playing at the Uptown."

"Well, they—they have two theaters there."

"Yes. And the other theater's playing a revival of *The Seven Samurai*. I don't think Adam Sandler was in that one either. I checked on what was playing there, Spencer. If you're going to lie to me, you should at least come up with a better cover story."

Spencer's back was against the door. She practically blocked his way into the rest of the town house.

"Sorry," he mumbled.

"Well, *sorry* isn't going to cut it here," she said. "You lied, Spencer, and I can't have that. Don't you understand? When you lie to me about where you're going or where you've been, all I can do is assume the worst. I got a strange phone call tonight. I'm pretty sure it was Troy Slattery. Whoever it was, they indicated you were up to no good tonight. Now, where were you? I know you weren't at the movies. And I know you weren't hanging around with Tanya and the cast of *The Pajama Game*. You don't even like her very much."

"I was following her," he admitted. "She said she was meeting someone tonight, and I thought it might be that Troy guy. So I followed her all night. My shoes got muddy, because I was spying on her from a construction site next door to her house."

Wide-eyed, Andrea stared at him. "Spencer, you could get arrested for doing that."

He shrugged. "I know."

"Well, okay, I'll bite," his aunt said. "Who did she meet?"

"Nobody," Spencer replied. "I guess the guy canceled on her. Anyway, I'm sorry I didn't tell you the truth. I figured you'd talk me out of it if you knew what I was doing."

"You're damn right I would have. So what else haven't you told me?"

"Well, okay, so today at school, Ron Jarvis threatened me." It actually felt good to tell her that.

"Ron Jarvis," she repeated.

"He's this big football jock."

"Isn't he one of the people who picked on Damon?"

Nodding, Spencer took off his jacket. "He picked on me, too—for a while. Anyway, he started getting texts and phone calls—just like Reed got right before he and his parents were killed. I guess somebody told him it was me."

"Probably the same creep who called me tonight," his aunt said.

"You think it's Troy?" Spencer asked. "Because I do. I have a theory—while he was dating Mrs. Shuler, he, Damon, and Tanya formed some sort of weird pact. Now he and Tanya are getting even for what happened to Damon."

He draped his jacket over the stairway banister.

"And it's not just the bullies they're killing. They're going after Luke, you, and me, too—everyone Damon mentioned in that speech, everyone who pissed him off. I wouldn't be surprised, once they're done with Ron, they go after Principal Dunmore."

"You could be right," Andrea said. "But Troy, Damon, and Tanya, that's an awfully strange trio. I'm not sure. Have Ron or his parents told the police about the calls and texts?"

Spencer nodded. "His parents reported it to the police. But I don't think they blamed me for it or we would have heard from the cops by now. Anyway, I'm pretty sure we've got it covered for the next twenty-four hours. This girl, Bonnie—she used to go out with Ron—she talked to him and got one of his teammates to make sure Ron doesn't go home tonight."

"And the police know," she said, apparently double-checking.

"Yeah," he said. "Do you think maybe we should call them and let them know about my theory?"

His aunt rubbed her forehead. "I don't think they want to hear any theories from either one of us, to tell you the truth." She sighed. "Did you get anything to eat tonight?"

"I had a slice of pizza at seven o'clock."

She sighed. "Go wash up and I'll fix you a sandwich." She stepped aside so he could pass.

She must have read his mind, because he had to pee. He started toward the powder room, but stopped and turned to her. He worked up a smile. "Thanks for not being too mad at me."

"Well, I'm hardly one to point fingers at anyone for

being secretive. Luke would attest to that, I'm sure. Along those lines, Spencer, I need to be honest with you. I've been busy 'being secretive' myself the last couple of days."

He frowned. "What do you mean?"

"I've been doing some investigating. I've uncovered a few things, but I still have a lot of questions. You might be able to help me with some of them."

"How so?" he asked.

"For starters, do you know who Doreen Carter is?"

He shook his head. "Why? Am I supposed to know her?"

"Not necessarily," she said. "What about Kirk Mowery or Richard Phelps?"

He shook his head again. "Who are they?"

"They're friends of a friend of yours," his aunt said.

"What are you talking about?" he asked, frowning.

Andrea sighed again. "Go get cleaned up. I'll make you a grilled cheese. And I'll tell you all about it while you eat . . ."


### Saturday, October 31—1:24 a.m.

He watched the light go out in the master bedroom on the second floor.

They'd left a lamp on in the living room just to throw off someone like him. It was the Mission-style lamp with the Tiffany shade. He'd noticed it while inside the house two nights ago around this time. They weren't throwing him off at all. He'd been here long enough to know nobody was in that living room—or on the entire first floor. The two of them had gone upstairs to their respective rooms about forty minutes ago. Though their bedroom lights were off, he was pretty sure neither of them was asleep yet.

He was parked across the street from the town house. He'd been there for almost an hour, and only twenty or so cars had passed him—none of them police cars. It was a far cry from three weeks ago, when this place had swarmed with cops and reporters. How quickly people forgot.

But he didn't forget. He held onto things. And, sometimes, they festered and he'd go a little crazy.

The two of them had foiled his break-in the night before last. But he would get inside that house again. It just wasn't happening tonight.

He grabbed the phone from the passenger seat and played the video again.

*"So, Troy's not home,"* Adrian was saying. *"I'm not sure when he's going to be back . . ."*

*"Well, I was hoping to track him down,"* Andrea Boyle said. The image of her in the bedroom doorway was slightly blurred and rickety—thanks to Adrian's unsteady hand. *"I'm a friend of Evelyn Shuler's . . ."*

His roommate—and sometime girlfriend—had surreptitiously recorded the beginning of Andrea's surprise visit to his basement abode. It was obvious that Luke Shuler's whore was trying to pin the hit-and-run on him. He wondered when she planned to go to the police with her suspicions.

Before that happened, he'd shut her up—for good.

He'd catch the two of them while they were home—when their guard was down.

And he'd go a little crazy.

# CHAPTER THIRTY-ONE

*Saturday—7:52 a.m.*

Carl Brubaker was running late. It had been his girl-friend Lolita's birthday last night, and they'd been out celebrating until one in the morning. She'd had her merlot, and he'd stuck with seltzer water all night long. Two years sober, so far.

He was just getting started on this building and had another floor of office suites to clean in a building in Madison Valley. Then he had to meet Lolita by four-thirty so they could take her little boy trick-or-treating. Usually, the clients in this building on Nineteenth Avenue expected a deep clean every weekend. That included emptying all the trash cans, washing the floors, watering the plants, dusting, and vacuuming the carpets. This weekend they would get what Carl's late mother called "a lick and a promise." He'd do some surface cleaning, make sure all the plants were watered—and then save the detail work for next weekend.

Unfortunately, there was already a wrench in his

plan. Someone must have thrown away something perishable into one of the office trash cans. He'd noticed the smell while spot-vacuuming the hallway. Even past all the perfume scents drifting up from the store downstairs, he could still tell something had gone bad—probably a milkshake or part of a tuna sandwich. People didn't seem to realize that a lot of office trash cans were just for trash—not food garbage. The smell seemed to be coming from Diane Leppert's waiting room. That was odd, because she was usually very tidy.

He got out his keys and unlocked the waiting room door. As he stepped into the anteroom, the stench hit him hard. He could tell it was something beyond the next door. He unlocked and stepped inside Dr. Leppert's office.

"Oh, Christ," he muttered, covering his mouth.

Someone must have rifled through the desk, because papers littered the floor. Lying facedown on the carpet, the therapist's body had swollen to twice her normal size. She looked like a beached whale. Her auburn hair on one side of her head was matted down with blood. A glass Saturn paperweight—splotched reddish brown—was on the floor beside her.

Carl knew this office well. The Saturn ornament was usually on the small table by the easy chair. Now in its place, he saw someone's paperback copy of *The Grapes of Wrath*.

*Saturday—10:14 a.m.*

"Hi, Doreen," Andrea said into the landline cordless phone in Luke's study. She sat in front of his computer. Hugh Badger Lyman's file on her was on the desk. "My name's Andrea Shuler, and I'm an attorney working for H. B. Lyman, a detective agency. I'm trying to track down a Richard Phelps. It's a private matter. In fact, he's in line to inherit some money. I was told you might know how to reach him."

"Not me," the woman said. "I don't know a Richard Phelps."

"Maybe you know one of Richard's friends, Garrett Beale or Kirk Mowery?"

"No, I don't. How did you get this number anyway?"

"I'm sorry I bothered you," Andrea said. "Thanks for your time."

She hung up, and scratched a line through the third "Doreen Carter" in Virginia—from her list of candidates. This one—from Fredericksburg—seemed to have some real "girlfriend" potential for Garrett, Kirk, or Richard. She was twenty-two, and had posted several slutty-looking selfies on Facebook.

Andrea had narrowed the list down to six women in Virginia. Now she had three Doreen Carters left. None of them looked too promising: a thirty-one-year-old single saleswoman at Ann Taylor at Tysons Corner Center; a Richmond-based, thirty-nine-year-old married dental hygienist with two children; and a twenty-eight-year-old married political consultant in Arlington. If none of them fit the bill, she would track down all the Doreen Carters in the Seattle area, and then Maryland.

It had taken her most of the morning to compose this first list of candidates, checking Google and Facebook, and then looking up the women's phone numbers.

Andrea had gotten up at six-fifteen. Her Fitbit showed two hours of heavy sleep, two hours of light. She envied Spencer for sleeping in. She'd heard him get up about fifteen minutes ago.

She wasn't sure who Doreen Carter was, but the name must have meant something to Evelyn's private detective. From what Dana had said, his boss might have scribbled down that name shortly before his death. And it was rather a bizarre death, too—an automobile-train smashup with no witnesses, and a combination of drugs and alcohol in the victim's bloodstream. How sure were the Seattle police that Hugh Badger Lyman's death was really an accident?

Andrea's entire morning hadn't been dedicated solely to tracking down Doreen Carter. She'd also tried the number H. B. Lyman had written down for Richard Phelps's older sister and guardian. But it was disconnected. Andrea had gotten the same result when she'd tried to call Kirk Mowery. She'd tried Kirk's mother and got an answering machine. She'd hung up without leaving a message.

She was dialing the saleswoman in Tysons Corner when she heard Spencer come down the stairs. Clicking off, Andrea put the cordless handset back in its cradle.

Spencer wandered into the study in jeans and a navy blue fisherman's sweater. He was carrying his jacket. His hair was uncombed and he looked a bit shaken.

"What's going on?" Andrea asked, leaning forward in Luke's swivel chair.

"Ron's dead," he replied numbly.

"The one you were telling me about yesterday? The jock?"

Spencer nodded. "I just got a call from Bonnie. She was crying. The police came to her house this morning. Ron hung himself—or at least, it was made to look that way. They found him strung up from a tree in the woods near Discovery Park. Some joggers found him. We—we thought he had it covered for a while. One of Ron's friends was supposed to look after him. I guess he left the party in a hurry. Bonnie—she's really torn up. She's pretty sure the police think I had something to do with it. I wouldn't be surprised if they were on their way here."

"Oh, my God," Andrea whispered. She watched him put on his jacket. "Wait—where do you think you're going?"

"I'm meeting Tanya," he said. "I just called her. She's the only one besides you who might be able to say where I was last night after eleven o'clock. That's when they think Ron was killed. I'm hoping Tanya might have seen me follow her home. She wouldn't say over the phone, but she agreed to meet me for brunch at the 5 Spot."

"Brunch?" Andrea repeated. She got to her feet. "What kind of nonsense is that? Why didn't Tanya just give you a straight answer on the phone? Why is she jerking you around like this?"

Tears in his eyes, Spencer shrugged hopelessly. "I don't know, but I'm hoping this time I'll get through to her. Maybe she'll finally open up to me. She said she'd wait for me at the restaurant. I need to leave—now, before the police get here."

"Well, I'm not letting you go there alone," Andrea said. "I'll drive you."

Located at the top of Queen Anne Hill, the 5 Spot was a fifties-style diner with wood paneling, red Naugahyde-covered booths and bar stools, and chrome edges everywhere. A partition separated the counter-bar from the main eating area. Every month they changed the menu to present foods from a different city or country. Above the partition dangled three piñatas—to celebrate their special menu from Mexico.

Even though she wasn't hungry and she'd already had three cups of coffee this morning, Andrea ordered a cheese omelet and a cup of coffee. She sat at the counter, where she could see Spencer and Tanya on the other side of the partition, seated in a booth near a six-foot replica of the Statue of Liberty on a pedestal. They were still ordering. Their waitress—like everyone else on the staff—was dressed for Halloween. She wore rabbit ears, a little Bugs Bunny nose-and-teeth mask, and a furry tail.

Andrea had brought along the contact list she'd collected for various Doreen Carters in Virginia. While she waited for her food, she called the saleswoman from Tysons Corner. She got an answering machine and left a message. Then she tried the married dental hygienist from Richmond.

The woman picked up: "Yeah, hello?"

"Is Doreen Carter there, please?"

"Yes, this is Doreen."

"Hi, my name is Andrea Boyle, and I'm an attorney.

I was told you might have some information regarding the whereabouts of a Richard Phelps. He's not in any kind of trouble. It's just the opposite. He's in line to inherit some money . . ."

There was a silence on the other end. Andrea wondered if she'd missed something due to all the chatter in the restaurant. "Ms. Carter? Doreen?"

"You're a lawyer?" she asked, sounding leery.

"Yes. I understand Richard was friends with a Doreen Carter. I'm hoping you might be the right Doreen Carter. As I said, Richard isn't in any trouble. It's a family matter. If you don't know Richard, perhaps you're acquainted with some friends of his, Garrett Beale or Kirk Mowery."

"Garrett?" she whispered. Andrea barely heard her over the noise.

"Yes, Garrett Beale," Andrea said. "Do you know him?"

The line went dead.

Andrea wasn't sure if the woman had hung up or if they'd been cut off.

The bartender, dressed like a cowboy, set a plate in front of her. "Cheddar omelet and whole wheat toast. Would you like some ketchup?"

"Ah, no, thank you," she said, the phone still in her hand.

He refilled her coffee cup and set a bowlful of Smucker's jelly packets beside her plate. As Andrea thanked him again her phone rang the "Hello, Goodbye" tune. She thought it might be Doreen calling back, but the caller ID showed: HARBORVIEW HOSP.

She clicked on. "Luke?" she said.

"Is this Andrea Boyle?" a man asked.

"Yes. Who's calling?"

"This is Dr. Stafford Lombard at the ICU at Harborview. I'm calling about Luke Shuler—"

"Yes?" she said anxiously.

"He developed an infection this morning. We hoped to keep it in check, but with his condition, it's very difficult. He has a fever of a hundred and four. He'd like you to come to the hospital. He said he'd prefer you to come alone. Um, do you have any idea where he keeps his will?"

"His will?" Andrea repeated. She was in shock. Luke had been doing pretty well last night.

"Yes, he'd like you to bring it," the man said. "Could you come right away? The sooner, the better . . ."

"I'm sorry to interrupt," his aunt said, putting her hand on his shoulder. She seemed nervous. Some of the color had drained from her face. "They need me at the hospital. Will you be okay on your own?"

"Is Luke all right?" Spencer asked.

She nodded. "He just needs me to bring some records from the house. I'll call you later. Okay?" She squeezed his shoulder. "When you're done here, I want you to go right home. Will you promise me?"

"Sure," he murmured. "Aunt Dee, are you okay?"

Across the table, Tanya was looking up at her, eyes narrowed.

"Yes. I'll call you later—at home," his aunt said. From her purse, she took out two twenties and handed them to him. "Here, this should cover your breakfast. And there should be enough for a taxi home. I know it's less than a mile, but I want you to call a cab."

"Okay, thanks," Spencer said. As he took the money, he noticed her hand was shaking.

His aunt turned to Tanya. "If you really cared about my nephew or Mr. Shuler, you'd be honest with us. Spencer's been decent to you. He deserves better. He deserves your help."

Tanya curled her lip. "What?"

His aunt turned and hurried out of the restaurant.

Tanya let out a stunned, little laugh. "What was that about? What's her problem?"

"She's worried about me," Spencer said. "I didn't get home until after eleven-thirty last night. Ron was killed near Discovery Park some time after ten forty-five. For most of those forty-five minutes, I was following you."

Tanya's mouth dropped open, and she blinked. "What are you talking about?"

Spencer thought she seemed to be overacting a bit. "I was worried about you," he lied. "And so I was following you last night—from the Thai place to your house to Kerry Park and back to your house again."

She laughed. "Oh my God, you were stalking me?"

"I was worried about you," he lied again. "I thought you might have seen me—near the end, when you called me. I was just down the block from your house."

She shook her head. "I had no idea."

"Are you sure?" Spencer pressed. "Tanya, someone is trying to set me up for Ron's murder. And the police are already pretty sure it was murder and not a suicide. They suspect me. If you saw me, then I have an alibi for where I was at eleven o'clock last night."

She took a sip of her water and said nothing.

"That's what my aunt meant when she said if you liked me, you'd be honest with me and help me out."

She shrugged. "I wish I could. But I didn't see you at all last night. You must be a pretty good stalker, because I didn't have a clue you were following me."

His eyes wrestled with hers. "You know something? I don't believe you."

"Well, it's the truth," she insisted. She shifted a little in the booth.

"Did you know Damon kept a journal?" he asked.

Tanya looked truly baffled. She shook her head.

Spencer could tell she wasn't acting this time. "I found it at Luke's house, and read parts of it—before it disappeared. I read about what Ron and Reed put him through—and what they put you through, too. It's horrible what they did. I have to admit, I'm not all that sorry they're gone. Four of the people Damon mentioned in that webcast are now dead, four people he hated. Maybe Damon planted the bomb that killed KC and Mr. MacAfee. But someone else had to kill Reed and Ron. And they did it for Damon. The police said that the murders of Reed and his parents looked like a two-person job. Now, I know you're not a killer. But in Damon's journal, he didn't mention any other friends—except you. Can you think of anyone else who might be doing this for him?"

Tanya's mouth twisted to one side. She nodded. "A couple of weeks before the explosion, I had a feeling

Damon had made another friend, someone he didn't tell me about."

Spencer was pretty sure she was telling the truth.

"I have absolutely nothing to back it up, but it was a feeling I got. It was like he started to cut me out of his life." She shrugged. "Then again, maybe he was already thinking about what he was going to do, and he didn't want me catching on . . ."

"You must have been hurt when he pulled away," Spencer said.

Tanya nodded.

"From everything you've told me—and what I read in his journal—you were a good friend to Damon."

"I was," she murmured.

"Here you go, folks," interrupted the waitress with the rabbit ears and nose. She set their plates in front of them. "Short stack for the lady, and eggs and bacon for the gentleman."

"Thank you," Spencer said.

Tanya didn't say anything. She didn't even look up. She had tears in her eyes.

The waitress set a syrup dispenser by Tanya. "Anything else for you folks?"

"No thanks, this is great," Spencer said. He watched the waitress walk away—her bunny tail wagging. Neither he nor Tanya picked up a fork.

"I know you're involved in these murders somehow," he said quietly. "Even if it's remotely, you're involved, Tanya. How well do you know Troy Slattery? Be honest with me . . ."

"I was telling you the truth. I hardly know the guy." With a sigh, she poured some syrup over her hotcakes.

"Do you really think a slick guy like him would hang around with me? Give me a break . . ."

Spencer watched her eat a couple of forkfuls of her pancakes. "Did Damon hire a couple of professional hit men before he killed himself? Did he give you the list of the people he wanted them to kill? Is that it?"

Tanya rolled her eyes and shook her head.

But Spencer thought he was on to something. "Did he make some sort of arrangement with you before he killed himself? Did he ask you to contact anyone or—or—"

"No, God!" she said. Her fork clanked on her plate as she put it down. "I already told you, I had no idea he was planning anything like that."

Spencer frowned at her. He started to eat his breakfast. "Okay, fine," he muttered between bites. "You realize you're helping to set me up for Ron's murder, don't you? Someone's using you. And you're taking a big chance getting involved with a couple of killers. Damon doesn't deserve your loyalty. Some of the stuff he wrote about you in his journal wasn't exactly nice."

"What do you mean?" she asked, suddenly sitting up.

Spencer could tell he'd struck a nerve. He stopped eating. "I don't want to repeat it. Just believe me when I tell you, it wasn't very flattering."

"Give me an example," she pressed.

He sighed. "All right, he mentioned that sometimes he was embarrassed to be seen with you."

"What else?" she asked. "What else did he say?"

"He said the way you dressed made you look 'frumpy,' and that you did it for attention, but it just made you subject to ridicule." Spencer didn't want to go on. He could see she was hurt, bristling.

"Well, don't stop now," she said with a tremor in her voice. "You're just getting started . . ."

"Okay, he sometimes blamed you for the fact that people didn't like him," Spencer said. "He wondered if he'd be better off if the two of you weren't friends . . ."

"That bastard," she grumbled. Her face was turning red. "He's going to have to explain—"

"What did you say?" Spencer asked.

Tanya hesitated, and then took a deep breath. "Sometimes, I—I forget he's dead. It—it's wrong of you to quote Damon when he's not here to defend himself."

Spencer just stared at her.

Tanya shook her head. "I know what you're thinking, and you're wrong."

"My God," he whispered.

Tanya grabbed her purse. The table rocked and silverware clattered as she quickly scooted out of the booth. Weaving around tables, she made her way to the door and hurried outside. Through the restaurant's big picture window, Spencer watched her almost knock someone over as she ran down the sidewalk.

He knew once she was far enough away, once she caught her breath, Tanya would call her only real friend.

# CHAPTER THIRTY-TWO

*Saturday—12:12 p.m.*

It started raining as she pulled onto Dexter Avenue. Andrea switched on the windshield wipers and then tightly gripped the steering wheel again. She told herself to focus on the road and watch the speed limit. If she had an accident or a cop stopped her, it would just delay her getting to the hospital. Luke was going to be all right. All this was just a precaution.

A fat, three-ring blue binder with "Estate Planning Portfolio" on the cover sat on the passenger seat. She'd found it in the closet in Luke's study. She was pretty certain he hadn't changed his will recently. He'd probably left everything to poor Damon. She didn't bother to check it. There was no time.

She kept resisting the impulse to press harder on the accelerator. The rain made the road slick, and besides, it felt like something was wrong with the car.

Andrea couldn't tell what it was, but she'd noticed

an odd buckling after she'd left the restaurant—almost like she'd run over an object in the road and it had somehow wedged itself under the car. When she'd gotten home, she'd quickly checked the tires, but hadn't found anything. Then again, she hadn't been very thorough.

Luke couldn't really be dying. Hospitals knew how to keep a fever in check, didn't they? What happened when someone's temperature went up to 105? Didn't they go into convulsions or something? She imagined getting to the hospital in time to see them trying to resuscitate Luke with one of those machines, the doctor with a pair of electrified paddles, hovering over Luke's broken, unresponsive body: *"Clear!"*

Andrea pushed harder on the accelerator. The rain was coming down faster now. She switched the windshield wipers to high.

She hadn't been thinking straight when she'd left the 5 Spot. She should have taken Spencer with her. Just because the doctor had said she should come alone, it didn't mean Spencer couldn't sit in the waiting room. She shouldn't have left him there in the restaurant. She couldn't be sure he'd actually go directly home after his meeting with Tanya. What if Troy Slattery was waiting for him when he got to the town house? Or maybe the police would come to question or arrest him while he was there all by himself. What if he tried to run away?

"Shit," she said under her breath.

Once she reached the hospital, she would call him and have him take a cab there.

Andrea sped up and sailed through a light as it turned

yellow. It felt like a tiny victory. She'd get to the hospital one minute sooner.

But then the car suddenly lurched and skidded. For an awful moment, the wheel seemed to lock on her. The VW veered into the oncoming lane. A minivan headed straight for her. A horn blared. Andrea pulled at the wheel again and swerved back into her own lane. She heard the tires screech. The blue binder flew off the seat and fell to the passenger floor. The car tilted to one side and rattled so much Andrea felt as if she were driving over a series of speed bumps. She realized one of the tires must have blown. Trying to get her breath, she tapped the brake to slow down. She switched on her indicator and pulled over to the side of the road.

Though she'd come to a stop, Andrea still clung white-knuckled to the wheel. She couldn't stop shaking. She told herself there was no time to start crying. She knew how to change a tire. She'd done it before—and in good time, too. She just hadn't ever changed a tire in the rain before—while someone she loved lay dying in the hospital.

She sat in the car for another minute, collecting herself. The windshield wipers squeaked a bit. Rain tapped on the roof, and other cars whooshed by. Andrea turned off the engine and switched on the hazard lights. She took a deep breath, then reached down under the dash and popped the trunk. Opening the door, she stepped outside and felt the cold rain hammering down on her.

She hurried around to the front of the car and opened the hood. Raindrops started to cover the spare tire—and something else that was in the VW's trunk, something that didn't belong in there. It was a navy blue and gray jacket, Spencer's school colors. The jacket wasn't his. It was a varsity jacket for someone on the football or basketball team.

Andrea picked it up and a few feet of slightly tattered rope fell out of the jacket folds. There was a big knot in the rope—like it might have been tied around someone's wrists or ankles.

She saw the *QA* sewn on the back of the jacket—a varsity letter.

"Ron Jarvis," she murmured.

*He's this big football jock . . . He picked on me, too—for a while.*

She remembered Spencer's muddy shoes when he'd come home last night. And she remembered what he'd told her happened to Ron: *They found him strung up from a tree in the woods.*

Had Spencer's shoes gotten dirty in those woods?

With cars sailing by, Andrea stood in the rain in front of her crippled VW and started to sob.

Spencer lingered outside the 5 Spot—in the shelter of its awning. The rain fell steadily around him, but he was dry.

He kept thinking of how Tanya had started talking about Damon as if he were alive. Spencer now knew that when she'd made that slip of the tongue, Tanya hadn't really forgotten that Damon was dead.

No, she'd forgotten for a moment *to pretend* he was dead.

Spencer studied the video on his smart phone.

It had taken him a while to find Damon's webcast.

The video had gone viral, but then was pulled off the Internet less than a day later because of its violent content less. Still, Spencer knew if he searched hard enough for it, he'd eventually find the uncensored video on some Web site. It was that way with practically everything on the Internet.

After only ten minutes, he'd found a site, www.grist-4-d-mill.com, with the headline: *Uncensored: Teen Suicide Webcast—Bullied High School Student Blows Up Mother & Self in Car!* Spencer hoped he didn't pick up some kind of virus downloading the video. The videocast was just over seventeen minutes long.

He moved the arrow at the bottom of the image until it was close to the end. He started at 15:40—fifteen minutes and forty seconds into the webcast.

It wasn't intentional, but Spencer started the video at the moment in which Damon was on the phone with his dad and mentioned Spencer: "You can marry that other woman—and be like a father to what's-his-name—Spencer." Though he was snide with that *what's-his-name* crack, Damon still seemed so sad and resigned to what he was about to do. His voice was a bit fuzzy on the video, and hard to hear over all the rain. "He's more like the son you always wanted than I ever could be. At the end of the day, you'll come out better than anyone else. And just think of the publicity, Dad. All those people who have never heard of you and never seen your plays, they'll know you after today . . ."

Damon fell silent as his father spoke to him on the phone. Spencer could only guess how much Luke was pleading with his son not to kill himself—or anyone else. With the phone to his ear, Damon kept nodding over and over. He looked so glum.

But then—at sixteen minutes and twenty-eight seconds—Damon suddenly hurled the phone into the woods. He opened the front door of the BMW, and then stepped to one side—out of camera range. After a moment, everything went out of focus as Damon repositioned the camera. It was directed toward the passenger side now. Damon stepped back into the shot, walking around to the front of the BMW to the door he'd opened on the driver's side. He bent down to climb into the front seat.

Spencer held the phone close to his face, trying to see inside the car. But it was too dark. Had Damon actually gotten in the front seat?

The driver's door slammed shut.

Spencer couldn't see any shadows or movement inside or outside the car.

Even though he knew it was coming, the bright flash still startled him. He paused the video just as the car burst into flames.

He told himself that this video had been seen by thousands of people. If anything about it had been faked, wouldn't someone have noticed? Or had most people watched it on the tiny screens of their smart phones? Had anyone carefully studied this video?

Spencer moved the arrow back to 16:42 and played it again. But his phone screen was too small to get a good look at every move Damon had made in those final seconds.

Switching over to phone mode, he dialed Bonnie Middleton's number.

She answered before the second ring. She didn't

bother to say hello. "What did Tanya say? Did you meet with her?"

"Yeah, we met," he said. "And I think she ended up telling me a lot more than she intended to. Listen. Do you live anywhere near the Five Spot?"

"My house is about six blocks away. Why?"

"Are you home?" he asked. "Or are you on your way to cheerleading?"

"I'm home. There's nothing to cheer-lead. They canceled the game, because of Ron—and the rain."

"Do you have a computer in your bedroom—with a big screen?"

"Yeah, I guess, eighteen inches," she replied. "It's not exactly enormous."

"Can I come over?"

"What for? Why are you asking about the size of my computer screen?"

"Because I want to watch Damon's suicide webcast," Spencer replied.

"You want to look at that *again*?"

"No, I want to look at it for the first time—on a big screen," he said. "I want to see if he actually got into that car before it blew up."


"I don't want to do this anymore," Tanya said into her phone.

It had started raining on her way home, and she didn't have an umbrella with her. So Tanya was cold and drenched as she turned down her block. Her sneakers from the Salvation Army were already soaked through, and her socks were wet. She was miserable—and hat-ing herself for that slip she'd made in front of Spencer earlier. She was almost certain he'd caught on.

She just wanted to get out of this. It had already gone way too far. She was tired of being a decoy and coconspirator.

She'd phoned twice and gotten the generic voice mail that came with those pay-as-you-go phones he was now using. Pimps and drug dealers used those types of phones. Other criminals used them, too. And that's what he'd become now. She'd become one, too: *an accessory to murder*.

On this third attempt to get ahold of him, she'd left a message. And the message was that she'd had enough.

"I could end up going to jail for my part in this," she said. She kept her head down—staring at the leaves on the wet sidewalk. Her hair was in damp tangles. "Spencer is starting to figure out what you're doing. It's obvious you're trying to frame him. And you know something? He doesn't deserve it. He never did anything to you—or me. He's a hell of a lot nicer to me than you've been lately . . ."

Tanya started to cry. "You won't even show your face to me! And listen, I know you're working with someone else. You've been lying to me about that. I want to see you . . ."

She took a deep, fortifying breath as she neared the walkway to her house. "I want to meet in person with you today—I mean it, *today,* face-to-face! Otherwise, tomorrow I'm going to the police and telling them everything. I'll cut a deal with them. I mean it . . ."

\* \* \*

Spencer saw her standing under an umbrella on the corner at the end of her block. Bonnie wore jeans and a dark blue jacket with a hood. She waved to him.

"God, you're drenched," she said as he approached her.

She offered to share the umbrella with him, which was sweet—but not really necessary. He couldn't have gotten any wetter if he'd gone swimming in his clothes. Still, Spencer didn't pass up the chance to huddle close to her. "Thanks," he said.

As they started down the sidewalk together, Bonnie warily looked around. "Like I told you over the phone, you're taking a real chance coming here," she said. "The police are still patrolling the neighborhood. And I have a feeling they're on the lookout for you in particular."

"Why? What do you mean?" Spencer asked.

"Last night at the party, Ron was going on and on about 'kicking your ass' to anyone who would listen. I guess enough people have told the police about it. It's clear Ron was jealous of you, at least the police think so. They figure where there's smoke . . ."

"I still don't get it," he said.

She looked at him and sighed. "I'm pretty sure the police think I'm your girlfriend. And they're expecting you to contact me."

"Oh," he heard himself say. "Wow."

"I'll take that as a compliment," Bonnie said. She glanced over her shoulder, and then across the street. "My mom's out. And my dad and brothers are down in the basement, watching TV. At least they were there when I snuck out of the house a few minutes ago. I'll go in first and make sure the coast is clear—"

"Why should we have to sneak around?" Spencer asked. "Why don't you just introduce me as one of the guys on the football team or something?"

"The police have your picture. It looked a few years old, but it's still a good likeness. Anyway, they showed it to my parents. I guess they wanted to make sure I didn't lie about you never coming over to the house. Anyway, that's why we have to sneak around."

She stopped in front of a driveway and nodded at a large, old Tudor-style house. "Here's us. I'll go in first. Wait here for me to signal to you, okay?"

Spencer nodded. She started to give him her umbrella, but he quickly shook his head and gave it back to her. "You're so nice," he said. "You're doing enough for me as it is. If you were my girlfriend, I should be so lucky."

She stared at him for a moment, and Spencer wondered if he'd been a little too honest. Was it creepy of him to have just said that?

Bonnie smiled. Then she turned and hurried toward her house.

Spencer smiled, too—for the first time since he got up this morning.

He watched her open the front door, collapse her umbrella, and duck inside the house. He heard a car coming down the block and looked behind him.

It was a police car.

He raced across the driveway and hid behind some evergreen bushes. He wondered if the cop had already spotted him. If that was the case, he'd just given himself away as a pretty damn suspicious character. He wondered if Bonnie's dad and brothers were watching him from inside the house, wondering who this guy was creeping around their house.

Crouched down by the shrubs, Spencer glanced back at the house. Bonnie had left the front door open a bit. He heard the police vehicle pass. At least, he thought it was the police vehicle. He didn't move. He checked the house again.

Bonnie came out to the front stoop and waved him in.

He darted across the lawn. She held the door open for him. "My dad and brothers are still downstairs," she whispered. "We'll go up the front way. Better take off your shoes . . ."

The house felt warm, and Spencer shuddered gratefully. He stopped to pull off his shoes in the front hall, careful not to make a puddle. He carried them as he followed Bonnie up the carpeted stairs. They crept down a long hallway past a couple of bedrooms. Bonnie's room was at the very end of the hall, by the back stairs.

It was mostly pink and white—with a lot of Paris-themed stuff, like the art on the walls and the Eiffel Tower bedspread. It smelled nice in there, too.

"You can put your jacket and shoes in the bathroom," she whispered. "Help yourself to a towel."

The bathroom had blue tiles on the walls, a tiled floor and a claw-foot tub with a shower attachment. The shower curtain had an Impressionist painting of water lilies on it. Spencer set his shoes on the floor and draped his soggy jacket over the shower curtain rod. His sweater was damp, so he took that off, too, and hung it next to his jacket. He still had on his T-shirt, but he started to shiver—partly because he was cold, and partly because he was nervous being in her room.

Wrapping a towel around his shoulders, he stepped back into Bonnie's bedroom. She'd taken off her jacket, too. She wore a black pullover with her jeans. She stood by her desktop computer. "I found a site that has a better, clearer version of Damon's webcast," she said, turning to type on the keyboard and adjust the mouse. "I got a chance to study it, and I'm pretty sure I know what Damon did . . ."

She brought up the webcast and moved the arrow along the bottom of the video to the last couple of minutes. She clicked on the size option, and the image filled the screen. Then she froze the frame. It showed Damon on the phone when he was talking with Luke.

She turned to Spencer. "Did you ever see *Sixteen Candles*?"

Drying his hair with the towel, he gave her a baffled smile. "Molly Ringwald?"

She nodded. "There's a scene near the end, when the grandparents are all piling into a car to go to the sister's wedding. If you look carefully, you'll see that one of the grandmothers doesn't actually get into the car. Maybe there wasn't enough room for her or it was a timing thing. But she doesn't really climb inside. She ducks behind the car and shuts the door. Check it out next time you see the movie."

"I don't understand," Spencer murmured.

She turned back to the computer and started the video. "Damon does the same thing here. You never actually see him climb inside the car. Take a good look . . ."

Spencer watched once again. At sixteen minutes and twenty-eight seconds into the video, Damon angrily threw the phone into the woods. On the larger screen Spencer could see three old, rural-style mailboxes in the background.

Damon opened the front door of the BMW, and then he moved out of camera range.

Bonnie clicked her mouse and froze the image on the computer. "Why do you think he opened the car door then? He opens the door, and then he goes and does something else. He doesn't climb in . . ."

She clicked the mouse, and the video continued.

Damon moved toward the camera and repositioned it. Everything turned blurry for a few moments. "It's a distraction," Bonnie said.

"Jesus," Spencer whispered. "He left the car door open for someone else . . ."

"That's what I was thinking, too. There's just enough time here for someone to load another body into that front seat." She pointed to the screen as the image went into focus again. "Look where he's moved the camera so we're seeing the passenger side of the car."

Spencer frowned. "Okay, but who do you think was helping him out? Tanya? I can't see her loading a dead body into that car in a matter of a few seconds."

"Why not? Tanya's a big, sturdy girl." Bonnie nodded at the screen. "Here's where he pretends to get into the car. I watched it three times before I figured it out."

Spencer studied Damon's every move as he bent down next to the car. The driver's door shut.

Bonnie backed it up and played it again. "You never

see him actually getting inside the car," she said. "He's just ducking on the other side of it . . ."

Spencer imagined Damon trying to get away from that car before they blew it up, crawling away on his belly like the fastest snake in the world.

"Whose body do you think they used?" he wondered aloud. "And—wouldn't the police be able to tell it wasn't Damon?"

She frowned. "Spencer, that body was sitting next to five sticks of dynamite. The police would have been lucky to find a few teeth. Besides—"

A knock on the door silenced her. "Bonnie?" a woman called.

Looking panic-stricken, Bonnie mouthed the words, *my mother,* and then she pointed to the bathroom.

"Bonnie? Who are you talking to in there?"

On his tiptoes, Spencer hurried into the bathroom. As he closed the door, he stole a glance at Bonnie, picking up her phone. He didn't close the door all the way. He figured if it was completely shut, the bathroom would be the first place her mother looked.

He heard the bedroom door open. "Bonnie . . ."

"Mom, I'm talking with Beth."

"Who?"

Spencer felt his phone vibrate in his pocket. He wondered if they could hear it. He quickly pulled it out of his pocket and shut it off.

"Beth Kinsella," Bonnie was saying. "I didn't know you were back. Is everything okay?"

"When you finish talking to Beth, your dad and I would like to have a word with you downstairs."

"This sounds serious," Bonnie said. "Am I in trouble?"

"Just—finish up your call, and come down to your father's study."

Spencer heard the bedroom door close. But he didn't move.

After a moment, Bonnie opened the bathroom door. "I don't know what's going on," she said under her breath. "Maybe a neighbor saw us walking down the block or something. You better stay in here, and don't move."

He nodded. Backing away, he sat down on the edge of the tub.

Bonnie retreated into the bedroom, and a few moments later, he heard the door shut.

Spencer switched his phone back on and checked his messages. The caller hadn't left one.

Then he checked the caller ID.

"Oh, Jesus, no," he whispered.

He stared at the words on the little screen: SEATTLE POLICE DEPT.

# CHAPTER THIRTY-THREE

*Saturday—12:43 p.m.*

Andrea stared at the varsity letter jacket in the trunk of her VW. She'd moved it aside, so it wouldn't get soiled by the dirty, deflated tire she'd just dumped in there—along with the tools for changing the tire.

She'd managed to replace the tire in about half an hour. But it still seemed to take forever. While toiling away in the rain with the jack, lug nut wrench, and tires, she'd been crying. She couldn't help it. She was soaked and chilled to the bone. She felt the roadside gravel digging through her pants into her knees. Her hands were wet, filthy, and numb. The whole time, she thought of Luke in the hospital, without a spleen, and the infection that was killing him. She thought of Spencer, and the too-real possibility that he'd killed again.

She realized right then that she needed to be with Luke. She couldn't help Spencer anymore, not if he'd murdered Ron Jarvis—and maybe Reed Logan and his parents, too. If that was the case, she was finished with him.

For the last six years she'd done everything she could for this kid who had shot her sister and brother-in-law. He'd murdered them. How much longer could she keep making excuses for him?

She often thought about how Viv had asked her to look after Spencer that evening in July six years ago. But she'd had a date, and she even made some snarky comment to her sister that she was trying to have *something resembling a love life*. It turned out the guy and the date were both unremarkable. If only she'd agreed to look after Spencer that night, none of it would have happened.

But her nephew wasn't really the guilty one. It was that other boy.

Spencer had always been so sweet and affectionate. He and Andrea had had a special bond. When he was a toddler, and she'd drop by her sister's house, Spencer wouldn't leave her alone. She always lapped up the attention from this beautiful little boy. He drew pictures for her, and wanted to show her his toys. When she was ready to leave, he'd always cry and cling to her leg. As Spencer got a little older, she loved being the cool aunt who took him to his first Redskins game, the Smithsonian, and on the White House tour. Viv and Larry made the most of the fact that she enjoyed baby-sitting for them. They would go away for a weekend about once every two months, leaving Spencer to stay with her. It got so that the tiny guest room in her Washington, DC, apartment became Spencer's room. Andrea never really considered it an imposition, but then she found herself turning down guys who wanted to go out with her, because she had to babysit while her sister and brother-in-law had another weekend getaway. So, on that Saturday night in July, 2009, although she relished the time she spent with her adoring nephew, she'd resolved to go on what would be an unremarkable date.

She knew in her head it wasn't her fault that Viv and Larry had been killed that night. But she couldn't help feeling somehow guilty. She also knew in her head—and in her heart—that Spencer wasn't a killer.

She couldn't turn her back on him. He had no one else. She kept remembering him as a toddler, crying and clinging to her leg as she was about to leave him.

Andrea shut the hood of her VW Beetle, and then climbed back into the driver's seat. Luke's estate planning portfolio was still on the floor. She reached down and set it back on the passenger seat. Starting the car, she switched on the heat and the windshield defogger. She couldn't keep from trembling as she pulled the phone from her purse. She clicked onto her last call— from that Dr. Lombard who had called from Harborview. She wanted to explain that she was on her way. Or was she too late already?

Andrea clicked on the number. She counted five ringtones. All the while, the rain was tapping on the car roof. The traffic on Dexter seemed to have gotten busier since she'd first pulled over. The cars were zooming by.

Finally, someone answered: "Harborview Hospital . . ."

"Hello, is Dr. Lombard there, please?" Andrea asked.

"Dr. Lombard?" the woman repeated.

"Yes, Dr. Lombard. He called me about Luke Shuler."

There was no response on the other end. All Andrea could think was, *Oh, no, Luke's dead, and they don't know how to tell me. They're going to connect me to the hospital chaplain or some social worker . . .*

She had a hand over her heart. "Hello? Are you still there?"

"You're calling about Luke Shuler?"

"Yes," Andrea said. "I know his condition was— critical this morning, and they were concerned. Dr. Lombard called me about an hour and a half ago . . ."

"Ma'am, we don't have a Dr. Lombard in our directory."

"But he called me from this number."

"The number you called is a patient room that's unoccupied. No one's picking up in there. So your call was automatically forwarded to me here at the switchboard. Would you like me to transfer you to Mr. Shuler's room?"

It took Andrea a moment to realize what happened. "Yes . . . please . . ."

It rang twice. "Hello?" Luke picked up, sounding groggy.

"Luke?"

"Hey, babe."

"Are you all right?"

"Well, outside of a headache that's killing me, I'm okay I guess . . ."

"So you didn't have an infection or a fever this morning?" she asked. She needed to hear from him that he was all right.

"No, just this lousy headache," he said. "What—what are you talking about?"

"Nothing," she murmured.

She glanced at the Estate Planning Portfolio, sitting on the passenger seat. She thought about the last agonizing hour and a half. She decided Luke didn't need to hear anything about it. She wondered why someone would call her from an empty room at the hospital, pretending that Luke was at death's door. Had the same person done something to her tire—after planting the varsity jacket in the trunk?

After all, she was sure to find it in there when she changed the tire. If she hadn't had the blowout, weeks might have gone by without her knowing the jacket was there. She'd thought it a bit bizarre the doctor told her to come alone. Did this creep want to make sure Spencer wasn't with her when she found the varsity jacket?

Or was all of this merely wishful thinking? Maybe the call leading her on this wild goose chase had nothing to do with what she'd found in the trunk. Maybe she was just trying to convince herself once again that her sweet nephew was incapable of murder.

"Honey, are you still there?" Luke asked.

"Yes, I—I'm on my way to see you . . ."

"Well, have you left the house yet?" he asked. "Because if you haven't left yet, why don't you just wait until later this afternoon to come visit? Right now, I was hoping to take a nap, maybe chase away this headache. Do you mind?"

"No, I—I haven't left yet," Andrea lied. "I can wait until this afternoon . . ."

After they hung up, Andrea called the hospital again. She explained that some stranger had called her from an empty room, claiming to be a doctor. She knew most of Luke's doctors. She should have questioned this guy. Her main concern was the security around Luke. If this stranger had snuck into an empty room, what was to keep him from sneaking into Luke's room?

The man she spoke with from hospital security apologized and then assured her they'd ramp up security on Luke's floor. She had a feeling he was placating her.

"I don't think this was just a prank," she pointed out. "I believe this person could be dangerous. He might want to harm Mr. Shuler."

"Well, if you truly feel that way, I'd contact the police about this if I were you," he replied.

"I—I'll do that," she said. "Thank you."

But as she hung up, Andrea thought about the varsity jacket in the trunk of her car.

Pulling into traffic again, she headed for home. She hoped Spencer was waiting for her there. Andrea told herself that once she got the truth out of him—whatever it was—she would indeed call the police.


"Now, we were both here when the police questioned you," her father said. "And we know what you told them. But I want you to tell us: Has this Spencer *Rowe-Murray*—or whatever he calls himself—has he contacted you at all today?"

"No, he hasn't, Poppy," Bonnie lied.

She sat on the ottoman, facing her parents, who

were on the sofa in her father's study. The police had met with the three of them in this same room a few hours ago—to tell her that Ron was dead. Bonnie wondered what the point was to this follow-up session.

Once again, she wondered if some neighbor had spotted her with Spencer outside and phoned her parents. If that was the case, her folks had just caught her in a lie.

"Sweetheart, the police called about ten minutes ago," her father said. "They're looking for your friend, Spencer, as 'a person of interest' in the murder of a therapist on Capitol Hill. She was bludgeoned to death earlier in the week. Her body was discovered in her office early this morning. The last client she had listed in her notebook was this Spencer person on Tuesday night. He even left a book behind in the office."

Bonnie shook her head. "Well, he couldn't have," she said. "God, it's not enough that they're trying to blame him for Ron's death—"

"The police are calling him 'a person of interest,' which means—"

"I know what it means," she interrupted. "They're trying to make him out like he's some kind of monster, and he isn't. Somebody must have set this up to frame him. If—if Spencer really killed this woman, do you think he'd be foolish enough to leave a book behind? Someone planted it there!"

"Bonnie, honey," her mother said. "I know you're fond of this boy—despite his history. Neither your father nor I am thrilled about it. But that's not important right now. If you know where he is, and you're trying to protect him, you aren't really helping him. The sooner he gives himself up and talks to the police, the sooner they'll straighten this all out."

Bonnie said nothing. She wondered if she was letting her attraction to Spencer warp everything. Was the sweet, handsome guy now hiding in her bathroom really a psychotic killer?

"This isn't a punishment or anything," her father said. "But for your own safety, you'll need to stay home today—and tonight."

She shrugged. "Well, after the news about Ron, I really didn't feel like going out anyway. I don't mind."

"The police said that starting this afternoon, they'll be keeping an even closer surveillance of the block," her father continued. "If this boy tries to call you, or text you, or Twitter or email you, I want you to let us know."

Bonnie looked him straight in the eye and nodded. "Yes, Poppy, of course."


Spencer sat on the edge of the tub in Bonnie's bathroom. He held his phone in his hand. He tried to convince himself that the police probably just wanted to ask him some questions—like where he was last night when Ron was killed. They weren't trying to hunt him down so they could arrest him. They just wanted to make some routine inquiries.

The phone vibrated again, startling him. He automatically switched it off.

He figured it was the police again. They weren't giving up. Maybe they'd uncovered some evidence linking him to Ron's murder. After all, Damon's accomplice had planted Reed's baseball cap in his locker in an attempt to link him to last week's murders. They could have found a similar way to frame him for Ron's lynching.

Would the police believe him if he told them Damon was still alive?

Hell, probably not. He'd be lucky if they even bothered to study the video again. If they did, they might not see what he and Bonnie saw. There was still no real proof that Damon *didn't* get into the car.

Why would they believe him—a kid who had murdered his own parents six years ago?

Spencer thought he heard footsteps. But he realized the sounds were coming from another part of the house, nowhere near Bonnie's room.

She seemed to be taking forever downstairs.

Biting his lip, he switched his phone back on. The message light blinked. It was from his Aunt Dee. He turned the phone volume down and played the voice mail: "I'm in my car, down the block from Luke's," she whispered, sounding grim. "There are three cop cars parked in front of the place. I have a feeling you aren't there. I have a feeling you came home, saw them, and turned around and ran. Spencer, what happened last night? Where were you really? Damn it, I wish you'd pick up. The police will want to talk with me. What am I supposed to tell them? I can't keep . . ." she hesitated. "Listen, call me, okay?"

Spencer heard someone coming up the back stairs. Switching off the phone, he stood up and listened.

It sounded like the person had passed Bonnie's room and continued down the hallway to one of the other bedrooms. Someone else was up here on the second floor now.

He put his phone in his pocket again. He didn't know what to do. He couldn't go back to Luke's. And his aunt didn't seem to believe him anymore.

And where the hell was Bonnie?

Earlier, the two of them hadn't heard her mother come home. Had she brought the police with her? For all he knew, there were a couple of cops downstairs, grilling Bonnie. He wanted to go over to the window and look outside for a police car. But it was one of those frosted bathroom windows, and he didn't dare make any noise attempting to open it.

Spencer reached up toward the curtain rod and felt his sweater. It was still a bit damp, but he put it on anyway.

He heard the bedroom door creak open, and he froze.

The door closed once again, and the lock clicked. "Don't worry, it's me," Bonnie whispered.

He stepped out of the bathroom. "What's going on? I heard someone come up earlier."

Bonnie nodded. "It's my brother. He went into his room. Listen, I need to tell you something . . ."

"What?"

Bonnie looked nervous. Her eyes searched his. "The police—they found your therapist."

"They got ahold of Diane?" he asked. "Did she vouch for me? She said she would—"

"Spencer, she's dead."

Dumbfounded, he stared at her. He felt as if he'd

just slammed into a wall. Everything stopped. He couldn't breathe.

"I'm sorry," Bonnie murmured.

Spencer let out a gasp, and quickly covered his mouth. But he couldn't hold back his tears. "No . . . no . . . no," he whispered.

She reached over and started to caress his arm. "I knew it couldn't have been you. I'm so sorry. They found her in her office this morning. She was killed earlier this week—bludgeoned. Spencer, somebody set you up. It happened some time after your last appointment. A book belonging to you was found in the office. The police are calling you 'a person of interest' in the case . . ."

He could barely comprehend what she was saying. He was still so torn up about Dianne. She'd been one of the few people he could trust, one of the few people who believed in him. And now she was dead.

"If Damon's the one doing this to you, I don't understand why," Bonnie said. "What did you ever do to him?"

Spencer just shrugged. Maybe it was because Luke liked him, and Damon couldn't stand that.

"We need to get you out of here—and soon," Bonnie said. "The police are planning to ramp up their patrol on this block in the next hour or two."

He pulled away from her and wiped his nose with his sweater sleeve. "I've got no place to go. I might as well give myself up. I'm screwed. Whoever's out to get me, they're winning. Maybe it's Damon, but we can't be sure. There's not enough in that video to prove he faked his death."

"Don't say that. We just need to hold off the police for a few hours, a day at the most. I'll work on Tanya, while you hide out." From her pocket, Bonnie pulled out a set of keys—on a ring with a four-leaf-clover medallion. "I lifted these from my dad's dresser drawer. They're the keys to the family boat. It's docked on Lake Union. No one will think of looking for you there . . ."

She turned and snatched a change purse from the top of her white dresser. "I have nearly fifty bucks in here," she said, looking inside the little purse. She fished out some bills and handed them to him. "You probably won't need it. You'll have all you need on the boat. It's got a bathroom, bedroom, and a galley—with cheese and crackers, soft drinks, and soup in the pantry. The instructions for operating everything on the boat are in the first drawer of the cabinet—on your left as you step into the galley . . ."

Bewildered, Spencer looked at the keys in his hand—and then at her. What she was saying came all too fast at him. But he kept nodding anyway.

"It's the South Lake Union Marina, pier seventy-nine, dock C. Can you remember that?"

He nodded again. He tried to remember: *seventy-nine and C.*

"The name of the boat is the *Bonnie Blue*—yeah, after me," she said, rolling her eyes. "I probably won't be able to get to you until early tomorrow morning. Maybe dawn, I don't know. I can't see you tonight. It's just too risky. You better not call me either. If you have to call, there's a pay phone down at the end of the dock, use that. Don't use your regular phone. You'll have to get rid of it. I'm pretty sure the police can track where you are through your cell phone number . . ."

She led him to the window by her desk. There was a tree outside, practically right beside the house. "This is probably too much information, but I snuck out one night about a month ago to meet Ron. From here, you can climb out on the tree and work your way down. It's not too far a drop from the bottom branch. And you'll land in the side yard, right by the dining room—so no one's going to see you. Are you up for it?"

"I think so," he said, still a bit dazed. "Pier seventy-nine, dock C. The *Bonnie Blue*."

Turning away from him, she opened the window. Spencer could hear the rain, but it seemed to have lightened up a bit. He stared at the tree branches outside the window, wondering which one he should climb onto first.

Bonnie turned toward him again and put her hands on his shoulders. Her face was just inches from his. "I'm going downstairs to make sure they don't wander anywhere near the dining room. Give me a good sixty seconds before you climb out the window. Leave it open. Once you reach the marina, give me a call from the pay phone. I'll put my phone on vibrate. Just let it ring once and hang up. Then I'll know it's you, and that you're okay."

He nodded again. "Thank you for all of this," he whispered, "and for believing in me."

Bonnie smiled at him and kissed him on the lips. "Give me a minute, and then climb down. And watch out for the police on this block. Okay?"

"Okay," he said, but he was thinking about that kiss. He was dazed and grateful.

Spencer waited until Bonnie had left the bedroom and quietly closed the door. He crept back to the bathroom and put on his damp shoes and jacket. Then he padded back to the window. He figured he'd already given her sixty seconds. He took a good, long look outside to make sure no one could see him.

Throwing his leg over the sill, he reached out for the closest branch and pulled himself outside. He dangled in the air for a moment, then swung forward and planted his feet on a lower limb. The tree seemed to shake with his weight, and a few twigs snapped and fell to the ground. Spencer winced at the noise. Did anyone in the house hear it?

He glanced down at the twenty-foot drop below. His heart racing, he worked his way down from one branch to another. He was looking right into their dining room window as he reached the bottom limb. The room was empty, thank God. He thought he heard someone talking inside the house—a slightly muted murmuring.

He sat on the branch and then lowered himself down. He had about a five-foot drop, which he could have done easily—if the grass weren't wet. The minute he hit the ground, he slipped and landed on his ass. It didn't hurt as much as it unnerved him.

He scurried to his feet and glanced back at the dining room window. It sounded like the voices inside were louder.

Spencer raced toward some bushes bordering the neighbor's property. Weaving around the shrubs, he cut through the neighbor's yard toward a side street. He didn't see any police cars down the road.

Catching his breath, Spencer forced himself to slow down. He figured people were more likely to notice him if he was running. At a brisk clip, he started down the sidewalk, and didn't look back.

"South Lake Union Marina, pier seventy-nine, dock C," he said to himself, as he felt the light rain on his face. "The *Bonnie Blue* . . ."

# CHAPTER THIRTY-FOUR

*Saturday—2:47 p.m.*

The phone on his bedside table rang—a reminder to Luke that he'd forgotten to turn it off.

He'd fallen asleep for a while, but didn't feel much better. When he'd told Andrea that he had a headache, it was a polite way of saying that he was in excruciating pain. Everything hurt. They were trying to wean him off the painkillers, and had lowered his dosage for the first time. He'd hated the sensation that he was all doped up. But right now, he'd have preferred to be a little out of it—instead of in this constant agony.

It was an ordeal just to reach for the phone with his good arm. From the night table, a get-well card—with a monkey in a nurse's cap on the cover—fell to the floor. He finally managed to grab the receiver on the fourth ring. "Hello?"

"Luke? Hi, it's Spencer. Did I get you at a bad time?"

"It's okay," he said, trying not to sound like he'd just woken up. "How are you?"

"I—I'm really sorry to bother you, but I'm in trouble," he said, his voice cracking. The words rushed out of him: "Ron Jarvis is dead—and my therapist, they killed her, too. They're trying to set me up. I can't call Aunt Dee. I'm pretty sure the police are with her . . ."

Luke closed his eyes. "Just—just slow down, okay? Where's Andrea?"

"At your place, I think. Last time she called—almost an hour ago—she said the police were waiting outside your house. They think I killed Ron Jarvis—and my therapist, Diane . . ."

Luke had seen something on the local news at noon about the death of Damon's former tormentor, but they'd reported it as a suicide. He'd had no idea Spencer's therapist was dead, too.

"They're trying to frame me," Spencer said. "They've set it up so it looks like I killed them."

"The police are trying to frame you?"

"No, Damon is," he replied. "Luke, I don't know how to tell you this without sounding crazy, but I'm pretty sure Damon's still alive. Check the video again. Look close. You never actually see him get into the car. I think he faked his death so he could get back at all the people who bullied him. And he's trying to make it look like I killed these people."

Luke sighed. "Spencer, this isn't funny . . ."

"I'm not trying to be funny. I know you don't want to hear this, and I hate telling you. I mean, he's your son. But check the video. Tell Andrea to check the video.

Damon opens the car door and then picks up the camera to reposition it. But that's all a distraction while Damon's accomplice loaded another body into the car. I think his friend Tanya might have helped him . . ."

"Spencer, I've heard enough," Luke said.

"After the explosion, there was nothing left to identify. Don't you see? He had it all figured out . . ."

"They found a couple of Damon's teeth," Luke said evenly. He was angry, hurt, and in pain. "The dental records matched, Spencer."

"Well, he could have knocked out those teeth ahead of time."

"You saw the webcast," Luke said. "Damon's mouth looked fine."

"He could have gone to a—a crooked dentist days or weeks ahead of time," Spencer argued. "He planned this thing, Luke. Look at how Reed died. He was trapped inside a refrigerator. That was Damon getting even for locking him inside a storage space. Ron, he was strung up from a tree. Ron threatened to string up Damon from a ceiling pipe in the restroom at school. They stripped Damon, too. Aunt Dee should ask the police if Ron was naked when they found him hanging from that tree—"

"Stop," Luke breathed. "Stop it. Just tell me where you are, Spencer."

"I can't say. I need to disappear for a while. Please tell Aunt Dee I'm okay. And she needs to look at the video. I'm sorry, Luke. I'm really sorry."

Luke heard a click on the other end. Then the line went dead.

\* \* \*

Spencer stood at one end of the University Bridge over Lake Union. The rain had tapered off to a light mist.

The bus had dropped him off one block from the drawbridge. According to the Seattle Metro route directions he'd gotten off his smart phone, the transfer bus would pick him up at the same spot in ten minutes. He hoped the police hadn't tapped into his phone yet. If they had, then they'd know exactly where he was headed.

He leaned on the bridge walkway railing with the phone in his hand. He hated upsetting Luke—especially when the guy was in a lot of pain. Luke had sounded furious with him. Why wouldn't he be? Three weeks ago, he'd watched his son die in a very public suicide. If that wasn't bad enough, the kid took Luke's former wife and two others down with him. And now here he was, telling Luke that Damon was still alive and out there killing even more people. It was a wonder Luke hadn't hung up on him.

He could see why Damon had gone after the people who had bullied him. And he understood why Damon, out of jealousy, tried to pin their murders on him. After all, he was sort of taking Damon's place with Luke.

But why kill Diane? What did she ever do to Damon?

His phone rang.

Spencer wondered if it was Luke calling back—or maybe Aunt Dee. The caller ID showed: CALLER UN-KNOWN.

He reluctantly answered: "Hello?"

"Hey, Spencer," the man said. "How are you doing?"

"Who is this?" he asked.

"Where are you right now?"

He realized it was probably a cop. "I didn't kill anybody," he said, a tremor in his voice.

"We know that," the man replied. "We just need to ask you some questions. Your aunt is very worried about you. We're all worried about you, Spencer. Tell us where you are, and we'll come pick you up. I promise we'll—"

Spencer clicked off the line.

He had a pen, and took a Seattle's Best Coffee punch card out of his wallet. On the back of it, he copied down Bonnie's phone number. He slipped the card back into his wallet and tucked the wallet into his pocket.

With a shaky hand, he set his smart phone on the railing of the bridge. He gave it a push and watched it drop into Lake Union.

Then Spencer went to catch his bus.

"Can't you see that Spencer's been set up to take the blame for these murders?" Andrea said, pacing around Luke's kitchen. "I mean, whoever's doing this isn't exactly subtle about it."

Detective Talwar, in a beige pantsuit, sat with a uniformed cop at the tall, glass-top breakfast table. Andrea had served her coffee in a Huskies mug. None of the other cops wanted anything to drink. Two more were in the living room with Deputy Marston—obviously waiting to pounce on Spencer the moment he came through the front door.

She'd given them permission to search Spencer's room. At this point, if he was hiding something from her, Andrea figured the police were welcome to it. She'd told them: "I'm doing you a favor allowing you to go through his room without a search warrant. Do me a favor, and try not to tear the place apart, okay? Please, put everything back the way you found it."

They hadn't found a thing—except Reed Logan's baseball cap, which had been bagged as evidence and now sat atop the kitchen counter.

She'd shown Talwar the varsity jacket and rope from the trunk of her VW, and another cop had already bagged them and whisked them away to their lab. Andrea had been trying to convince Talwar that someone had framed Spencer. But the policewoman didn't seem to believe a word she was saying.

"Let me put it this way," Andrea said, stopping and putting a hand on the kitchen counter. "Do you think it was just a coincidence that I got a blowout after being sent on a wild-goose chase across town by someone pretending to be a doctor? They did something to my tire. If I hadn't gotten a flat, I wouldn't have found the rope and that jacket in my trunk. Don't you see? Those items were planted there. Someone wanted me to think Spencer killed Ron Jarvis."

"And who would that be?" Talwar asked.

Andrea sighed. "I told you. Talk to Troy Slattery— and maybe check on some of his roommates at that dump where they live on Capitol Hill. You'll probably find a ton of stolen property in there. Troy's a meth addict. He had an affair with Evelyn Shuler, and he hates Luke. Check that Mazda CX-9 for his prints and traces of crystal meth. I wouldn't be surprised if he has a record and his fingerprints are on file. I'd say he's your best candidate. Find out where he was the night Luke was mowed down—and when all the murders took place. I'm pretty sure he's the one who broke in here the other night, too . . ."

Detective Talwar frowned. "Why in the world would he want to frame your nephew for these murders? And what motive would he have for killing high school kids?"

Andrea was stumped. "I'm not sure. These were people who bullied Damon. Maybe he and Damon had a friendship—and he's doing it out of revenge. He was close to Evelyn, and she wanted to make my life miserable. Troy could be carrying on her mission. I don't know. I really wish you'd ask him."

Andrea glanced at the baseball cap in the evidence bag on the counter. "We've been up front with you from the very start," she said, nodding at their "find" after searching Spencer's bedroom. "Spencer told you about someone leaving that hat in his school locker, and you dismissed it as some classmate's joke. And now you're accusing him of killing his therapist. Good God, if you knew how he depended on that woman. She did so much to help him. Why would Spencer kill her? Diane was like a second mother to him."

Detective Talwar put down the coffee cup. "I'm sorry, but didn't he serve time for killing his mother?"

Andrea sighed. "That happened when he was eleven years old—and there were extenuating circumstances. He's already paid his debt for that. He isn't—"

Her cell phone rang.

Andrea grabbed it off the kitchen counter, and checked the caller ID: HARBORVIEW HOSP.

"Who is it?" Talwar asked, hopping off the tall kitchen chair.

"It's from Harborview," she said. "It could be the same guy who called me earlier, the one pretending to be a doctor . . ."

"Put it on speakerphone," Talwar urged her.

Andrea clicked on the phone, and then switched to speaker mode. "Hello?"

"Hey, babe, it's me," Luke said, sounding groggy.

She gave a wary glance at Detective Talwar and the cop by the breakfast table. Marston and the two other policemen came to the kitchen doorway. They must have heard the phone ring.

"Hi, Luke," she said. "I have you on speaker. You remember Detective Talwar? Well, she's here—along with a few policemen. We have a—a situation here."

"Well, okay," he said. "Does it have to do with Spencer?"

"It does," she replied.

"He called me about twenty minutes ago," Luke said. "He said someone was framing him for murdering his therapist—and Ron Jarvis. Last I heard, this Ron person committed suicide. But maybe that's changed. Is that right, Detective Talwar?"

She hesitated, and then spoke up loudly. "Yes, we now have reason to believe it may have been a homicide."

"Spencer says he didn't do it," Luke said. "He says he hasn't killed anyone, and I believe him . . ."

"Did he give you any indication where he might be?" Talwar asked. But then she suddenly seemed distracted. Her phone must have been on vibrate, because she reached for it.

"He wouldn't say where he was," Luke answered. "He—well, he thinks Damon is still alive. He says Damon faked his death. He wanted you to look at the webcast video again, Andrea. He claims Damon never really got in the car . . ."

"What?" Andrea gasped.

"I don't believe it either," Luke said. "But it's clear to me that Spencer does."

Andrea glanced at Detective Talwar, who clearly wasn't interested in what Luke had to say about Spencer's fantastic theories. In fact, she wasn't even listening. She was holding her phone close to her face and murmuring into it.

She wasn't the only one. Marston and another cop were on their phones, too.

"Spencer wasn't making much sense to me," Luke said. "He went on and on about how Damon was pretending to be dead so he could kill the people who bullied him—or something like that. I'm afraid I wasn't very patient with him . . ."

There was a buzz throughout the room. A couple of the cops whispered to each other. The others were still on their phones. Andrea could hardly focus on what Luke was saying.

"Ah, you said he called about twenty minutes ago?" she asked him.

"Yeah," Luke replied. "Spencer said he had to disappear for a while, and then he hung up. I tried calling him back—three times—but didn't get an answer, not even his regular voice mail. It was an automatic recording from the cellular company . . ."

"Tell Luke you'll call him back," Talwar whispered, giving Andrea a nudge.

Andrea frowned at her. "Pardon me?"

"Mr. Shuler, something's come up," the detective announced. "Andrea's going to call you back."

"Oh, well, okay, I guess," he said, obviously confused. "Um, I'll be here." He clicked off.

Andrea switched off her phone. "What's going on?"

"He sounds pretty strong," Talwar said. "Can he sit up? Is he in any condition to be moved?"

"I doubt it. Why?"

"He's at Harborview, isn't he? Do you think the doctors there could at least wheel him down to the morgue?"

"The morgue?" Andrea's eyes narrowed. "What are you talking about?"

"We need him to identify his son's corpse," the detective said. "They just found someone they think is Damon Shuler in a shallow grave in the woods—not too far from where that jogger discovered Ron Jarvis today. He was shot in the back of the head."

Stunned, Andrea stared at her.

Talwar let out a long sigh, and then she spoke into her phone: "Can you transfer the body to the Harborview morgue? We'll notify the father and set up identification there. Thanks."

Clicking off the phone, she frowned at Andrea. "So, unless he was there in the woods last night when Ron and Damon were killed, how do you suppose your nephew knew—before anyone else—that Damon faked his death three weeks ago?"

* * *

"I know Damon's alive," Bonnie said. She stood on the front stoop of Tanya and Mrs. McCallum's bungalow. "I looked at the video, Tanya. He never got into the car, did he?"

Dressed—pretty normally—in a sweatshirt and jeans, Tanya stood in the doorway. She'd refused to let her inside. Bonnie could hear a TV blaring in the living room. It sounded like some old game show. Tanya glared at her, but occasionally seemed distracted by the idling car in front of her house.

Bonnie knew her parents wouldn't allow her to go out on her own. So she'd asked her mother if she would drive her to their old block—and Tanya's house. She'd said that Tanya might be able to help them—and the police—find Ron's killer. And she hadn't been lying about that. "I promise I'll only be a couple of minutes," she'd said. "I just need to ask her a few questions face-to-face, that's all."

But Tanya had ready a standard response to every question—and every time Bonnie tried to put her on the spot. Half hidden by the partially open door, Tanya just scowled, shook her head and grumbled: "You must be crazy . . ."

After Bonnie said she knew Damon was alive, Tanya embellished the rejoinder a bit: "You must be crazy. It's probably due to all the purging you do after every meal. It's bound to corrode your brain eventually . . ."

Bonnie rolled her eyes. Maybe Tanya thought she was poking a nerve with her anorexia wisecracks, but she wasn't. Bonnie never would have dreamed of saying anything to Tanya about her weight, because it would have been mean and catty. Maybe Tanya somehow knew that and was just pushing her to cross the line.

"You're not going to distract me with that bulimia crap, Tanya," she said. "I know Damon's alive. You and he probably feel justified in killing the people who have bullied you—and maybe that includes me. Maybe you think KC, Reed, and Ron all had it coming. But you and Damon are trying to pin the blame on Spencer, who never did one mean thing to either one of you. He was nice to you—and I know from experience, Tanya, that it's not always easy to be nice to you. You can be awfully overbearing. I pushed you away, but Spencer hasn't. He's a decent guy. And you're hurting him, you're persecuting him. You're turning into a bully, Tanya—the very thing you hate . . ."

Tanya continued to glare at her, but she had tears in her eyes. Bonnie thought maybe she was getting through to her.

But then Tanya stepped back and shut the door in her face.

She locked the door, then went to the dining room window and peeked out beyond the curtain. She watched Bonnie walk back to the car that was waiting for her. She looked a bit defeated. And that made Tanya smile.

Past the incessant TV noise, she heard her phone chime. Someone had sent her a text. She hurried into the kitchen and swiped the phone off the counter. She'd been washing dishes when Bonnie had knocked on the door.

The text was from an unknown sender, but Tanya knew who it had to be:

Tanya, U R my 1 & only pRtnR. I caR bout U mo thN
Spencer eva c%d. Yes, I haven't met w U n prsn since
aL dis started, bt that's Bin 4 yor own protection. f U insist,
I'll MEt w U @ 7:30 2nt @ d Galer Crown Stairs.
Meanwhile, don't BlEv NEthing U hEr on d news bout me.
I'm OK. I'll explain wen I c U 2nt.

Tanya wasn't sure what he meant about hearing things on the news about him. But she texted back:

OK, I'll MEt U @ d top of d Galer Stairs 2nt. Meanwhile, U
shud knO dat both Spencer & Bonnie hav figured out dat U
R alive. See? U nEd me.

She almost wrote that if he'd done away with Bonnie when he was supposed to, then he wouldn't have this problem. Maybe now he'd take some action, and finally put that bitch out of her misery.

One thing Bonnie had said that stuck with her—it was about a part of Damon's plan she really didn't understand. Tanya always wondered why Spencer had to be the fall guy in all of this. Bonnie was right about that. Spencer had never done anything mean to either one of them.

She couldn't help feeling it was someone else's idea. But she remembered what he'd said at the beginning of his text: *You are my one and only partner.*

Tanya wished she could believe that was true.

# CHAPTER THIRTY-FIVE

*Saturday—4:58 p.m.*

Spencer hadn't expected to fall asleep. He remembered stripping off his wet clothes down to his undershorts. Then he'd covered himself with an itchy blanket and flopped onto the bed in the boat's tiny stateroom. He'd been shivering. He might have started crying, too. He couldn't be sure.

He heard the water lapping against the side of the *Bonnie Blue*. He could also hear—in the next room—Bobby Darin singing "Mack the Knife" on the radio. It was some oldies station obviously targeting people over sixty. When he'd first tuned into it earlier, most of the ads had been for retirement villages, vitamin supplements, and hearing aids. It was the only station that came in without a ton of static.

At least he'd gotten the generator started. He'd found the Catalina 36 owner's manual just where Bonnie had said it would be—in the top drawer of the cabinet on the left as he'd stepped down into the galley. He'd located the boat pretty easily, too. But he wasn't much of a sailor. Even with the instructions, it had taken him nearly an hour to figure out how to get the electricity and water working. With the flick of each switch and every button he pushed, Spencer kept thinking he might blow up the boat or something.

Even now, he detected a slight gassy smell and wondered if that was normal. He couldn't be sure. Hell, he wasn't sure of anything.

He'd tracked down the pay phone Bonnie had told him about. He'd called her number, let it ring once, and then he'd hung up. So she'd gotten the signal he was okay. Spencer wished he'd worked out some kind of signal with his Aunt Dee to let her know he was all right—for now.

In no hurry to get up, he lay there under the warm but scratchy blanket. There were some books, but no TV on board. He'd gotten the computer started, but then it had asked for a password. If he could figure out how to work the stove, he'd heat some soup for dinner and then maybe read one of the books.

Spencer hadn't noticed lights in the windows of any of the other boats. He didn't want to call too much attention to the *Bonnie Blue*. So he figured on keeping just one or two lights on tonight.

Bonnie wasn't coming by any time before dawn tomorrow. Spencer knew he had a long night ahead.

Bobby Darin finished up his song. Spencer heard the news come on. *"In Seattle,"* the announcer said, *"a fourth student from Queen Anne High School has died. The body of seventeen-year-old Ronald Jarvis was found hanging from a tree near Discovery Park. Just one week ago, a junior at the high school was murdered along with his parents. Police are looking for another student, Spencer Murray, as a person of interest in the case. He is also wanted for questioning in the death of a fifty-eight-year-old woman on Capitol Hill . . ."*

Just hearing the announcer say it, Spencer felt as if he were guilty. Certainly, everyone else seemed to think he was.

He was tired, and it felt warm under the blanket. There was no reason to get up. His clothes were probably still damp. But Spencer knew he couldn't sleep a wink, not now. For at least the next twelve hours, he would be alone here—listening to every noise outside, waiting for the police to bust in on him, and worried that the next local news item he heard might be about the death of someone he really cared about.

Yes, it was going to be a long night—one of the longest in his short life.

The big disadvantage to snorting cocaine in a parked car at night was that he couldn't quite see what he was doing—and exactly how much was getting up his nose. But there was a distinct benefit to indulging here instead of in his apartment. He didn't have to share. If crystal meth was top sirloin, then coke was filet mignon. And Troy didn't feel like divvying it up with any of his stupid roommates. He'd gotten this stash from one of the more wealthy cougars among his regulars. "Gigolo swag," he called it. Right now, the money he "borrowed" from those older bitches was his main livelihood.

He was parked half a block from the apartment building. Leaning back in the driver's seat of his old Jetta, Troy closed his eyes and relished the bitter-tasting drip at the back of his throat from that last snort.

All at once, someone knocked on the window.

Startled, he gaped through the glass at his room-mate, Adrian. She looked even more like a train wreck than usual. Wearing her hooded sweatshirt, she leaned close to the window, fogging it up with her breath.

Troy started the car to lower the window. "You scared the crap out of me," he said over the humming as the window descended. "You look strung out again. What's going on?"

"The police left, like, fifteen minutes ago," she whispered. "And I don't think they've completely gone either. I have a feeling they're watching the building—at least in the back. I wouldn't be surprised if one of them was following me."

"Well, what do they want?" he asked.

"They were looking for you. They think you mowed down that Luke What's-His-Name, the playwright you can't stand."

"Shit," he muttered. "What did you tell them?"

"Nothing, God!" she exclaimed. "Why? Did you do it?"

Troy didn't answer her. He kept rubbing his mouth. He was fuming.

"They took fingerprints off stuff in your bedroom and the kitchen," she said.

He hit the steering wheel with the bottom of his fist.

"They made me sign something," she said, half crying. "And they took Skeet away—in handcuffs. Anyway, you better not come back to the apartment. They're looking for you. If I were you, I'd get out of town and lay low for a while. One of the cops said something about the Miami Police looking for you, too. What happened in Miami?"

Troy shook his head over and over. "That bitch Andrea Boyle did this. She shot her mouth off to the cops."

"I heard one of them mention her," Adrian said, nodding. "What are you going to do?"

He was screwed. If they'd hauled away his roommate, Skeet, that was it. He was as good as dead. Skeet knew most of his deep, dark secrets—including how he'd plowed into Luke Shuler with that hot Mazda CX-9 last week. Skeet also knew about Miami, where two years ago, Troy and another pal had hustled this old guy. They'd gotten him to take them back to his mansion, where they'd robbed him. Only things got a little rough, and the old guy ended up dead. Skeet had a long list of outstanding warrants. Troy figured he wouldn't hesitate spilling his guts to the cops about Miami and a lot more if he could work out a plea bargain for himself.

Troy kept thinking this was all Andrea Boyle's fault. Well, he wasn't going to run—not just yet.

He'd been trying to hide his cocaine stash from Adrian. But now he took a pinch of it and sniffed.

"Hey, where'd you get the coke?" she asked.

"You can't have any," he muttered, reaching for the switch on his armrest. "I'm swapping it for some ammo." Troy raised his window.

"Wait a minute!" Adrian said. She started pounding on the glass and yelled something he didn't hear. She jumped back as he pulled away from the curb.

He had a friend who was house-sitting for a guy who had a regular arsenal in a secret closet off his den. For a little coke, his buddy might let him take out a weapon on loan. The house was in South Seattle.

That would be Troy's first stop.

Then he would pay a visit to the town house in Queen Anne.

And he'd put that bitch down for good.


*Saturday—7:19 p.m.*

"Do you want any makeup?" someone asked.

Andrea shook her head.

"Let Deborah put some base on you—just so you don't look all pasty under the lights."

"Fine," Andrea muttered. She sat in the corner of the sofa in Luke's living room. Someone had dragged the tall potted ficus tree over behind her. They must have figured it made for an interesting backdrop. She had a mic clipped to her collar. The wire for it ran beneath her sweater and over her bra. It was attached to a receiver box clipped to the back of her pants. She tried not to squint at the spotlight they were shining on her.

A twenty-something blonde came up to her with a pad and a jar of foundation powder. The woman started applying it to Andrea's face.

"Deborah, see if you can do something about her hair!" yelled the same disembodied voice behind the glaring lights.

Andrea wished to God she hadn't agreed to this. But they'd caught her in a very weak and vulnerable moment. She'd been at the hospital, where she'd just helped a battered, sickly Luke identify his son in the morgue. Someone had wrapped a towel around the back of Damon's head to conceal the bullet wound. It looked like he was wearing some kind of weird, oversized turban. Luke had asked the attendant if Damon had all his teeth. But they'd been one step ahead of him. The three teeth found in the burnt rubble and ashes that remained after the explosion of Evelyn's BMW were indeed missing from the back of Damon's mouth.

Luke was barely able to get through the ordeal. For him, it must have been like Damon had been killed all over again.

Worse, the police seemed to think Spencer was involved in Damon's murder. Neither she nor Luke wanted to believe it. He told her that he wanted to be alone—and she was probably better off going back to the town house to wait for Spencer in case he tried to contact her.

While Andrea was at the hospital, two policemen stuck close to her. One of them told her not to talk to any reporters about the purpose of her visit here. The police still hadn't notified the press about the second body found near where Ron Jarvis had been killed. She didn't think they'd be able to keep a lid on the news much longer.

Two more policemen and a reporter were waiting

for her near the hospital's elevator. They wanted her to tape a brief announcement for the news, asking Spencer to turn himself in. The police promised that, at this point, they just wanted to question him. If he were scared, desperate, and contemplating doing harm to himself or others, a level-headed plea from his aunt might be just the reassurance he needed. If she truly believed in his innocence, the sooner he was in police custody, the sooner they'd clear him of all charges.

So Andrea had agreed to make a brief video, which would be featured online and during tonight's local eleven o'clock newscasts. One of the cops told her there was a chance CNN would be picking it up. He acted as if that was supposed to make her happy or something.

Now, between the camera crew and the police, there were about ten people crammed into Luke's living room—along with the sound equipment and the spotlight. Cable lines ran along the floor everywhere. Someone was drinking water from Luke's Bruce Lee mug, which would not have gone over well with Luke.

TV news vans and dozens of onlookers had gathered outside the town house. Andrea noticed some people had stopped with their kids, who were dressed in costumes for their trick-or-treat rounds. Several people had their dogs on leashes.

One of the strangers in Luke's living room asked her if she'd talk to the reporters outside—after they'd taped her spot. Andrea was reluctant until he told her: "It'll improve your chances of getting the message out to your nephew. And besides, after you go out and talk to them, most of them will leave. If you keep them

YOU'LL MISS ME WHEN I'M GONE 463

waiting out there, that's just what they'll do. They'll wait out there . . ."

So Andrea agreed to talk to the reporters outside, too.

The same man asked if she knew what she was going to say.

"Not really," Andrea muttered. The makeup woman was still hovering over her.

"Well, let's shoot it, and you can talk off the top of your head," he said. "Sometimes the best takes are the unrehearsed ones."

He backed up, turning around just in time to avoid tripping over a cable. "All right, let's try a take!" he announced.

The makeup woman gave her one final pat and then moved away.

Andrea sat up.

"Okay, Andrea," the man called. "On three! One, two, three . . ."


"They're talking about your boyfriend on CNN," announced her brother Tim. He stood in her bedroom doorway. "Mom and Dad are watching it downstairs."

Bonnie almost knocked him over as she ran out of her room. Racing down the back stairs, she hurried to the family room off the kitchen. Her mother was on the sofa. Her dad was in his lounge chair. And Spencer's aunt Andrea was on the big-screen TV.

Even if Bonnie hadn't seen the pretty brunette's family resemblance to Spencer, she knew who she was thanks to the caption—right above the blue-strip newsfeed at the bottom of the screen. It read: ANDREA BOYLE, TEEN FUGITIVE'S AUNT AND GUARDIAN.

*"This message is for my nephew,"* Andrea said. She sat in what looked like someone's living room. She appeared collected—but just a bit brittle. *"Spencer, I know you're scared right now. So am I. But I want to stress to you—and everyone else who's watching—that you haven't been accused of anything. The police just want to ask you some questions. A lot of new evidence has come up that confirms what you and I have already told the police. If you keep hiding, people are going to assume you're guilty of things you didn't do. And that puts you in a—a dangerous situation. So please, please get in touch with me as soon as you can. I miss you, Spencer. Thank you."*

The image on TV switched to the handsome anchorman. Behind his right shoulder was a photo box with a picture of Spencer in it. Bonnie guessed the photograph had been taken a couple of years ago—maybe while he was incarcerated. He looked slightly gawky, but still cute.

*"Spencer Murray is also known as Spencer Rowe,"* the anchorman said. *"At age eleven, he was convicted and served five years for the murders of his parents in Virginia . . ."*

"Well, just one look at him and you can tell he's a creep," Bonnie's father muttered.

"Honey," her mother whispered. She shook her head at him and then gave a nod in Bonnie's direction.

*"Rowe was released from a state facility in Arlington in May of this year,"* the anchorman continued. *"He was allowed to move to Seattle with his aunt and*

*guardian, provided he continued to see a mental health specialist. His therapist, fifty-eight-year-old Diane Leppert, was murdered earlier in the week. Her body was discovered in her office this morning. Stay tuned later in this hour for* The Sally Justice Show. *Sally, you'll be talking about this complex case with some expert criminologists . . ."*

The TV picture went to split screen—with the dapper anchorman in one half, and a fifty-something woman with bad Botox and straight, bleached-blond hair in the other. She wore a pink blazer and held a pen in her hand, which she waved emphatically as she spoke. *"What I'd like to know, Rob, is what's wrong with our criminal justice penal system?"* Sally ranted. *"Here's a little monster who shot both his parents in cold blood back in 2009. So they let him out of jail and allowed him to travel to another part of the country! And what does he do when he gets to Seattle? He changes his name, so no one knows him. Even sex offenders have to register! And what does this 'reformed, rehabilitated' killer do less than five months after his release? He starts killing again and again . . ."*

Bonnie felt her throat close up. Tears came to her eyes.

Despite what his aunt had just said in her televised plea, it seemed Spencer had already been convicted by the police and the press for all these murders. She was almost glad there wasn't a TV onboard the boat. If Spencer saw this, it would kill him.

Bonnie quietly turned and withdrew toward the back stairs.

But Sally Justice's voice on TV followed her up the

steps, taunting her: *"He's responsible for five recent deaths—that we know of. I hope after they catch him, he's tried as an adult. I don't care if he is seventeen . . ."*

Even after Bonnie closed her bedroom door, she couldn't quite shut out what was being said about Spencer.

*Well, just one look at him and you can tell he's a creep.*

She flopped down on her bed and told herself that it just wasn't true. None of what they were saying about Spencer was true.


Tanya stood at the top of the old Galer Crown Stairs. With 785 concrete steps, the wide stairway had three landings and a pipe railing down the middle of it. Surrounding trees and bushes formed a near-complete arch over the stairs, which seemed to go on indefinitely. But at the moment, it was too dark to see much beyond the first fifty or so steps.

She was early for their 7:30 appointment. She'd put on some lipstick and mascara for him. Except for a few joggers and a handful of others, no one else was using the stairs at this hour. While Tanya waited, she kept thinking about what a creepy, lonely spot this was.

She had her phone to keep her company. Online, she'd watched Andrea Boyle's public plea for her nephew to turn himself in. She wondered what "new evidence" had come up to "confirm" what Spencer and his aunt had already told the police. Did it have anything to do with her—or Damon?

She thought of what her ex-friend Bonnie had said: *You and Damon are trying to pin the blame on Spencer, who never did one mean thing to either one of you. Spencer has been nice to you . . . He's a decent guy . . . You're hurting him . . . You're turning into a bully, Tanya—the very thing you hate . . .*

She'd tried to call Spencer, but got some automated recording: *"The cellular customer you're trying to reach is unavailable right now . . ."*

She checked the Internet for any news updates. On CNN Live, some reporter talked about Ron Jarvis, making out like he was some kind of boy-next-door, honor student, star athlete—instead of the dumb jock a-hole he was. After the segment on "Saint Ron," they finally cut back to the anchorman, who announced, *"We have word of a new development in this case. Seattle Police have now confirmed that a second body was discovered in the woods where high school varsity quarterback Ron Jarvis was murdered. They haven't yet released the identity of this second victim. The police are still looking for another Queen Anne High School student, Spencer Murray, for questioning in connection to these murders . . ."*

The same photo of Spencer that CNN had used earlier came up in a box behind the announcer's shoulder.

*"CNN will give you continued coverage of this situation in Seattle. Stay tuned now for* The Sally Justice Show *. . ."*

Tanya didn't understand what they were talking about. Who besides Ron was killed in those woods by

Discovery Park? Why wasn't she told about it? In his text earlier, he'd said she shouldn't believe what she heard on the news about him. She wondered if this had anything to do with that.

She glanced at her Betty Boop wristwatch and realized he was already twenty-five minutes late. Tanya phoned him and got the generic recording. She left a message: "Well, it's practically eight. I've been waiting here at the top of the steps for over a half hour now. By the way, your handiwork is all over CNN. Congratulations, you've gone national. They're talking about a second body in the woods. Was this the thing I was supposed to ignore? I really wish I knew what was going on with you. Anyway, I give up. It's obvious you're not coming. I'm out of here."

Tanya clicked off and started for home. She was just slipping her phone into her coat pocket when it chimed. Someone was sending her a text. She stopped to read it:

SBTA bout d delay. Couldn't b helped. Go om & KEp a lookout 4 me @ d bk dor. I shud b ther v s%n.

Tanya texted back a terse *OK*. Clicking off again, she shoved the phone back into her pocket and continued toward home.

She wanted to ask him about that other body in the woods. Was it another innocent bystander—collateral damage like Mr. and Mrs. Logan? She'd known he was going after Reed, but it had thrown her for a loop that the parents were killed, too. When she'd asked him about it on the phone, he snapped back: "Well, you knew I was going to cram him inside the refrigerator and attach a lock to it. Did you expect his parents to sleep through all that?"

But she didn't understand why Spencer's therapist had to die. And now there was this person killed along with Ron.

He hadn't spoken to her since last night, before he'd killed Ron. Today, he'd just sent texts in response to her voice mail messages. Why was that? What had happened to him?

All day long, she'd had this strange feeling. She wanted to hear his voice. She wanted to see him in person again—finally. She wanted to be face-to-face with him when he told her about that second corpse in the woods.

Kicking leaves out of her way, Tanya ambled down the sidewalk. She missed their lunches together, and watching bad TV at her house when her mother wasn't monopolizing the set. She even missed suffering with him at the hands of those bullies. It had been a lot more fun thinking of ways to kill them when it was just a fantasy.

She hadn't actually seen him since he was supposed to have died three weeks ago. He kept talking about how they were going to get together when all of this was over. But that seemed like an empty promise.

He'd probably keep her waiting at the back door half the night before she got another text saying he'd meet her later.

Tanya had an awful feeling she'd never see her friend Damon again.

\*    \*    \*

There were cops all over. He'd parked his Jetta across the street and half a block down from the town house. It was a mob scene in front of the place.

The police were still looking for him. They'd called twice, leaving a message once and hanging up a second time. Adrian had called and left a message, too.

A few minutes ago, he'd wandered amid the forty or so onlookers and reporters. Even with all the cops around, it had been easy for him to get lost in the crowd. He'd overheard one of the reporters say that Andrea Boyle was supposed to come out and talk to reporters sometime soon.

Troy had expected to catch her coming back from the hospital by herself. He hadn't anticipated this three-ring circus in front of the town house. And yet the Kompakt .233 assault rifle he'd chosen among his friend's friend's secret arsenal was perfect if he wanted to go out in a blaze of glory. He even had a slightly oversized trench coat under which he could conceal it—right up until the last minute.

Back in the car now, he made sure no cops were around. He took one last hit of cocaine, using it all up. It strengthened his resolve.

He was ready for this.

The truth was he'd always wanted to be famous. And he'd never really made it as an actor.

But after this, everyone would know who he was.

The actor in him never stopped studying human behavior—even now, while high. He could mentally go outside his own skin and look at himself. Troy knew, thanks to the coke, he was now in that manic, jittery, euphoric stage in which he truly believed he could do anything.

And he could.

He reached under the driver's seat and grabbed the Kompakt .223. His hands were shaking, and he took a few deep breaths—like an athlete about to run the high hurdles. He wasn't scared or nervous.

Troy climbed out of his Jetta. He'd parked close to a row of shrubs on the driver's side, so he had some camouflage as he put on the baggy trench coat and then hid the assault weapon inside it. Shutting the car door, he started toward the crowd in front of Luke Shuler's town house.

He'd never felt more powerful in his life.

The damp, chilly air kissed his face. He watched the police escort Andrea Boyle out the front door. More than a dozen reporters raising their handheld microphones formed a human podium for her. She put on such a pious, long-suffering look as she approached the cluster of mics.

He merged with the rest of the onlookers. None of them seemed to notice him. They wouldn't see him until it was too late. They had their cell phones out to record this moment for Facebook and Twitter. They had their children in cute Halloween outfits. They had their dogs on leashes. He wondered how many would be struck down by the storm of bullets within the next minute.

As he weaved through them, Troy couldn't stop smiling. He barely heard any of their mindless chatter. He was looking at Andrea Boyle in front of all those microphones. Clutching the Kompakt .223 under the floppy coat, Troy started to move faster toward his target. He bumped into onlookers and reporters, and impatiently pushed others aside. Their startled cries and admonishments fell upon deaf ears. No one was getting between him and that bitch.

He was just a few feet away from her now.

Luke Shuler's whore looked up from the microphones and seemed to lock eyes with him. Clearly, she recognized him.

Troy broke into a grin and whipped out the gun.

He saw her open her mouth to scream.

He squeezed the trigger and fired off the first round. Shots echoed out.

People started shrieking. Children cried out in terror. Everyone ran in different directions. Dogs yelped and barked furiously. Along with the kids, the animals had it the worst—as the mob trampled and tripped over them to get out of the line of fire.

By the town house's front stoop, the wall of microphones toppled. All at once, the cops swarmed around Andrea Boyle. They fell into a human pile on the front stoop.

Troy couldn't see her amid all the bodies. He couldn't tell if he'd killed her or even drawn blood. He was about to fire off another round at them to make sure she was dead. But suddenly he heard gunfire—and it wasn't from the assault weapon he brandished.

Troy felt the bullets ripping into him, electric jolts of pain in his chest and at the base of his throat.

He'd wanted to go out in a blaze of glory.

But as he fell to the hard pavement, the last thing Troy heard—past all the screaming and crying—was a man's voice, louder than anyone else's. "They got him!" he yelled. "They killed the scumbag . . ."

As she turned down her street, Tanya half expected to see a line of police cars in front of her house. It was just a matter of time before they caught up with Spencer. Once they did, he'd tell them his theories about her and Damon. He had his aunt on his side—and Bonnie, too. The police would have to listen. They'd have to follow it up.

Tanya was still a block away. But so far, she didn't see any patrol cars.

She wished she could just disappear—like Damon had.

When they were picked on at school, she and Damon sometimes talked about how sorry people would be if they committed a double suicide. "They'll miss us when we're gone," Damon used to say. Tanya was never completely sold on the suicide fantasy. She always had more fun daydreaming about the different ways they'd kill certain bullies and mean girls.

Around the second week of school, when Damon pulled away, Tanya had no idea what she'd done to upset him. But he was acting differently toward her. That was when she started to suspect he'd made a secret new friend.

She was pretty sure it wasn't Troy Slattery. Tanya had met him a few times and found him rather fascinating and edgy. But Damon never liked him all that much. She couldn't see them pairing up as "partners in crime." Besides, his mother had stopped dating Troy by the end of the summer. By September, she was seeing a much younger man, and apparently, it wasn't very serious. Tanya never met the guy.

Maybe Damon didn't have a second partner in all this. Maybe she was indeed the only one. It would make sense that he'd have to isolate himself to plan for October 8. He wouldn't have been able to keep it secret from her had he not pulled away a bit.

His suicide webcast three weeks ago had taken Tanya totally by surprise. She was devastated—and quite hurt that he'd do something like that without first telling her.

Then three days later, she'd started getting hang-up calls from UNKNOWN CALLER. After the umpteenth call, Tanya finally clicked on the line, ready to give a tongue-lashing to what she assumed was a persistent telemarketer. She greeted the caller with a curt, "What the hell do you want?"

"I just want to talk to an old friend," she heard Damon say on the other end.

At first, she thought it was some cruel joke, the type one of those a-holes from school might pull. Someone had figured out how to imitate his voice perfectly. But he kept insisting he was the genuine article.

"What's the last thing we watched on TV together?" she demanded to know.

"The *Glee* '*Rocky Horror Picture Show*' episode," he answered without hesitation. "You got the DVD at the library. And I kept telling you to shut up, because you talked during the whole thing."

Tanya burst into tears. "I thought you were dead!

How could you do this without telling me? What happened?"

What happened was he'd found out his mother had paid Reed Logan to pick on him—starting shortly after his parents had broken up. She'd manipulated much of the bullying in order to get his father's attention. It was one way to make sure she saw his dad—at the meetings with Principal Dunmore.

"So she's really dead?" Tanya said, nonplussed. "You killed her?"

"She deserved what she got," he replied.

Damon explained he'd found the perfect stand-in for himself—a nineteen-year-old drug overdose case, who had been recently buried on Lopez Island. "I dug him up," Damon said. "Can you believe it—me, a grave robber? Oh, Tanya, it was so disgusting. The whole time, it was all I could do to keep from calling you and telling you what I was doing . . ."

What he did was knock out all the corpse's teeth. He said it was good practice for knocking out three of his own teeth that Friday night, six days before the webcast. A pint of bourbon and some painkillers got him through it. But he was still sore and sick on Monday, which was the real reason he'd missed school that day. "One advantage to having had a mother that didn't give a shit about me is that she didn't question why I came back from Lopez Sunday night looking and feeling miserable," Damon told her.

He said the cadaver went into the big freezer they had in the garage at the Lopez Island house. He drove back over to the island with his mother in the trunk on

Wednesday night. He'd slipped her three Ambien to knock her out and then tied her up.

"I thawed out the toothless nineteen-year-old the night before the webcast," he said.

"What?" Tanya asked, incredulous. "After he'd been in a deep freeze for a few days? That's a whole body you defrosted. It should have taken at least a couple of days to thaw out . . ."

"I guess he—well, yeah, he was still pretty stiff when I loaded him in the car," Damon replied.

Tanya wondered if he was hiding something from her about this body he'd dug up to stand in for him. But before she could ask, he went on about how he'd fooled everyone during his webcast. He told her all it took was some trick camera angles and a little sleight of hand to load the body into the car at just the right time. Tanya asked if he'd had any help planning or carrying out this scheme. She couldn't believe he'd pulled off that webcast deceit all on his own. But Damon insisted he'd worked alone. He was counting on her to be his link to the outside world. They couldn't risk meeting in person for a while. He had a room in a cheap hotel just outside the city—and was spending some nights at the Lopez Island house.

Damon asked if his tormentors at school were sorry, now that he was gone.

Tanya had to tell him the truth—that Reed, Ron, and the others were actually joking about it.

That was when Damon suggested making their former daydreams of revenge a reality. "I'm dead," he said. "It'll be easy for me to get away with murder."

He never said anything about making Spencer Murray his live scapegoat. But she wasn't surprised when Damon instructed her to plant Reed's baseball cap in Spencer's locker. What surprised her was that she went along with it. She'd always kind of liked Spencer, but could tell he wasn't interested in her. Damon resented him for moving into his father's house. He'd told her early on about Spencer spending time in Virginia mental institutions and juvenile detention centers for killing his parents. Damon's mother had found that out from a private detective she'd hired to look into Spencer's aunt.

Tanya felt conflicted about what they were doing to Spencer—especially since, for the last three weeks, ever since the webcast, she'd stopped feeling close to Damon. He was just this voice on the phone. It got so he only talked to her about killing. At least Spencer was there. He was cuter than Damon, and hell, he'd even been following her around the last couple of nights. She'd lapped up the attention. It was almost like having a guardian angel.

But her loyalties stayed with her soul mate, her partner in crime. It was exciting to know Damon was alive, when everyone else was so utterly clueless. Tanya relished witnessing the panic that swept through the school after Reed's murder. All the while, she remained calm and above it all. It was a dizzy, powerful feeling. And in a way, they were making the school a better place. Each murder was a fantasy fulfilled. Damon called them "grand deeds." The last time they'd actually spoken, he'd told her: "I'm making last-minute preparations for tonight's grand deed with our friend Ron . . ."

Despite all their scheming, they never really had a

solid plan for their future—except disappearing after a while. Tanya imagined it would be like their lunch periods—the two of them slipping away someplace together where no one would bother them. They'd never planned what to do if someone found out Damon was alive and pulling off these murders. And, indeed, someone knew.

She figured they could discuss it tonight. Damon was taking a real chance, showing up at her house—if he did show up at all.

Tanya turned down the walkway to her front door. She kept a lookout for someone hiding in the shadows. Maybe Damon had arrived early. Or perhaps Spencer was spying on her again. She stopped and glanced over at the house under construction next door—a dark shell.

She hurried up to her front door, unlocked it, and stepped inside. As usual, the sound of the television set in the living room greeted her. But something was wrong. It wasn't the Game Show Network or one of her mother's other favorite channels. It sounded like the news.

"Mom?" she called.

"*. . . Seattle police are confirming that the second body discovered this morning, buried in a shallow grave near Discovery Park, is indeed Damon Shuler, who apparently faked his own death three weeks ago . . .*"

Tanya stopped dead in the hallway. Ahead, she could see the flickering TV light in the otherwise dark living room. Had she heard it right? Damon was dead?

She remembered what he'd said in his text: *Don't*

*believe anything you hear on the news about me. I'm*
*okay* . . . This had to be what he meant.

But how did he do it?

On the TV, she heard them break for a commercial
for some prescription antidepressant. She had only a
partial view of the dim room. A shadow swept across
the carpet.

"Mom?" she said again.

But there was no answer.

Tanya stepped beyond an archway into the living
room. Her mother was on the couch, dressed in her
homely, chartreuse bathrobe—as usual. The TV table
was littered with dirty glasses and plates. The television's light flickered across her beleaguered face. Her
eyes were open, but not quite looking at the TV set—
or at her. She wasn't blinking either. Blood from the
slash across her throat had spilled down the front of
her ugly robe. It stained the white bed pillow behind
her head.

Tanya gasped.

"Spencer hasn't gotten in touch with you, has he?"
someone asked.

Tanya swiveled around and saw a stranger in the
corner of the room. He wasn't much older than her.

"Do you know where Spencer's hiding?" he asked.
"Come on, Tanya. Talk to me! Damon's always going
on about what a chatterbox you are. Where the hell is
Spencer?"

"I—I don't know," she whimpered, backing away.
She realized he was the one who had sent her those
texts today.

The stranger took out a hunting knife from inside his jacket. "You'll have to cooperate with me, Tanya. I have a feeling the police will want to talk to Damon's best gal pal—now that he's really dead. They could be here at any minute. So I really need your help."

"What do you want from me?" she asked, her voice cracking.

"I want you to die easily, Tanya," he whispered.

She shook her head.

"Don't struggle. Damon said you talk all the time. You never shut up. So I think it's only fitting you go the same way your mother did . . ."

Her back against the wall, Tanya realized who this stranger was—this young man who was about to slit her throat.

He was Damon's secret friend.

# CHAPTER THIRTY-SIX

*Sunday, November 1—4:52 a.m.*

With a start, Andrea woke up on the sofa in Luke's study.

She hadn't planned on sleeping. She'd just needed to close her eyes for a few minutes. So she'd grabbed an old cardigan Luke sometimes wore when he was writing, draped it over herself, and curled up on the couch. A sofa pillow with a palm tree on it had been perfect for resting her aching head.

From the antique clock on Luke's desk, it looked like four hours had passed. Andrea's right shoulder felt like it was on fire. It took her a moment to remember what had happened. They'd brought her back from the hospital in a patrol car last night. She'd been treated for a flesh wound. Troy's shooting rampage had put one cop on the critical list. Two more policemen, a reporter, and a woman bystander had also been wounded. A number of people had sustained minor injuries in the scuffle—one of them, a child. As Luke had said, "Why would someone bring their kid to a place where the press was covering a murder story?"

She'd visited with Luke after getting stitched up and bandaged in the hospital. He was still devastated about Damon. Not only was he dealing with his son's death all over again, but he also had to struggle with the very real possibility that Damon had planned and carried out all these brutal murders.

But he couldn't have done it alone. Andrea was pretty sure about that.

She'd been right about Troy. His fingerprints were all over the interior of the stolen Mazda CX-9 that had barreled into Luke. It was far from his first offense. He'd been arrested several times, including once for breaking and entering. And the police had found out from Troy's roommate that a while back Troy and a friend had killed a man in Miami while robbing him.

Damon and Troy, both dead, were now considered the leading suspects in the murders of Reed Logan and his parents, Ron Jarvis, and possibly Diane Leppert. The police were investigating Troy's actions on the nights of those murders.

Andrea had told the police that Tanya McCallum knew both suspects and seemed to be concealing inside knowledge about the killings. A pair of detectives went to Tanya's house to investigate, and found Tanya and her mother with their throats slashed. As of a few hours ago, the police still hadn't determined the exact time of death for the mother and daughter.

The murders may have happened some time before Troy Slattery had opened fire on her and the crowd just outside Luke's town house—or perhaps *after* Troy was already dead.

So Spencer wasn't completely off the hook yet. Despite all the new developments and her videotaped plea, she still hadn't heard from him. Her heart broke when she thought of him in hiding, feeling hunted, lonely, and scared.

Getting up from the sofa, she threw Luke's sweater over her shoulders. She could smell him on it. It gave her a bit of comfort, and for a few seconds she could forget that her shoulder hurt like hell. She shuffled to the window and glanced outside.

Only nine hours ago, it had been utter pandemonium in front of the house—what with the crowd, the ambulances, several squad cars, and even a fire truck. Now all Andrea could see was one police car.

She wandered into the kitchen and got herself a glass of ice water from the dispenser on the refrigerator door. After downing two Excedrin, she noticed her phone on the breakfast table. The message light was blinking.

She checked and found an email from Detective Talwar. It had been sent at 1:17 a.m., with the subject line *Update*.

Andrea,

Thought I'd let you know that Troy Slattery was stopped for speeding in Spokane around 1 a.m. on 10/24—the evening the Logans were murdered. This puts him 294 miles away from the crime scene. So this eliminates him as a suspect in those homicides.

We still very much need to talk with your nephew. I'll
be in touch.

Det. Maya Talwar

"Damn it," Andrea muttered. That explained why
the one police car was still parked outside. A part of
her had always considered Damon and Troy an unlikely pair. Troy's grudge was against Luke and her—
not some high school bullies.

That meant the person who had killed Damon—and
killed *with* Damon—was still out there.

She moved into the family room, grabbed the remote, and switched on the TV. She found the local
early morning news on channel 104.

Troy's shooting spree and Damon's "second death"
were the top stories. A pretty, Asian anchor with bangs
and a red blazer warned viewers, *"The following video
contains some disturbing images. Viewer discretion is
advised. Our KING-5 correspondent Deborah Neff is
here with the story . . ."*

Bleary-eyed, Andrea watched as the station reran
snippets of the webcast "suicide" to show how Damon
had indeed killed his mother, but didn't actually climb
inside the car with the explosives in it. *"As you can
see, the young man's mother, Evelyn Shuler, is clearly
helpless here,"* the reporter said. They showed Evelyn
bound and gagged in the backseat. *"Once again, as
Lori warned, these images are disturbing . . ."*

Andrea hadn't watched the webcast since seeing it
live. It was somehow even more gruesome to look at it
now, knowing what would soon happen to Evelyn.

With his camera, Damon had zoomed in for a close-up of his mother's hands, tied at the wrist, in back of her.

Andrea saw something she hadn't noticed before. The reporter didn't comment on it. Why would she? Andrea was the only person who would have noticed. She put down her water glass. Luke's cardigan slipped off her shoulders and fell to her feet. But she barely noticed.

The close-up had lasted only a moment or two. Andrea couldn't be sure of what she'd just seen. Grabbing the remote, she played back the live broadcast. She pressed the pause button and stared at Evelyn's hands.

Andrea recognized the cocktail ring on the third finger of Evelyn's right hand. The last time she'd seen that ring, it had been on her sister's finger. It was the "fruit salad" ring.

After checking so many pawnshops and junk stores in Virginia for so many years, Andrea had finally found her mother's old ring.


Every step on the back stairs seemed to creak as Bonnie made her way down to the first floor. The house was dark, but she didn't turn on any lights. She didn't want anyone knowing she was up. She was pretty certain her parents and brothers were asleep. In fact, she was counting on it.

She'd drifted off for a couple of hours last night, but mostly just tossed and turned. Every once in a while, she'd gotten up and padded downstairs to glance out the front window. She'd figured out the police had a patrol car checking the house every fifteen minutes. Sometimes, they even turned on the searchlight as they cruised along the street.

From the coatroom off the kitchen, Bonnie grabbed her jacket and threw it on. Then she tiptoed to the front of the house. She waited there for about five minutes and saw the squad car slowly drive by.

She grabbed her mother's car keys from the bowl on the table in the front hall, and then quietly slipped out the front door. She wondered who would be the first to notice the family SUV wasn't in the driveway—her parents or the police?

The headlights blinked as she unlocked the SUV with the remote device. After climbing behind the wheel, Bonnie switched off the headlights and carefully closed the door. She glanced up at the house and the windows on the second floor. No lights had gone on yet.

With her eyes on the side mirror, she backed into the street. There wasn't any traffic at this hour. She waited until she was half a block away from the house to switch the headlights on. She didn't see a cop car anywhere.

Bonnie figured she'd be at the marina on Lake Union in about fifteen minutes. The last communication she'd had with Spencer had been twelve hours ago, when he'd called her from the pay phone and hung up after one ring. That had been their signal to let her know he'd found the boat and he was okay.

There was a radio on the boat, but no TV. And if Spencer had thrown away his smart phone like she'd suggested, then he probably had no way of knowing about the shooting rampage in front of Luke Shuler's town house, or the murders of Tanya and her mother. Spencer probably didn't realize that his theory about Damon faking his death was spot on, and that the police now suspected Troy Slattery had been involved in the recent string of murders.

It was probably okay for him to give himself up now. She needed to let him know it was safe. She couldn't wait to tell her parents how wrong they were about him. Then again, they'd probably be furious that she'd harbored a fugitive. Maybe the less said about it, the better.

Bonnie pulled up to the marina, and parked the SUV in the car lot. In the distance, down the dock, she could see the lights on inside the *Bonnie Blue*.

She switched off the engine. In the sudden quiet, she heard something rustling in the backseat. She glanced in the rearview mirror.

Someone popped up behind her.

Bonnie let out a little shriek.

She saw his eyes staring back at her in the rearview mirror.

Then she felt the point of a knife at the side of her neck.

"I knew you'd lead me to him," the man whispered.


Sitting at Luke's desk, Andrea stared down at the mug shots of Garrett's two friends from the Virginia Juvenile Correctional Institution in Richmond: the baby-faced Kirk Mowery and swarthy Richard Phelps.

For years, she'd been looking in pawnshops for her mother's cocktail ring. Many of the other pieces Garrett Beale had taken the night of the murders had been sold or hocked. But he must have kept the "fruit salad" ring—and hidden it well.

But not so well that his two pals didn't find it.

She remembered what Dana had told her, based on Hugh Badger Lyman's research: *About two months before Garrett was sprung, his parents' house was robbed while they were away on vacation. They never caught the thieves. But Hugh always wondered if Kirk and Richard had anything to do with it.*

One of them had held on to that ring. Was it the dark-haired boy who had completely disappeared—or the angel-faced blond, who was the last person Hugh had interviewed before his mysterious death? One of the two must have made his way to Seattle and gotten friendly with Evelyn, at least friendly enough to give her the cocktail ring he'd stolen.

Luke had mentioned a while back that after Troy, his wife had started seeing an even younger man. Evelyn had joked with him about feeling like a cougar.

Richard or Kirk must have gotten friendly with Damon, too. Andrea couldn't quite see chic, smart Evelyn sporting that slightly garish ring—unless she was expecting a visit from the young man who had given it to her. Evelyn's sometime boyfriend must have helped her son in abducting her, tying her up, and killing her. Richard was a firebug. Did he know something about explosives? Andrea could imagine Evelyn finding the nineteen-year-old Richard sexy enough—despite the age difference.

Poor Evelyn had joked about being a cougar. But she'd had no idea who the real predator was.

Hugh Badger Lyman hadn't been able to locate Richard since the fire that killed Garrett and his parents in April. And Andrea didn't have a working number for Richard's older sister and guardian.

But yesterday, when she'd phoned Kirk's mother, Hannah Mowery-Jansen of Charlottesville, she'd gotten an answering machine and hung up. It was eight-twenty on the East Coast, kind of early to call on a Sunday. But Andrea picked up the cordless phone on the desk and dialed the number for Kirk Mowery's mother.

A woman answered after two ringtones. "Hello?"

With the phone to her ear, Andrea stared down at the mug shot of the blond boy. "Yes, hi, is Kirk there, please?"

"He isn't home," the women answered. "Who is this?"

"Well, you don't know me. But my name's Andrea Boyle. Can you tell me how to get in touch with Kirk?"

"I was hoping you could tell me," the woman said. "I saw that two-oh-six area code and figured you must know him. You're calling from Seattle, I take it?"

"Yes . . ."

"Well, when did you last see him?" Kirk's mother asked.

"I haven't seen him at all, but I'm acquainted with some people who might know him," Andrea said. "Did Kirk ever mention a Damon Shuler or an Evelyn Shuler?"

"Hmm, no, I don't think so," the woman replied.

Andrea glanced at Hugh's Post-it: *Check on Doreen Carter—Girlfriend?* It had been attached to Richard Phelps's rap sheet, but she had stuck it on the list of

*Doreen Carters* she'd been calling all yesterday morning.

"Did Kirk happen to have a girlfriend by the name of Doreen?" Andrea asked. "Doreen Carter?"

The woman laughed. "You must not know Kirk very well at all."

"What do you mean?"

"Do you have any contact information for this Damon or Evelyn Shuler you just mentioned?" asked Kirk's mother. "I'd really like to get in touch with them."

"Well, you can't," Andrea said.

"Why not?"

"Because they're dead," Andrea admitted. "I have—well, I have reason to believe that Kirk was involved with Evelyn Shuler."

"That's ridiculous," the woman replied. "And Kirk can't be involved with this Doreen Carter person either. My son's gay, Ms. Boyle. And he's never hidden it. That's what I meant when I said you couldn't know him very well. Now, what's this all about?"

"Did he know a boy named Richard Phelps?" Andrea asked.

"Yes, but the police already asked him about Richard. Kirk hasn't seen him or heard from him since early last spring. And if you're trying to connect Kirk to that fire in Fairfax, you can't. He was with me at the time—in Williamsburg at a family reunion."

"But he knew Garrett Beale."

The woman sighed. "Know him? He worshiped him. He would have followed Garrett to the other side of the world."

"Did Kirk ever mention to you anything about a private detective named Hugh Badger Lyman?"

"Yes, Mr. Lyman talked with both of us shortly before Kirk took off for Seattle."

"What about? Do you mind my asking?"

"He wanted to know about Richard and the fire that killed Garrett and his parents. This detective thought Richard may have started it. Both Kirk and I had to agree with him. I think Richard stole enough money to disappear, and made sure to burn the place down as he left." Andrea heard her sigh on the other end of the line. "I threw away Mr. Lyman's number. Maybe I shouldn't have. He's from Seattle. Maybe he could help me track down Kirk."

"Ah, I don't think he's available," Andrea said, deciding to leave it at that. "When did you last hear from Kirk?"

"Well, he left in mid-September," the woman answered. "He'd always been interested in Kurt Cobain and the grunge or grungy movement there in Seattle. So when he won some money at the racetrack, he decided to fly out there on the cheap. He was very good about keeping in touch, too—right up until the first week in October, and then suddenly, nothing. Even his phone doesn't answer now. I'm worried sick about him. You see, Kirk got himself into trouble once. Well, I guess you know—if you know about Richard and Garrett. Anyway, I can't help thinking he's in trouble again—or worse. Because of his problems with the law in the past, I've put off calling the Seattle Police about his disappearance. But I—I can't wait any longer. I'm positive something's wrong . . ."

All Andrea could think about was that Kirk had disappeared just around the time Damon had faked his death in the car explosion.

"Ms. Jansen, I'd like to help you if I can," she said. "Would it be all right if I called you back later today?"

"Why, sure," she replied. "I'd appreciate anything you could do to find my son . . ."

After she hung up with Kirk's mother, Andrea stared at the list of Doreen Carters. The last one she'd called, the married dental hygienist from Richmond, had hung up on her.

Yesterday, in the morgue, Luke had asked the police about Damon's missing teeth. His son had made sure three of his teeth were found amid the ashes, bone fragments, and rubble from the car explosion.

She remembered what Dana had told her about the fire that swept through the Beales' house: *There was hardly anything left of the place—or the three corpses in it. They had to identify them all from dental records . . .*

Andrea didn't think she'd get any answers out of Doreen Carter of Richmond. So she started up Luke's computer and went onto Google. She found Doreen's current résumé on LinkedIn. Doreen had been working at Cuyer-Paul Dentistry in Richmond for the last three years.

Andrea looked up the phone number for the dentist. She knew they wouldn't be open on a Sunday morning. But she grabbed Luke's cordless and dialed the number anyway.

"Cuyer-Paul Dentistry," a woman answered.

"Hello, I have a dental emergency," Andrea lied.

"My son broke his tooth and he's in a lot of pain. But I'm not sure if this is the right dentist. If I give you my son's name, could you check to see if he's a patient there?"

"This is the answering service," the woman said. "But Doctors Cuyer and Paul check in regularly. If you leave your name and phone number with me, I'll have them get in touch with you."

"Ah, well, my son was at the Virginia Juvenile Correctional Institution last year," Andrea said. "He had some dental work done there. Does Dr. Cuyer or Dr. Paul handle the dentistry for inmates at the facility?"

"Yes, they're on the client list. Now, if you leave your name and phone number, I can have one of the doctors get in touch with you—"

"Thank you very much," Andrea said.

She clicked off and then immediately dialed Doreen Carter of Richmond.

Doreen picked up after three rings: "Yes, hello?"

Andrea could hear a child griping about something in the background. "Hi, Doreen," she said. "I called you yesterday, but we got cut off."

There was no response for a moment.

"What do you want?" the woman finally growled.

"I'm an old friend of Garrett Beale's, and I believe you were acquainted with him, too—when your dentist was doing work at the correctional facility."

"I—I don't know what you're talking about," the woman stammered.

"I don't care whether or not you had sex with him," Andrea said. "Your secret's safe with me, Doreen. But just tell me this. How did Garrett persuade you to switch the dental records? You swapped Richard Phelps's records with Garrett's, didn't you?"

"Who are you?" Doreen whispered.

This time, Andrea hung up on her. She had her answer.

Richard Phelps hadn't really disappeared after the fire that killed Clinton and Denise Beale. His was the third corpse in that house.

Garrett's first friend disappeared after Garrett "died" with his parents in that blaze. And his second friend disappeared after Damon "died" with his mother in that car explosion. In both cases, the only means of identifying the remains were by examining the victims' teeth.

It was Kirk Mowery's body that was blown to bits—along with Evelyn Shuler—when the BMW exploded.

Kirk's mother said her son would have "followed Garrett to the other side of the world."

But Kirk only got as far as Seattle.


In the powder room, Andrea splashed cold water on her face.

It all started to make sense. She could see it now. A pattern was there. Garrett had manipulated—*forced*, really—Spencer to kill his parents, and he'd manipulated Damon into killing his mother.

Andrea knew Damon only remotely. He was a troubled kid, but he hadn't seemed like a killer. It had taken someone like Garrett to push him over the edge and become one. She imagined him helping Damon fake his death. After all, Garrett had gotten away with faking his own demise a few months before. She could see slick, charming Garrett working on both Evelyn and Damon, playing mother and son against each other.

It made sense that Garrett would want to frame Spencer for these murders. Six years ago, he'd expected Spencer to take full blame for killing Viv and Larry. He never thought he'd be held accountable for his crucial role in those murders. What better way to get even with Spencer and his meddling aunt than to set up his old friend for these new murders?

Andrea was drying her face with a small hand towel when she heard her phone chime. Someone had just sent her a text—at 5:40 in the morning? She hurried into the kitchen, where she'd left the phone on the counter. She checked who it was: B. MIDDLETON. Spencer had mentioned Bonnie Middleton a few times. It was clear he had a little crush on her.

Andrea checked the message:

Andrea, my nAm iz Bonnie Middleton. I'm Spencer's frNd. I hv him hiding on my parents' boat @ d lAk Union Marina, Pier 79, dock C. Cn U brAk awA & MEt us? Don't brng d police. I'm Afrd Spencer wiL do somTIN drastic f d police shO ^ hEr. He hz my father's gun. I can't git Thru 2 him dat things wiL b OK. He needs U. Plz, cum @ once—no police.

With a shaky hand, Andrea phoned her back. She wasn't going to waste time texting her. It rang once and then went to voice mail. *"Hey, this is Bonnie, and you've reached my voice mail,"* she said on the recording. *"Sorry I can't pick up. You know the drill. Leave a message. Thanks. Bye!"*

Andrea waited for the beep. "I need to hear your

voice," she demanded. "I'm not coming there based on some stupid text." With the phone to her ear, she hurried into the living room, and glanced out the window. The police car was still parked in front of the town house.

"I need to hear you or Spencer tell me to come there," she continued. "Someone could have stolen your phone . . ."

The call-waiting signal beeped. Andrea switched to the other line.

"Come, and don't—don't bring the police," the girl said. It sounded like she was crying. "Please, hurry . . ."

There was a click, and the line went dead.


Past the sound of water lapping against the boat and the pilings, Spencer heard footsteps on the dock. He was lying on the bed in the stateroom, with just his shoes off and the itchy blanket over him.

The last twelve hours had dragged by. His clothes had dried, and he'd put them back on. He'd figured out how to work the stove, and heated up some Campbell's Chicken Noodle soup, which he ate with some saltines—comfort food. Last night at nine o'clock, the oldies station—the only station that came in clearly on the radio—went to nonstop infomercials without any news breaks. So while he'd gotten all sorts of information about a cruise line's various destinations, a great vitamin supplement to help boost his energy, and how to guard against identity theft, he had absolutely no idea what was happening out there right now. Were the police closing in on him? Were Aunt Dee and Bonnie okay?

He'd been too keyed up and worried to focus on any of the books the Middletons had on board. He'd discovered the toilet worked, thank God. But upon flushing, it dispensed some kind of air freshener, the scent of which made him a little nauseous. He noticed they had Dramamine and NoDoz inside the bathroom's medicine chest. He almost popped a Dramamine, but rode out the slight case of seasickness. He felt like such a nautical wimp. The boat was still in its slip, for God's sake.

Spencer had also discovered where they kept the tools in the cabin and the storage box on deck where they kept the flare gun and extra flares. At one point, he'd actually stepped off the boat—just to stretch his legs and keep from going stir crazy. He'd wandered to the pay phone and almost called Aunt Dee, but decided against it.

He'd had several false alarms—with the sounds of different people coming down the dock. The squeaky planks were a dead giveaway each time. He hadn't heard anyone out there since midnight.

But he heard someone now.

Throwing back the blanket, Spencer climbed off the bed. He stumbled into the galley, switched off the cabin light, and peered out the window. He listened to the dock planks groaning under footsteps. It sounded like more than one person. Had the police found him?

He didn't see anything, and tried the next window. In the darkness, he spotted Bonnie coming toward the boat—with a man at her side. She wore a hooded jacket and jeans with sneakers. Spencer didn't recognize the man. He didn't look old enough to be her dad, and from the way he was dressed—army cargo pants and a leather aviation jacket—he didn't look like a cop. The man carried a backpack in one hand. His other hand was behind Bonnie.

As they got closer, Spencer noticed that Bonnie was crying.

Maybe the guy was a cop after all.

They stepped onto the boat. Spencer moved to the cabin steps. "Bonnie?"

Tears were streaming down her cheeks. "I'm sorry," she whispered, cringing.

Behind her, the man gave Bonnie a forceful shove. She cried out and toppled down the companionway steps, slamming into Spencer. They fell onto the cabin floor in a tangle.

Catching his breath, Spencer managed to sit up. Bonnie winced and rubbed her elbow. She sat up, too. He could see she wasn't hurt too badly.

Bewildered, he gazed up at the man at the top of the steps. "Who are you?" he asked.

"Don't you recognize me, Spence-o?" the man replied, smiling. He had a slight southern accent. He took a gun out of his jacket pocket and started down the steps. "Don't you know your old pal?"

Spencer hadn't heard that voice in over five years.

And the sound of it now made him sick.

# CHAPTER THIRTY-SEVEN

*Sunday—5:49 a.m.*

From the darkened living room, she stared out the window at the police car, still parked in front of the town house.

"That's right," Andrea said into her phone. "I'll be at Max's Mini-Mart at the bottom of Queen Anne—off Olympia. How soon can you send someone?"

"Ten minutes," the Orange Cab dispatch woman said. "Is this a good number?"

"Yes, it is," Andrea said. "Thanks very much."

She clicked off the line. For a moment, she once again contemplated calling Luke. She wanted someone to know where she was going. Maybe she could work something out with him. If she didn't call back in a half hour, he should phone the police and send them to the marina. But he was probably sleeping right now. Late last night, after the rough day he'd had, the nurse had said something about giving him a sedative and letting him sleep in this morning.

Besides, Luke would try to talk her out of going. He'd want to call the police. He'd say she was walking into a trap—and she probably was. There was every possibility she'd go there and find Spencer and his friend already dead—and Garrett waiting for her.

But as long as there was a chance Bonnie's text was true, she couldn't send the police to the marina. She had to check it out first.

She decided to let Luke sleep.

The closest thing they had to a gun in the house was the prop revolver on his desk from one of his plays. It looked and felt real enough. Andrea stashed it in her purse. She figured it might buy her some bargaining power—for a few minutes anyway. She transferred her little canister of pepper spray from her purse to the pocket of her jeans.

She took one last look out the window at the patrol car. Then she headed into the kitchen and quietly slipped out the back door.

"That's it, that's the stuff," Garrett said, leaning against the galley counter with the gun in his hand.

Bonnie was holding up a sixteen-ounce plastic bottle she'd pulled out of his backpack. The bottle said Sprite, but was three-quarters full of a pale brown liquid.

"Now, you help your boyfriend guzzle down about a third of that," he said.

Aboard the Middletons' Catalina 36, Garrett was call-ing all the shots. All the curtains were drawn, and there was only one small light on—in the main cabin. That was where Spencer sat on the sofa-bench. At gunpoint, Bonnie had been instructed to tie a rope around his ankles—and around his hands in back of him. The rope pinched at his skin. Garrett had warned Bonnie not to leave any slack. He'd tested her work and seemed satisfied.

Spencer almost didn't recognize the nineteen-year-old as the tan, handsome young teenager he'd known six years ago. Garrett's looks had hardened—as if he'd grown old way too fast. He'd spiked his hair and dyed it blond. A dark patch of beard stubble covered the bot-tom half of his chin.

"This is a little cocktail I came up with—Valium, diluted window pane, and some other good stuff," he explained, nodding at the bottle in Bonnie's hand. "It chills you out, makes you very cooperative. You might even trip out or fall asleep for an hour or two. Go on, honey, make him swig it down."

Seated on the sofa bench across from Spencer, she hesitated.

"Better do what he says," he murmured.

Pushing aside the backpack, she got to her feet and twisted off the bottle cap. She tilted the Sprite bottle toward his mouth.

Spencer reluctantly drank it. The stuff tasted like root beer gone flat and bad. There was too much corn syrup in it. He tried not to gag. Some spilled down his mouth. She took the bottle away. He started coughing.

"Another couple of gulps," Garrett said.

But Spencer turned his head away and looked at him. "Why are you doing this?"

"Well, I'll answer that question with another question, Spence-o," he said. "How does it feel to have everyone blaming you for murders you didn't commit? How does it feel to be walking around in my boots? Your aunt—that bitch—she got me put away for killing your parents. I didn't shoot the gun. You did. You're the one who killed them—and I got sent to jail for it."

"You—you pushed me to do it," Spencer said. "I didn't want to. Your hand was on the gun . . ."

"But it was your finger on the trigger—and I took the rap for it." Garrett's eyes narrowed at Bonnie. "Give him another couple of swigs, honey . . ."

With a sigh, she tipped the bottle toward Spencer's lips again.

He forced it down.

"We used to make this stuff for a good buzz when I was in juvie," Garrett said. "I gave some to my friend Richie that night back in April, right before we bashed my father's head in and set fire to the house. I spiked Richie's last few sips with some real crazy shit. He was pretty much paralyzed when I left him behind. It was kind of funny to see him on my bedroom floor, not giving a crap—with the bed and the drapes on fire. I made off with twenty thousand in jewelry and techno toys. I'd planned the whole thing back when I was at the joint. I even got someone to switch our dental records—so everyone thought he was me."

"Nice," Spencer said, frowning. "Who stood in for Damon when you guys detonated the car?"

"Well, if you'd asked your pal, Tanya, she would have said it was a nineteen-year-old drug addict who overdosed and got buried on Lopez, but that was just Damon's cover story. The corpse belonged to another friend of mine, Kirk. After we killed him, we yanked out all his teeth. Then I helped Damon yank out some of his own—to plant in the car."

Twisting the cap back on the bottle, Bonnie curled her lip at him. "You're one terrific friend, aren't you?"

Garrett just grinned. "Put that bottle on the table. You might be having a sip yourself a little later, honey. It's good stuff. It kept Evelyn docile for several hours while we had her on Lopez."

Bonnie wordlessly obeyed him.

"I suppose you're right about Kirk," Garrett admitted with a cavalier shrug. "It wasn't very friendly of me. He got a raw deal. He was good enough to let me know that some detective from Seattle was sniffing around, asking about me and the fire. So I followed the private dick here from Virginia, and I found out who he was working for . . ."

He twirled the gun on his finger. "You know, Spence-o, you and your aunt did a pretty good job disappearing. I was looking for you guys. And Evelyn Shuler's private dick led me right to you. He led me to Evelyn and Damon, too. After that, he really wasn't any use to me. In fact, he was a liability. When I killed him, he was getting dangerously close to figuring me out."

"How—how did you work it with Damon and his

mother?" Spencer asked. The drug was already working to slow down his senses. He felt so tired—and warm. "Go on, enlighten us. You love it. You love telling us just how clever you've been . . ."

"What can I say?" he chuckled. "I had them both wrapped around my little finger. I started out fucking the mother and ended up fucking the kid, too. It was a real trip, man. I was doing them both at the same time—and they had no idea."

Bonnie just stared at him and shook her head.

"But it's not about the sex for you, is it?" Spencer asked. He remembered what his therapist, Diane, had said about Garrett. "It's not based on—on attraction or anything like that. It's got to do with power . . . manipulation . . ."

"Huh, you sound like my shrink in the joint," Garrett said, smirking. "That Damon, he would have done anything for me. He looked up to me—the way you once did."

"Did you get him to trust you—and take you into his confidence?" Spencer asked.

Garrett nodded. "Him and the mother," he said. "It was fun to pit them against each other at times. It was easy persuading Damon to kill her—especially after I told him that his mama had been paying a guy to bully him. We were partners in crime, him and me. He was a hell of a lot better partner than you ever were. The little son of a bitch got damn enthusiastic when he started bumping off some of his classmates. He liked the idea of pinning everything on you, too. The one glitch was he wanted to have his friend on board—that idiot, Tanya. I didn't want her to know about me. I couldn't control her—except through Damon. She contributed some, but mostly she was just a pain in the ass. Anyway, as of yesterday, they'd both outlived their usefulness to me."

Spencer numbly stared at him. "You mean—you killed them?"

Garrett just shrugged again and chuckled offhandedly.

Spencer looked at Bonnie, and she nodded. "It was on the news. Damon was shot in the head and left in a shallow grave near where Ron was killed. And last night, Tanya and her mother were killed. He slit their throats." She turned to glare at Garrett. "You're a real piece of work. Talk about a lowlife. When they bury you, they'll have to dig up."

Garrett stepped forward and suddenly punched her in the face. She flopped back and crashed down on the floor.

Spencer jumped to his feet, but he immediately lost his balance and fell back onto the bench. Maybe it was the drug, but he couldn't get up again. He just lay there, helplessly watching Garrett as he stood over Bonnie.

With her hair in her face, she curled up on the floor and whimpered in pain. Spencer caught a glimpse of blood at the corner of her mouth.

Garrett pulled some more rope from his backpack. He grabbed her arms and jerked her to one side so that she was facedown on the cabin floor. She let out a groan of protest.

"Now, you're going to make yourself useful, honey," he muttered. Hovering over her, he started tying her wrists together. "You're going to help me kill his bitch of an aunt . . ."

"No!" Spencer yelled. It was all he could do. His legs weren't working. He felt as if he was paralyzed.

"You know, you really screwed it up last time we did something together," Garrett said, still binding Bonnie's wrists together. He stopped to grin at Spencer. "This time, I'll show you how it's done—and you'll take the blame, my friend."

Then he went back to work.

It started to rain as the cab pulled into the South Lake Union Marina.

The parking lot was only half full at this hour. Andrea figured the vehicles belonged to people who had already set sail, because she didn't see another soul in the wharf area. None of the boats moored off the docks had an outside light on. She wondered if Spencer's friend Bonnie had given her the wrong pier number.

Then again, she couldn't help feeling someone was watching the cab pull up to the pier. Inside one of those boats, Garrett Beale was waiting for her. Was Bonnie Middleton still alive? Was Spencer even here?

Her cell phone rang. She checked the caller ID. It was Bonnie again.

Andrea clicked on. "Hello?"

"Get out of the cab," the girl whispered. "Pay the driver—and—and send him away."

Andrea heard a click.

It sounded as if someone had been feeding Bonnie those instructions. Andrea gave the taxi driver forty dollars for an eleven-buck fare. "Can you do me a favor? After you pull out of the lot, could you park halfway down the block?" She glanced at the phone number on the placard with his photo on it. He had a thin face and a dark cocoa complexion. "Just wait there, and if I don't phone you in ten minutes, Dashawn, call the police. Tell them where you dropped me off. My name's Andrea Boyle—"

"Yes, I have it," he said. "You gave it to the dispatcher. But I don't know what's going down here. I'm not up for any big adventure this morning. I'd like to help you, but I can't."

Andrea sighed and took another forty dollars out of her purse and handed it to him. "That's all I have on me," she said.

"I can help you," he said, sticking the bills in his shirt pocket.

"Good," she said, a little out of breath. "Also tell them you found Spencer Murray. Could you do that for me, please?"

"I can do that for you." He turned back and smiled at her. "Whatever it is you're doing, be careful, lady."

"Thanks," she said.

Andrea climbed out of the cab and shut the door. Her stomach in knots, she stood there in the cold drizzle and watched him drive away.

Her phone rang again. She clicked it on. "Yes?"

"Dock C—to the left of the shack," the girl said.

The line went dead again.

Andrea took a deep breath, and walked toward a small, shingled lean-to near the dock. The streetlight beside it was out, and the area beyond that to the water was shrouded in darkness. She clutched the collar of her jacket around her neck. She could hear the rain on the lake, and water lapping against the dock pilings.

Andrea reached the shed and started to turn the corner.

They were waiting for her in the shadows on the other side of the shed.

She gasped and stopped in her tracks.

The long-haired, pretty girl had a red mark on her face, as if she'd just been slapped—hard. Tears welled in her eyes. "I'm sorry," she whispered.

Andrea recognized Garrett Beale. He'd gotten old before his time and looked rough around the edges. He stood behind the girl, holding a gun to her head.

"Where's Spencer?" she asked with a tremor in her voice.

Garrett smiled. "Like you, he's just where I want him."

Spencer willed himself to stay awake.

He'd feigned sleep while Garrett had pulled Bonnie from the floor and led her up the companionway steps. He'd listened to her moaning in pain at one point. It had been all Spencer could do to ignore it. He'd waited until he could barely hear their footsteps on the dock. Then he'd rolled off the sofa and hit the floor with a thud. It had hurt like hell, but it had helped wake him up, too. Spencer had tried to wiggle his hands free, but the rope was too tight. He'd dragged himself to the head.

He was in there now, bent over the toilet, breathing

in that sickening air freshener. He couldn't stick his finger down his throat, so this was the only thing he could do. But it worked. He started to feel nauseous and then gagged. He kept gagging—until he finally threw up.

He hadn't thrown up since that night he'd killed his parents. He'd forgotten how horrible it felt—the churning pain from his groin up to his throat. He threw up a second time. After flushing the toilet with his chin, he closed the toilet seat lid the same way. A waft of the air freshener hit him, and he started to gag again, but held back.

Some of the drug was still in his system. Fighting light-headedness, he inched over to the sink and managed to straighten up. His legs felt wobbly. With his chin, he pried open the medicine chest. He stared at the bottle of NoDoz for a moment and then tried to grab it with his teeth. A container of eyedrops and a prescription bottle fell into the sink with a clatter. But Spencer finally caught the NoDoz bottle in his teeth and dropped it in the sink. Then he turned his back to the sink, squatted down, and retrieved the bottle with his hands. He started to feel dizzy, but fought it. His mouth tasted horrible. If he could have, he would have bent over the sink and tried to turn on the water for a drink. But there was no time. It seemed to take forever simply to unscrew the damn safety cap to the NoDoz, but he finally got the lid off. Then he tipped the vial over the edge of the sink. He heard the pills spilling out on the small counter. Turning around again, he bent down and gobbled up at least three pills—maybe more. He couldn't tell. He fought his gag impulse again.

Leaning against the sink cabinet, Spencer lowered

himself to the floor. He crawled over the head's raised threshold. Then just past the doorway, he braced himself against the wall and managed to straighten up again. He hopped toward the front of the cabin, where they kept the tools in a drawer. He'd noticed a box cutter in there earlier. With every hop, he could feel the boat rocking a little—and he wondered if Garrett might notice it from wherever he'd taken Bonnie.

Just as he reached the galley, he stumbled and fell, banging his arm into the edge of the table as he went down. Flailing on the cabin floor, he started to cry—from the pain and frustration. Maybe the drug had something to do with it, too. The boat seemed to be spinning. He dragged himself the rest of the way to the front of the vessel, and then struggled to his feet. He turned around and pulled the drawer open.

He swiveled back again to see where the box cutter was—on the right side, near the drawer's edge. He turned and started feeling around for it.

"Come on, come on, come on," he whispered. Tools clanked as he pushed them aside—until he finally located the box cutter. He had it in his grasp.

As he closed the drawer with his hip, Spencer heard the dock planks groaning. From all the footsteps, it sounded like three or four people—and they were getting closer.

"Shit," Spencer muttered. He hopped back toward the sofa and collapsed on it. He kept the cutter tight in his fist and turned on his side so that Garrett couldn't see his hands.

The boat rocked, and he heard Garrett's voice: "First thing I want you to do once we're down below is call that cabdriver and tell him to get lost. You think I'm blind, bitch? I can see him parked on the other side of the marina . . ."

Frank Middleton woke up at six-fifteen every day—including weekends. This Sunday morning was no different—until he reached for his wristwatch on his dresser. He kept the watch in a pewter bowl—along with his change and keys. The watch, loose change, and house keys were all there. But he didn't see his keys to the boat.

He tried the top drawer, the one with the compartment dividers. It was where he kept his socks and extra keys, tie clasps, cufflinks, and junk. The boat keys weren't there either.

"Megan?" he said, glancing in the mirror above his dresser.

She was in bed, still sleeping.

"Honey?" he said, louder. "Have you seen the keys to the boat?"

She stirred. "Yeah, I have them right here under my pillow," she groaned. "What do you think?"

Frank walked over to the bedroom window and glanced down at the driveway. The family SUV wasn't there. "Oh, shit," he muttered. "Honey, wake up . . ."

He turned and ran out to the hallway. He didn't even knock on Bonnie's door. He flung it open. His daughter's bedroom was empty.

"Son of a bitch," Frank whispered.

He didn't have to guess where Bonnie was—and who was with her.

"I'm sorry," she heard Bonnie murmur.

Her back straight, Andrea sat on the sofa bench. She felt Bonnie, behind her, pulling and knotting the rope around her wrists. Across from them on the other bench, Spencer had passed out, but obviously he was in the throes of a nightmare. He kept twitching and groaning.

"He's tripping," Garrett said, slouched against the cabin steps. He tossed her purse on the galley counter. Andrea had watched him go through it. He'd found the prop revolver almost immediately and seemed to think it was real. At least, he'd pocketed it. But he still held on to his own gun.

He'd already patted her down, but hadn't found the pepper spray. He'd focused on her jacket—along with the waist and the cuffs of her jeans. He must have been looking for another gun or maybe a knife. Or perhaps he'd just gotten distracted, because while pressing the gun barrel under her chin, he'd fondled her breasts.

Andrea had said nothing and resisted the impulse to spit in his eye. She figured, for the time being, she'd just cooperate. She'd already sent the cabdriver away. Garrett had made her talk to him on the speaker phone, so he could hear the driver's responses and know she wasn't trying to use any kind of code with him.

She was biding her time, hoping to loosen the ropes around her wrists. Maybe then she could get to the pepper spray. Right now that was her only plan. She wished Spencer's friend hadn't tied the knot so tight. But the girl didn't have much of a choice. Garrett had said he would check her work. And her own hands had been tied behind her—up until just a few minutes ago.

Bonnie finished tying her up, and then put her hand on Andrea's shoulder. The rain seemed to be coming down heavier now. Andrea heard it pelting the boat deck—and the lake's surface. The vessel rocked slightly.

Across from them, Spencer let out another moan and shifted on the couch.

The clock on living room wall read 6:20. It would be light soon, and even with the rain, there would be a few people coming to the marina. She turned to Garrett. "Can I ask what you're planning to do?"

He studied her and smiled. "You know, sitting there right now with that expression on your face, you remind me of your older sister—right before we shot her."

Andrea swallowed hard and said nothing.

Someone's phone rang. Andrea knew it wasn't hers, because it didn't chime out the Beatles tune.

Garrett snatched the phone off the galley counter and glanced at it. "*Middleton, Frank*—looks like Dad, wondering where his little girl is."

"He's probably already figured out where I am," Bonnie said.

"That's why you're going to get us out of here," Garrett replied, tossing the phone back on the counter. The ringing stopped—the call had gone to voice mail. "You're taking us to Lopez Island."

"Are you crazy?" Bonnie shook her head. "Just because my father owns a boat, it doesn't mean I'm this maritime whiz. I've never done any sailing on my own. And the rain out there is getting worse. I can't do it. I'd get us all lost—or drowned."

"The Shulers' cabin on Lopez has its own dock,"

Garrett explained. "We'll get the latitude and longitude off the computer. You'll take us there."

Bonnie shook her head again. "No, I'm sorry, I can't. I won't risk it."

"Then what good are you to me?" he asked. "What's to keep me from killing you and tossing you overboard right now?"

Cold rain and wind whipped across Bonnie's face as she stood at the helm. She wore a life preserver over her jacket, but she was still shivering. She held on to the wheel and maneuvered the Catalina 36 out of the mooring area. She'd never been at the controls before, not without her dad somewhere on deck.

Instead of her father's help, she had to contend with this creep watching her every move. He stood at the top of the cabin steps with the gun pointed at her. He kept glancing over his shoulder—down at his two captives belowdecks. The canopy above him flapped in the breeze as the boat started to pick up speed. Bonnie could see small whitecaps on the water, and knew it would be much worse once they sailed farther out.

Past the churning motor and the rain, Bonnie heard a siren in the distance.

Was there a chance her father had figured out where they were? He would have called the police. Was this them? From the pier, they might be able to see the *Bonnie Blue* heading out to Puget Sound. Maybe they'd contact the coast guard. She knew how to operate the control panel in the cabin and send an SOS from there. But she couldn't do it here on the bridge. The flare gun and cartridges were in a locked box on the port side of the boat. As long as Garrett was standing there, she couldn't get to it.

Garrett must have heard the sirens, too. He glanced toward the pier. "Quit dawdling," he barked. "Let's pick up some speed . . ."

She glanced back and saw three squad cars pulling into the marina lot, their red and blue lights flashing. But the promising show of police force only got farther and farther away as the boat motored north.

"Put up the sails, for Christ's sake," he said. "Let's get this mother moving . . ."

"I told you, I'm not very experienced at this!" she shot back. She'd only worked with the sails a couple of times—and that was with her father walking her through every move. "Let me get to the Sound, and then I'll crank the sail up . . ."

As she navigated the boat through the Fremont Cut, Bonnie kept thinking she'd capsize the boat. It was already tilting too far portside. The ride got rougher past the Cut. If she, Spencer, and his aunt weren't murdered by this maniac, then they'd all end up dead at the bottom of Puget Sound.

Garrett peeked back inside the cabin, and turned toward her. He smiled.

The boat started rocking in the choppy water. Waves splashed against the bow. The spray mixed with the rain pelting her.

"Your boyfriend is still tripping down there," he yelled—over the sound of the flapping canopy. "So, have you two fucked yet?"

Bonnie ignored the crude question. She was trying

to stay balanced on the rocky boat. With one hand still clutching the wheel, she grabbed hold of the cord handrail on the starboard side. The wheel was fighting her.

"Are you one of those chicks who are into serial killers?" Garrett asked, continuing to taunt her. "Did the idea that he'd killed both his parents turn you on? Is that it?"

"I knew he must have been forced into doing it," she answered loudly, still struggling to keep the wheel steady. "I—I read up on the case. You know, Spencer's finger might have been on the trigger, but you were the one in control. You were wrong earlier. You got what you deserved. Spencer—he's the one who was screwed. Then again, that seems to happen to anyone who becomes your friend."

He laughed. "Oh, you're so sure, huh? You read a few articles online, and suddenly it's like you were there, and you know every little detail about what happened . . ."

She glanced at him for a moment and then focused again on the treacherous horizon. "Just one minute with Spencer, and I knew he couldn't intentionally hurt anybody," she shouted defiantly—over the howling wind gusts. "The same way in that after just one minute with you, I knew you were a cold-blooded, murdering bastard."

"Feisty," he said, cackling. He swayed with the unsteady boat. "You're a brave girl."

"No, I'm not," she yelled, clutching the wheel. "I'm scared shitless right now."

Bonnie looked over her shoulder again. She could

barely see the lights on the shore. In front of them was the whitecapped, turbulent water. It seemed endless.

"Spencer, wake up!" Andrea said.

He felt his aunt kick the sofa bench.

"Please, wake up, for God's sake!"

"I'm awake," he said, opening his eyes. "I—I'm okay . . ."

That wasn't quite true. He was dizzy and light-headed—partly from that awful drug concoction, but also from seasickness. His hands were covered in blood from the countless times he'd nicked himself with the box cutter blade over the last half hour. Every time he twitched and groaned, he'd been hacking away at the rope—or slicing into his own skin. But he'd managed to cut the ropes.

"I—I just got my hands free," he said. "I grabbed a box cutter earlier . . ."

"Thank God," Andrea murmured.

He glanced at Garrett, whose back was to them. He was standing on the top step of the companionway. With the wind gusts, the boat's motor churning, and the waves crashing against the bow, Spencer couldn't make out what Garrett was saying to Bonnie. He figured it was safe for Aunt Dee and him to whisper to each other.

"I'll get to you in a second," he said under his breath. "I just need to free up my feet . . ."

He bent over to work on the rope around his ankles. He heard Andrea gasp—probably at the sight of his bloody hands. With the cutter, he furiously hacked away at the thick rope. But then he saw Garrett take a step down the companionway.

Spencer immediately pulled his hands behind his back and feigned sleep. With his eyes half-closed, he watched Garrett peeking into the cabin at them. "How are you doing down here?" he asked, grinning. His face was wet from the rain and spray.

Glaring at him, Andrea didn't reply. Her hands behind her, she rocked from side to side along with the unsteady boat.

"Think you're feeling uncomfortable now?" he asked. "I haven't even gotten started on you yet. Just wait . . ."

Spencer watched him turn and take a step toward the top deck again.

Bonnie struggled with the wheel, trying to execute a slow, wide U-turn back toward the marina. She prayed Garrett wouldn't notice. But the rain would be coming at him from a different direction. That might be a dead giveaway.

The Catalina bucked as it changed course in the choppy water. She braced herself for each jolt.

Once he'd ducked down into the cabin, Bonnie reached for the keys on the navigation panel. With her hands shaking, she pried the lock key from the four-leaf-clover ring. She needed to get to the box with the flare gun. But even if Garrett stayed down in the cabin for a few minutes, she couldn't leave the wheel. She might lock it in place with the helm brake, but in this weather, the boat could start careening. It might even capsize.

She saw Garrett stepping back up to the deck, and she quickly shoved the key into her jacket pocket.

He looked slightly annoyed.

She wondered if he'd caught her hiding something in her pocket. Or had he figured out she was changing course?

"Why haven't you put up the sails yet?" His eyes narrowed at her.

"It's too dangerous with this wind," she answered.

She noticed a light in the sky, and it filled her with hope. He couldn't see it, because it loomed on the horizon behind him. And he probably couldn't hear the helicopter, because of the canopy above him, flapping wildly.

"You know what you'd do if you were smart?" she called. "You'd get out the life raft, camouflage it with one of these black sail covers, and get out now. Leave us onboard. We're still close enough to the shore. You can make a clean getaway while the police chase after us. They've already spotted us. It's only a matter of time before they catch up with us. Even in the open water, they have the advantage—police boats with better sailors, the Coast Guard . . ."

"You talk too much," he growled.

"I'm just saying we're never going to make it to Lopez Island."

He stared at her and said nothing.

Bonnie watched the helicopter descend a bit. It was zeroing in on them.

Garrett took a step down and checked on Spencer

and his aunt again. After a few moments, he came back up. She could see the wind was blowing rain in his face.

"I think you're right, honey," he yelled. "It's not what I had in mind for tonight, but you've given me a great idea. The police aren't looking for me. They're just after you and your boyfriend. I can slip out of here, and they won't be any the wiser, isn't that right?"

She nodded several times. "Yes . . ."

"Of course, that doesn't work out so well for you, because I'll have to kill the three of you." He chuckled. "But hell, that's a win-win for me. I'll make it look like Spencer did it—a murder-suicide. Funny, I set something like that up just three weeks ago . . ."

"But—there's no time," she said. "You have to get the raft and get out of here now . . ."

He smirked. "Come back and kill another day? No, it doesn't work that way." He nodded at the wheel. "Does that thing have a lock to keep it steady?"

"Yes, but in these conditions, you—"

"Shut up and lock it," he said, raising the gun.

Bonnie obeyed him, and applied the helm brake.

He motioned at her with his free hand. "Come here," he whispered.

She could hardly hear him over all the noise. Warily, she moved toward him. She was trembling as she stepped under the canopy.

All at once, he hauled back and hit her in the face.

Bonnie flopped down onto the deck.

Stunned, she lay there and listened to him starting down the cabin steps again.

\*   \*   \*

"C'mon, c'mon," he heard his aunt whispering.

Spencer was bent over, frantically working the cutter blade on the thick rope around his ankles. He'd sliced about halfway through. His shoes and white socks were splattered with blood from the cuts on his hands.

The boat pitched, and the blade slipped. He nicked his leg. Spencer let out a little cry, but he kept hacking away at the rope, now soaked crimson.

"Spencer—" his aunt started to say.

He looked up and saw Garrett at the bottom of the stairs.

"Well, what the damn hell?" he chuckled, waving the gun. "Aren't you the sneaky bastard?" Then the smile ran away from his face. "I got a question for you, Spence-o. I've always wanted to know. Did you have your eyes closed when we shot your mother? Because I want you to keep them open now, okay? I want you to see this . . ."

He pointed the gun at Andrea.

"No!" Spencer screamed.

A sudden blinding light poured in through the windows. The loud churning of propellers came with it.

The box cutter in his fist, Spencer leapt off the sofa bench and lunged at his old friend. The rope around his ankles tripped him up. He slammed into Garrett. The boat rocked violently, and they banged against the galley cabinets. Andrea's purse—and everything inside it—flew off the counter.

Frantically brandishing the cutter, Spencer kept trying to slash him.

He heard the gun go off—twice.

Each time, he felt a burning jab in his stomach.

In a fury, he kept wielding the cutter—and finally connected, making a deep slice in Garrett's arm. Blood sprayed in Spencer's face.

Garrett howled out in pain. He dropped the gun, and it slid across the cabin floor—under one of the benches.

Spencer heard his aunt screaming. All he could think about was saving her—and Bonnie. Maybe it would make up a little for his parents.

His stomach was on fire, but like a crazy man, he kept jabbing away at Garrett—until the box cutter flew out of his hand. Or maybe he'd just dropped it. He'd lost feeling in his hands and arms.

Everything was shutting down. His legs gave out.

As he collapsed onto the cabin floor, Spencer could feel Garrett over him.

All his fighting hadn't done any good.

His old friend was still standing.


Andrea screamed. She saw Spencer fall to the floor at Garrett's feet.

She tried to get up from the sofa-bench, but the boat suddenly lurched to one side. She went crashing into the table and then toppled to the floor. Andrea had barely gotten her breath back when she felt Garrett's hand slam down on the top of her head. He dragged her up by the hair.

With her wrists and ankles still tied, she was utterly helpless. She tried to struggle as he pulled her toward the stairs, dragging her over Spencer's body. She couldn't tell if he was still breathing. Under him, blood billowed out on the cabin floor.

The boat careened out of control. Rain came in through the opening at the top of the companionway. The sky was bright white from the helicopter's spotlight. All the while, someone was yelling over a PA system—maybe from the helicopter or a nearby ship. A man shouted out something that sounded like a warning. It was indistinguishable past the wind, waves, and flapping canopy.

"Goddamn you both," Garrett muttered as he hauled Andrea up the steps.

As they reached the deck, he pulled a gun out of his jacket pocket. It was Luke's prop revolver. He jabbed the barrel into the side of Andrea's neck.

Under the canopy, she couldn't see the helicopter hovering directly above, but she knew it was there. A police boat approached the port side, shining a spotlight on them. It was blinding. For a few moments, Andrea didn't see Bonnie, who was steadying the wheel with one hand and holding a flare gun with the other.

"Get out! Get away from here!" Garrett shouted at the police on the watercraft. "Turn off that goddamn light—or I swear I'll kill her!"

Andrea felt the gun barrel scraping against her jaw, taking away a layer of skin.

With the rain and wind whipping at her face, Bonnie kept the flare gun aimed at Garrett. She was shaking.

Garrett turned to her. "Put it down, bitch."

"Don't listen to him!" Andrea yelled. With all her might, she pushed herself away and fell down in front of the wheel.

She left Garrett with a fistful of her hair—and a fake gun. He tried to fire it several times before he seemed to realize he'd been duped.

Andrea saw him looking at the gun, dumbfounded.

For just that moment, only she and Garrett knew the gun was a prop.

The police and Bonnie had no idea.

Bonnie fired off the flare with a loud pop. Spewing a tail of flames, the cartridge hit the side of Garrett's neck and lodged under the collar of his jacket. Sparks and smoke exploded around his head. He screamed out in agony.

Three shots rang out from the police boat. Garrett's body twitched and convulsed with each bullet that ripped through him.

He staggered blindly to the edge of the boat and teetered against the railing. All the while, he was whimpering and crying. It was a pathetic sound.

Garrett toppled over the handrail.

He was still wailing—until the water swallowed him up.

# EPILOGUE

Bonnie stood at the graveside in a black trench coat she'd borrowed from her mother. She was dry-eyed. Her face was still slightly bruised from when Garrett had punched her on Sunday morning, but she'd managed to conceal it with some makeup.

Andrea stood at her side, looking somber—and a bit frayed.

It was a beautiful fall afternoon. The sun had just started to set as the minister opened his book for the reading. About twenty others were in attendance, a few of them classmates. The memorial service earlier—at a nondenominational church on Capitol Hill—had drawn about forty people. Bonnie had spotted a few more fellow students there. They must not have felt close enough to the deceased to make the trek here to the cemetery.

Ron's funeral had been yesterday, and he'd drawn a huge turnout—with several teachers, his teammates (all wearing their varsity jackets with ties), and at least half the junior class. Reporters and TV news vans had waited outside the cemetery gate. The grave site was surrounded by flowers, creating a riot of colors. Over Ron's coffin, the minister had read A. E. Housman's poem, "To an Athlete Dying Young," and everyone had been in tears—including Bonnie. She'd become the reluctant center of attention there. Ron's parents had insisted she sit with them at the church—and stand with them by his grave in Lakeview Cemetery. They'd acted as if she'd never broken up with him. After the burial, a reception had been held at a country club.

In comparison, today's service seemed so shoddy and furtive.

Bonnie kept thinking she should have said something to the minister about the reading. The choice seemed so generic, and his recitation was uninspired. Someone should have read an excerpt from *The Perks of Being a Wallflower*. Bonnie remembered Tanya referring to the novel and "the island of misfit toys" at the memorial for Damon—the *first* memorial for him.

Bonnie remembered it was where she'd had her initial conversation with Spencer. She'd also met Damon's father for the first time there, too.

Neither one of them were here for Damon's second send-off. She'd heard Mr. Shuler's condition was improving, but apparently the doctors thought it was too soon for him to be moved around—even in a wheelchair.

She'd just visited Spencer this morning. He was doing better, too. They were supposed to move him out of intensive care later today—into a room down the hall from Mr. Shuler.

It was just as well neither of them had made it here. Mr. Shuler was still dealing with the fact that his son had taken part in murdering at least nine people. Bonnie figured he wasn't ready to face the public and all the reporters.

Meanwhile, the press ate up the story of the two teenage killers who had faked their deaths. In profiling Garrett Beale, the media had to remind everyone that as minors, both he and Spencer Rowe—aka Spencer Murray—had each spent five years in juvenile detention centers and psychiatric facilities for the murder of Spencer's parents in 2009.

Bonnie felt horrible for Spencer, whose guarded secret was now common knowledge. She was glad he wasn't at school to hear all the talk, the snickers, and the sick jokes.

She'd gotten close to Spencer's aunt in the last few days. A crisis could do that with strangers. She'd helped Andrea get over some of the hurdles in arranging this double funeral. Luke had already scattered what everyone had thought were Damon's ashes—along with Mrs. Shuler's. This proved to be a problem for the mother of Damon's "stand-in," Kirk Mowery, but there wasn't much the poor woman could do about it.

The real problem was Tanya. Her twice-married mother had expressly wished to be buried beside her first husband in Colorado Springs. She'd made no arrangements for her daughter—from husband number two. Tanya's estranged father refused to take on any responsibility for her interment. The fact that she'd been an accessory to several murders had seemed like a good reason. But Bonnie had a feeling it was just a pretext for staying uninvolved in his daughter's life—and death. No one else wanted to take on the responsibility.

It was Bonnie's idea that Tanya be buried beside her friend, Damon. Mr. Shuler paid for everything. She and Andrea had made the arrangements.

Bonnie hoped maybe all her efforts somehow helped square things with both Tanya and Damon.

A chilly wind stirred up, and she shuddered. She gazed at the pair of dark bronze coffins, side by side—suspended above two holes in the ground. The caskets were held up by two hand-cranked bracketed mechanisms that would later lower Damon and Tanya into their neighboring plots.

Bonnie began to cry. She couldn't help it.

She thought of the two misfits at school, slipping away during lunchtime—someplace where no one would bother them.

### Thursday, November 26—6:08 p.m.

"Excuse me," Luke murmured.

Andrea heard him past the clinking silverware and polite conversation at his dining room table. She'd made Thanksgiving dinner for Luke, Spencer, three people from Luke's new play who had nowhere else to go for the holiday, and a fourth guest. Andrea had also invited Spencer's friend, Bonnie, but she was with her family tonight. Despite everyone's assurance that the cuisine was sublime, Andrea knew she'd overcooked the turkey. Plus the mashed potatoes were kind of lumpy. But the stuffing and other side dishes weren't bad. She'd just served up the ice cream and a pumpkin pie from Metropolitan Market.

She'd been keeping an eye on Luke for any signs of fatigue ever since two-thirty, when the driver from the non-emergency ambulance service had wheeled him up the front walkway. This was Luke's first time back home since the night he'd been mowed down by Troy Slattery in that stolen car. His arm and leg were still in casts. He also wore a back brace—along with one of those ugly, padded neck braces that made even the coolest person appear pathetic. But the bruises and swelling had disappeared—and he almost looked like his old self. He was in an upbeat mood, cracking jokes with his theater friends. But because of his medications, he couldn't have any wine. At dinner, he sat at the head of the table, and fed himself. Andrea had cut up his turkey ahead of time, sparing him that indignity in front of their guests.

On the subject of indignities, Luke had warned her that he would need help going to the bathroom. He'd made it clear he didn't want her or Spencer stuck with that duty. It turned out his driver from Mobilecare Services was qualified to do the job. Andrea had invited the young, East Indian man to join them for dinner, but he said he was required to stay with his vehicle unless the patient needed him. They'd hired the service until seven-thirty. That was when Luke's doctors at the rehab facility wanted him back.

After his quiet "Excuse me," Andrea figured Luke

needed to take a bathroom break. But then she looked across the dinner table at him. On the other side of the flickering candles and the cornucopia centerpiece, she saw him leaning to one side in his wheelchair. He was as pale as chalk. His eyes were half closed. "Andrea?" he said—just a bit louder. "Hon, could you—could you wheel me to the bathroom? *Now?*"

She sprang up from her chair. "Excuse me," she announced, hurrying around to the other end of the table. As she pulled Luke's wheelchair away, she glanced down at his place setting. He hadn't touched his pie. And she'd noticed earlier that he'd only eaten about half of his meager portion of dinner.

At the same time, Spencer and one of Luke's theater friends both asked if she needed any help. But Andrea chimed back, "We're fine!" Then she pushed Luke in his wheelchair into the kitchen—toward the powder room.

"I'm going to throw up," he said under his breath.

Stopping, Andrea grabbed an empty bowl off the counter and held it under his chin. "It's okay," she whispered.

She heard him take a few deep breaths. "Jesus, could I be any more pathetic?" he finally muttered. "I think you can take the bowl away now, hon."

She set the bowl back down on the counter, and then patted him on his shoulder.

Luke sighed. "Oh, brother, once I'm finally walking again, you won't want to touch me. If our sex life survives this, it'll be a miracle."

"I think we'll survive," she said, bending down to kiss the side of his face. "If it's any reassurance to you, so far, I've asked your doctor only six times how long before I can make a conjugal visit."

It was true. She missed him terribly. She missed having his strong arms around her.

"I guess I just had a little too much excitement today," he said. "I feel like the kid who stayed too long at the fair. You better have the ambulance guy take me back . . ."

By the time she was ready to wheel Luke out to the ambulance, his three theater friends had made their excuses and their very polite, hasty departures. Andrea planned to ride back to the rehab facility with Luke and make sure he was settled in. That left Spencer alone with their fourth guest—Hugh Badger Lyman's assistant, Dana. Like their other guests, Dana had nowhere else to go on Thanksgiving. He'd been so helpful to Andrea, and she didn't want him to be alone on the holiday. She hadn't been sure how he'd mix with the others. But it turned out one of Luke's theater friends wanted to write a play about Vietnam, and Dana had spent most of the night talking with him.

Andrea called a cab for Dana before she headed out the door with Luke and the ambulance driver. She told Spencer not to bother with the dishes. She'd clean up when she came back in about an hour.

It was damp and chilly out. She could see her breath. She'd covered Luke with a plaid blanket. It kept slipping down from his shoulders while the driver wheeled him up the ramp into the back of the ambulance. Once inside the van, the young man strapped Luke and the wheelchair in place.

Waiting outside the vehicle, Andrea shivered and

turned up the collar of her trench coat. She stole a glance at the house.

She'd planted some new bulbs in the front garden a couple of weeks ago. By spring, they'd be blooming. She'd gotten Luke's town house ready for his homecoming by moving in some of her own furniture, art, and knickknacks. She'd been taking photos of each new addition to show him and to get his input and feedback. And they'd shopped on line for other things together. She wanted the town house to be theirs.

In Troy Slattery's apartment, the police had found the silver frame with her mother's photo in it.

It now had a place in the living room—*their* living room.

After all that preparation, Thanksgiving seemed like one big disappointment. Everything had started out so nicely this afternoon. Luke had seemed thrilled to see—in person—the changes in the town house. He kept saying how wonderful the dinner smelled, and how great it was to be back.

And now he looked so miserable.

Once the driver stepped outside, Andrea climbed into the back of the ambulance. She sat down on a bench across from where Luke was anchored in his wheelchair. She readjusted the blanket. He closed his eyes and winced.

"You still feeling nauseous?" she asked.

He nodded, and took a few deep breaths. "I just overdid it today," he murmured.

Andrea felt the ambulance starting to move down the street. She stroked his good arm. "I'm the one who overdid it," she said. "Your first day back should have been something more low key. I shouldn't have had all those people over. And the turkey was dry . . ."

He let out a weak chuckle. "Oh, shut up. Everything was great. Thank you for a wonderful Thanksgiving."

She let out a tiny laugh and touched his cheek. "Well, okay, you're welcome."

Andrea felt a few bumps in the road as the ambulance picked up speed.

The color was coming back to Luke's face. He gave her a tired smile. She knew it would be a while before he was his old self again. Then they could start over.

Until then, she'd just be patient.


The last guest to leave—the guy named Dana—helped Spencer clear the dining room table. He'd said he wanted to make himself useful until the taxi arrived.

Spencer tried not to stare at his mangled hand with the missing digits. But he was fascinated by how Dana still managed to pick up and hold on to things with just a thumb and a row of nubs. He didn't let it slow him down much. While they cleaned up, Spencer watched him carry glasses, silverware, and plates into the kitchen. Spencer was careful not to be caught looking. He knew all too well what it was like to be on the receiving end of prying, judgmental stares.

He'd started back to school two weeks ago, and those first few days were rough. Everyone now knew his horrible secret. His teachers and fellow students treated him like a freak or some kind of dangerous character. Or they did their damnedest to ignore him. But it was starting to get easier. He was seeing a new therapist, whom he liked.

Still, he missed Diane.

He was also seeing a lot of Bonnie. In fact, he was in love—at least, he thought it was love. They were taking things slow. Bonnie wanted it that way. Her parents were still a bit wary of him. Plus everyone at school expected her to carry on like she was Ron's widow or something.

Spencer knew her popularity was waning because of her association with him. But Bonnie insisted she didn't give a damn. At lunchtime in the cafeteria, she no longer sat at the cool table. She sat with him.

He was really disappointed she hadn't come over tonight.

This Thanksgiving had been kind of a letdown for him. He'd spent his last five Thanksgivings incarcerated—either in a psychiatric hospital or a juvenile detention facility. He'd had such high hopes for this first holiday someplace that didn't have bars on the windows.

Luke's town house seemed like home now. Aunt Dee had redecorated while he and Luke had been in the hospital. It was a mix of things he knew from Luke's place, knickknacks he remembered from his aunt's apartment in Washington, DC, and stuff from his parents' house. Luke had told him to make the guest room into his room. So once out of the hospital, Spencer had taped his Bill Murray movie posters on the walls—and on the bookshelf, he'd displayed framed photos of his parents.

He told himself this was as close to *home* as he'd ever get.

For company tonight, he'd put on a pressed blue shirt, a tie, and clean khaki cargo pants. Even though they all knew about him, everyone was nice. Aunt Dee had busted her chops to prepare a terrific dinner. Luke seemed in a great mood—for a while anyway.

But it was weird for Spencer to be *home*—and not have his mom and dad there. No one really understood that he missed them horribly. Until his arrest, his holidays had always been with them—and Aunt Dee. He missed his grandfather, who used to dote on him. And now the bitter old man refused to talk to him.

The cab arrived for Dana. Spencer took Dana's threadbare jacket off a hanger in the closet, and gave it to him at the door. "Well, thanks for helping me clean up," he said. "Happy Thanksgiving."

The strange-looking man smiled at him. "I read so much about you before I met you," he said, putting on his jacket. "And I came to the conclusion that you were a pretty good kid who got a raw deal. I know now that I was right. Happy Thanksgiving, Spencer."

"Well, thanks," Spencer said, shaking his good hand.

He stood at the door and watched the man hurry toward the waiting taxi.

Then Spencer stepped back inside—to the empty, messy house. He shut the door behind him. He suddenly felt so lonely, he wanted to cry.

His phone rang. He pulled it out of the pocket of his cargo pants. He saw on the caller ID that it was Bonnie. He cleared his throat, and clicked on the phone. "Hey," he said.

"Hey," she said. "What's going on there?"

"Absolutely nothing," he replied, wandering toward the kitchen. "I'm alone. My Aunt Dee took Luke back to the rehab place. There are two slices of pie left and about a million dirty dishes to wash."

"Well, can I come over for some pie? I'll help with the dishes."

He smiled. "That would be great."

"I'm on my way," she said.

"See you soon," Spencer replied. He clicked off, and then slipped the phone back into his pants pocket.

He turned on the hot water, and started washing off the dirty plates. He thought of his parents again. He was always going to miss them, and he would always be horribly sorry for what happened.

Spencer looked down at his hands holding a plate under the stream of hot water. He thought of Dana's mangled hand.

Some people had scars on the outside, and others carried them around inside. They would always be there.

He figured the trick was learning to live with them.